Praise for Jenny J

D0055266

"In the third installment in the Charmed , Bella Kirkwood is back on the case, this time with a wacky sidekick, in a laugh-out-loud, romantic mystery. Bella's hilarious antics coupled with her witty repartee will have readers begging for more."

—*Romantic Times* 4-star review of *So Over My Head*

"In *So Over My Head*, Jenny B. Jones hits a high note. You'll laugh, you'll cringe, you'll shake your head in wonder at the wacky but believable situations in which Bella finds herself. Grab anything you can by this author! The Charmed Life series is a great place to start!"

—Nicole O'Dell, author of the *Scenarios for Girls* interactive fiction series

"[*So Not Happening*] will certainly charm its way onto the bookshelves of any lover of chick lit and fun, light-hearted fiction.

—titletrakk.com review of *So Not Happening*

"Who wants to keep up with the Kardashians now that Bella Kirkwood is starring in a reality show? No need for Nancy Drew when Bella is on the case. This second in the Charmed Life series has everything: mystery, romance and comedic shenanigans. It's crazy, preposterous good fun! What's not to like?"

—*Romantic Times* 4.5 star review of *I'm So Sure*

"A novel by Jenny B. Jones isn't just good entertainment for your mind...it's laughter for your soul. With unforgettable characters and a story to keep you turning pages into the wee hours of the night, the second installment in "The Charmed Life" is better than the first."

—deenasbooks.blogspot.com review of *I'm So Sure*

"Brilliantly written, charmingly witty and deeply emotive, this book is a treasure to be read many times over."

—RelzReviewz review of *Just Between You and Me*

so Over my Head

other books by Jenny B. Jones include:

Just Between You and Me

YOUNG ADULT SERIES

The Charmed Life Series

So Not Happening

I'm So Sure

The Katie Parker Series

In Between

On the Loose

The Big Picture

QG 12-03-15

SO OVER MY HEAD

A *Charmed Life* Novel

JENNY B. JONES

THOMAS NELSON
Since 1798

NASHVILLE   DALLAS   MEXICO CITY   RIO DE JANEIRO

© 2010 by Jenny B. Jones

All rights reserved. No portion of this book may be reproduced, stored in a retrieval system, or transmitted in any form or by any means—electronic, mechanical, photocopy, recording, scanning, or other—except for brief quotations in critical reviews or articles, without the prior written permission of the publisher.

Published in Nashville, Tennessee, by Thomas Nelson. Thomas Nelson is a registered trademark of Thomas Nelson, Inc.

Thomas Nelson, Inc., titles may be purchased in bulk for educational, business, fund-raising, or sales promotional use. For information, please e-mail SpecialMarkets@ThomasNelson.com.

Publisher's Note: This novel is a work of fiction. Names, characters, places, and incidents are either products of the author's imagination or used fictitiously. All characters are fictional, and any similarity to people living or dead is purely coincidental.

Library of Congress Cataloging-in-Publication Data

Jones, Jenny B., 1975–
  So over my head / by Jenny B. Jones.
    p. cm. — (Charmed life)
  Summary: Oklahoma seventeen-year-old Bella Kirkwood wages a full-scale war to win Luke back from his ex-girlfriend, tries to save her father from a diva with shady motives, and investigates the disappearance of a murdering magician.
  ISBN 978-1-59554-543-5 (softcover)
  [1. Dating (Social customs)—Fiction. 2. Remarriage—Fiction. 3. High schools—Fiction. 4. Schools—Fiction. 5. Journalism—Fiction. 6. Christian life—Fiction. 7. Oklahoma—Fiction.] I. Title.
  PZ7.J720313Spg 2010
  [Fic]—dc22   2010000617

Printed in the United States of America
13 14 QG 0 9 8 7

This book is lovingly dedicated to my cute
sister-in-law, Laura. She is a ray of sunshine in
our family, as well as our missing piece, fitting in
just perfectly to complete the picture.

I love you, girl, and am so glad you saw something in
my brother. I personally don't get it, as all I ever saw
was someone who always stole the front seat as well as
my allowance, but whatever. To each her own. May
God richly bless you with laughs, love, and cute shoes.

here's the scoop

Dear Reader,

I am super excited you picked up *So Over My Head!* Not only do I think you'll have fun with Bella as she tries to bring chic to the circus, but I have added a little behind-the-scenes info to certain parts of the book, just for you. Thomas Nelson (my publisher) is calling it "All Access," but I tend to think of it as a glimpse into the glamorous life of an author as she is writing a novel . . . or watching YouTube for hours on end.

So, as you're reading along, keep an eye out for this symbol : *. That means there's a little note from me to you at the back of this book (starting on page 313). And remember, this conversation is just between you and me.

> Happy reading!
> Jenny B. Jones
>
> www.jennybjones.com

chapter one

*I*f my love life was the knife toss at a circus, I'd have Luke Sullivan speared to the wall with an apple in his mouth.

"Ladies and gentlemen! The Fritz Family welcomes you to the greatest show on earth!" A man in a top hat stands in the center of a giant tent, his curlicue mustache as delicate as his voice is strong. "Prepare to be amazed. Prepare to be wowed. Allow us to entertain you with sights you've never seen, horses whose feats will astound you, and death-defying acrobatics!"

On this first night open to the public, the crowd stands in a swarm of shouts and applause.

I stay seated and jot down some quick notes for the *Truman High Tribune.* Or at least that's what I'm pretending to do. In actuality, it's taking all my energy just to be civil.

"I just don't see why you had to invite her."

From his standing position, Luke glances down. "Are we back to that again?"

"You and I are working on the carnival story. Not Ashley." Ashley Timmons, a new girl who joined the newspaper staff last week, has become my least favorite person on the planet. She's not quite as awful as those on the top of that list—namely the handful of people who've tried to do me bodily harm over the last year. But icky nonetheless. Fresh from Kansas City with her brother, Ashley thinks she is to journalism what Edward Cullen is to vampires. She's disgustingly cute, and worst of all, she's Luke's ex-girlfriend. She moved away for two years, but I can tell she's ready to rekindle anything they used to have. It doesn't take a keen reporter's intuition to see that. Just anyone with at least one working eyeball.

"We've hung out with them all week, Luke."

"I haven't seen Kyle in a long time, and he'll be leaving soon for college." Luke searches my face. "I've included you in everything. Have you felt left out?"

"No." I just want *her* left out. I don't mind the return of his friend Kyle at all. But where Kyle is . . . there you'll find his sister. "Tonight isn't about hanging out with your friend, though. He's not even here. You invited Ashley for the paper."

"You've been ticked at me ever since your last article. But it was weak on verbs and lacked your usual creativity." He sits down and trains those intense eyes on mine.

"Yeah, and then you proceeded to show me some piece of writing wonderment your new recruit produced." Ashley came with glowing recommendations from her former journalism teachers. Everyone on our staff thinks she is, like, the greatest thing to writing since the delete key. Everyone but me.

"You know what your problem is, Bella? Number one, you're jealous and insecure—"

"Of her?" I toss my hair and laugh. "Maybe I just don't like the way she's thrown herself at you from the second she stepped into the classroom. I'm not insecure, but I'm also not stupid."

Luke's mouth twitches. "I meant insecure of your writing abilities. But now that you mention it, you probably are jealous of my talking to her. That would fit."

"Fit what?" A band of clowns ride unicycles in the ring, but I don't even bother to watch.

"It would fit with the Bella Kirkwood pattern." He lifts a dark brow. "You are completely distrusting of the entire male species. I guess one couldn't blame you, given your dad's history *and* your experience with your ex, but I have no desire to get back with an old girlfriend."

"This is outrageous. I do *not* have trust issues with guys! And you know what else?"

"I'm dying to hear more."

"I think you're enjoying all the attention from Ashley." All Luke and I have done lately is fight. While digging into other people's business might be my spiritual gift, I'm beginning to think arguing comes second.

"Ever since we've been together, you've balked at my every comment in journalism. You can't stand to be criticized—even when it's for your own good. And"—his blue eyes flash—"you're just waiting for me to cheat on you like Hunter. You think I don't see that?"

Hunter would be my ex-boyfriend from Manhattan. This past fall I caught him doing the tongue tango with my former best friend Mia. And then not too long ago I considered getting back with him. He swept me up with this new version of Hunter Penbrook, told me he had started going to church, said all the right things, bought me coffee. It's a little hard to resist a cute guy bearing a mocha latte with extra whip, you know? Luckily, at prom two weeks ago, I saw the light and let that rotten fish off my hook.

"I'm not worried about you cheating on me, Luke. I'm tired of you bossing me around and acting all 'I'm in charge.'"

"I *am* in charge. I'm the editor."

"Not of our relationship."

"I'm back!" Ashley chooses that very moment to flounce back to her seat. "I got you a cotton candy." She hands the pink confection to Luke. "Bella, I figured you're like most girls and need to watch your weight, so I didn't get you anything. What'd I miss?"

Luke holds me down with his arm. "Don't even think about it," he whispers.

The crowd *oohs* and *ahhhs* as the Amazing Alfredo begins juggling two long silver swords. I applaud politely when he pulls a third one out of his hat and tosses it into the air with the rest. I'd hate to think where that sword was *really* hiding.

Like a distant relative, the Fritz Family Carnival comes to Truman, Oklahoma, every April and sets up camp on land that, I'm told, goes way back in the Fritz genealogy. They stay at least a month—working on additional routines, training new employees, giving the local elementary teachers a nice afternoon field trip— and don't leave until they can ride out bigger and better than the year before. And while that might be odd, it's nothing compared to the fact that I'm sitting on the bleachers between my boyfriend and a girl who has been openly flirting with him. That chick needs to learn some boundaries.

"Bella, Luke said you might need some help with your article."

He holds up a hand. "I just thought it would be interesting to get our three perspectives. Bella will still handle the interviews."

"It's been so great to work with you again, Luke." Ashley's smile could charm the shirt off Robert Pattinson. "Just like old times, huh?" Her eyes gaze into his. Like I'm not even there. "Kyle's really enjoyed hanging out. Too bad he had a study session tonight."

Luke leans close, his mouth poised near my ear. "Just because we're dating doesn't mean I'm going to slack off on your writing. You're still a staff member. And you *know* I do not boss you around any other time. I have been nothing but respectful to you." He returns his attention to the ring. "Did you write down the fat lady's stats?"

"Of course I did." I scribble something illegible on my paper. No, I didn't get her stats. I'm too busy fighting.

"She's seven hundred and twenty-nine pounds, in case you missed it," Ashley chirps.

"Thanks." *Lord, help me be kind to this girl.*

"You always act like I can't handle the writing assignments," I whisper for Luke's ears only. "I think I have more than proven I can. Not only can I write, but I can crank out some award-winning articles *while* crime solving."

After I moved to Truman, I accidentally became the Nancy Drew of Oklahoma. Now that I'm known for my mystery solving skills, friends and strangers want me to help them out. Just last week I tracked down a stolen iPhone and did a little spying for a suspicious girl who thought her boyfriend Buster was cheating. It's true he hadn't been going to football practice like he said; I found him at Margie Peacock's School of Ballet, lined up on the bar doing pirouettes and high kicks. I hear he makes a heck of a swan in Margie's recital.

"I'm not doubting your writing skills." Luke claps as the magician leaves, and Betty the Bearded Lady bows before starting her performance.

I'm transfixed by the hair on her face, and it suddenly makes me feel a whole lot less self-conscious about the fact that I didn't shave my legs last night. The audience claps in time to the spirited music as the woman's collie jumps through her hula hoop, then dances to the beat on its hind legs.

I shoot a pointed look at his old flame. "Let's talk about this later."

Ashley reaches around me and puts her hand on Luke's knee. "I forgot—I have my latest assignment on my laptop in the car. You told me to spice up my verbs, and I revised it. I wanted you to look at it." She returns to clapping for the Bearded Lady.

"Yes, Luke. She wants you to check out her spicy *verbs.*"

"At least she takes constructive criticism well." His voice is just loud enough for me to hear.

"That girl wants you back. Period."

"I'm not Hunter. And I'm not your dad."

"I have to go interview Betty the Bearded Lady." And I stomp down the bleachers to find her trailer outside. When I glance back, Ashley has scooted down.

And taken my place.

chapter two

The April night air smells of animals, popcorn, and a hint of rain. I feel like a storm is brewing in my head. Luke is such an egotistical jerk sometimes. Is he really so blind he can't see what Ashley's up to?

"Betty?" I knock on the trailer that has the Bearded Lady's face painted on the side. Speaking of gross. If I had a face full of fur I don't believe I'd be going on the road with it. Maybe I should give her the number of a good waxer in Manhattan.

The door swings open and bangs into the metal trailer. "Yeah?"

"Um . . ." *Focus on the eyes. Not on the whiskers.* "I'm Bella Kirkwood. I contacted the owner of the circus about interviewing some of you guys. I'm doing a piece for the—"

"Get in here, you." She pulls me up the short steps and hugs me to her ample bosom. "I haven't been interviewed since 1995, when I accidentally set my face on fire after I had to fill in as the human cannonball." She closes the door and points to a seat. Her collie stands at attention beside her.

Her living quarters are small and dim, but clean. As I take a seat on a gingham cushion at her table, I get a sniff of Pine-Sol and discount store candles.

"Would you like something to eat?" Betty opens a small fridge and extracts a pie that is topped with about two feet of meringue. "I tend to bake on the road. The rest of the crew practices, but it's not like my tricks take much work. Old Peg never fails, do you, girl?" She makes kissy noises toward the dog and places the pie on the table.

As she slices into her creation, I think about hygiene and stray hairs. But this is pie, and I don't want to be rude. I need info for the article, after all.

Betty reaches behind her to grab two forks, and I allow myself to really look at her.

And it's just as bad as I thought.

But beneath the hairy face are kind eyes that twinkle and make me feel instantly welcome. A mouth permanently poised in a smile.

I take my first bite and savor the flavor on my tongue. The woman can bake like a dream.

Pulling out my notebook, I get down to business. "I understand the carnival comes to Truman every year."

"Yes. We normally don't set up the midway while we're here, but Red wanted to. Seems like a waste of money to me, but he doesn't seem concerned with that." She purses her lips. "Pointless."

"It is an unusual setup you guys have. My stepdad says you always spend early spring here in Truman."

"Yep. It's a tradition started by the original Mr. Fritz. We travel through Florida in the winter, then take some time off in April and May to regroup and learn new tricks. It's not always a profitable approach, but this carnival's always been about quality and unique-ness. So it works."

"How long have you been living the circus life?" I ask.

She blots her own mouth, and I can't help but stare at her face again. "About twenty-five years. I'm the oldest one in the show. High school wasn't exactly a good time for me, and I dropped out at sixteen and thought my life was over. Then Old Man Fritz saw me at one of his shows and asked me if I'd like to be a star." Betty chuckles at the memory. "I told him I would indeed like to be a star. I worked for him, then when he retired, I worked for his son." Betty's eyes lose some of their gleam. "Then when Junior Fritz and his wife, Shelly, were tragically killed last year, I stayed on to work for Red Fritz."

"Junior's older brother." I had done my research.

"Yes. He has custody of Junior Fritz's daughter, but she stays with me in my trailer. I'm kind of the carnival mom." She smiles and grabs a picture off the counter. "Cherry is twelve, soon to be thirteen. I took over homeschooling her when her parents died." Betty shakes her head. "That kid means the world to me. I would do anything to protect her."

"I'm sure it can be dangerous sometimes on the road."

Betty laughs, but her eyes dim. "Sometimes it doesn't matter where you go—the trouble seems to pack up and move with you. But nothing's going to happen to Cherry." She settles the frame back in its place. "Not on ol' Betty's watch."

I quickly scribble down her words and try to get her back on track. "Tell me about life with the carnival. Is it just like one big family here?"

Betty absently strokes her dog's ear, sending Peg's dog tags to clanking. "Family? There are some of us who are mighty close. But others"—her hand stills—"you'd rather have as far away from you as possible."

"But I've been watching the show. You guys seem to be having such a good time—like it's one big party."

"Trust me, kid. In the carnival life, things are *not* always what they seem."

Before I can prod further, a knock on the door has Betty standing.

The ringmaster and owner, Red Fritz, pops his head in. "Three minutes 'til the second act. Get a move on."

"I know what time it is." Betty fluffs her hair, turning her back on the man. "I'm doing two appearances in the program tonight, so I have to scoot. Why don't you come back after the show, Miss Kirkwood, and we'll finish this conversation?"

"I think that time would be better spent minding your own business and coming up with a new routine for the dog here. People are getting bored with all that stupid stuff you do," Red says.

"My dog is a crowd pleaser, and you know it."

Red Fritz narrows his eyes. "If your fuzzy face isn't out there on time, it's coming out of your pay. Again." With a parting glance at me, he slams the trailer door.

When Betty turns around, the smile is back in place. "Forget him. Now, let's walk back together, shall we? I have a great story about a clown mishap I can share as we go."

A flash of blonde in the distance catches my attention as I stand in the doorway. "I'll catch up with you later, Betty. I need to check out something in the parking lot."

My feet press into the gravel path, and as Ashley's car becomes more visible, so does its owner. My stomach drops like the floor in the gravity barrel out on the midway.

Under the streetlights, I watch my nemesis wrap her arms around Luke and seal her mouth to his. His hands move to her wrists.

"Working on a new story?" I cross my arms over my chest and feel the fire beneath my skin.

"Bella!" Luke shoves Ashley away. "I—I didn't—"

"Know I was standing here? Obviously."

He steps toward me. "It's not what you think. I wasn't kissing her. I—"

"It's my fault," Ashley purrs. "We got to talking about old times, and I got carried away. Don't blame Luke."

Yeah, she looks real contrite.

Humiliation and hurt battle in my head. "Forget it. I have work to do." I walk away as fast as my shaking legs will move.

"Wait." Luke runs to catch up. His hand clasps my arm. "Bella, hold up."

I round on the boy, my eyes flashing. "And you said it was all in my head—that she wasn't chasing you. Now is my idea so crazy?"

"Ashley didn't mean it."

I blink. "You're taking up for her?"

"No, I—" He sets his jaw and stares at the ground. "This is what you've been waiting for, isn't it? You've just been waiting for me to screw up—like all the other guys in your life."

"Don't turn this on me, Luke. You're the one who had your lips plastered to a girl who is *not* your girlfriend."

"I was pushing her away."

"I can't work with her. I *won't* work with her. I want Ashley off the newspaper staff."

He reaches out again, but drops his hand. "You know I can't do that."

"Then we're through. It's her or me."

"There's no choice here." His voice snaps with electricity. "Ashley's not going to do anything like that again. I'll make sure of it. But she stays on the paper. I can't fire someone for attempted kissing." He steps so close I can't help but breathe in his earthy cologne. "You know I would never cheat on you."

I watch an airplane soar through the night sky. "I need some time."

"For what?"

I bite the inside of my cheek. "Time to figure us out . . . and time to get that image of you two out of my head."

"I know you're mad. You have a right to be. But this boils down to trust—you either trust me or you don't."

I slowly nod and look into the face of the boy I've waited for all year. "I guess right now I don't."

Luke stares past me to the big top. "This is really what you want? Because it seems to me like you're just running scared instead of dealing with what happened—with us."

Pain gives my words a biting edge. "I know it's a big blow to your ego, but I really think a break would do us both some good."

He takes off his glasses and nods. "Good luck with your interview. And your space." Hands stuffed in his khakis, he walks away.

Leaving me standing in the midst of a hundred cars. And one broken heart.

I return to the main tent just as Alfredo the magician is working his way out of some chains. Soon all of them fall, and he's left with nothing but a pair of handcuffs. Finally they, too, drop to the ground, and the audience goes wild. But at the moment the man could completely vanish and I wouldn't be impressed.

"And now, ladies and gentlemen, feast your eyes on the lovely Cherry Fritz, our reigning princess of the trapeze!" Red Fritz waves his arms grandly toward the ceiling as a young girl flies through the air.

Ugh, men. Who needs them? There's my cheater ex, Hunter, and my dad who is planning a wedding even though he's the last person on the planet who needs a wife. And my stepdad? Life majorly changed when he won a professional wrestling reality show. Like having a stepfather who wears spandex on a regular basis isn't stressful enough. Where are the normal guys? I thought Luke was one of them. He's cute in that Clark Kent, Abercrombie sort of way. He's freakishly mature and smart. And he's not just a nerdy brainiac—he's even the captain of his soccer team. I thought I wanted nothing more than to be his girlfriend. Ever since I arrived in Truman this fall, we've been drawn together like two magnets. But tonight his magnetism's pulling in one too many girls.

Feeling absolutely miserable, I sit through the rest of the show. A guy walks on a tightrope. A girl does a handstand on a prancing horse. A small clown gets shot from a cannon. But all I can think about is Luke.

God, what am I supposed to do with all this?

Before I know it, all the lights come up and people are exiting the bleachers. I sit for a while longer and watch the workers go into action sweeping, removing the animals, and clearing the grounds. Finally I gather my purse and head out back to Betty's trailer. A breeze flutters over my skin, and I pick up the pace. Though I would never admit it to Luke, it is a little creepy out here now. Few cars remain in the parking lot, and I wonder at the sense of coming back here alone.

I pass two smaller trailers before coming to Betty's bigger one. The door hangs open, and light spills out.

I knock on the swinging door. "Betty? Hello?"

No answer. I stand on the step and knock louder. "Betty? It's Bella!"

Nothing.

Then my ears twitch at the tiniest of sounds. A distant whimper. An animal. From the back of the trailer.

"Betty?" I step inside just as her collie leaps out. "Peg! Hey, here girl!" I turn back to the trailer.

And feel my stomach drop to the floor.

My scream pierces the air.

Betty the Bearded Lady sits at her table, nose down in her pie.

And one shiny sword in her back.

chapter three

~~~~~~

*J*ust take deep breaths, Bella. Deep breaths."

I don't know how sticking your head between your knees and staring at your own crotch is supposed to help anything, but here I am. Trying not to pass out. Trying not to bawl uncontrollably.

Mark Rogers, friend and member of the Truman PD, pats my back as we sit on the arena bleachers. The rest of the police force combs through Betty the Bearded Lady's trailer. I've already answered a hundred questions, and I have a feeling they are just the tip of the iceberg. *Why me, God? How will I ever get that image out of my mind? All that blood.*

My breath hitches and Mark does more patting. "Think nice thoughts." Tonight his voice is as high pitched as a flute. "Go to your happy place."

"I thought I was *at* one. Then I saw a dead woman." I want this to be one of those overly realistic dreams you wake up from. The kind that makes you happy to be awake, realizing it was all just a vivid dream, and you are safely tucked in bed.

I hear the crunching of a wrapper and raise my eyes. Mark sticks half a Snickers in his mouth.

"What?" His eyes go wide. "I'm a stress eater. Want some?"

My stomach does acrobatics at the thought of food. "You have no idea what you're doing here, do you?"

"Not every day I see a bearded lady murdered." He eats the last bite. "Seriously, that is some freaky stuff in there. The only dead body I've ever seen was my Great Uncle Morty. And he was ninety-six, so it wasn't a real shocker that he went, you know? He keeled over at the nursing home square dance. He just did one too many do-si-dos. But still"—he shivers—"he was awfully pale and wrinkly. Kinda cakey looking."

"Thanks for sharing." I cover my face with my hands and rock back and forth. Mark's hand plops on my head. "Stop patting me!"

"Well, pardon me." He sniffs. "It works on my schnauzer."

"Bella?"

At that familiar voice, I stand up. "Luke." He walks past two cops, and I run straight into his arms.

"Shhh." He holds me close, and I breathe in the scent of him. His shampoo, his cologne, the smell of his clothes. Him. "Officer Mark called me."

"Please don't leave me." *Let's forget we broke up. Just for now.*

"I'm not going anywhere." He caresses the back of my head, and I hang on like he's my lifeboat off the *Titanic*. "Your mom and Jake are on their way. It's just going to take them a little bit from Oklahoma City."

My stepdad Jake's on the road a lot with the wrestling circuit, and Mom goes with him whenever he's close. Why couldn't he have been in Philly or Phoenix tonight? Seeing a dead woman definitely qualifies as one of those moments a girl needs her mother.

"She died . . . in her pie." My breath catches. "Why would someone kill her and let her die in her meringue?"

"I don't know." Luke's voice is calm, reassuring.

"It was good pie too."

"I'm sure it was, Bel."

I sniff on his shoulder. "If I die over pie, I want it to be coconut cream."

"She's a little shocky," Officer Mark says. Like I'm not right here. Like I'm talking crazy. But who, I ask, would want her last breath to be taken nose-deep in raisin pie? Or a meat pie? It would be my luck to go in a big ol' bowl of peas.

Luke steps back, keeping his hands locked with mine. "Do you think you can tell me about it?"

"I'd like to know too." A girl in a sparkly leotard appears, her blonde hair slicked into a ponytail. Though she still wears stage makeup, her face is pale. Her eyes haunted.

"This is Cherry Fritz," Mark says. "She's the owner's niece."

"This was my parents' circus." Watery eyes meet mine. "Betty was my godmother." As she steps closer I can see she doesn't look quite so harsh beneath the makeup. "Do you think she—she . . . suffered?" Cherry's tears inspire some of my own.

"I don't know. It didn't really look that way." Except for the sword the length of my leg sticking out of her back. "She did have dessert, if that's any consolation." Wow. My ability to comfort is just . . . awful.

"Betty didn't have any enemies. I just don't understand. There has to be some mistake." Cherry turns to Officer Mark. "Who would m-murder her?" Tears make tracks down her painted face.

"We'll get to the bottom of it." Mark clears his throat. Probably has a peanut stuck in there.

"Cherry!" The ringmaster explodes through the big top entrance. "Where have you been? We have a killer on the loose, and I couldn't even find you!"

I move closer to Luke as Red Fritz's piercing brown eyes land on me.

"You the one who found her?"

"Um . . ." I swallow past a lump and nod. "Yes."

The seconds stretch as he watches me. I look away, my skin tingling.

"Well, I'm sorry you had to see that." Red stands beside Mark. "We are a family here at the Fritz Family Carnival. And I can't imagine who would do such a vile thing. Surely it can't be one of our own, that much I know."

Officer Mark jots down some notes. "Mr. Fritz, Miss Betty's trailer will obviously be unusable for a while. Will Cherry be staying with you?"

"My son Stewart lives with me in my own trailer, so space has always been too tight for the kid. I've contacted a distant family member in Truman to take Cherry until she can move back into Betty's."

Ew. Like she'll ever *want* to live in the place where her godmother was murdered.

A policeman enters the tent, getting Red Fritz's attention. They speak in hushed tones. Red glances at his niece, then nods.

"What family member, Uncle Red? I can't go stay with a stranger."

A moment later the entry flap opens again and Dolly O'Malley, my mom's best friend, is escorted inside. She nods her head toward the ringmaster. "Red."

He tips his hat. "Looking as lovely as ever."

"How are you doing, Bella?" Dolly hugs me to her. "I can't imagine what kind of night you kids have had." She smiles at Cherry. "My, my. Aren't you the spitting image of your mother. Do you remember me?"

Cherry shrugs. "Kinda."

"Your mama was my second cousin. We used to play together when we were about your age." She brushes a hand over Cherry's hair. "I have a big house and lots of horses. Your Uncle Red thought it would be a fun place for you to hang out for a couple of days." Dolly turns to Officer Mark. "Bella and Cherry will be going home with me. I assume the police are done talking to them?"

"For now, but I'm sure there will be more questions tomorrow."

I follow Dolly and her cousin outside. Though it's April and the night is warm, I shiver a little.

"Wait—what's going on?" Cherry breaks from us and runs toward a police officer. "Stop!"

"The Amazing Alfredo," Luke says, pointing. "It looks like they've cuffed him."

I strain to see him in the dim carnival lights. "Does this mean he—"

"He's been arrested." Officer Mark joins us, staring straight ahead. "It was his sword that pierced Betty's heart. And we have Red's son, Stewart, who claims to have overheard a heated argument within twenty minutes of Bella finding the body. There are some other suspicious details I can't get into, but we're taking him in and waiting on the prints."

The officer pulls a crying Cherry off the magician. "No! He didn't do it!"

Alfredo says something to Cherry, and she steps back, shoulders heaving, and watches the policeman put Alfredo in the car.

"I'm going to get Cherry. We'll meet you at the house, Bella," Dolly says, walking to the girl.

Luke curls an arm around me, pulls me close, and presses a kiss to my temple. "I know you hate people telling you what to do, but try and get some sleep tonight."

"Right." I slide my arms around him until we're locked in a hug. I just need one moment of safety. To breathe in his strength and pretend that all is well. "Thanks for coming back and staying with me."

"That's what ex-boyfriends do."

"Luke?"

"Yes?"

"I have to find out for sure who killed Betty the Bearded Lady."

He sighs into my hair. "I was afraid you were going to say that."

chapter four

The Monday morning alarm goes off, and it's everything I can do not to throw it across the room. My mentally challenged cat, Moxie, peeps open one eyeball, decides she'd rather not get up, and curls into the blanket.* Lucky thing.

I didn't sleep a wink all weekend. Every time I closed my eyes, Betty the hairy dead lady was there. Visions of her eating pie. Visions of her dog jumping through a hoop. But mostly . . . visions of someone plunging that sword into her back. There's only one thing to be said for it all.

I, Bella Kirkwood, will be Betty the Bearded Lady's avenger.

After I have some oatmeal.

I go through the motions of my morning routine and finally walk down the stairs to the kitchen. We live in an old farmhouse that looks like an Oklahoma twister sucked it up, thought better of it, and tossed it right back out. It's rough, it's worn, but it's become home. The interior is not much better. Aside from the kitchen, which got a remodel last fall due to an arsonist's fire, the house is like something out of 1975. But Mom has promised that the reign of shag and wood paneling is almost over now that Jake has made it to the big time in wrestling.

"Hey, honey." My mother stands at the toaster and kisses me as I walk by. "Did you sleep any?"

"Yeah. I'm fine," I lie. I've been on lockdown all weekend, and I have *got* to break out of here and see civilization. If you'd have told me just last year that I'd consider the small town of Truman, Oklahoma, worthy of being called civilization, I would have laughed in your face and then gone shopping with my daddy's credit card. But those days are over. Now it's dirt roads, sweet tea, and the occasional run to Target. The sweet tea I've gotten used to.

"Are you sure you're okay to go to school?" My mom ponytails my long brown hair in her gentle grip. "We could just hang out here at the house."

I sit down at the table, stifling an eye roll. I know she means well.

"I feel a little traumatized myself." My stepbrother Budge reaches for the syrup, his big red 'fro especially buoyant this morning. "Maybe I should stay home with Bella."

"We have a test in junior English, if you recall." I turn determined eyes to my mom. "Can't miss that." Not that I got the chance to study much the last few days. Mom was busy keeping me purposely distracted with her weekend of board games and family movies. "Besides, if I have to play Monopoly or see *Shrek* one more time, somebody is gonna get hurt."

My youngest stepbrother enters the room, wearing a Spider-Man T-shirt and a red cape. "You're just mad because I beat you. All ten times." He taps his head. "It's all about strategy."

"Whatever," I say. "I totally let you win. You're the youngest— that's what we're supposed to do." Robbie is in first grade, and if Harvard knew about him, they'd be recruiting.

Twenty minutes later I climb into my VW Bug and drive to school, grateful for the change of scenery.

~~~~~~~~~

I struggle through a test in English, my mind on facing Luke for the first time at school. With a confidence I don't feel, I sail into the classroom, greet some fellow reporters, and head straight for the safety of my beloved Mac.

Ten minutes into my typing frenzy, a shadow falls over my keyboard.

Luke looms, his blue eyes ever serious. "You don't look like you've slept much."

I stare at the screen as if my own writing is the most engrossing thing ever. "Thanks. Your concern is touching."

"Of course I'm concerned."

"Really? Because practically all of Truman High came to visit me this weekend—but you." Shoot! I was *not* going to say that. I was going to play it cool that he didn't so much as call me after we left the carnival Saturday night. No call. No text. No e-mail.

"We broke up. Remember?"

"Right." I lift my chin a notch. "And I thought we'd still be friends, but maybe you're not mature enough to handle that."

"I heard about all the people stopping by over the weekend, so I didn't want to *smother you.* I know how you hate that."

Nothing like having your words thrown back at you. Like a big spitty paper wad.

"And I didn't know it would bother you to not hear from me." He has the nerve to look smug. "Missing me already?"

"It didn't bother me." I meet his challenging gaze. "My mom was asking about you. That's all." Ugh. I need a scarlet *L* for liar.

Luke sits his Hollister-clad legs on the edge of my work station. "I do have some news that will probably upset you."

"You're stepping down as editor, and Zac Efron is taking your place?"

Luke's eyes narrow a fraction before he continues. "You're being reassigned."

My hands slip off the keyboard. "What did you say?"

"I'm taking over the series on the carnival."

"Um, no, you're not."

He blinks down at me. "Yes. I am."

"But I—"

"I'm the editor, and that's final."

My mouth opens in a sputter. "I . . . but you . . . this can't . . ." I stand from my chair. "I'm going to talk to Mr. Holman." Our advisor will straighten this out.

Luke stops me with a hand on my arm. "I've already discussed it with him. He's in complete agreement."

I put my nose inches away from his. "I cannot believe you would stoop this low." Where's the sensitive guy who came back for me Saturday night? Because this boy right here needs a good, swift kick in the—

"Bella, you're a good writer. We both know that. But you're also reckless and tend to run headfirst into danger."

I glance at his ex-girlfriend, whose blonde hair is disgustingly perfect. "If you assign her to this, so help me—"

"Ashley Timmons has nothing to do with this." His eyes darken. "She has nothing to do with *anything*."

"Didn't look that way in the carnival parking lot."

"Let that go. She and I both have. Ashley's already apologized. She feels terrible."

I'm sure she's doubled over with grief. More like she's planning her next make-out attack.

"I've already finished the first article." I punch my finger in his solid chest. "You can't just rip me off this story."

He grabs my hand, holds it suspended. "Yes. I can. And I just did. We'll run your interview with Betty, but I've e-mailed you the details of your new assignment."

"You are *such*"—I wrench my hand free—"a jerk."

Luke quirks a black brow. "Then I guess I've finally lived up to your low expectations."

I bite my bottom lip to keep from yelling like a banshee. Not that the class would notice. Everyone is writing away and listening to their iPods. Except for one.

Ashley Timmons.

I glower in her direction, and she snaps her attention back to her computer.

"Is this in retaliation for breaking up with you?" My voice is a whisper.

"You know me better than that. This is for your protection—because when you get nosy, you tend to get into near-death situations." He brushes a finger on my forehead. "There's something brewing in there. Admit it."

"Yeah, it's called dislike for my editor and a certain opportunistic reporter."

"We'll revisit this in a few weeks and see if we need to reevaluate." Luke opens his mouth to say something, then changes his mind. "I'll leave you to your new assignment."

My eyes shoot poison darts at his back as he saunters away.

By the time lunch rolls around, I'm in a mood worthy of a category four hurricane.

"He said *what*?" Ruthie McGee cuts into her burrito with the contraband pocketknife she keeps in her boot. Today her hair is a shocking shade of electric blue, teased to Marge Simpson heights and tied off with a camouflage headband.

"Luke took me off the carnival story." My head pounds inside my skull, and I regret not taking my mom up on her idea to stay home.

"Bella, that sounds very thoughtful to me." This from Lindy, the first friend I made at Truman High. She hung out with me in exchange for my giving her a makeover to catch a boy. The makeover and friendship stuck, but Matt Sparks, her best friend and unrequited love, has never treated her as anything more than a sister. "He knows how awful Saturday night was for you—finding that woman . . . um, you know—"

"Nose deep in meringue?" Ruthie crunches on a chip. "Gone to that great Gillette razor in the sky?"

"I mean Luke probably knows how traumatic all that is going to be for you for a while. So I think it's very thoughtful of him to take you off the story." Lindy eyes Matt Sparks, sitting next to her, lost in his burger. "Romantic even."

"And they arrested that Alfredo guy," Ruthie says. "So I guess it's not like you need to go back to the carnival and investigate."

I focus on peeling the label off my water bottle. "Right."

Ruthie gasps, clutching her throat of a hundred necklaces. "I've seen that look before. Like at prom when you and my dream muffin Budge saved us from that psycho who wanted to blow us all up."

"Bella, no." Lindy frowns. "Can't you just lay low for a while? In the short time you've been at Truman, you've almost been killed twice."

"Yeah." I wave off Lindy. "Don't worry about it. I'm sure the police are on top of everything. I just—" I pause as a tall boy stops at our table. He holds out a Gatorade.

"Hey, Lindy." He swallows visibly. "I just wanted to thank you for sharing your water at track practice yesterday." He hands her the bottle. "I wanted to return the favor. I noticed this is your favorite."

Lindy accepts it, a small smile on her face. "Thanks, Bo."

The senior's cheeks pinken. "I'm on my way to check the next practice schedule. Um, in case you'd want to walk with me to the gym."

"Yeah." Lindy laughs and fingers the collar of her T-shirt. "Yeah, I would." Clutching her Gatorade, she follows Bo Blades, THS track star, out of the cafeteria.*

"I'll clean up your tray." Matt picks up Lindy's trash, his movements jerky, his brow furrowed.

Ruthie and I exchange a look.

"Bo is so cute." She sighs. "Not as cute as my Budgie—but still a hot number."

"Especially in those running shorts," I add. "Mee-yeow."

"Lindy had pizza on her shirt again," Matt huffs. "But I guess Bo won't even notice." He stomps away.

I chew on a carrot stick. "Well, that was interesting."

"Indeed. It seems Lindy has an admirer and her BFF is *mucho* jealous. Either that or he just has PMS." Ruthie pats her big hair. "It happens to the best of us."

I see Luke Sullivan enter the cafeteria with Kyle and some of his soccer buddies. Walking by his side is Ashley Timmons. She tips her head back and laughs at something he says. Whatever small appetite I had is now officially gone. He's hanging out with her?

"That girl is too cute," Ruthie says, then catches my expression. "Er, I mean, no. She's *so* unattractive." Her face scrunches in disgust. "I've seen dog butts prettier than her."

"Luke and I have broken up. He can flirt with whoever he wants." Never mind the feeling of a million pinpricks to my heart. I'm sure it's just indigestion. Cafeteria gas.

"So what are we going to do to solve this carnival mystery?"

I blink at Ruthie. "What? *We're* not going to do anything. And besides, like everyone says, it's probably all wrapped up. Just waiting on the sword prints. No mystery."

Ruthie leans over the table, getting closer. "Bella, you're up to something, and I want in on it."

"No."

"Aw, come on! Batman . . . Sherlock Holmes . . . Scooby Doo—do you know what they all have that you don't?"

"Testosterone?"

"Sidekicks!" Ruthie nods her blue head manically. "You need me. I could be the muscles behind the operation, and you'd be the brains. Plus it could be like my graduation present."

"You're a walking arsenal and would probably get us arrested." Why the Baptist preacher's daughter feels the need to carry around brass knuckles and the occasional knife is beyond me.

"Some of the Fritz crew go to my daddy's church every spring when they're in town." She waggles a single eyebrow. "I could get us part-time jobs at the place."

"I'm sure I can get my own job—not that I was thinking of doing that." Item number one on my after-school to-do list: head to the Fritz Family Carnival . . .

"Mr. Fritz might not want to see you around . . . since you bring all that bad mojo and all." Ruthie shrugs. "But my dad could probably talk him into anything."

"I don't bring bad mojo."

"Face it, you got dead girl juju."

"Fine. Talk to your dad."

"About what?" A masculine voice asks.

Luke.

Fabulous.

"You could've told me he was standing there." I swivel to face him. "Did you need something?"

"You wouldn't be making plans to get up close and personal with the Fritz gang, would you?"

"Nope." Ruthie answers for me. "But if she was, I'd be her new sidekick." She picks up her tray and stands up. "I'm probably going to need to get me some business cards. And a logo—I need one of them logos. Maybe a snappy sidekick catchphrase." Still talking to herself, Ruthie walks away to throw out her trash.

Luke slowly shakes his head. "You just can't leave well enough alone, can you?"

"Funny." I shoot a glance toward a watchful Ashley Timmons. "I was about to say the same to you."

chapter five

~~~~~~

*N*ow we're just going to check on Cherry. That's all. Don't act all weird and suspicious or anything." I hang a left to the Fritz Family Carnival.

Ruthie rolls down the passenger window in my Bug. "Me?" She snorts. "I'm cool. Queen of ice right here."

"Stick close to me and let me do all the talking."

"Duh." She pats a thick book. "That's what assistants do."

"What is that?"

"A manual for sidekicks." She pops her Bubblicious. "Got it off the Internet."

I pull into the gravel parking lot, and we get out. We walk past the Tilty Spin and the Zipper roller coaster.

"That looks awesome." Ruthie points to the twisted tracks of the coaster. "Nothing like being upside down, eh, boss?"

"I'm not your boss." *Or I would've already fired you.* "And you will never see me on one of those things."

Ruthie stops midstride. "Is *somebody* afraid of heights?"

I hold back a shiver as I look at all the rides. "Just when I'm on a ride that looks to be held together by duct tape and rubber bands."

"Ever kissed a boy on a Ferris wheel? It's so romantic." She sighs and looks toward the giant ride in the back of the lot. "Except for that time I puked on Sammy Stutes, which just proves corndogs and the Tilty Spin do *not* go together."

We walk into the big top, and I check out the area. I'm not sure what exactly I'm doing. I guess I'm hoping I'll know it when I see it.

"Can I help you?"

Ruthie and I look to the ceiling. There above us on a platform stands Cherry Fritz, trapeze in hand.

"Actually," I call out, "I just stopped by to check on you. I'm Bella Kirkwood. We met the other night." *You know, the night I found your godmother all dead and stuff.*

She lets the trapeze swing and skitters down the narrow ladder.

"How are you doing?" I ask as she walks to us. "Back to work already?"

She glances up to her trapeze. "I needed to get my mind off things. The show is closed until tomorrow night, but I decided to work on a new stunt with our downtime." Cherry frowns. "Betty wouldn't have approved, but I want to do it."

"Because it's too hard?"

"Almost as hard as the stunt that killed both my parents." For a moment the hollow look returns to her gaze before she shakes it off. "But my uncle says it's what we need to take the circus to the next level. Times are hard. People don't come see us like they used to. He says we have to make this season's show more dynamic."

I look over my shoulder and find Ruthie has vanished. Fabulous. She's either sneaking a free ride on the bumper cars or patting down a suspect.

"How is it working out at Dolly's?"

Cherry smiles. "It's okay. I mean, it was weird at first—we're distantly related and didn't really know each other that well. But she's been amazing. It's been nice to have a home-cooked meal instead of something from one of the food trailers. And Dolly's really easy to talk to."

Dolly has plenty of mother experience. She lost her two young daughters many years ago in a car wreck when she was still married to Mickey, my stepdad's manager. My mom says there's been a big gaping hole in Dolly's heart ever since, so I'm sure she's loving the company at her house.

I startle at the sound of raised voices from the opposite side of the tent.

"I'm through. This place is going under, and I've had it." A man about as tall as my armpit stomps out of a partitioned tent, a clown wig in his fisted hand.

Another guy, who could be his twin, follows close behind. "I can't make a living here. More and more work—and for what? Less pay!"

They bolt through the exit flap, and Cherry shakes her head. "That's our fourth employee to walk today. Where in the world are we going to get two clowns on such short notice?"

The Lord parted the Red Sea for the Israelites. Me? He gives a clown job. "I'll do it."

Cherry blinks. "Are you serious?"

My fake smile wobbles on my face. "Yeah. I'd love the job." *What have I done?* "And my friend Ruthie would too."

"I don't know."

"I'm a great worker." I can't believe I'm having to convince someone that I'd be a worthy *clown*, for crying out loud. "And Ruthie is so dependable and smart."

"Is that her?" Cherry points to a far corner where Ruthie McGee lies prostrate on a magician's table.

A man waves his hands over her. "Abracadabra! Shalla-kazaam! I will now cut you in half, then magically piece you back together."

"Oh boy." Cherry takes off for the couple, and I follow. "Bart!"

He stops, his hand saw held high. Ruthie's eyes go wide as funnel cakes.

"How many times have I asked you not to touch Alfredo's props?" Cherry rips the saw out of Bart's grip. "Especially the sharp ones?"

Ruthie bolts to a seated position. "What? You're not a magician?" Cherry rolls her eyes as Bart runs away. "He's a mechanic."

"He was going to cut me in half!" Ruthie straightens her biker jacket and sniffs. "I thought something was fishy when he asked me if I had any lug nuts."

"Cherry, I wanted to ask you a few questions about Betty, if you think you're up to it."

She frowns. "I guess."

"You mentioned that Afredo couldn't have killed Betty—"

Her answer comes quickly. "Because he loved her."

"They were a couple? For how long?"

Cherry twirls a piece of her white-blonde hair. "Maybe three months. They had worked together for years, so for them to fall in love was totally out of the blue and unexpected." Her face stretches into a contented smile. "Betty had never been happier. She'd never really had a lot of attention from the guys because—"

"Her man-beard?"

Cherry shoots an annoyed look at Ruthie. "Because she devoted her life to the circus—then to me."

"Did she get along with everyone here?" I ask. "Any enemies? Any fights or disagreements lately?"

She considers this. "No, no one. Well, everyone has the occasional fight with Red, so that's nothing different."

I perk at this. So Betty didn't get along with creepy guy. "What problems could there be between Betty and Red?"

Cherry lifts an eyebrow. "Why do you want to know?"

Ruthie chortles. "Don't you know who this is? She's a famous crime—"

I elbow my friend. "I'm just concerned. If I'm going to be working here and all." I smile at Ruthie. "By the way, how do you feel about red honking noses and rainbow wigs?"

Ruthie pats her blue hair. "That was so last year."

"I'll introduce you to my cousin Stewart." Cherry motions for us to follow. "He's in charge of hiring hourly workers."

She leads us outside to the largest travel trailer on the grounds. This looks like the Hilton on wheels compared to the rest—even Betty's.

After one knock, Cherry swings open the door. "Stewart?" she yells. "I brought you two clowns."

I think I might be offended.

We step up into the trailer. It's much newer than Betty's—large and spacious. The front half is an office of desks and file cabinets. A TV hangs suspended from the ceiling, showing real-time footage of the big-top grounds.

A tall, lanky guy stands up from one of the two desks. He looks like he's a few years older than me, and is just as slender as Red is rotund.

"And what have you brought me today, dear cousin?" He grabs my hand, shakes it, and holds it longer than necessary. "I don't get to see too many beautiful girls on the road." He *tsks*, his beady eyes darting to Cherry. "The carnival really isn't for the pretty."

I draw back my hand. It's everything I can do not to wipe it on my jeans. Ew.

Stewart turns his attention to Ruthie. His smile falters just a bit, but he recovers. "And you"—his eyes trail up to the tippy top of her hair—"also a vision." He tries to capture her hand, but Ruthie deflects.

"You don't want to shake my hand. I just got over a bad case of the runs."

"Stewart, these girls would like a job while we're here in Truman." Cherry's voice takes on a different tone as she talks to her older cousin. The voice my mom uses when reading her grocery list. "We just lost two more clowns—the Bingworth twins. So I thought maybe—"

"Of course, we need the help." Stewart steps closer to me, and prickly chills dance along my arms. "You look familiar."

"Bella is the one who"—Cherry swallows—"found Betty."

Stewart tilts his narrow head, sending his black hair falling over his eyes like a curtain. "How terrible that must've been for you." His sigh sounds loud in the metal trailer. "I'm sure this is the last place you would want to work. And we respect that."

"She wants the job." Cherry softens her face, and I watch in awe as she steps into a new role. Her full lips push into a pout and her head drops. "I just thought with Betty gone, the woman who was like my mother, it would be nice to have some older girls around to talk to." She regards him through her lashes. "That way I won't have to come to you and Uncle Red with my questions about cramps and tampons."

"Okay, okay, okay!" Stewart holds out a hand. "We'll give it a trial period, all right?" I feel Stewart's eyes travel the length of me and resist the urge to shudder. "But I'll be keeping a close eye on you two . . . just to make sure that it's not too much." He sends a slow wink my way. "Especially you—with all you've been through. We wouldn't want to cause you any further unhappiness."

"I'll be fine." It comes out like a squeak. "I'm pretty tough." I nudge Ruthie. "Aren't I?"

My friend nods. "I've seen her kill a rattler with her teeth."

I quickly turn the topic back to our new roles as clowns and get the rundown on the job, which mostly consists of interacting with the audience and assisting the performing clowns. Fifteen minutes later my head is swimming with information, and I feel like going home and taking a good, long shower to rid myself of Stewart Fritz cooties.

"You Truman High students sure are a helpful bunch," Stewart says as we step down from his trailer. "All but one of our positions have been filled now. I think things are looking up for us. And don't forget, Bella—I'll be keeping a special eye on you."

I cough to cover up the retching noise. "See you tomorrow." Pulling Ruthie along, I speed walk away from him.

"Bella," Ruthie says. "The Lord gifted me with the ability to see things in people that others don't. So this information may come as a surprise to you, but Stewart Fritz is one spooky dude."

"Your insight into the human soul is clearly just God-given."

"I know, right?" Ruthie jerks as I pull her to the left. "Where are we going?"

"I want to check out Alfredo's trailer. I noticed they took off the police tape."

"Oh, cool!" Ruthie rubs her hands together. "Are we gonna riffle through some drawers? Dust for any prints the cops might've missed? Set up some hidden cameras?"

"No. *I'm* going in. And you're going to keep watch."

"That's lame. My dynamic duo guidebook says I have to make sure you don't crowd me out of the action."

"Look, I have not said you're my partner yet. So consider this like part of your interview—a test. Did that book tell you that being lookout girl is one of the most crucial steps to being a sidekick?"

Ruthie shuffles a rock with her toe. "No. But I've only read the pages with pictures."

"Well then." I scan the area for anyone who might see us. "Stand outside this trailer while I go in. If you see anyone headed this way, I need you to call out 'good afternoon' really loud, okay?"

Ruthie chews on her lip, blue with a lipstick that complements her hair. "That's not very original. How about I sing a few lines from *The Wizard of Oz?*"

"No."

"And then I could say, 'The monkeys are coming! The monkeys are coming!'"

"Just stick with my plan." I look back over my shoulder as I peel open the door. "Consider this phase one of your test."

"Man, I hate tests. They give me the burps."

The door gives a little squeak as I shut myself inside. *Dear God, if there were a breaking and entering prayer, I would so say it right now.*

The shades are pulled, blocking out the afternoon sun. I slip a tiny flashlight out of my purse and shine it around the trailer. Looks like more than one guy lives here. Each side is split into bunk beds. I take it the stripped bed is Alfredo's. I wave my light around until I see a small chest of drawers on his side. I ease the top drawer open and peer inside. Car magazines, a Snickers, a few pictures. I take one out. Alfredo and a woman. A beardless woman who is definitely not Betty. They're staring into each other's eyes and laughing. Extracting my camera, I snap a shot of the front and back of the picture. My heart races as I listen for sounds outside. I have to hurry. The life of crime is really not my thing.

Moving on to the bottom drawer, I find jeans, T-shirts, socks. Nothing out of the ordinary. I can't imagine having to live with so few belongings. I mean, five T-shirts to your name? If Alfredo is guilty of anything, it's a crime of fashion. I quickly run my fingers over the drawer seams, looking for any sort of hidden compartment. What? It works on TV.

"Somewhere over the rainbow!"

Ruthie's voice from outside jolts me like a cattle prod. I drop my flashlight, and it skitters across the floor, under the far bed. Oh no—I have to get it! I have to hide! My brain scrambles for a rational thought. *Think, Bella! What do I do?*

I must get that flashlight. It was a present from Luke and has my name on it! I leap for the other side of the trailer and throw my hand under the bed, reaching with my fingers.

"The monkeys are coming! The monkeys are coming!"

I hear the door handle being lifted.

Not much farther. Almost got it. I can see the flashlight.

The door groans.

I shoot up to my feet.

Just as Stewart Fritz steps inside.

chapter six

"iss Kirkwood?"

Fall leaves in Connecticut could not shake harder than I am as I face Stewart Fritz.

He flicks on the lights. "What are you doing?" He takes large steps until he's but a breath away.

"I—I—" I was trespassing and searching through things that didn't belong to me. "I was told there was a bathroom in here." I do a little dip. "It's kind of an emergency. But I couldn't find a thing in the dark." Especially with my flashlight under the bed.

Stewart's small hazel eyes narrow like a snake's. "We have Porta-Potties all over the property."

I toss my hair and laugh. "Oh, silly man! I could never use one of those. And since I'm an employee here now—"

"This is one of the men's trailers you're in."

I look around. "Is it? Why I couldn't tell *what* it was in the pitch black." I giggle some more.

Stewart stares at me as the seconds tick painfully by.

Finally his face breaks into a sly smile. His voice is a low ebb. "Any time you need some help, you ask for me."

Gulp. "Thank you. I tend to get lost often. I'm a little bit air-headed at times."

Stewart rests his hand on my shoulder. "All the more reason for me to keep my eye out for you. I'd hate for you to get hurt out here. The carnival life isn't always as safe as it looks."

"I'll keep that in mind." I try to skirt past him, but his body blocks my way.

"How old are you, Bella?" His eyes dip to my chest.

"Seventeen." If he asks my bra size, I'm knocking him in the teeth.

"I'm twenty-one." His grin reminds me of the Joker in *Batman*. "Do you like older men?"

I take one step around him. "I really have to get back outside. My friend is waiting on me."

"The crazy girl who was yelling outside?"

"Yep. That's the one." I force a smile and take another step. "She's not well today. Her, um, antidiarrheal meds are really messing with her head. She can't be left alone for too long . . . or she could start singing *Rent* any second." What am I saying?

"Sounds serious."

He moves just enough that I make a break for it, sliding past him, hissing as my body has to touch his. Finally I reach the door.

"You want to be careful when you're alone in the dark," he says, as I fumble with the latch.

I shut the door and leap off the steps. Passing Ruthie, I grab her elbow and take off in a jog. "Ew, ew, ew!" Definitely taking a shower when I get home. Extra soap.

"What happened in there, boss?"

"Just keep moving." I shuck off some of the fear as I spot my lime-green Volkswagen. "What happened to the original signal we planned on?"

"I freaked! I think I had test anxiety or something. You're lucky I got 'Somewhere Over the Rainbow' out—the first tune that came to my head was 'I Like Big Butts.'" She shakes her head. "And I cannot lie."

My phone rings before I can unlock my door. Luke Sullivan.

"Yes?" My voice is as calm as a trickling brook.

"Any reason you and Ruthie McGee are sprinting away from the carnival grounds?"

I throw my purse on top of my car, desperate to get a grip on my keys and unlock this thing. Can't seem to make my fingers work. "Um—"

"Let me try."

I jump at the voice behind me.

Luke steps from behind the van next to us. He walks to me, his face tight. Grabbing onto my hand, he gently pulls my fingers apart. He doesn't let go as he clicks my keychain.

Ruthie scrambles inside and buckles herself in. I see her dive to the floorboard for her sidekick guide book.

"Now why don't you tell me what's brought you out here."

"I—"

Luke holds up his free hand. "And be crazy and try the truth."

"I stopped by for a visit." I don't need to explain myself to him.

A Rihanna song pours out of the car as Ruthie rolls the window down. "Tell him about our new job!"

I grit my teeth until my jaw aches. "She's a little out of her mind today."

Ruthie hangs her blue head out the window. "And Bella went snooping in Alfredo's trailer."

I give Luke my haughtiest glare. "I was here to check up on Cherry."

"And that Mr. Creepy Pants caught her!"

"Ruthie, *would* you study your book and leave the talking to me!" I roll my shoulders, straighten my posture, and face my ex-boyfriend—whose eyebrows are lifted as high as his forehead will allow.

"What do you think you're doing, Bella?" His words are like

sandpaper to my nerves, and he cuts me off before I can reply. "Never mind. We both know exactly why you're here."

I cross my arms over my chest and glare my editor down. "You took me off the story, Chief. But that doesn't mean I can't do my own digging around."

"What was Ruthie talking about? Who caught you snooping?"

I glance at my watch. "I really have to run. Lots to do." *And I need to be somewhere I'm not breathing your cologne.* Breaking up with him was the right thing to do, right?

Luke's hand curls around my arm. "Start talking, Bella."

"I might've gotten lost and found myself in the magician's trailer." I watch Luke's eyes darken. See the flex in his jaw and know he's not going to let this die. "And Red's son walked in." I rush on before Luke interrupts. "But I told him I was looking for a bathroom, so it's no big deal." Minus the pink flashlight with my name on it I left in the trailer. Definitely going to have to go back and find that first chance I get.

"I stood guard!" Ruthie shouts.

Yeah, for all the good *that* did.

"Bella, you were taken off the story for your own good—to protect you."

"I don't need protection. I happen to be excellent at taking care of myself."

Luke's laugh is bitter. "Says the girl who snooped through someone's possessions and then got caught in the process."

"I think the important point here is that I talked my way out of it." Yep, that's the part of the story I personally like.

"And Red Fritz's son bought your story?"

Well, probably not, but it got me out of there. "Luke, it's over. I handled it."

"So I guess the next question is . . . did you find anything?"

"As if I'd tell you!" I'm so sure. "You can't pull me from the story, then expect me to hand over all my information."

Luke inhales slowly and considers the blue sky beyond me. "Just promise me you'll be careful."

"Careful is my middle name."

Ruthie's head appears from the driver's side. "I figured it was something like Myrtle or Helga."

Luke holds me with his eyes. "Take care of yourself, Bella."

Must. Look. Away. Broken up couples do not have long moments of meaningful eye contact!

Say something snarky. Something wickedly intelligent to one-up him.

"Um... I gotta pee." I jump into my Bug, banging my head a few times on the steering wheel.

Ruthie smacks her gum. "Everything okay, boss?"

"Nothing a brain transplant wouldn't cure." And I drive the car far away from Luke Sullivan.

~~~~~~~~

Later that evening the family sits down at the dining room table. We make a circle with our hands as Jake says a prayer over the meal.

"And Lord, please be with me and my family as I begin to travel even more. Give Jillian the strength and wisdom to take care of everything in my absence. Amen."

His absence? What is that about?

I lift my head and gawk at my mom. She folds her napkin in her lap and trails a nail down her water glass. Last year that nail was fully manicured and polished. Now it's neatly trimmed and ink-stained from writing notes for her psych class at the Tulsa Community College.

"What do you mean, 'traveling even more'?" I pass Budge the peas. I do not eat small, green squishy things.*

Jake casts a quick look at Mom. "I have a few more weeks left of training, but after that I'll hit the road full time. I've seen the schedule, and I'll be gone for most of the remaining year."

Robbie lets out a little whimper.

"I knew it would be a lot," Jake says. "I just didn't know it would be almost every day of the year." His mouth spreads into a grin. "When Captain Iron Jack gets more established, I can set my own schedule."

Mom wears the same plastic smile she wore the day she told me my dad was leaving us. This is not good. My dad traded my mom in for a string of bimbos. What's Jake getting? Night after night of spandex wedgies and a stiff neck from the tour bus?

"Budge, you might have to ease up on your hours at the Wiener Palace to help out around here more."

My stepbrother chugs his root beer. "I'm six hundred dogs away from wiener seller of the year. I can't slow down now."

"Maybe I could cut back on my television watching," Robbie says, his face solemn. "I could give up one Superman cartoon and the financial network."

"Nobody's giving up anything." Mom's spine is straighter than a dry spaghetti noodle. "We'll be fine. I'm going to finish up my class at the community college, then take a little break."

"But you've waited your whole life to go back to school."

"It's fine, Bella." She pats my hand. "All things in time. I can pick it back up some other time."

"We'll discuss that later," Jake says. "I do have some good news for you, Jillian."

I don't know if she can take any more.

My stepdad proudly throws his arm around my mom. "You can put in your notice at Sugar's. I'm officially on the payroll. The first check hits this week—and it's a good one."

"Are we rich, Daddy?" Robbie claps his little hands.

Budge grabs a piece of bread. "Can I have a pony?"

"Not rich, kids. But I'm definitely going to be making more than I did at Summer Fresh."

Um, yeah, Summer Fresh would be the factory where Jake previously worked. He made pads. As in lady business. My own father is a plastic surgeon to the rich and famous in Manhattan, so it took quite awhile before I could hold my head up every time I went back to New York City.

"Well, at least we can start updating the house, huh, Bel?"

"Yeah, Mom." I give her my most encouraging face. "It will be fun."

Four hours later I've flossed, moisturized, and read my homework for English—another Charles Dickens novel. It's like Death by Dickens. Lately any time I can't sleep, I just pick up ol' Chuck and next thing I know, I'm drooling on my pillow.

Leaving Moxie snoring on the bed, I walk downstairs to the kitchen to get a bottle of water.

I slip a Dasani out of the fridge, then head back up.

"You could've warned me."

My foot pauses on the third step. I follow my mom's voice through the living room and toward her bedroom. I lean my ear to the partially opened door.

"Jillian, the management just sprang it on me. What did you think this was going to be like? We knew it was a full-time commitment."

"There's a difference in being gone three hundred days of the year and being gone a few days a week."

Ew. Fighting makes my stomach all knotty and squishy. It reminds me of that last year before my dad left.

"This won't last forever. We have to ride it out until things calm down," Jake says.

"Until things calm down? You said that could take years."

"I thought you wanted me to live my dream."

"I do!" Her voice is almost a yell. "But what about mine? At what point did this go from me supporting your dream to you leaving me alone to raise three kids?"

My heart thuds in the following silence.

Finally Jake speaks. "Do you want me to quit? Say the word, and I will."

"Don't make me the bad guy, Jake. Of course I don't want you to quit. What I do want is for this family to be our priority. Find a way to make it work." I hear bare feet on the floor and the rustling of sheets. "I'm sleeping on the couch tonight."

I just get to the living room as my mom opens the bedroom door.

"Bella?" She stands at the end of the small hall, her pillow in her arms.

I freeze, stubbing my toe on the couch. "Ouch!" My breath hisses between my teeth. "Oh, hey, Mom."

"What are you doing?"

"Me? Um . . . just came down to get a bottle of water."

"In the living room?"

"I thought maybe I'd sneak some David Letterman." I shake my finger at her. "But you caught me."

She tilts her head and sighs. "You're a horrible liar."

I get that a lot.

"Good night, Bella." She flops onto the couch and picks up one of her college textbooks.

I walk back toward the staircase but turn back at the first step. "Are we going to be okay?"

"Of course." She flips a page. "It's just going to be a big adjustment. But it should be . . . fun."

"Um, Mom?"

She looks up from her book. "Yes?"

"You're not so hot at lying yourself."

chapter seven

The divorced-parent visitation thing can be a little stressful. Especially when you have an eight-year-old clinging to your dad and sticking her tongue out in five-minute intervals when no adult is looking.

Dad holds open the door to the famous Manhattan restaurant Nobu, and I file in behind his girlfriend and her bratty sister.

"So, Bella, like I was telling you"—my dad pulls out my chair and then sits down—"the show won't air until next year, but it's going to be huge." Huge like his smile. Huge like the hole in my heart every time I'm here, seeing my dad drifting further and further away from me.

Christina, the live-in girlfriend, opens her menu. "Your father is so excited. Our whole family is." She pats her sister's hand.

Ick. A family. After my dad left us, he went on this dating frenzy. At first that bothered me. Then he decided to keep one, and now I long for the rotating door of bimbos. Christina is a talent agent, and currently represents my dad and his dream to bring his plastic surgery skills and advice to the small screen. All he talks about lately—besides their approaching wedding—is his upcoming gig in Brazil. But after his accountant ran off with a ton of his money last year, at least he's not still harping on that.

"So are you going to have to move there?" I take a sip of water and crunch down on a piece of ice.

"Just for six months during filming." Dad surveys me over the top of his menu. "But don't worry, Bel. We don't start shooting until August. And we'll fly you in for some long visits."

"And you and Marisol can play on the beaches of Rio de Janeiro, my homeland." Christina gives her order to the waiter. "Won't that be fun?"

Marisol bats her little eyelashes toward my dad. "I can't wait to get to know Bella better."

"Isn't she precious?" he asks.

Preciously nauseating.

"Bella, I will be running some errands tomorrow." Christina pulls her long, dark hair until it drapes over the other shoulder. "Wedding details, you know. I was wondering if you would be a dear and keep an eye on Marisol."

Beside me Marisol makes little gagging noises. My thoughts exactly. "I guess—"

"I know," Dad says. "Why don't Marisol and I go to the park, and you two girls can do wedding stuff together?" He beams like he just invented a new wrinkle filler. "Christina, you've been talking about how you need some help with the planning."

Her smile is tight. "I meant like an assistant."

"My Isabella is amazing at anything involving style, fashion, and decorating." Dad pats me on the back. It's been so long since I've had a compliment from him, I just run it over and over in my mind, savoring his words.

"I think Bella would be bored and—"

"I can't wait." Anything to get out of monster-sitting. "It will be a fun time." Okay, that was probably too much. But if Christina gets to shop, I know Dad will let me charge a thing or two as well. And there is a new BCBG skirt I'm dying to hang in my closet.

Later I silently eat my lobster salad as the *family* becomes consumed with wedding chatter.

"Roses or calla lilies?"

"Seven bridesmaids or nine?"

"But I don't want Josh Groban to sing for us."

"Don't forget our ballroom lesson next Tuesday."

"Yes, Marisol, I think flowers in your hair."

I push my nearly empty bowl away. "How 'bout those Yankees?" They keep talking amongst themselves. "Anybody seen any plays lately?"

They don't even hear me.

"I found a dead body."

Christina's fork clanks to the floor.

My dad chokes on his water. "What did you say?"

"I, um, found a murdered woman last weekend."

Dad says something that would make my mom flinch. "Why didn't you tell me?"

"You didn't call me this week."

He sits up straighter. "Yes, I did."

"Leaving a message on my phone doesn't count." The words are out before I can pull them back in. I try to soften my tone as I quickly fill him in. Christina holds her hands like muffs over Marisol's ears. Probably a good idea. We don't need any more evil inclinations in that kid's head.

"I had no idea." Dad shakes his head. "I can't imagine."

"That must have been so traumatic for you, Bella. Probably still is." Christina's accent rolls off her tongue. "You should stay at home tomorrow and rest."

"Actually, I've been looking forward to shopping for quite a while." Is she just trying to ditch me so I'll stay at the house and bond with her sister?

"Just what she needs." Dad hands me the dessert menu. "You two will have a great time." He winks. "Just go easy on my friend MasterCard."

The New York sky is dark by the time we finally leave the restaurant. My dad hails a cab, and Marisol and Christina climb in.

"You sit in the back with the girls," he says. "I'll sit up front." A breeze blows his brown hair, and I remember how handsome I thought he was when I was a little girl. I wanted to grow up and marry a man just like my daddy. He's still as cute as any Brad Pitt or George Clooney, but I don't want to end up hurt like my mom.

"Bella?" He holds the door.

I blink and pull myself out of my gloomy thoughts. "Yeah?"

"I'm sorry I haven't called lately."

I lift a shoulder. "It's okay." But really . . . it's not. It's just not. I want him to *want* to call me. I want him to wonder what his daughter is doing, how the math test went, what bands I'm listening to this week. Know the names of my friends. Know that I broke up with my boyfriend last week, and I'm still a jumbled mess.

On Saturday morning I wake up to the smell of pancakes and sausage. I follow the scent downstairs to the kitchen, where Luisa, my old nanny, stands at the stove.

I throw my hands around her voluminous waist and smack a big kiss on her cheek.

She chuckles and kisses me back. "Hello to you too, *niña*. I hear you are going shopping with Christina today, so I make you big breakfast." She jabs her thumb toward the living room. "That one only eats grapefruit and spinach drinks. That's no way to start a day."

"It's probably how they do it in the homeland." We share a laugh as I grab some orange juice.

"I heard that." The little munchkin lurks in the doorway.

"Good morning, Marisol." Her outfit is clearly high-end, and I think about the Target clothes I've been reduced to. I will not be jealous. I will not be jealous. *God, help me handle this girl*—without *showing her the new wrestling move Jake taught me.*

"Luisa, fix me some eggs," the little girl barks. "And hurry up."

My mouth forms an O. "You do *not* talk to Luisa that way. She's not a servant to be bossed around. She's family." *Real* family.

Marisol curls her pink lip. "You don't tell me what to do. I *live* here. You don't."

I charge toward her, gaining some good momentum, until Luisa steps between us. "Girls, stop." Luisa looks over Marisol's head, her brown eyes pleading with mine. "*Please* just drop it."

"No! She can't talk to you like that."

Luisa awkwardly pats Marisol on her black head. "Why don't you go in the living room and watch TV, eh? I will call when it is done. Will be ready soon."

"Hmph!" Marisol sticks her nose in the air, throws me one of *those* looks, and sashays out of the kitchen.

I just stare at my nanny. "What was—"

"Leave it alone, *mi corazón*. Is none of your business. Your Luisa is fine."

"I'm going to talk to Dad, and he'll—"

"No!" She blocks my exit. "You must not," she whispers. "Things are different here now, Bella. There is a new woman in the house, and things change. I will roll with it." A small smile spreads. "I will—how do you kids say it—be cool?"

"But if you'd just let me talk to Dad."

"No." She shakes her head. "Promise me you will not. Not now."

"Okay." I take a deep breath, and my pulse still beats a wild staccato. "But just for now. I don't know what's going on, but I'm not putting up with anyone treating you like that."

Her nod is brief. Then she waddles back to the stove and fixes my plate.

"Whoa, I can't eat that much," I say as she piles on a mound of food.

"Trust me." Luisa hands me my breakfast. "You're going to need it to keep up your strength."

~~~~~~~~~~

I've been shopping for four hours, and not only have I not had a chance to buy anything, but Christina hasn't stopped once for food, drink, or tinkles. And I'm in desperate need of all three.

I stand in the third wedding boutique as my dad's girlfriend schmoozes with the designer. She tries to impress Enrique with my dad's history on the E! Channel and his famous clientele, and I have to turn away and get the eye roll out of my system.

"Bella, I have two bridesmaid dress possibilities here. Perhaps you should try on the floor samples, and Enrique and I will decide if they work." She pats the little man's bicep.

Christina delicately rests two outrageous frocks on my arms, and I clutch them to me.

"No, no, no." Her head shakes like a bobble. She unlocks the dresses from my grip. "Gently. These are not mere dresses. Enrique's designs are works of art. You would never hold a fine oil painting so tightly."

I chew on my gum to keep from saying something I'll regret, but at this rate, there's not enough Juicy Fruit in the whole state of New York to last me the entire day.

A few minutes later I stare in horror at my reflection in the mirror. I can't seem to make myself open the dressing room door.

"Bella, do you have a dress on yet?" Christina calls from the other side.

"Um . . . I can't seem to find the arm holes."

"There are not any," she says. "You wrap those two boas around your arms and neck. Isn't that genius?"

Genius? It looks like Enrique raided a six-year-old's dress-up stash and hot-glued a bunch of feathers together. I can't be seen in public in this.

"Come on out. We don't have all day." Christina is getting testier the longer we shop.

"If you say so." I ease open the door and step out.

Christina gasps and covers her mouth with both hands.

I see myself in the three-way mirror. "I know, right? It's—"

"Amazing!" She closes her eyes like she just bit into a truffle. "I think my bridesmaids will look stunning in this."

Enrique sniffs, his chest puffing. "It was all the rage at my show in Milan."

It's about to put me in a rage. "I think you should keep looking."

Christina's perfectly shaped brow lifts. "You don't like it?"

A feather piece slips off my shoulder, and I scramble to hold the dress together. "I couldn't even tell which end was up when I was putting it on."

Enrique sputters. "This is art! Who are you to tell me my dress is not anything but superior? I had Madonna contact me just yesterday for a gown fitting." He turns on Christina. "I told Taylor Swift to call back just so I could make this appointment with you. And *this* is how I'm treated?"

"No, Enrique. She didn't mean it." Christina sears me with her eyes.

"Yeah, I'm sorry. The dress is fine." Oh no. Feathers up my nose. "*Ah-ah-achoo!*" Tiny plumes go floating all around the three of us.

"Leave my shop!" Enrique yells. "You have two minutes to get her out of that dress and out of my store!" Remnants of the dress land on his bald head.

Christina pushes me toward the dressing room, hissing hurried instructions.

Ninety seconds later we stand on the corner in front of Enrique's House of Design.

"And stay out! You are forever banned from wearing my creations!" Enrique slams the door and locks it behind us.

"Achoo!" I hold a tissue to my nose and a giggle escapes.

"You're laughing?" Christina asks, her hands curled into fists. "I was just publicly humiliated and you're *laughing*?"

I can't help it. I turn my head as the laughter pushes tears out of my eyes.

"I am blacklisted, Bella."

"By a man who decorates with things I could find on the floor of a chicken house?"

Her chin inches higher. "Well, I guess it didn't take long before Oklahoma seeped into your blood. But in upper Manhattan, we care about style and cutting-edge fashion."

I need another piece of gum. "In *Oklahoma* they don't believe in wearing things that require health code inspections and a tetanus shot."

Christina opens her mouth, and I prepare for the verbal thrashing. "You little—" Her phone sings, startling both of us. She takes a deep breath and answers it. "Yes. Uh-huh." Her voice is low, controlled. The opposite of what it was seconds ago. "I see." She glances at me, then back to the ground. "Yes, Mr. Smith. I will check my calendar and get back with you immediately. Give me a few moments."

"Business?" I ask, as she slips her phone back into her purse.

"Yes." She pulls out a ten-dollar bill and presses it into my hand. "Why don't you run over to that coffee shop and get yourself something while I make a few calls. I think you and I need a little cool-down time anyway."

Though I'm mad at Christina, I could weep with relief for the break.

She points to another boutique down the street. "Meet me at that shop in ten minutes."

I all but run to the coffee shop.

God, why do I let that woman get me so riled up? But you know, in my defense, today I'm seeing a totally different side of her. I always knew she wasn't some cuddly, sweet thing. But now she's like Bridezilla . . . on steroids. Maybe I should talk to my dad and suggest a nice Vegas wedding. That feathery concoction would probably fit right in.

A bell chimes overhead as I step inside. I inhale the rich aroma . . . and breathe out the guilt.

The least I could do is go back and ask Christina if she wants anything. Surely even size zero talent agents need food.

I turn right back around and head in the direction I left her. She stands one door down from Enrique's, staring at the opposite end of the street.

I'm just about to call out to her.

Then a yellow taxi pulls up to the curb.

I stop in my tracks as a woman steps out, one long leg at a time. Her giant sunglasses cover her eyes, and a large brimmed hat sits low over her forehead.

Christina looks around, and I duck behind a minivan.

I will be the first to admit I was born with more than my fair share of nosiness. I mean, what's a girl to do? I figure if God gave it to me, then I should use it.

I step into the crowd on the sidewalk and weave my way closer to Christina and her acquaintance. The two talk, their faces intense. Their mannerisms rushed.

Ten feet away from them, a group of teenage girls stands in a huddle and chat. I inch toward them and hover on the outside of their circle. My ears perk at Christina's voice.

"I tried to come alone today. You think I wanted to bring her?"

Oh! How rude! I should have just let her have it and not wasted the gum.

The other woman's voice is so low, I can't even hear it.

"I said I'd work on it, and I am. These things take time. I'll give you the account numbers later."

The woman with the giant shades mutters something, but it's lost in the honking of a car.

Christina throws up her hands. "I haven't been blinded. I know what my job is, and I'll do it. We're partners."

She's a one-woman agenting operation. Partners in what?

"Nobody crosses us and gets away with it."

The girls beside me dissolve into loud giggles, covering up what the stranger says.

"Do you want something?"

I turn and one of the girls stares at me. Like I'm some sort of creepy lurker. Well, okay, I am. But whatever.

"Do I know you?" she asks.

I smile. "Well, you might've seen me and my family on TV recently. We were on a reality show, and—"

"That really wasn't a question." She backs up, her eyes suspicious. "That was code for 'go away.'" She pushes her friends forward. "It's just not safe on the streets anymore. Let's go girls."

"Bella?"

I jump at my name and find Christina behind me. I look around, but the stranger is gone.

"What are you doing?" Her voice has an edge sharper than a stiletto.

"I—I, um, came back to see if you wanted any coffee." I wave my hand toward the group of disappearing girls. "But then I ran into some old friends and stopped." To eavesdrop.

Christina studies me, her mouth in a firm line.

"Did you run into a friend too?" I ask.

Her eyes widen a fraction. So small you had to be looking for it—and I was. "No." Christina licks her glossy red lips. "I did not."

"Oh." Hunger has robbed me of all subtlety, so I push on. "I thought I saw you talking to someone."

Christina glances over her shoulder, in the direction the taxi went, before swiveling her razor eyes back to me. "You are mistaken. The only person I have a need to talk to is your father—to tell him how you've ruined my day."

chapter eight

On Monday morning, my friends sit around me in the courtyard, and I catch them up on my weekend craziness before the first-hour bell.

"So did you tell your dad what Christina said to you?" Lindy puts the finishing touches on an English assignment and sticks it in her bag.

"No. My dad and I really aren't in a good place right now. I didn't feel like I could talk to him with nothing to go on but my suspicions. I just had this feeling like I should wait and collect more information first. But I know something is going on."

"I totally would've had to put that woman in her place." Ruthie leans on my stepbrother Budge, her head on his shoulder, her bouffant hair covering up his smiling face.

"I'm surprised you didn't put her little sister in a choke hold too," Matt says.

"Luisa asked me not to. But I can't get that out of my mind. Christina is bad news, and I'm going to get to the bottom of it—the sooner the better."

"I had a date last night."

All heads swivel to Lindy.

"What?" My voice scares off a nearby bird. "With who? And why didn't you call me?"

She laughs, her skin turning a light shade of pink. "It was very last-minute. After church, Bo Blades called me and took me out for pizza and ice cream."

Ruthie sits up. "And you spent the rest of the evening staring into each other's eyes and were so caught up, you couldn't so much as text us." Her voice is a sigh.

"Um, no." Lindy's grin is as big as an Oklahoma cornfield. "But after he drove me back home, I called him. And then we just talked for hours."

"About what?" Matt scowls. "What could you possibly have to talk about after hanging out?"

Fire dances in Lindy's eyes. "Lots of things. I could talk to Bo for days and never get bored. Some guys know how to have a conversation with a girl."

Matt snorts. "Whatever. He probably just wanted your homework answers."

"Bo finds me interesting, for your information, Matt Sparks." Lindy gives her best friend her shoulder. "Not that it's any of your business." She turns her excited face back to me. "We're going to run together tonight."

"How romantic." Running. That's right up there with watching documentaries or double-dating with your parents. All definite dating *no*'s in my book.

"I don't know about him, Lindy," Matt says. "You should really be on your guard."

"Why?" Lindy barks. "He's on the honor roll. He took us to state in track last year. He plays the guitar in his church. Um, which part of that do you find so shady? Because I must be too caught up in it all to see it."

I watch in fascination as Matt sputters for an answer. He is so jealous. I wonder if he even realizes it. This is perfect.

"Forget it. Have a nice *run*." Matt grabs his backpack and storms toward the double doors.

"Is anyone thinking what I'm thinking?" Ruthie asks, her voice giddy.

My eyes dart to Lindy. "That Matt Sparks is jealous?"

Ruthie frowns. "No, dudes. It's meatloaf day in the caf."

Luke completely ignores me in journalism. Which would be just fine except instead of harassing me, he's giving all his attention to Ashley Timmons.

The man stealer leans over his computer and laughs. "Oh, Luke. You're so funny!"

Behind my monitor, I mimic her girly giggles.

The girl tosses her angelic blonde hair and moves in closer. "You're so smart. That's exactly what my article needed. Thank you!"

Thank you! You're so smart! Ughhh. It's like I need to start taking antinausea medicine before I come to class now.

"Ashley, you're a great writer," Luke says. "You just have a few skills that need some polishing."

"Ohhh." I swear I see her bat her lashes. "Would you work with me? I'd love to get some tips for improving. Your articles are always so perfect."

Luke laughs. "Well, not perfect."

"No." Her hand lands on his bicep. "They totally are."

I'm out of my seat before my brain has time to register that my legs have moved. "For the good of the rest of the staff, could you guys please keep it down?"

Ashley sits up straighter. "We're just working here."

"Really?" I throw her a pert smile. "Is that what you call it?"

"Luke and I were simply talking. He was about to help me with some weak areas."

It's everything I can do not to blast her with a retort on her weak areas. "I need Luke to look over my article, so maybe this one-on-one tutoring could happen later?"

Ashley opens her glossy mouth, but Luke stops her. "It's okay, Ashley. I'll check your copy and prioritize the areas you need to focus on."

I don't miss her look of venom as she saunters back to her work station.

Luke turns the full force of his stormy gaze on me. "Don't you *ever* do that again."

"What? Stop you before you drooled in front of your entire staff?"

He takes a step closer. "Don't ever disrespect me when I'm working with a staff member."

"Since when does flirting fall under the category of work?"

Luke breathes out his nose. "I'm the editor, Bella. And helping my staff improve their writing is what I do. I was not flirting."

I can't stop my laugh. "Whatever."

"Why don't we take this outside?"

"Let's."

I follow him out into the hall where he takes off his glasses and looks down his nose. "I don't bring our personal life into the paper, so I expect you to be professional enough to do the same."

I point between us. "*We* have no personal life, if you remember."

"How could I forget?"

"You're hanging out with her." The words sound pitiful to my ears. Too late to take them back.

"I'm hanging out with her *and* her brother." Hard eyes stare back at me. "Ashley hasn't had time to get reacquainted with anyone yet. I'm strictly being a friend."

"Her methods of getting reacquainted are quite original. Aggressive even." I have got to let this go. I'm annoying myself.

"Obviously you don't have enough to do on the paper, so why don't you copyedit everyone's work for the next week?"

"So I hit a nerve, and to punish me, you're going to put me on grammar duty?"

He shrugs. "One of the joys of being in charge."

"That and flirting with your reporters?"

His head dips low as he plants one hand on the wall over my head. "You are so jealous."

"Nuh-uh." That sounded more mature in my head.

"You know what I think this is all about?"

"That Barbie doll three computers away from me?"

He slowly shakes his head. "It's about the fact that you miss me."

I gaze into his clear blue eyes. "You're right. I do miss you, Luke." I watch his arrogant mouth curve. "Like cramps."

"Still running scared." He pushes off the wall. "That's too bad."

"Or maybe I'm just completely over you." I pat his chest. "It's a bitter pill to swallow. I understand."

Luke's eyes drop to my mouth, then slowly trail back up. "Whatever you need to tell yourself to keep it safe, Bella. You do that." He reaches for the doorknob and glances over his shoulder. "But keep your insecurities out of my paper and don't ever attack one of my staff members again." He winks. "Oh, and better brush up on your commas."

~~~~~~~~~~

"I don't know if I can do this." I stare into a mirror at my clown garb. I can hear cars pulling up outside the big top.

"It's too late now." Ruthie straightens my big red nose. "The circus is going to start in twenty minutes."

"This might've been my dumbest idea ever."

She fluffs her rainbow wig. "My dumbest idea was when I tried to ride my bicycle down the slide in my backyard."

I laugh. "How long ago was that?"

Ruthie rubs her rear. "Yesterday."

Cherry Fritz pops her head in the door. "You guys ready?"

She looks so beautiful in her makeup and glitzy leotard. And here I am in clown paint, shoes made for a giant, and a wig that looks like it suffered a bad encounter with a lightning bolt.

"All you have to do is go into the crowd and meet and greet the little kids." She hands each one of us a bucket of suckers. "And Ruthie, don't throw them like you did when we practiced earlier. We don't want anyone losing an eye."

"Personally I think that would be kinda cool."

At Cherry's worried look, I try to reassure her. "She'll be careful. I'll watch her."

"Your cue to come out of the crowd is when the clown car starts honking. Remember, all you have to do is run down to the center and open the door."

"And we act like we're gonna shut it, but more of those clowns keep coming out." Ruthie acts like it's painful to recall her few instructions.

"Right. And that's it. You'll be great." Cherry gives each of us a brief hug. "Dolly's coming tonight and taking me for a burger afterward. Maybe you guys could come with us."

Raw hope brims in her eyes. How could I possibly say no? "Sounds fun." If I live through tonight and don't kill myself in these shoes. Or die of mortification.

Ten minutes later I'm on the top bleacher talking to a little boy who doesn't know whether to laugh or cry at my hair. "Here you go. Have fun!" I hand him a sucker and make my way down to the bottom row.

My eyes scan the arena, looking for anything unusual or suspicious. Two midgets and a pig in a tutu walk by. I probably need to narrow my definition of suspicious.

"Nice outfit."

I follow the voice to the ground. Luke.

"Though the makeup's a little heavy."

"What do you want, Luke? Or let me guess—you're here to work on *my* story and just stopped by to gloat." I stomp my giant foot. It tangles with the other shoe, and suddenly I'm airborne, headed for the ground. "Whoa!"

Luke steps up, and I land with an *oomph* in his arms.

Face redder than my bulbous nose, I pull my eyes up to his. "Um . . . thanks."

His arms stay locked around me as he lifts me off the bleacher and sets me on the ground.

"Glad to help."

"Hey, hands off the clown." Stewart Fritz stops, just as his dad takes the center of the ring. "You're needed in the sound booth." His eyes leer.

"Me?" I ask.

"No." He jerks his head toward Luke. "This guy." His eyes linger over my form for a moment too long before he walks away, snapping out commands into his headset.

"So I guess he's kind of like the producer?" Luke asks.

"Um . . . you're working here? Since when?"

"Same day you got hired." He shrugs. "I needed something else to fill my time."

"You work for the local paper."

"And now I work here."

I smell a rat. "Yeah, well, just stay out of my way."

He laughs. "Isn't that what the police are always saying to *you?*"

chapter nine

~~~~~~

The work of a circus clown is never done.

During intermission, I rush backstage, careful not to trip over my giant shoes. Ruthie and I grab water bottles for those just finishing and pass out props for the next round of performers.

"Serena, I think your hair would look really good with a few strips of magenta," Ruthie tells the lady who does horse tricks. "Maybe tease it up another six inches or so. I have some hairspray that will shellac that stuff right in place. It's like cement."

I brush off her partner's jacket with a lint roller. "So, um . . . anyone heard from Alfredo?"

The man's laugh is a mean staccato. "Yeah, right. Like we'd want to talk to the guy who killed Betty."

"But what if he didn't do it?"

He waves my idea away. "Look, kid, his prints are on the sword."

"The forensic results came back?"

"Yeah." He smirks. "Alfredo may be the master of magic, but even he can't make scientific evidence disappear."

"Besides," Serena says with a southern twang. "Alfredo was a dirty crook. He didn't really love Betty. Everyone saw right through him."

"What do you mean?" I ask.

Serena runs her hand over her tight updo. "Betty and Alfredo were the weirdest couple ever. And I'm telling you . . . something wasn't right from the beginning. At first he didn't even act like he liked her. It was like he was forcing himself to date her."

"Life does get lonely out here on the road. And it's not as if there're lots of options for chicks."

Serena smacks her partner. "You got something to say to me?"

He shakes his head. "Nah."

"Maybe you wouldn't get lonely if you'd clean up your messes in the trailer. If I didn't have to follow you around like I was your mother instead of your wife, then I'd have more time to spend with you. Eh?"

"But back to Alfredo and Betty—"

"Ladies and gentlemen!" Red Fritz announces the second half, and Serena and her husband run toward the center of the ring, still arguing over housekeeping.

I glance at Ruthie. "That was strange."

"Nah. Men are slobs. Nothing weird about that. She shouldn't have to put up with socks and tightie-whities on the floor."

"I meant what Serena said about Alfredo not acting as if he liked Betty."

"Not everyone is as kind and sensitive as my Budge."

I think of my stepbrother, who just this morning burped the entire *Star Wars* theme song at the breakfast table. "Yeah, he's just a dream of perfection."

"Did you ever get the flashlight you lost in Alfredo's trailer?"

I inwardly cringe. "No. Someone's always in there." But I've got to get it. Soon.

"Yeah, well, don't cut me out of that. I have a few ideas on how to get inside." Ruthie's eyes glisten. "It involves rope, WD-40, and some mace."

"You forgot one thing in that list."

"What?"

"A warrant for our arrest."

Fifteen minutes later I'm working the crowd and passing out a few balloons as Cherry and two others take to the trapeze. Just looking up there makes my stomach flop.

Feeling prickles of awareness, I look across the arena and find Luke watching me from the control booth. And Stewart Fritz. The two are talking, but both have their eyes trained in my direction. It's not every day a girl gets the attention of two boys. But in this case, one makes me so mad I want to throw him in the middle of one of Jake's wrestling matches. And the other . . . makes me want to douse myself in hand sanitizer.

Red Fritz announces his niece and the trapeze act, and a hush falls over the crowd as they watch them fly through the air.

In his usual garb of top hat and tuxedo jacket, Red walks off the floor and over to the control booth, his large stomach leading the way. He pulls his son aside and whispers near his ear. Luke keeps his eyes on the trapeze, adjusting the lighting and sound controls, but I know that boy. And I know he's doing everything he can to listen in to the father and son's conversation.

Red walks away, exiting out the main entrance. I'm passing out my last balloon when I see Stewart leave the same way.

"Hey, I want my balloon in the shape of a dog."

I pull my eyes from the door and down to the kid below me. "Sorry. That's all I have."

"I want a dog!" he yells.

I yank his balloon back, give it a few twists, and hand it to him again. "There you go." I have to follow Stewart and his dad. Something could be up.

"No!" the kid shrieks. "That looks like a four-leaf clover!"

"Well, then give it to your mom." I pat the little brat on the head. "She obviously needs the luck."

I maneuver my way back down the bleachers. Easier said than

done in a wig that keeps drooping in my eyes and shoes that could knock out an entire row.

The carnival rides flash their rainbow of lights as I step outside. Screams pierce the night as one of the roller coasters swings everyone upside down.

"Two tries for a dollar!" a guy calls out from the basketball toss.

Following a distance behind Stewart, I pass a row of food trailers and inhale the smell of hamburgers.

He hangs a left, disappearing for a moment from view. I keep a nonchalant look about me, as if I'm just taking in the sights and sounds of the carnival. Like it's every day I walk about the carnival grounds in full clown makeup.

When I hear Red Fritz's voice, I stop. The two guys stand talking by the Ferris wheel.

"What do you want?" Red asks. "I gotta close out the show."

I take a step back and hide behind the edge of another game trailer.

"Did you talk to Alfredo?"

"Yeah, I talked to him. Do you think I can't handle him, Stewart? I've got his situation under control. Has anyone seen Betty's stupid dog?"

"She's long gone."

"Well, if you find her, put her to work, then take care of her—permanently. Son, you do your job right, and this could all be yours." Red's voice is barely audible over the rising carnival noise.

I lean out a bit to get a better view.

Stewart laughs, a menacing sound that lifts the hair on the back of my neck. "Whatever it takes. This is a family business, after all. *Our* business."

Red spits on the ground and nods. "Gotta get back. I need to keep my eye on Cherry. She's been acting weird, and I don't trust her."

I gotta go! Move, clown feet. I lift the left, only to be jerked back by the right. I'm stuck! Omigosh. *God, help me!*

Their voices get nearer as I bend over, jerking on my shoe. It's snagged on some sort of canopy pin.

"Maybe I should have a talk with little cousin Cherry."

Oh no, I cannot explain my way out of this one, Jesus. How about a Harry Potter cloak of invisibility right now? Please help me.

I take a giant breath and pull with all my might. Aughhh!

Too late. Two sets of feet appear.

"What do you think you're doing?" Red Fritz demands.

From my stooped position, I lift my eyes. "Um . . . I was just—"

"Waiting for me."

I jerk upright as Luke appears at my back. He sends me a warm smile and curls an arm around my shoulder. "Our first date was at the county fair. And it was on a Ferris wheel just like this that I knew I had found someone special. I thought we'd take a ride tonight and celebrate old times." Luke rushes on before Red can interrupt. "It's my break time."

Oh, he is so full of bull.

And I couldn't be more grateful.

"You shouldn't be walking around out here like this," Stewart says to me. "Alone and all. You never know what might get a pretty thing like you."

"Thanks." Ick.

A short man in a dirty Metallica T-shirt limps over to the Ferris wheel control. "Oh . . . um, hey, boss."

Red Fritz pierces him with an icy glare. "What have I told you about leaving your ride?"

Luke takes the opportunity to drop his keys to the ground. "Oops."

"I know, boss. I, um, had to go to the bathroom real bad and there wasn't anyone around to cover."

Luke yanks on my shoe, and I find freedom. *Thank you, Lord. I totally owe you one.*

Stewart turns his attention back to me as Luke picks up his keys. "How long had you been standing there—waiting?"

"Just got here, Stewart." My voice rises an octave. My heart still thunders like a wild stallion in my chest. "Yep, just found the Ferris wheel."

"I could give you a ride. On the house." The short man attempts a smile for Red. "If that's okay. Then I'll shut it down for the night."

Stewart jerks his head toward Luke. "Is this your boyfriend?"

Luke pulls me to his chest. "It's complicated. We're still working out some kinks." His hand digs into my rib cage. "Right, Bella?"

"Right." Get me out of here. "Just can't seem to stay away from each other." I pat his chest.

"Then by all means, take a romantic spin around a few times." Stewart's eyes have me snuggling even closer to Luke. "I'd hate to get in the way of true love."

"No, that's okay." I look up at the tall ride and swallow. "We're just going to go back to the big top and finish up."

"Nonsense." Red smiles, and I notice a few back teeth missing. "Fire her up, Will. Bella here is the one who found Betty. Stabbed. Dead." His tongue peeks out as he punctuates each word. "I guess the least we can do is give her and her boyfriend a ride."

"He's not really my—"

"Great." Luke pulls me toward the entry ramp. "Thank you." He presses a kiss to my cheek as we walk. "Play along or we both lose our jobs."

"I heard them talking," I say through gritted teeth.

Luke grins and waves to the three carnival workers. "Imagine that. You eavesdropping."

Will runs up ahead of us and holds open the door to the seat. "Hop in."

I freeze in my steps and feel Luke's hand pressed to my back. "Um, maybe we could do this another night. I should get back to the circus."

Luke's tone is pseudo-friendly. "But Red and Stewart are watching us to make sure we get that ride we wanted."

I step one long shoe into the cart and take a deep gulping breath. "Okay. Okay." I can do it. But if this thing stops at the top and dumps me out onto the cold, hard concrete, I'm going to be so mad.

I fumble my way into the seat and plaster my body as close to the wall of the cart as I can get.

Luke throws an arm around me again and pulls me close. "Eyes are watching us," he says under his breath.

The man named Will locks and secures us in, then slaps the cart. "Here we go! You ready? This one goes pretty high!"

"Oh. Great." Why couldn't I have eavesdropped near a kiddie ride? A little choo-choo train would've been nice.

Will runs back to his post and yanks on a lever. The entire ride chugs and shivers.

"Try to look like you're not repulsed by my very presence," Luke says.

"Uh-huh."

"Lean my way."

"I'm good."

He lets out a huffing breath. "Bella, you're—" I watch his face change from frustrated to bemused. "It's not me, is it?"

"Nuh-uh."

I clutch the handlebars until I can feel my nails tear into skin.

Luke's chest shakes with his laughter.

"This is not funny," I hiss. "What kind of dumb story was that? We met at the county fair?" We're going up. So not good. I want my mom. And a parachute.

"Are you afraid of heights?"

"No." Just rides that *involve* heights.

"Then why are your eyes closed?"

"I'm praying?"

His laugh is softer this time. "Bella, they're watching us. I don't know why, but they are. I'm pretty sure Stewart Fritz is considering carving out some time in his schedule to stalk you, so if you could help out in any way, that would be great."

"What do you want me to do?" My voice is whinier than Robbie's when he gets a Superman video taken away.

"Just lean in my way."

I pull my shoulder off the wall and put my weight on Luke. He takes my hand in his and holds it tight. "You're shaking."

"Your powers of deduction are red-hot tonight, Chief."

"They're still watching. I don't think they believe you came out here to meet me."

I tuck my head into the space beneath his shoulder and study the fairy tale motif on the ride. "How did you know where I was?" Okay, seriously. We're at the top now. I squeeze my eyes shut again.

"I followed you." His chest rumbles where my ear is pressed. "I knew exactly what you were up to. And if we're not careful, they will too."

"They want Betty's dog for some reason—and not for the show. Red told Stewart to put her to work, then kill her. What kind of people do that?"

"Not nice ones. That's why I don't want you messing around here. Bel, open your eyes. You look like you're a flight risk. Can't you dig down deep and find some acting skills in there? Just get your mind off how high we are."

"Just get my mind off it?" I squeak. "How?"

Luke leans his head down, turning his body slightly. "Remember when we were chased by some football players out at the lake last fall? Remember our plan B?"

My eyes pop open just in time to see Luke's face hover over mine. His smile is slow and lazy.

"Plan B?"

He nods. "Just for the sake of our cover, you understand."

"But we're broken up."

"Break over." His nose brushes mine. "Kiss me like you mean it."

I open my mouth to protest, but his lips capture mine. His arms pull me tight. I'm vaguely aware of Will hooting in the background. I sigh and just give in, letting his warmth surround me. He changes the angle of the kiss, and I follow. My hands work their way up his neck to his face, and all visions of plunging to my death fade away.

Luke pulls back, his eyes searching mine. "Still scared?"

Of him or the Ferris wheel? "Yes."

My heart stutters at his roguish grin. "Then we should continue"—he kisses each cheek—"for the cause."

"For the cause." I thread my fingers through his dark hair, loving the way it curls slightly at the ends.

Luke's head lowers, his mouth a breath away from mine. His eyes roam over my face, my hair . . . the ground below?

"They're gone." He drops me so fast, my head smacks the back of the seat. "Stop the ride, please," he calls.

I sit up straight, mentally counting to five.

"You okay?"

I straighten my wig. "Perfect. You?"

Some of the arrogance leaves his face. "You were a pretty good sport."

"Sometimes we do what has to be done." I sound like my grandmother.

Luke brushes a piece of rainbow fuzz from my cheek. "Admit it, you miss me."

I move in close. Closer. "Luke?"

"Yeah?" He draws out the word, leaning in.

"You have clown lipstick on your face."

chapter ten

*A*ny peace I found in my Wednesday morning quiet time has long since evaporated.

"Luke, I would have never thought to put that sentence there. It makes the article so much better!"

Ashley Timmons sits right next to our editor and coos over every single thing he says like it's the winning number to the Lotto. You know, just because I don't want to date the guy doesn't mean that I want to see other girls throw themselves at him. Especially her. It's so unclassy. I mean, where's her self-respect? Her dignity? Her—okay, if she doesn't take her hands off his shoulder, I'm going to grab that halo of blonde hair and yank until I see roots.

"I think that would be a great idea, Ashley," Luke says, snapping me out of my dismal thoughts. "And I know just the person to help you with it." He swivels in his seat to face me. "Bella? Would you come over here please?"

I watch Ashley's face fall as I approach. "Yes?"

"I was telling Ashley about the carnival, and she wants to do a feature on Cherry Fritz."

"Uh-huh." *How much did you tell her? Did you mention your lips were locked with mine on the Ferris wheel? Because I'd hate to dampen her little crush.*

Luke rolls up his shirt sleeves on forearms tanned from soccer.

"Since you know Cherry better than I do, I want you to introduce Ashley to her tomorrow night before the show."

"Yeah, Bella." Ashley smiles prettily. "I hear you work as a clown. That must be a little embarrassing to have the whole town see you like that."

"Luke didn't seem to mind Monday night." I send him a saucy wink. "I suppose I could introduce you to Cherry. She's kind of a private girl, though. And she's been through a lot lately, so, you know, go easy on her."

Ashley's laugh is light and airy. "That's cute—your advice. I've been working on a newspaper staff for three years and won five national awards." Her smile never falters. "You've been writing for how long?"

Lord, you're going to want to move her out of my way, for the sake of her health and general well-being. "I guess I shot up in the ranks at the *Truman High Tribune* so fast, it seems like I've done it forever. At least that's what our advisor, Mr. Holman, says." *Take that, you she-devil.*

"And before coming to Truman, Bella had a regular gossip column at her old school," Luke says, his face a mask of innocence.

"*Advice* column," I spit out. "And helping hundreds of girls with their problems did prepare me for a lot of things—like writing." I lift a haughty brow. "And learning to read people. I can pretty much size up a person in minutes."

Ashley holds her assignment to her chest. "Luke, I'll see you at my house after school." Her smile is total movie star seductress. "Kyle said to tell you he'd be a little late getting there for your afternoon run."

Oh, and I'll bet you can think of all sorts of things to pass the time. "Speaking of super fun get-togethers," I say to him, "Dolly wanted me to invite you to her house tonight after church. She's having a birthday party for Cherry and wants anyone who can make it to be there." I glance at Journalist Barbie. "But if you have other things to do—"

"I'll be there." His eyes bore into mine. "In fact, Ashley, what are you doing later this evening?"

What is he thinking? "I believe Dolly wants Cherry to be surrounded by friends and family only." And not girls with fangs.

"It would be the perfect place for Ashley to interview Cherry."

"Another great idea!" Ashley claps her hands. "I would love to come. Luke, pick me up at seven fifteen." She gives him a playful punch in the shoulder. "You're going to love my new dress." She saunters away, and I barely resist the urge to stick my finger down my throat and make those mature little gagging noises.

"It's strictly business," he says.

"I didn't say a word." I look down at my editor.

"Just remember—you're the one who broke it off."

Pull yourself together, Bella. "And I meant it. I'm sorry your pride is still so wounded." I pat his back. "It will heal in time. At least that's what all the boys tell me."

Luke stands up to his full six feet. He takes off his glasses, giving me the full effect of his ocean-blue eyes. "All those boys, huh?"

"Right." I nod. "A whole line of them. I could fill a notebook with all the hearts I've left broken."

His grin is tigerlike. "There's been Hunter who, I will remind you, cheated. Oh, and lied to you repeatedly. And then there's been me, who you're afraid will treat you like Hunter. You remember me, right? The guy who kissed you on the Ferris wheel last night?"

I struggle to swim through the spell Luke's weaving and find something coherent to say. "Oh . . ." I swallow. "Yeah?"

"Yep."

No, I will deflect his über-hot words. Time to fight dirty. Time to fight with sass. "Actually, I just remember feeling pukey on that ride." I pause to consider. "Or was it your attempt at a kiss? I believe it was."

"You don't believe that for a second." He leans closer to me. "I know exactly what you do when you're lying. You give yourself away every time."

"I don't have any idea what you're talking about, and it offends me that you would suggest I am anything but the very virtue of honesty." At least fifty percent of the time.

"You twist your hair." He reaches out and stills my hand, my fingers curled around my locks.

I wrench my hand back. "I twirl my hair because you make me nervous—it's hard to act all friendly to you when you're obviously still not over me."

He tosses his dark head back and laughs. "Oh, but don't you wonder, Bella?" The air sizzles around him. "Ashley and I will see you tonight. We can't wait."

After church, I ride to Dolly's with Budge and Ruthie. My mom, who gets starry-eyed anytime there's a party to organize, is already out there, no doubt making sure every detail is just perfect. She's been really distracted lately, so having Cherry's birthday to plan has been just what she needed.

"Youth was awesome tonight, wasn't it?" Ruthie asks from the front of Budge's hearse. Yes, my stepbrother drives a hearse, as in a vehicle formerly used to haul dead folks to their final earthly destination. But it is handy for cramming in lots of people, which we're doing tonight.

I stare out the window and watch a dark, rainy Truman pass by. "It was okay."

"I thought it was interesting too. Dude, why didn't you tell me youth group was so good? I would've gone a long time ago." Budge eyes me in his rearview. "I've totally been missing out on Little Debbies and mochas."

"It's true." Ruthie skips a song on Budge's screamo CD. "Nights we have Oatmeal Cream Pies seem to be especially inspirational. What didn't you like about it, Bel?"

"I don't know. I guess my mind was just on other things. It seemed kind of irrelevant to me."

"Um, it was about trusting God." Ruthie bobs her blue hair to the music. "I think that pretty much covers everyone. Besides, you got some issues."

"I do not."

"Yeah. I knew it from the first time I met you."

"Right back at you." The first time Ruthie introduced herself, she asked me to find out who was passing around pics of her making out with someone who was *not* her boyfriend, and I agreed just so she wouldn't beat me up.

"Nah, I mean for real. You don't trust anyone." Ruthie nudges my stepbrother. "Budgie, did you know Bella's also afraid of carnival rides?"

He sighs and turns into Matt Sparks's driveway. "Add that to the list of her insecurities."

"My—my—what?" I should've walked. Ten miles in the rain wouldn't have been that hard. "You've had your girlfriend a matter of weeks, Budge, so I don't think that makes you any expert. I'm merely a cautious person, as life has taught me that—"

"Dude, I love this song." Budge cranks it up and plays drums on the steering wheel.

"Me too!" And Ruthie sings the chorus to "Lizards: They're Not Just For Breakfast Anymore."

At Budge's honk, Matt runs out of the house. He climbs in the back, next to me.

"Welcome to the Death Mobile," I say. "Let's go pick up Lindy and Bo."

"What?" Matt snaps his seatbelt. "Bo Blades is coming?"

"I heard they went out Friday night—after the track meet." Ruthie wiggles her eyebrows. "They've been seeing each other like a week." She sighs and grabs Budge's arm. "Do you remember our week-a-versary?"

"Do I ever." He pats her knee and stops at a four-way. "I took you to the Dairy Barn for ninety-nine–cent burger night. Seems like it was just yesterday."

"It was last month!" This romance crap is about to make me yak all over myself. "Can we just talk about something else?"

"I agree." Beside me Matt fumes. "People just rush into relationships these days. What happened to being friends and taking things slow?"

"Budgie's pretty much my BFF," Ruthie says. "And believe me, we're taking things slow. Right, poopsie bear?"

He stops in front of Lindy's house. "Sure thing, muffin top. Nothing but first base for us."

Ruthie cranks around in her seat. "No homeruns in this ballgame of love."

"Oh my gosh, stop! Ew!" I shove open my door and jump out so Lindy can get in the seats behind me.

"Hey, guys!" Lindy sails out of her house, pulling a smiling Bo Blades by the hand. "Bye, Dad! And I promise I won't break curfew tonight."

"What?" I hear Matt mutter. "She broke her curfew?"

"Very roomy." Bo stares in wonder at the hearse as he climbs in.

Budge grins. "Just one of the many perks."

"Plus a nice, chemical pine smell." Ruthie inhales. "It's just like I'm in a fake forest."

"Nothing but the best for my girl."

I sink into my seat as we back out, listening to both couples whisper and giggle.

I roll my eyes. "I should have taken my own car."

"I wish you had," Matt mumbles. "I would have paid you to run me over."

I can't help but laugh. "Just ten more minutes and we'll be there." I nudge him with my elbow. "Are you okay?"

"Yeah. Fine. Great." His mouth is grim as he glances back at Lindy, absorbed in her own world with Bo. "I guess I just miss my best friend."

chapter eleven

The sight of Dolly's house never fails to make me smile. As a side-hobby, my mom's friend works at Sugar's Diner downtown by day. But in her off-time she's a champion horse breeder, which has paid for the giant sprawl of a home and her many acres.

"Come on in before you get wet!" Dolly's big eighties bangs blow in the warm breeze as she holds open the door. "Cherry's in the kitchen." Dolly leans close to my ear. "She's a little nervous about not really knowing everyone that well, so anything you can do to perk her up would be appreciated."

"No problem. The food smells good." I follow the scent into the kitchen and give Cherry a side hug. "What are we having?"

"Whatever Mickey Patrick is fixing," she says, gesturing to the back door with a carrot stick. "He's grilling."

My mom stands next to the sink, and I kiss her on the cheek and begin putting ice in cups.

I turn my curious stare to Dolly. She and her ex-husband have been hanging out some in the last few months. Maybe more than I thought. "Mickey's here?"

"Yeah." Dolly shrugs it off. "Now that Jake's made the big time, Mickey's not training as much. He's focusing more on managing."

"I wish Jake could've been here tonight. His plane got delayed in

Kansas City." My mom drops some flowers into a vase, then carries it into the giant dining room.

"Anyway," Dolly says, "I had a problem with the grill, so Mickey came over to help."

I bump my hip into Dolly's. "Lighting your grill—is that what you kids call it these days?"

She laughs and swats me with a towel. "I have to go check on the burgers."

"So, Cherry, are you having a good birthday?" I ask.

Her smile almost meets her eyes. "Yeah. The carnival family gave me a party earlier today. So it's just Dolly and you guys tonight."

"I know you're missing Betty today—and your parents." I hug her again. "I'll introduce you to some people. If you're going to be staying in Truman, you need some friends." Heaven knows I did.

"What I wish I had is Peg."

"Who?"

"Betty's dog." Her eyes tear up. "I just think about her out there alone without me or Betty." She sniffs. "I mean, what if she's hurt? Or hungry? What if someone took her?"

"I'm sure she's okay." I pat her arm and try not to twirl my hair.

"Why hasn't she come back, then?"

I don't know, but it's a good thing she hasn't. How do I tell the girl that her uncle and cousin want to kill her dog? "Are you doing okay out here at Dolly's?"

"Yes." Cherry pours herself a Dr Pepper and takes a long drink. "It's been nice. Dolly's so cool—it's like we've known each other forever. She—she makes me miss my mom. But I also feel bad for imposing on her like this because we *haven't* known each other forever. I'm a distant cousin. She's even taken over my homeschooling. And now she says she's taking a leave of absence from Sugar's."

"The diner is just her social time. Something to do to fill her hours." Dolly makes a small fortune with her horse farm. "Cherry, you know Dolly and Mickey had two girls a long time ago. They were killed in a wreck."

"I didn't know."

I refill her cup. "So you being here—it's not an imposition to her. In fact, I'd say it was God helping her out."

"Why?"

"Because she's been so lonely. I know she loves having you here."

Cherry looks around, then grins. "I have the best bedroom. It's huge! And it's all mine."

I laugh. "And don't forget the pool!"

"You'll have to come over one day and swim with me. When we're not working, that is."

"Um, speaking of work." A thousand questions rush through my mind. "What did you think about Alfredo?"

She shakes her head. "I don't know. I thought I liked him. At first I didn't—at least not for Betty. It was all so sudden, and they just jumped into this relationship. I couldn't believe how fast they moved. But then he really grew on me when I saw how happy Betty was. She told me Alfredo was talking marriage."

"Did you ever hear Alfredo mention it?"

"No. But he seemed to really like her—toward the end. So it was pretty shocking when . . . well, when—"

I finish the thought. "He killed her."

"Yeah. I still can't believe it."

"What if he didn't do it?" I ask, moving closer.

"It was his sword. His fingerprints. People heard them fighting. Still, it doesn't seem like him at all . . . I don't want to believe he did it."

"Had you noticed Betty not getting along with anyone else lately? You mentioned that she didn't exactly see eye to eye with Red."

"Yeah, but that sums up everyone. Nobody gets along with Red." Cherry sputters on her drink. "Do you think Red did it?"

"No!" I say quickly. "I mean, I don't know. Right now everyone seems kind of suspect to me. I just don't think Alfredo and Betty's story adds up."

"It's true no one trusts Red—or Stewart." Cherry's voice dips to a whisper. "Including me."

"Was there anything special about Betty's dog?"

She shakes her head at my weird question. "Peg was the best. She jumped through hoops and learned all of Betty's routines really quickly. A really smart dog. I guess she knew a lot of commands. Why do you ask?"

"No reason. But if you see anything weird, let me know."

"Bella, I'm thirteen and I work in a circus. All I know is weird."

Cherry and I walk to the living room together, just in time to see the front door swing open and a herd of giants stampede the foyer.

"We heard there was a party here!" Jake breaks through the pack, his eyes landing on my mom. "Thought we'd stop by."

Mom squeals as he picks her up and twirls her around. "What are you doing here?" She looks beyond Jake's shoulder to his friends. "*All* of you."

Jake sets Mom down, his large hands remaining on her shoulders. "I was missing you. There were all these traffic delays due to the weather, and our flight got cancelled. The next one to Dallas was tomorrow morning, so we just got a car and drove here."

Mom laughs as Jake kisses her cheek. "So where is everyone staying?"

Robbie comes bolting through in his red Superman cape and hugs his dad's leg. "With us! Can they stay with us?"

"We shouldn't be too much of a problem, Mrs. Finley. The Truman Inn is booked." A man taller than the doorway holds out a hand. "Vicious Viper—but you can just call me Larry."

The other six men introduce themselves.

"Of course you can stay with us." Mom hugs Jake. "I'd hate to disappoint Robbie."

Jake hoists his son into his arms.

"Daddy, I taped this great documentary we can watch together. It's called *Commodities and Stocks in a Bear Market.*"

"Maybe next week, Robbie. I'm only in for tonight, okay?"

"Oh." Robbie's smile melts. "Yeah, okay. I guess Jillian can watch it with me."

Mom sweeps his hair from his eyes. "I'd love to, sweetie." She glances at her husband once more. "I have work to do." And she walks away.

The doorbell rings again, and I run to answer it.

"Luke."

"Hello, Bella." He has the nerve to stand there smiling with Ashley Timmons by his side.

"Sorry we're late," she gushes. "We got to talking and lost track of time."

Shoot me now. I cannot watch her drape herself all over him the entire night. "I hope Luke didn't bore you with his favorite topic of ballet. That boy can talk pirouettes and tutus all night. Or his other favorite pastime—mud wrestling."

"Nice." Luke's jaw is taut as he pulls an uncertain Ashley past me to join the crowd.

"Have a good time now!"

An hour and a half later I'm sitting in a lounge chair by the pool with everyone else. I'm stuffed with cake and amazed at the princess theme my mom threw together at the last minute. There are lily pads floating in the pool, tiny pink lights in every visible shrub, and I can see Cherry's tiara sparkling from here. I'd say the birthday party was a success.

At least for Cherry.

As for me, I've spent the entire evening watching couples— Budge and Ruthie, Lindy and Bo, and now Ashley and Luke. Seriously, if that girl scoots any closer to him, they'll be Siamese twins. Even Mickey Patrick hasn't left Dolly's side. I don't know if they're seeing each other again, but the war seems to be over. I've also been working overtime keeping Ashley away from Cherry. I've intercepted her, like, five times. This is Cherry's birthday. She doesn't need to be hassled by an obnoxious reporter. Unless it's me.

Deciding I'm about ready to call it a night, I gather up some plates and make my way across the yard toward the back door of the kitchen.

"Jake, you saw your son's face."

I stop at my mom's voice. She and Jake stand on the deck, the porch light spilling over her worried features.

"I'm here tonight, aren't I? Instead of sitting in that airport, I came here to be with you and the kids. This is overwhelming to me too. Do you think I like being gone this much?"

"Whether you like it or not doesn't change the fact that this family is suffering. I don't enjoy being the mother *and* father here. How do you think your sons feel when I have to be the disciplinarian? Just like last weekend—Budge stayed up for forty-eight hours straight playing some stupid video game that had just come out. Guess who had to pull the plug on that and be the bad guy?"

"We'll talk about this later."

"When?"

"When I have time to deal with it."

My mom shakes her head. "This family deserves more than visits between layovers. Your *later* might be too late."

chapter twelve

Where else would any fun-loving American teenage girl be on a Friday night? Probably at the mall or the movies. But me? I'm poised over a dunk tank.

"Nobody's knocked you down yet, boss. How awesome is that?" Ruthie tosses a baseball in the air and catches it. "Plus we're getting some extra dough working a few additional hours before the show."

"Yeah, a brilliant idea."

"Dude, I need all the money I can get. I'm graduating next month, you know."

I swing my legs and look on with dread as I see Luke Sullivan getting out of his 4Runner in the parking lot. Of course he would be here early. "And why is it I'm up here instead of you?" I ask my friend.

"Because I have to be all ready for my unicycling debut tonight."

"Your what?" I watch as Luke stops to talk to the roller-coaster operator, making his way closer to us.

Ruthie clutches the ball to her chest. "I just wasn't feeling personally fulfilled with our basic clown work. I needed more. I wanted to feel challenged, alive, and—"

"In the spotlight?"

"I happen to have a gift to share with the world." She stuffs a piece of stray hair back into her wild updo. Gone is the neon blue, replaced with an eye-blinking shade of violet.

"So you're going to ride your unicycle around for a few minutes?"

"Ride it around?" Ruthie harrumphs. "What I do is called art. I will be performing a unicycle ballet I choreographed myself. I call it 'Love Is Squishy.'"

I'm spared the chance to comment as Luke appears. "Hello, ladies."

His casual tone sends Ruthie to chatting. But when he glances at me, I see something lurking beneath that's about as friendly as a derailed coaster.

"Ruthie, will you give me a minute with Bella?" His steel eyes find mine. "I need to talk to her about some homework."

Homework? Not unless the assignment is wringing my neck.

"Sure thing." Ruthie sets the ball down. "I have some important performance preparations to tend to anyway." She takes off in the direction of the nearest funnel cake trailer.

"Dunk tank?" Luke steps closer until he's standing right in front of me. "Anything for the job, huh, Bella?"

"That's your motto—hanging out with Ashley. It's all about the job, right?" I swing my legs, shrug, and study my nails.

Luke reaches through the fence between us and captures a foot. "Want to tell me why you blew off her attempts to talk to Cherry Wednesday night?"

"I don't believe I like your surly tone. So no." I jerk my foot back. "I don't think I do."

"The *Tribune* is still my paper, and I'm still your editor."

"You know, I was going to get that tattooed on my butt, but you say it so many times, I've decided to go with something more original."

A muscle in his jaw ticks. "It's one thing to disrespect me. But it's another to get in the way of one of my staff members' work."

"Disrespect *you?*" I toss my head back and laugh. "If anyone's been disrespected here, buddy, it's me. That girl kisses you, you protest your innocence, but yet you're with her all the time—as *friends.* Then you rip the carnival feature from me—something I was totally wrapped up in—only to hand over part of it to your new girlfriend!"

He lifts his head. "I'm letting her do an interview with Cherry. Not a full-blown series on the Fritz Family Carnival." Luke's voice dips. "And Wednesday night you blocked every attempt Ashley made to speak to Cherry."

"It was the girl's birthday. It wasn't the time or the place to ask her twenty questions about her lonely life as a trapeze performer or how she felt about losing yet another person in her life."

"You know what I think?" He leans onto the chain link fence cage around me, his tan fingers curling around the wire. "I think you're so eaten up with jealousy, you can't even see straight."

"I think you're beating a dead horse. A bloated, maggoty, dead horse. We are clearly so over. So if you want to date—"

"Journalist Barbie." He throws my words back at me with a slow grin.

"If you want to date the stinking queen of England, I don't care. Just don't expect me to do her any favors. Ashley Timmons can figure out her own way to talk to Cherry."

"Number one, while the queen's orthopedic shoes are a huge turn-on, she travels too much to truly be there for me." He picks up a ball and tosses it in one hand. "And number two, I am telling you that you better figure out a way to cool it with Ashley."

"Or?"

He lopes away, his dark jeans slung low over his hips. "Or I'll cool it for you."

I catch the wicked gleam in his eye and go on alert. "Oh no you don't. You wouldn't!"

And with lightning speed, a smiling Luke Sullivan pivots and throws a fastball right toward the bull's-eye.

I stand shivering outside the trailers, cursing Luke Sullivan and thanking God for the millionth time I didn't wear a white shirt today.

Well, maybe my luck just changed. I spy one of Alfredo's old roommates weaving through the trailers, talking to Luigi, one of the ticket takers. It's time to reclaim my flashlight—if it's not too late already.

"Hey, you're Johnny, right?" I call out.

The small man just grunts, but he stops.

"You were really great last night—balancing like you did on that horse. I've never seen anything like that."

His cheeks turn as pink as a cherry limeade.

"I got roped into dunk-tank duty and really came unprepared. I wondered if I could maybe borrow your hair dryer?" I twist my long hair into a rope and water drips onto the ground.

"I guess my roomie has one you can use." He steps toward his trailer when a voice stops us both.

"I don't think that's such a good idea."

I turn around and find Stewart eyeing my wet form.

No! It's a great idea. I have *got* to get back into that trailer.

Stewart runs a hand over his prickly goatee. "If you have to be in anyone's sleeping quarters, I'd prefer it be a member of management's." He crooks a skinny finger. "Follow me. You can dry off in my trailer."

How in the world am I going to get that flashlight back? "Um . . . okay. But I think I'll run and get Ruthie to keep me company."

"She's rehearsing. Can't bother her now."

Fine. Assuming Red's not in there, this will give me a chance to search the Fritzes' trailer. Praying for protection from sheer creepiness, I follow Stewart to his home on wheels, looking behind me for Ruthie the entire way. But no help comes.

"After you, my lady." He opens the door with one hand and sweeps his other before him like some sort of gallant duke.

I step inside, my nostrils flaring at the smell of stale smoke and burnt microwave popcorn.

"It's not much, but it's home." He brushes past me, taking me through the office space into the living quarters. "Would you like something to drink? A Coke? Water? A beer?"

"I'm seventeen."

Stewart's laugh reminds me of a hyena. "I won't tell if you won't."

"You know, I think my hair's dry enough. And I'll just borrow a towel from one of the ladies."

"No way." He smiles, and I try not to shudder again. "Whatever you want, it's yours."

I wind my purse strap around my hands. In case I need to launch a good swing toward Stewart's head.

"Thanks," I say as he sets a towel and blow dryer on the tiny counter of the bathroom. He moves out, so I can step in. I pick up the beige towel and blot my neck and arms, trying to ignore his lurky presence.

"You have beautiful hair." He stands right there, an arm braced in the doorway. "You know, Bella, circus life can be a lot of fun. I could—"

"Hey, Stewart, you must be really busy." *Being a full-time perv and all.* "Don't let me keep you. I know how important you are around here."

He moves forward until he's blocking the door, crowding out any space left in the bathroom. I reach for a hand mirror. I am the stepdaughter of Captain Iron Jack, wrestling phenomenon, and I know how to use this thing for more than checking my lipstick.

"I know you've got that boyfriend, Bella. But word is you two are having problems." Stewart leans back against the wall, with mere inches between us. "So any time you want to stay after the show and get a few free rides on the Ferris wheel, you let me know. There are all kinds of privileges of dating a carnival manager."

Knock! Knock!

I sag with relief when the door flings open.

"Stewart?" A voice calls.

"Sounds like someone needs you." And it sure isn't me.

I pop my head out to see Luke standing in the office. His eyes flit to me, then to Red Fritz's son.

"There's a problem with one of the horses. The trainer said he needs you immediately."

Stewart's lazy gaze travels back to me. "I'm sorry. I guess we'll have to pick up our conversation later. But you get all nice and pretty in here, and I'll see you after the show." He slides out of the bathroom, his chest puffing as he passes Luke. "Don't you have work to do?"

When Stewart shuts the door behind him, my shoulders all but fall to the floor in relief.

"What in the *heck* do you think you're doing?" Luke demands. "Never be alone with that guy. Are you crazy?"

"He wasn't going to hurt me. Besides, I wanted to peek around in here."

"Oh, I'm sure he has plenty to show you." Luke shoves his fingers through his hair. "When I couldn't find you and someone told me they saw you going in here with Stewart—" He shakes his head. "You have no idea."

"I'm not even speaking to you, so you can just leave now."

"Not without you."

Had he not dunked me in the tank an hour ago, I might've found that hot. "Look, I have things to do here."

"Like what?"

"I have hair to fix and drawers to open." I wave my hand. "So unless you're going to help, get out."

Luke looks back over his shoulder toward the door. "What are we looking for?"

I make quick work of drying my hair, then join Luke in the office, where he sits at a computer.

"See anything?" I open a file drawer and thumb through each one, checking the window for anybody walking by.

"No suspicious e-mails that I can find. Though Red seems to have an online girlfriend."

"I'm sure the top hat is a huge turn-on." I move on to the few folders and files on the desk. Bills. Check stubs. "Wait. What is this?" I flip through a giant-sized checkbook.

"It's Red's pay system. Looks like he still writes his checks by hand."

Curious to see how much Betty was paid, I flip back a month. "That's strange. Betty had been with the circus longer, but Alfredo made quite a bit more."

Luke stands near and peers over my shoulder. "Looks like Alfredo made more than everyone." His hand snakes around me as he runs a finger down the book.

Between Luke's light cologne and the fear of getting caught, my heart beats loudly enough to scare the circus animals. I flip through the pay book backward. "Look—in November Alfredo got paid less than Betty and most of the others. But by December, his check got a major bump."

Luke's voice rumbles near my ear. "Maybe he took on more work."

"What, made more rabbits disappear?" I turn my head and draw in a breath at the closeness of Luke's face. If I just leaned the slightest bit, our lips would be touching. *Omigosh, focus!* "Um . . . but December would be about the time Alfredo started seeing Betty."

Luke lifts a brow, seemingly unaffected by being a breath away from me. Of course, he wouldn't be. He's got Ashley Timmons now.

"Could be just a coincidence." Luke's voice at my ear sends chill bumps down my neck.

"But it might not be."

"You think he was paid off for seeing her?"

I slowly nod. "That was my thought."

He pulls an errant piece of hair away from my cheek. "Any other thoughts in there?"

Just that I'm an idiot to let myself feel this for you. That you draw me in like a sale at Bergdorf's, and I can't stand the thought of you and Ashley. "Nope. That's it."

"You know what I think about?" His voice is as soft as cotton candy.

"That it's a shame girls don't want to talk about the SATs and chess on a date?"

"I think about that night on the Ferris wheel."

"Really?" Ohhh, he's playing dirty. "I don't."

He sighs and smiles, pulling my twirling finger from my hair. "I believe you do. And I think you want a relationship, Bella. But just like that big ol' Ferris wheel—it scares you. And first chance you get, you jump off. It's too easy to believe I cheated on you."

"We really should get out of here."

"Not every guy is out to break your heart."

"They all have." I suck in my bottom lip, knowing I just fell for his bait. "I don't want to talk about this."

"I'm sorry about your dad. I'm sure it hurts to be left out of his life."

"My dad has nothing to do with this."

"Then there's Hunter." Luke takes the payroll book out of my hands. "Total idiot."

"And where do you fit in, Luke Sullivan?" I turn all the way around and look up into his face.

"Right here." He angles his head as his arms go around me. His head lowers, and my eyes flutter closed.

The door flings open, slamming the outside of the trailer. "Hey!" Luke and I jump apart as a pair of hostile eyes take in the scene.

"The time for secrets is over. Tell me why you're here. Now."

chapter thirteen

My tongue freezes at the roof of my mouth. But Luke moves fast. He steps away from me and shoves the payroll book behind his back.

"Hey, Cherry."

Her eyes take in the interior of the trailer. This girl who flies through the air and relies on perfect timing for a living doesn't miss a thing. "I knew you two were up to something."

I finally find my voice. "I came in here to dry off from the dunk tank. Luke followed to check on me. That's all."

"I meant from the very beginning." She closes the door with a slam. "You with all your questions." She gestures at me with her chin. "And this one always prowling and hanging around way after we're closed for the night."

I glance at Luke. "Really?"

He nods proudly. "Yeah."

Cherry stomps her foot and breaks the moment. "I want the truth or I scream my head off for my uncle."

"You don't want to do that." Luke sits down at the edge of the desk. "We're here to help."

"Help yourself to my uncle's checkbook?"

"No." Luke flips it back open and hands it to her. "About the time Alfredo started dating Betty, he began receiving a substantially larger paycheck."

She scans a few pages. "So?"

"Nobody else's pay seemed to go up," I say. "Cherry, everyone we've talked to has commented on how strange Alfredo was with Betty when they first got together. Even you said it. What if he was being paid to date her?"

"That's ridiculous. Anyone could see he loved her. Especially in the last few weeks."

I decide to let go of my best information. "I overheard Red tell Stewart to find Betty's dog. But then . . . Red wants Peg dead. These guys are not to be trusted. He said he had Alfredo's situation under control."

"What? No!" Her face pales beneath her stage makeup. "Uncle Red would never kill Peg."

Luke steps closer to her, as comforting as a big brother. "Bella and I are here to solve Betty's murder. We know you want justice more than anyone."

"But the police say Alfredo did it. I didn't want to believe it, but we can't argue with the evidence. His prints were on the murder weapon."

"Why wouldn't they be?" I ask. "He handled those swords every day. He claims he's innocent—what if he's telling the truth?"

Tears gather in Cherry's kohl-lined eyes. "But my uncle loves me." She rubs her hand over her nose. "I mean, he's never been like a dad or anything. But he took me in when my parents died. He saved me from an orphanage—he's told me about those places."

"And I'm sure he does love you," Luke says so convincingly even I almost believe it. "So we don't want to upset him with anything until we have more evidence, okay?"

"But you think my uncle had something to do with Betty's murder?"

"It's really important we find out." I move toward her and swipe away some dripping mascara on her cheek. "But we need you to act like you know nothing, okay? Can you do that?"

She stares down at the floor, where she makes a figure eight with her shoe. As if she has the weight of the world on her shoulders, she lifts her head. "Uncle Red and Stewart are heading out somewhere after the show tonight. I don't know where. I just heard them talking about looking for something."

Luke's eyes dart my way, but I focus on Cherry. "You can trust us." I pull her into a quick hug. "Everything is going to be okay."

"You promise?"

I stare at the girl who's seen too much sadness in her thirteen years. "I promise."

Thirty minutes after the evening's final performance, I walk out of the tent into the dark night with Ruthie.

"What an evening, huh?" She holds out her arms and spins. "I unicycled like I have never unicycled before. Did you see the finale?"

"It was riveting." All I can think is I hope Cherry doesn't rat me out with her uncle and cousin. I am so toast. This whole thing is.

"Did you see the last part where I fluttered that ribbon behind me? I added that in at the last minute. It was symbolic, you know? I mean, there was a message in there."

"Shakespeare couldn't have said it better." I check my watch. Ten thirty. I'm so tired it might as well be two in the morning. And the night is far from over. "So, I'll see you tomorrow."

As my car comes into view, so does Luke. He sits on the hood, lounged back on his muscular arms. Geeks should not be this devastatingly good-looking.

"What are you doing?" I ask.

"Thought we could hang out." He doesn't move from his lazy recline.

"I'm sure Ashley Timmons is waiting for your call. Besides, I'm just going home."

"Sure you are."

Not once have I ever wished for a crime-solving partner. Not one time.

Ruthie throws a leg over her motorcycle. "You know, maybe it's because it's been a night of emotional expression for me and I'm extra-sensitive, but I'm picking up on some vibes here. Yeah"—she waves a finger between us—"I think you two are up to something. And it ain't no date."

"Good night, Ruthie." I open my car door. "And Luke."

He jumps off the hood and grabs the door. "Not so fast. We're a team."

"A *team* member wouldn't dunk me in a water tank." Every time I think about that, I get ticked. "I'm working solo." I direct my glare at Ruthie too.

She hops off her bike and scurries to my car. Pushing Luke out of the way, she slides into the backseat. "Where are we going?" She bestows Luke with her haughtiest stare. "I am the sidekick, you know, so don't get any ideas about taking my title. I have the book and everything."

A corner of his mouth quirks. "I know a place where we can park the car out of sight and keep an eye out for anyone leaving."

"Oh, espionage!" Ruthie claps her hands. "I love it. Hey, should I have brought my slingshot?"

"No!" Luke and I yell simultaneously.

After texting my mom that I'm going to be hanging out with Ruthie and Luke, I steer the car onto a side road, and we wait.

Ruthie whiles away the time by humming. "Can you guess that tune?"

"Sounds just like the last three." Luke rubs the bridge of his nose.

Ruthie sighs. "Did I tell you the story about the time I stapled the church secretary's skirt to a pew?"

"Yes. And when she stood up to sing 'Just As I Am,' her skirt fell down and she farted. Good story." Ugh, I just want to go to sleep. And get away from Luke. Seriously, the guy almost kissed me tonight. Right? I'm sure he was going to. But why? Maybe now I'm just some challenge to him. I know Ashley sure isn't.

Luke jerks his seat up straight. "There they go—Stewart and Red."

We all watch Red's old Ford F-150 pull out of the carnival parking lot.

"Start the car," Luke says. "But keep the lights off."

"Omigosh. This is so CSI!"

I roll my eyes in the dark at Ruthie, and at the count of ten I put the car in drive.

We follow them through downtown, staying back a comfortable distance. They drive to the city park, and I stop the car across the street.

"What are they doing?" Ruthie whispers.

I reach into my purse and get out my little pink binoculars. "They've got shovels."

"They're stopping at the memorial fountain."

"Probably gonna scoop up some pennies," Ruthie says. "I sneak out here and do that every once in a while myself. You don't get much, but it's a good way to fund a beef jerky and Yoo-Hoo purchase."

"They're digging all right." I hand my binoculars to Luke. "Right next to the fountain."

Thirty minutes later father and son climb back into the truck, armed with nothing but their shovels.

"Whatever they're looking for, they didn't find it." I work out a kink in my neck. "Maybe this is what they wanted the dog for—to find something."

"I totally should've brought snacks." Ruthie pops in her fifth piece of gum. "Some bean dip would really hit the spot."

We all duck down as the truck goes by, its headlights shining through my Bug.

"They're turning down Hall Street." Luke straightens to a seated position. "Let's go."

Over the next hour Red and Stewart stop at a pig farm, the Dairy Barn, and a used car lot. Finding nothing at the water tower, the two guys toss the shovels in the bed of the truck.

"Wait a minute. What's that?" Luke adjusts the binoculars and zooms in. "A piece of paper. They're reading off some sort of instructions or something."

"Maybe it's a treasure map!"

I'm so exhausted I laugh out loud. "Ruthie, this isn't *Pirates of the Caribbean*."

Luke shifts in his seat, his body humming with renewed energy. "She could be right."

I lean on my armrest and yawn. "Buried treasure?"

As we follow the truck back to the carnival grounds, Ruthie voices what we're all three thinking. "Buried *something*."

chapter fourteen

The rest of the weekend flies by, with Ruthie, Luke, and me staking out Red each night after the carnival. Saturday night we followed Red and Stewart out to the lake where they continued their strange digging, but they took Sunday off. I guess even suspicious creepy guys need a day of rest.

"I still don't understand why I'm going to Dad's again." I zip my carry-on as Mom pulls a shirt out of my closet to borrow. "I just saw him two weekends ago."

"We went over this Monday, Bella. And Tuesday." Mom holds the shirt up and studies herself in the mirror. "I want to see Jake's first official show in Los Angeles. He needs my support."

"Why can't Budge and I go? Robbie gets to."

"Because Budge is staying with friends. He's one wiener medal away from Employee of the Month, and I can't take that away from him. Plus, you and Robbie can afford to miss three days of school. Budge can't."

"But I could go with you. Or stay with Ruthie."

"Your father was nice enough to get Ruthie a ticket too, so don't push it." Mom leans over and kisses the top of my head. "I don't like how things have been between you and your dad. This is the perfect opportunity to get in some additional father-daughter time."

"He's just going to foist me off on his fiancée or make me watch the Disney Channel with Marisol." Plus, I need to be here. I could miss something at the carnival. Even though Red and Stewart didn't take any late-night drives with their shovels Monday or Tuesday evening doesn't mean they won't resume them tonight. What if they find something and I'm not there? When I asked Red Fritz for the rest of the week off, he jumped on the idea. Why would he be excited about me leaving town? Because I'm definitely an asset to the circus. My clowning skills are pretty much priceless. Yet he dismissed me for the week as if the show can just carry on without me. I mean, yeah, I might've mistakenly popped a kid with a balloon Saturday night. And maybe that four-year-old *was* crying because I accidentally hit him with my shoe, but that's no reason to be glad I'm gone. What if Red knows I'm onto something? That man is connected to Betty's murder. I'm just not sure how. Or why.

I give my mom the same wounded expression that used to get me what I wanted—from new shoes to jaunts to Paris. I pout my lips. I blink until my brown eyes have a misty sheen. My voice is as sweet as the tea at Sugar's Diner. "Mother, please let me stay in Truman."

By two p.m. I'm standing at the LaGuardia baggage claim with my dad.

"Hey, sweetie." He crushes me in a hug, then I introduce him to Ruthie.

"I don't believe in plastic surgery, sir," she says, handing him her bag. "I'm all about keeping things as natural as the good Lord intended."

As she walks in front of me, I stare at her striped beehive that's a security risk all by itself.

Three hours later Ruthie and I are watching TV in my bedroom.

"Dude, this room is scary." She points toward the trio of cherubs on the ceiling above my bed. "I can hardly watch the movie for thinking any minute one of them is gonna swoop down and stab me with a pitchfork."

"One of my dad's ex-girlfriends decorated the house." That would've been two hundred ladies ago. "Every room has a theme."

Ruthie picks up the lamp in the shape of lips. "What's the theme in here—scary movie props?"

"Love," I sigh. "Anymore, I think it's pretty dead-on. This room gives me nightmares and a stomachache. So do boys."

"Aw, you just gotta find the right guy. Like my Budgie-umpkins."

Before I can totally gag, little Marisol sticks her head in the door. "Guess what?"

The monkeys from The Wizard of Oz *are at the door, and they've come to claim you?* "What?"

"This is going to be my room."

I nearly fall off the bed. "I don't think so! You have your own room down the hall." In the lovely theme of vegetables that are purple.

"But when the baby comes, I'll move into this room."

"Baby? There's no baby." Oh no. My dad can't even keep up with me, let alone another child. I sit down hard on the bed. "Right, Marisol?"

She shrugs a shoulder and sniffs. "Well, there will be one day. I mean, they are getting married soon."

"My dad's already done the baby thing. Me." And I turned out fabulous, thank you very much. "So don't get your hopes up."

"But I heard them talking about it yesterday when they met with Christina's lawyer over the prenup."

How sad is it that an eight-year-old even knows what a prenup is? "So . . ." I pat the space beside me on the bed in invitation for her to sit. She skips into the room, straightens her bow, then takes a seat. "What else do you know about their prenup?" I glance at Ruthie, but she's absorbed in an old Reese Witherspoon movie.

"Nothin' really. After the lawyer lady left, my, um, sister was in a really bad mood."

Hmmm. Maybe it didn't go so well. Good. I hope my dad stuck

it to her and made sure Christina walks away with nothing of his if they divorce. But it's odd only one lawyer was involved. Surely Dad's guy was in on it too.

"I wouldn't set your sights on my bedroom yet." I pat her on her dark head. "Let's get them married first, okay?" Or not.

Marisol's forehead draws into a frown. "They have to get married. She says she's worked too hard for it not to happen."

I blanch. "What do you mean?"

"Marisol!"

The girl perks at her sister's voice. "Christina's home!"

I reach for her. "Marisol, wait—"

She races out the door . . . taking her secrets with her.

Dinner is low-key, with pizza and chips at the dining room table.

"Tomorrow we'll go out for dinner." Dad takes another slice of pepperoni. "Bella, are you going to show Ruthie your city?"

"I thought we'd hit the Statue of Liberty tomorrow. Maybe the NBC studios and Rockefeller." Squeeze in some shopping.

Ruthie chomps on a bite, oblivious to the string of cheese dangling from her chin. "I want to see if I can talk to the guys at *Saturday Night Live*. I have this skit idea they're gonna love. It involves a talking asparagus."

"Kevin, will you cut my pizza into bites?" Marisol slides her plate toward my dad.

"Of course, pumpkin."

"You're the best in the whole wide world."

Like a slo-mo sequence from a horror film, I watch as she leans toward my father. He meets her half way. And they rub noses, giggling. Giggling!

"Aren't they sweet?" Christina asks, like we're in the middle of a Hallmark movie. "She loves him so much." Her smile wobbles for a brief moment. Like a sad memory walked across her mind.

Christina jumps as her phone rings.

"Don't get that." Dad's voice is resigned. "Let it go."

"I can't." She reaches into the pocket of her tailored jacket. "Hello? Oh. Yes, just one moment." She puts her hand over the phone. "I'm just going to take this in the other room." Christina rolls her almond-shaped eyes. "It's a client."

Dad rubs a hand across his deliberately stubbly face. "She's had to work a lot lately. But that's why she's the best. Ruthie, did Bella tell you about the TV show deal Christina got me? It's like *Extreme Makeover*, but in Brazil. And I'm the show's plastic surgeon."

"That's cool, Mr. Kirkwood. I don't watch much Brazilian TV. But sometimes I turn on the Latin soap operas. You should think about getting on one of those." She looks at me and whispers behind her hand, "Kinda weird your dad *and* stepdad have both been on TV. How cool is that?"

"It's the coolest," I deadpan.

"I'm sorry." Christina's heels tap on the dining room floor. "But I have to go. I have a client who's in the middle of a crisis."

"Again?" Dad asks. "This is the third night in a row."

She trails a hand across his shoulders. "I have to be available to my clients whenever they need me. And this particular one is just a little high maintenance."

Dad stands up and brushes the pizza crumbs from his lap. "Then I'll go with you. The girls can watch Marisol."

"No!" Christina checks her gold watch. "I'll be back in no time. Just going to call a cab." She walks away, disappearing into the hall that leads to the master bedroom.

Something is just not right with this chick. I feel the need for a little surveillance. Heaven forbid I go twenty-four hours without tailing someone.

"Wow, I am seriously craving a frappuccino." I kick Ruthie under the table. "Aren't you?"

She pops another pepperoni in her mouth. "Whipped cream gives me gas."

"Starbucks has great water." I stand up and pull her with me. "I'll just grab our purses." I run upstairs like a rabid pit bull is chasing me. When I make it back down, Christina is at the front door.

"I'll see you all in a bit."

"Wait! Ruthie and I are going to grab a coffee. Let's share a cab."

Christina's eyes widen. "No, you two take your own so you can have your girl time."

I move ahead of her and open the door. "We must think green and protect Mother Earth." Not to mention my dad.

"You guys have fun!" Dad yells as we spill onto the sidewalk and into the cab.

My dad's fiancée is quiet during the ride as Ruthie babbles on about things she knows about New York City. "And my mom told me to carry my money in my bra because that would be the last place a robber would look."

"Here you go," Christina says as the taxi pulls up to Starbucks. "Have fun."

We shut the door, and I watch her give instructions to the driver.

"Come on." I pull Ruthie away from the coffee shop door and flag down another cab.

"What are we doing?"

I yank open the door of the yellow sedan. "Follow that cab ahead. But keep at a distance."

Ruthie's eyes widen as she buckles herself in. "Are we tailing Christina?"

I fill Ruthie in on the mystery woman from two weeks ago. "It could be nothing, but my gut says Christina is up to something."

Ruthie rubs her stomach. "My gut says I shouldn't have had that root beer."

My head bobs with every stop and go. Even at night, there's no downtime for New York traffic. It's always rush hour.

"Turn down that street to the right, please," I say to the driver as Christina's cab stops at a hotel a half a block away. I pay the fare and scurry out.

Peeking around the corner of the building, I watch as Christina nods to a doorman, then sails through the revolving doors and enters the Broadway Heights hotel.

"Follow me, but act cool, okay?"

Ruthie and I walk nonchalantly to the door. When I roll on through, I'm emptied into a large lobby with green botanical carpet.

And completely alone.

"Ahhhh!"

With a moan of dread, I turn around. Ruthie runs in circles, banging on the glass. "It won't let me out! Crazy spinning portal! You won't suck me in!"

I stop the glass door and grab my friend by the wrist. "You really have to get out of Truman more often."

"That thing is evil!" She glares back at the offensive entrance. "Evil, I tell you."

I plaster my hand over her mouth and jerk her behind a large potted palm. "Be quiet, would you? Getting us kicked out is kind of counterproductive to following Christina."

Beyond the front desk and across the expansive lobby, my dad's fiancée presses a button for an elevator. With a ding, the doors slide open, and she steps inside. From the glass front, I watch her rise and count the floors.

"Eighth floor." I pull on Ruthie again. "Let's go."

Praying we won't miss Christina, we scurry across the green carpet and get in a waiting elevator.

"Keep your head down just in case she looks over here."

When the door swooshes open, I throw out my arm, stopping

Ruthie's full-speed-ahead departure. "Quietly. Slowly." I point toward the hallway and wave her on.

On tiptoes we walk down the long row of doors with no Christina in sight. When the hall veers right, I follow it, then immediately freeze to a stop.

"Oomph!" Ruthie plows into my back. "A little notice, if you please."

"Shhh!" I point around the corner. "Christina," I whisper.

I watch as she knocks on the door of room 857. "It's me," she calls in her light Brazilian accent.

The door swings open and Christina rushes inside.

"Can I help you?"

Ruthie and I jump as a man carrying a briefcase appears behind us, his face scrunched with suspicion.

"What exactly are you two ladies doing?"

Ruthie goes on the defense. "What are *you* doing? Sneaking up on two teenage girls like that. You ought to be ashamed of yourself."

"Ruthie." I jab her with my elbow. "It's okay. We were just walking through."

"Yeah," she huffs. "Walking through to inspect this place for our dad's pest control company." She leans closer to the guy, dropping her voice. "For some of the bigger jobs where the bugs are more obvious, he sends us to assess the damage." She whistles, her eyebrows going high. "And these here? Freaky big."

The man clutches his briefcase and takes a step back. "You can't be serious."

"This floor seems to be the worst." Ruthie shakes her head mournfully. "You better get in your room and lock the door. My partner and I are on duty for another two hours, so we won't let anything near you. But if you come out"—she lifts her shoulder in a shrug—"we are not responsible for what might happen."

Torn between not buying a word Ruthie said and afraid not to, the man rolls his eyes, dismisses us with a flop of his hand, and walks away. Quickly.

"Nicely done," I say.

"You should probably give me a raise."

"I don't pay you as it is."

"My people will call your people." Ruthie turns her attention back to the hall.

One hour and two sore butts later, the door to mysterious room number 857 creaks open.

"Stick with the plan," says a voice from inside, the accent similar, yet stronger than Christina's.

"She's going to see us," Ruthie whispers, pointing frantically to the door. "Let's go."

I nod in agreement and turn toward the joining hall.

"I don't want to hurt him anymore."

That's Christina! I stop.

Ruthie tugs on my arm. "Come on, Bella. Running out of time here."

Who's "him"? I have to know! What if it's my dad? Or the president? I don't know this woman. She could be planning to take over the world for all I know.

The woman from inside the room speaks again. "We've come too far for you to bail now. You're integral to this plan. And you know you owe me. You owe this family."

"Bella, come *on!*" Ruthie sees I'm not budging. "I'll see you in the lobby."

I wave her on, desperate to hear more of this conversation.

"I'm not backing out," Christina says. "But it's not too late to change our minds. This isn't going to plan."

"And whose fault is that?"

Yeah, whose?

I see Christina drop her head, her gaze focused on the floor. "I have to go."

Oh crap. Here she comes.

My feet beat the floor as I sprint down the hall. I slap the elevator button, but the nearest one is on floor twenty-two. I'll never make it.

I hear the light scuff of Christina's heels on the carpet. Think! Think!

Two wingback chairs sit on either side of the elevators. I aim for the left, then switch and decide on the right. Muttering a prayer, I dive behind it and crouch low, willing myself to breathe quieter. Hoping she can't hear my galloping heartbeat.

She digs through her purse as she waits.

"Darn."

Omigosh. She's dropped her lipstick. If she bends down she'll see my feet.

Please God, please God, please God. I'm trying to do some good here . . . really. Don't let her see me. I need help. Maybe a miracle. Oh, I know! A guardian angel!*

I see the sheer pink sheen of Christina's nails as her hand nears the floor. Just a millisecond more and I'm outed.

Ring! Ring!

Christina's sigh fills the hall.

Her hand disappears, and I hear her rummage through her purse again. "Hello? Oh, hi, um, Ruthie. Kevin gave you my number? Isn't that nice." She reaches again for the lipstick, her fingers curling around the tube. Completely oblivious to my legs beneath the chair. "Bella's been in the Starbucks bathroom for twenty minutes? Have you checked on her?" The elevator pings and opens. "Sounds like she's having serious stomach problems then. Yes, I'll stop by and get some medicine. See you at the house." And the doors shut, sending the elevator whisking south.

I sag against the chair for a moment before calling Ruthie. "Stomach problems?"

Ruthie laughs on the other end. "It was all I could think of."

"Are you telling me you couldn't come up with anything better than giving me the runs?"

"It worked, didn't it? I watched her come down the elevator."

"Yeah, it worked. Horrible story . . . but strangely enough, perfect timing." I end the call and decide to take the stairs.

Ruthie McGee—my guardian angel of deception.

Maybe she does deserve that raise.

chapter fifteen

On Monday morning I sit at the kitchen table reading the back of the Cinnamon Toast Crunch box and contemplating my life.

Dad was so busy with his TV show preparations, he barely spoke to me. Christina is one big weird mystery I can't seem to unravel—especially when I spend all my time in Truman. And my snooping skills must be getting rusty because I couldn't find a trace of any prenuptial agreement in Dad's office. He's probably keeping it some place I would never suspect. Like his Bible. My dad is not a believer, and I really wish he would get with it. If anybody needs some Jesus, it's him.

My mom shuffles in, still in her robe. She wraps her hair in a ponytail and heads straight for the coffeemaker.

"Running a little slow today?" Normally she's up, dressed, and completely lipsticked way before the rest of us roll out of bed.

She fumbles for a coffee mug and pushes her bangs out of her eyes. "Didn't sleep much last night."

Robbie pads in, his Superman cape over his Spider-Man shirt and jeans. "Did anyone catch that CNN report last night on Middle Eastern politics?"

Mom and I both just stare.

Robbie shrugs and sits down by his bowl. "Your loss." He pours out some cereal, keeping an eye out for the prize.

I help Robbie with the milk. "How was Jake's big show?"

My stepbrother frowns. "He was good. But we didn't get to see him much except from the stadium. Dad's real busy."

Mom pours her coffee and says nothing.

"But he did smash someone's face in."

I ruffle the top of Robbie's head. "I know you must be proud."

He thumbs through some mail on the table, pulling out his *Superheroes in Training* magazine.

"What's this?" I pick up a letter that sticks out. "A note from your advisor at Tulsa Community College? Mom, you didn't get detention or anything, did you?"

Robbie giggles but Mom focuses on adding creamer to her mug. "It's just a reminder about late registration for the next term. No big deal." She grabs the paper and crumples it in one hand, sending it to the trash can in a perfect arc.

"You shouldn't quit school. You love going."

"It's not like I know what I want to major in anyway." She pats me on the back to soften her words. "Maybe next fall."

"My daddy's gonna be superfamous then!"

I glance at Mom, but her face is blank. Is there one area of my life not on the verge of falling apart? Just one?

When I get to journalism second hour, I notice Luke isn't there yet. Disappointment flutters in my chest as I take my seat at my computer. I wanted to grill him on all that happened at the carnival since I've been gone. And that's seriously the only reason I'm sad he's not here. I haven't missed him or anything.

"I talked to Cherry this weekend."

I lift my eyes from my screen and see Ashley walking toward me. Her shorts defy the school dress code. Not that the administration ever does anything about it. But still, it tempts me to make a citizen's arrest for crimes against decency and good fashion.

"Glad you got to talk to her." Which means Ashley went to the carnival. Where Luke was. I blink a few times to block out the vision of them sharing a jumbo popcorn.

Ashley props a hip on the corner of my table. "She really didn't have a lot to say. Did you warn her not to talk to me?"

"No." I type a few sentences on a story outline. "But I do have this little remote in my purse, and occasionally I use it to control her."

Ashley's laugh trumpets the room only to end with a hard glare. "I already apologized to you, so what is your problem?"

"I don't have a problem with you." *As long as you don't talk, move, or breathe.* "You're completely on your own with Cherry. She's young and she's been through a lot. You can't blame her for not wanting to give you the Oprah interview version of her life. Or maybe she didn't talk to you because she didn't warm up to you." *Because it seems like Luke is the only one who can stand next to you and not get frostbit.*

She stands up, one hand to her hip, one hand pointing dangerously close to my face. "Look, things got out of hand that night at the carnival. And your relationship with Luke obviously wasn't strong enough to take it, so I'm not going to take responsibility for one tiny kiss." Her glossy lips curve in a smile. "But now he's single, and I'm single. And since you dumped him and are ridiculously incompatible, there's nothing standing in the way of us going out again."

"Did he say we're incompatible?"

Ashley rolls her eyes. "Luke and I have talked about all sorts of things." She lets the sentence hang, and my mind races with various scenarios of them hanging out, chatting on the phone, texting to their little hearts' content. Just how many times has he LOL'd her?

"I'm kind of busy here." I force a smile. "Was there something specific you wanted?" *Or were you just needing to gloat?*

"I want to do what's best for this paper and for Luke. So let's just all try and get along, okie dokie?"

She is about one *okie dokie* away from me steamrolling her

into next week. I stand up and get ready to tell her what to do with her bossy, pseudo-positive attitude. "You know what, Ashley? I think—"

"Good morning, girls." Luke sails through the classroom, his mouth pulled into a grin. "Glad to see you two working together." As he talks, his strong hand latches onto my shoulder and forces me to my seat. "I know how much professionalism means to you both." With a hand at her back, Luke leads Ashley back to her computer, chatting amiably about her current assignment.

I'm halfway through my outline when Luke returns. "You want to tell me why I walked into this room and found you ready to slam Ashley to the mats like Captain Iron Jack just took over your body?"

"That girl is a viper."

"I like her."

Let me just pick this arrow out of my heart. "Clearly."

"I meant as a friend." He sits on the very same spot his little protégé vacated. "She's a good writer, Bella."

"Then tell her to stick to writing and leave me alone."

His mouth curves in a wicked grin. "Can't handle her?"

My eyes narrow on his handsome form. "I don't know what she's like when you two are alone, but with me, she's as friendly as a Manhattan mugger."

His laugh is quiet, but I hear it nonetheless.

"Go away, Luke. I have work to do." I have an article to write for my next column, a future stepmom to investigate, and all sorts of loose ends at the carnival.

He takes the empty seat next to mine and rolls toward me until we're shoulder to shoulder. Looking straight ahead at my computer, his voice is still so close it sends chill bumps dancing down my spine. "If I went away, then I couldn't tell you Red and Stewart went on their treasure hunt every night you were gone."

"Seriously?" I lower my voice. "Keep talking."

He turns his head at an angle, leaning his square chin on his hand. "Unfortunately, that's all I know. They act more agitated every night. And never seem to find anything."

I stare at the ceiling and contemplate this, trying to block out the clean scent of my ex-boyfriend. "Nothing else happened?"

"Surveillance wasn't the same without you."

I look into his piercing blue eyes. "Really?"

"And Ruthie." His wicked grin is back as he gets to his feet. He gives my shoulder another squeeze and walks on by. "See you tonight."

chapter sixteen

~~~~~~

"This Bozo wig is giving me a scalp rash." I stick the thing on my head and tuck any loose hair into the elastic band.

"I like mine." Ruthie gives a curlicue a tweak. "I was thinking of wearing it to graduation. It would look better than those stupid hats they pass out. Hey, did you see all the people out there? I think the whole county's here. Obviously they've gotten wind of Ruthie the unicycle wonder." She pops her bowtie, sending it to spin. "Everybody's here but Budge."

"He's a workaholic." I pat her arm. "He'll show up one of these nights."

"I hate the Weiner Palace. It's his real true love. I just can't compete with relish, onions, and pressed pig parts."

"Hey, girls."

"Cherry!" I pull the girl into a loose hug. "How's it going?"

Her nervous eyes dart around the backstage area, looking for eavesdroppers. "It's hard to act natural around Uncle Red and Stewart. Are you *sure* you didn't misunderstand what they said about Peg?"

"Bella's got good ears. And if she said she heard"—Ruthie makes a noise and drags her finger across her throat—"then that's what she heard."

"We'll figure it out." I inject as much confidence in my voice as I can. "Have you overheard anything suspicious lately?"

"Not really."

"Could you try?" The words slip out of my mouth before I can reel them back in. "Er, that is, nobody's closer to those two than you. They won't think anything of you hanging around listening to the occasional conversation."

"I'll see what I can do." She peels back one of the curtains. "Dolly's here."

"She watches you almost every night without fail." I follow the direction of her gaze. "Whoa—and Mickey's with her?"

Cherry nods, the glitter in her hair catching the light. "Yeah, he's been coming over for dinner some. And he was here Thursday and Saturday night. He's cool. And I think Dolly likes him—a lot."

I smile at my own hopefulness. I would give anything to see those two reunited and happy. It's like life's been pulling them back to one another for years.

"Red thinks I should move back into Betty's trailer," Cherry says. "He says he'll move one of the other girls in with me. But I really like it at Dolly's. It's like a home to me." She waves away the idea. "It's stupid to get attached though. By the end of May, we'll be rolling out."

"But I think no matter what, Dolly will always be in your life now."

Cherry bites her lip and smiles. "I think so too."

Ten minutes later I'm passing out balloons to kids and greeting the crowds. "Welcome to the Fritz Family Carnival!" I pat a little boy's head. "Have fun!"

"Clowns are stupid."

I bend to his level. "Clowns are actually a very misunderstood, underappreciated group of individuals who bring joy and gladness to boys and girls of every race, size, and creed." I step up two more bleacher rows. "Disrespectful mutant."

"Bella!"

"Hey, Lindy." I huff out a breath, sending a few multicolored curls flying. "Hi, Bo." My eyes adjust to the sight of my friend holding hands with a boy.

"How's it going, guys?"

"It's awesome." Bo's smile is so big, his cheeks are ready to pop off. "I heard there's a heck of a unicycle ballet. I'm totally stoked for that."

"Yeah." I glance toward the arena floor where Ruthie does leg kicks for her warm up. "Who wouldn't be?"

"Bo"—Lindy pats his knee—"will you go get me some popcorn?"

He jumps to his feet. "Sure. How about a Coke?"

"Sounds good."

"I bet a candy bar would hit the spot too. Be right back!" Her track-star boyfriend nimbly makes his way down the packed bleachers.

"I like him, Lindy. He's such a good guy to you."

She stares toward the door where Bo holds open the flap for a family. "He's perfect. He lets me pick the radio station in the car. He carries my books. Notices my hair. Prays for me."

Shouldn't she be smiling? "You don't sound very happy."

Lindy shakes it off and pulls out a slow grin. "Of course I am. It's exactly what I've always wanted in a guy. I wasn't even looking for him, and he found me."

"I'm glad for you." I think. "Well, duty calls. I have balloons to twist and kids to terrorize." I leave my friend and walk away with an unsettled feeling awhirl in my brain. Just another one to add to the collection.

After another grueling show, I run to the backstage area and take off my makeup with a wipe. Peons like Ruthie and me don't get trailer privileges. We get a mirror tacked up on a tent pole next to a hook for our wigs.

As I walk out, I catch Luke's eye from where he stands at the sound-control table, shutting things down for the night. He gives a curt nod, a signal that we will be doing some undercover surveillance tonight.

The evening air hangs with the strong odor of impending rain. I inhale deeply, loving that heavy smell that will usher in green pastures and sprouting flowers. And hopefully an end to this case. I'm just not convinced the Amazing Alfredo is our guy.

I spot a group of people I have come to know and love, and meander in their direction. Ruthie, still in clown uniform, stands surrounded by Officer Mark, Cherry, Dolly, and Mickey.

"Good job in there." Officer Mark pats Ruthie's polka-dotted shoulder. "When you wheeled out, it was like watching Cirque du Soleil."

Her posture straightens as she considers this. "Well, I don't know who that is, but if they ever need pointers, I guess you could send them to me."

"There's another one of our favorite clowns." Dolly catches sight of me and hugs me tight. "You did great in there too."

"Yeah, I think I only made three little kids cry tonight." A huge improvement from last week.

As Cherry talks with Dolly and Mickey, I pull Officer Mark off to the side. "How's the investigation going?"

He rubs a hand over his badge and shakes his head. "Just once I'd like to be greeted with 'Hi, Officer Mark. How are you?' You don't even pretend to be courteous." He flashes a smile under the carnival lights.

"Any progress? Anything you can share?"

"You know the answer to that. I can't give you anything. But I don't know much anyway. The county's got this one covered. And for all intents and purposes, Alfredo's our man."

"I want to talk to him. Could you arrange that?"

"Only family."

"I'm his circus family."

Mark laughs. "That's just a creepy thought."

"If Alfredo did it, I don't think he acted alone." I share with Mark all I know, leaving out nothing except my prowling through trailers. I still need to go back and try to find my flashlight. That's a loose end I've got to tie up.

"Bella, you know the routine. You stay out of it and let the professionals do their job."

"But I'm on the inside. Your professionals are sitting behind desks thinking they've got their man." I back off when I see his fierce scowl. "Just relay my information to whoever's in charge. I think this case is deceptively simple."

"That's the only kind you stumble onto, isn't it?" He blows out a breath, briefly shifting his eyes to look at something over my shoulder. "I'll pass on your information, but they're really tied up with a series of gang incidents in Tulsa. Your job is done. If you've got a burning in your heart to be a clown, that's your freaky business, but otherwise, I think you better consider retiring from the carnival life."

"And miss all the satisfaction I get from spreading joy and happiness to circusgoers?"

Officer Mark snorts as he steps away. "Butt out, Bella. I mean that."

When I return to the group, I see Luke has joined them. As Dolly talks about homeschooling, Luke doesn't take his eyes off her. But I know he knows I'm there. It's that whole magnet thing. I think we could find each other in a dark tunnel, even if we were on opposite ends. I don't know that I like being that aware of someone.

"I hear Jake had another great night last night," Mickey says, his voice laced with pride. "I'm going to fly out to Seattle and see him next week."

"How's your mom doing?" Dolly asks, her eyes sharp and knowing.

"I guess she's struggling with him being gone so much. Seems to be stressing everyone out." And when I say stress, I mean as in the kind of pressure that can fracture something. Like a marriage. "Jake says he's still trying to find his balance. I hope he finds it soon."

Dolly smiles. "He's a smart guy. I have faith he'll figure it out."

"Sometimes it's easy to take your family for granted," Mickey says, his expression guarded as he looks at Dolly. "And sometimes it takes doing without to see what you had."

At this, the conversation lapses. Around me I hear the sounds of families making their way to vehicles, the roller coaster still zipping, and carnival workers calling for someone to take a chance for a buck.

Dolly wraps her arm around Cherry and kisses the top of her head. "You did so good tonight, girl. Ready to go home?" They head toward the south parking lot.

I turn to Luke and motion for him to follow. "My car's out this way too."

We all walk together and say our good-byes for the evening next to Dolly's Jeep.

She unlocks the vehicle just as Cherry squeals. "Peg!" Cherry points through the crowd, and I see the collie tearing toward her. "Oh my gosh! You came back!" Cherry drops to her knees as the dog pounces, running into her outstretched arms like a lost child. She licks her cheeks, her nose, her chin. Cherry giggles and pulls her closer.

"I can't believe it," Dolly says. "Where in the world has that dog been?"

"It's a miracle." Tears glisten in Cherry's eyes. "Dolly and I said a little prayer for you, Peg, and you came back. It's a miracle, isn't it, Dolly?"

I walk around the Jeep and run my hands through the dog's fur. "Wherever she was, they didn't extend bathing privileges."

"Dolly?"

I feel my blood drain at Red Fritz's scratchy voice. "Go! Distract him!" My whisper comes out in a frenzied rush as I push Cherry toward the other side of the Jeep. Toward Red.

Red's voice grows a bit stronger. "Cherry, it's time you came back home. I know the loss of Betty was a shock, but as we say, the show must go on. Your home is with us."

"She's thriving with me," Dolly says, just as I slink into the back of the Jeep, scooting along the floorboards.

Luke picks up the dog, and she gives a little bark.

"What was that?" Red demands.

Luke shoves the dog at me, then throws back the seat. "Just smashed my finger in the door." I watch Luke shake out his hand as he shuts me inside the Jeep.

Where the dog goes crazy.

"What's going on in that car?" Red asks.

I stick my head up. "Just me! I'm changing clothes!" I make swirly motions with my one hand and hold down Peg's head with the other. "No peeking!" Omigosh. *God, please don't let this dog bark again.*

"We'll talk about this later, Red," Dolly says. "I've got to get Cherry home now. She needs her rest."

"This isn't over, Cherry. You know where you belong. Stewart and me—we're your real family."

My whole body jerks as seconds later the door is flung open.

The first person I see is Luke, staring into the floor. He's surrounded by Dolly, Cherry, and Mickey.

Luke's mouth quirks. "If you smother the dog, Bella, you're the one who'll have to perform mouth-to-mouth."

I look down to see I'm completely rolled on top of Peg, with all four limbs wrapped around her like a vise, both hands clamped on her snout.

"Not a word, Luke Sullivan. Not one word."

chapter seventeen

~~~~~~

*A*s I drive to the carnival after school Tuesday, I punch the button on my phone with as much consideration as one would give the command for a nuclear bomb.

"Bella?"

"Hey, Hunter. It's me. I know, surprise, right?" Never thought I'd be calling my ex-boyfriend, pond-sludge sucker that he is. "Yeah, I'm good. Um, there's kind of a reason for my call."

"Missing me?"

Boys. Do they *all* think they're God's gift to the planet?

"No, I do *not* miss you."

"Give it time. You will."

Yeah, like the flu. I turn down my stereo as Hunter Penbrook prattles on about changing, turning his life around, mending his ways. Blah, blah, blah. Heard it all before. Even fell for it once. But never twice.

"Hey, Hunter, I hate to interrupt your dissertation on your virtues, and I think your new vegetarian diet is very noble, by the way, but I need your help."

Silence.

"The last few times I've been to see Dad, things have been pretty weird." I explain my odd Christina moments. "There is definitely something going on there, but I can't be in two places at once. Time is of the essence because Dad's getting married in June. So if Christina's not on the up-and-up, and I strongly suspect she isn't, then I need to get proof of that soon. I can't just go to him with suspicions."

His deep voice fills my ear. "So what do you want me to do about it?"

"Remember the last time you were in Truman—you know, when you were pretending to be someone you weren't because Jake's reality show was paying you?"

His excuses and apologies come in sputters.

"Save it. I do recall, though, that in one of your crying fits one of the things you said was that you'd do anything for me. Remember that, my little dumplin'?"

His sigh blows into the phone. "I didn't cry."

"Okay." I guess now is not the time to bring up his sordid, teary-eyed past. "Well, I need your help."

"Name it."

Nice. If only Luke were this biddable. "I need you to find out who's staying in that hotel room."

"What's in it for me?"

"I'll send you a Christmas card this year."

"You sent me one last year."

"I promise not to stick my tongue out in this one. Can you just help me out here?"

"How's the new boyfriend?"

Um. "Fine."

"That didn't sound fine. Trouble in nerd paradise?"

"Luke is not a nerd." Only *I* can call him that. "He's brilliant, studious, while also being conveniently buff."

"So you two are happy?"

"Every day is another twenty-four hours of bliss."

Hunter laughs. "Bella? Our maids play poker together. I know you broke up with that guy."

"Can you find out who's in room 857 or not? I'm not asking you to save the world here—just do a little snooping around, a little stake-out in front of her door."

"Did I ruin you for anyone else?"

Now it's my turn to laugh. "Yeah, your cheating ways are so hot, I can't bear to be with anyone else now." If I were standing in front of the guy, I'd have to gouge out his eyes just on principle.

"No. I mean you were already leery of trusting anyone. And then I pushed you over the edge with all the crap I pulled." His voice is strangely sincere.

"Twice."

"Twice." More silence. "You know, even after two years of dating, you always did hold back."

"If this is about that night at your parents' lake house, I *told* you I had my boundaries."

"He's not me, but I thought that Luke character was a pretty good guy. You should've seen the way he looked at you at prom. And when he saw you hurt—" Hunter expels a ragged breath. "Never mind. What do I care?"

I pull into my spot at the carnival and turn off the Bug. "Hunter, you're the last person I'm going to take relationship advice from. Are you going to help me or not?"

"I'll do it. Because I really am a better person these days."

"Uh-huh. Well, keep me updated. And . . . thanks."

"Bella? Give the guy a chance. Anybody who's saved your life a couple times can't be all that bad. What are you afraid of?"

The line goes dead, and I sit there with my head on the steering wheel. Hunter Penbrook just went all love-doctor on me. Oh, the irony. It's like taking advice on conservative attire from Britney Spears.

When I walk into the big top, there's a small crowd beneath the trapeze.

"What's going on?" I ask.

Melvin, the fire-eating midget, points toward the ceiling. "Red's making Stewart and Cherry do the Praying Mantis."

"Since when does Stewart know the trapeze?"

"He was raised on it. Trained by Cherry's parents. He just took a few months off to try his hand at managerial duties. But his dad has put him back on as an aerialist starting tonight."

"So what's the Praying Mantis?"

His brown eyes darken. "It's the routine that killed Cherry's parents."

Dolly is gonna freak. "Is it incredibly dangerous?"

Melvin shakes his head. "It's not impossible. That night her parents died, there were equipment malfunctions. And her dad removed the nets—he insisted. He wanted to take the trapeze team to a new level. He thought it would put our carnival up there with the best of them."

I watch Red yell at Cherry and sigh. "And then the Fritz Family Carnival became memorable for all the wrong reasons."

"You got it. But Red wants to change that."

Cherry misses Stewart's outstretched arm.

"You idiot!" Stewart hisses. "Do you need glasses?"

"Pay attention!" Red yells. "This isn't a game."

"I know!" Cherry stands in the nest. "I—we just haven't worked together in a while. Can't Rusty and I do this? He's been my partner since March."

"No." Red curls his mustache between his fingers. "You are both of Fritz blood—circus royalty! It must be you two. Take a ten-minute break." Red claps his hands at Cherry and Stewart like he's a lion tamer.

I do a quick turn when a hand latches onto my shoulder.

"Jumpy today." Luke stands there, an arrogant smile tugging on his lips.

"I was watching Cherry and Stewart." I take a few steps away from the dissipating crowd. "Cherry talked Dolly into taking the dog home, by the way."

"Didn't Dolly want to know why they weren't returning it to Red?"

"Cherry explained it's what Betty would've wanted. Told her she'd heard Red was done with the dog, and his idea of retiring an animal wasn't too pretty. That's all it took for Dolly." I pause. "Luke, um, I need a little favor."

"I'm not going to like this, am I?"

"Would you mind getting my flashlight where I left it?"

"I guess." He shrugs. "Where'd you leave it?"

"In Alfredo's trailer."

"*What?*"

"Shhh!" I clamp my hand over his mouth. "It was an accident."

Luke pries my fingers from his face, keeping my hand hostage. "An accident that you were in there or that you left it?"

"Yes."

"Bella . . ." His growl is scarier than my clown routine. "How did it get in Alfredo's trailer?"

"I might've dropped it a few weeks ago when I was digging around." I rush on to explain. "There hasn't been a single chance to get it. I've tried."

His left eye twitches as he rolls this through his oversized brain. "Would this be the flashlight I got you? With your *name* on it?"

The one that came with a card that said, *Your laugh lights up my day.* "That's the one. And I really want it back."

"You *need* it back, you mean. So they won't know where you've been." He lets my hand fall like he can't stand the connection any longer. "So within weeks of getting my gift, you ditch it in Alfredo the Killer's trailer. I can tell it meant a lot to you."

"That's not fair. For your information, that flashlight did mean a lot to me," I snap. "I thought of you every single time I prowled through someone's belongings."

Luke closes his eyes and stares at the ceiling. "The likelihood of it still being there is slim. I cannot believe you took a chance like that."

"Someone was coming, and I had dropped it. Just find a way to sneak into Alfredo's trailer." I soften my voice. "Please? If you do, I won't insult your favorite blonde reporter one time tomorrow." I pat his chest and give him some more directions. "Be careful, 'kay?"

Ruthie arrives on the scene, cutting off any blistering remark Luke might've had. "Yo, carny dudes. What's up?"

I grab Ruthie by the hand. "Come on. We need to go talk to Stewart while he's on break in his trailer."

"We do?"

"Bella—," Luke warns.

I shoo him away with my hand as I pull Ruthie along. "Godspeed, Luke. May the force be with you. Oh, and also, if you'd provide a distraction for Stewart in about three minutes, that'd be swell." I give Ruthie a hard yank. "Move quickly before he comes after us."

"What's going on, boss?"

"We're going to go talk to Stewart about an idea you have for your unicycle ballet."

"But I don't have an idea."

"You have about ten seconds to get one."

chapter eighteen

uthie and I disappear around back, and I take us straight to Stewart's trailer. My hand shakes only slightly when I knock.

"What do you want?"

I pull open the door. "Stew?" I reserve my prettiest voice for only the creepiest of men. "Can we come in?"

His gruff tone changes instantly. "Of course." He swabs his neck with a towel. "I can always make time for two beautiful ladies."

Gag. "Ruthie has a great idea for adding to her unicycle routine. She'd like to describe it for you." I jerk my chin toward Red's son. "Tell him that amazing idea you were sharing with me." *Make something up, Ruthie. Come on.*

"Um, yeah." She clears her throat and forces a dreamy look into her eyes. "Imagine this. I'm decked out in swan feathers ..."

As she paints her unicycling scenario, I scan the office for any sign of a piece of paper that looks like a much-used list. If I had to put money on it, I'd bet the paper Red and Stewart have been using in their search is a map. And since he's standing here in spandex pants and no shirt—ick!—then it sure isn't on him now. So unless Red has it, it has to be in this trailer somewhere.

". . . And then Melvin the Midget and Wilhemina the Wondrously Tall Woman will come out and serenade me with Celine

Dion's 'My Heart Will Go On.' Then they'll start throwing the rose petals, of course ..."

I could start with the desk. Then his sleeping quarters. I hate to search through his undie drawer, but if it has to be done ...

A sharp rapping stops my roaming eye.

Stewart stalks to the door and throws it open. "What?"

Luke peeks through. "Red said to come and get you. Someone's let the horses out, and he needs your help."

Stewart hesitates as he looks at me and Ruthie.

"He said to hurry, Stewart."

Stewart rushes to the back of the trailer and returns with a shirt. "All right, everyone out. I have to go."

"But what about my ideas?" Ruthie calls as we exit onto the grass.

Throwing up a dismissive hand, Stewart runs toward the animal trailers.

I regard Luke with a tiny amount of disdain for his lack of improv. "That was gutsy. Red said the horses were out? Like he's not going to know that's a lie in a second."

"Wasn't a lie. The horses really are loose. Kinda crazy over there." He rocks back on his heels. "By the way—no flashlight."

"Are you kidding me?"

"It's gone." And he's ticked. At me.

Great! Whoever has it knows I was in that trailer.

Luke looks past my shoulder. "Are we going to stand here all day or go back in?"

"Ruthie and I are going in. You stay out here and keep guard." When he starts to protest, I beat him to it. "If Stewart can forgive anyone for being in the trailer, it's us—seeing as how we're girls and all."

Luke clenches his jaw. "Hurry up. And don't leave anything this time."

"Oh, you're funny."

Five minutes later I jump as Luke sticks his head in. "Anything?"

"No!"

"Hurry, Bella. You're driving me crazy." *Slam!*

"There's nothing here, Ruthie. We might as well call it a day. Maybe we'll get another break and try again later."

"Snooping stresses me out. I need a snack." She peels open the small fridge on the counter.

"Get out of there!" I shove it closed. "We have to go."

"I saw chocolate-covered Oreos!" Her eyes twinkle. "Come on. You have to let me have just one. Nobody can walk away from that temptation."

"One. And I'm leaving." I speed walk to the door.

"Who would've thought Stewart was a boxer guy, huh? I had him pegged as more of a—" Ruthie gasps. "Omigosh!"

My hand freezes on the door.

"I found it." She holds up a yellowed piece of paper. "I found a treasure map!"

Brain in overdrive. Heart beating out of my chest. Think! Think! I don't know what to do.

I turn a full circle around the trailer. The printer. I'll make a copy!

"Ruthie, keep an eye on the door." My pulse races, the sound echoing in my head. If we get caught . . . I don't even want to think about it. I slap the paper down on the machine and close the lid. The printer sounds too loud in the silence of the small office.

When someone bangs on the door, Ruthie and I both squeal.

"Hide!" comes Luke's voice from outside.

My eyes flit to the desk. To the sleeping area in the back. Maybe under the dining table?

"Come on. We must have company." I grab Ruthie by the arm and pull her into the bathroom. Shutting the door, I follow her into the cramped shower, where we stand close enough to be PG-13.

"Don't think I usually do this on the first date," Ruthie whispers. "You're an exception."

I hear the trailer door open. Then Stewart's voice. "I don't have time to talk right now."

"But I have some questions about the lighting for Ruthie's ballet," Luke says, his volume raised.

"Look, I have bigger things to deal with than some unicycle act."

Ruthie's mouth drops into an O. I squeeze her arm and shoot her a warning look. *Do not say a word!*

Luke tries again. "If you could come out here and look at the light board—"

"You were told to help with the horses. Now get out there or leave the grounds and don't come back."

I hear Luke expel a harsh breath, then the door slams again, rocking the trailer.

He's gone? Now what? I left the map in the printer. I'm such an idiot! I could've at least grabbed that. We could be stuck in here with a potential killer. My mom is going to be so mad!

I raise my mouth to Ruthie's ear. "Work together. Follow my lead."

I wrench open the bathroom door. "Surprise!"

Stewart jumps straight up, and a string of curses split the air.

I launch into song. "Happy birthday to you! Happy birthday to you!" I clap my hands and walk toward him as Ruthie helps me finish the tune. "Yay!"

I hug Stewart, waving madly with my hands to my friend. *Go get the maps!*

Stewart leans his scrawny self into me and pulls me close. Ew. Ruthie fumbles with the printer as time stretches into an eternity.

Must stall. "Stewart, close your eyes," I purr.

"Oh? Really?"

"Now, no cheating. I'll be mad if you do." I take a step back. "You don't want me angry, do you?" I pucker my lips in a saucy pout.

"No," comes his breathy reply.

"I didn't think so. Because I have a birthday present for you."

"But it's not really my birthday."

He closes his eyes, and I change places with him, turning him away from the office. "I guess I must've heard wrong then." I place my hands on his shoulders and squeeze. I'm totally washing these hands in bleach when I get home. "How about a birthday shoulder massage!"

"Uh . . ." His voice is a deflated balloon. "I guess."

Yeah, that's all you're getting. What was he thinking? Creep.

I let out the breath I'm holding as Ruthie slowly extracts the map and picks up the copy, which disappears down her shirt. I jerk my head toward the refrigerator. *Go!*

"What's all that noise?" Stewart asks.

"That's just Ruthie warming up her hands. She's a whiz at shiatsu. Keep those eyes closed!" As Ruthie moves, I shift Stewart until he's facing the office again. "You have such strong shoulders!" And bony. Almost skeletal in fact. *So* not hot.

I check over my shoulder to see Ruthie in the fridge.

And that's when the trailer door busts open again.

"Dad!"

I drop my hands. "Mr. Fritz!"

"This is treachery! It will *not* be tolerated!" Red's mottled face radiates with fury. It's all over.

"Dad, I—"

Ruthie and I look at each other, and somehow I find my voice. "Mr. Fritz, if you'll let me explain—"

"I'll have his head on a platter!" Red roars.

Stewart stands up uncertainly. "I'll find out who let the horses—"

"Horses?" With wild eyes, Red shakes his head. "I'm talking about Alfredo."

I blink. "Huh?"

"Alfredo DeLucci. He escaped from prison this afternoon." Red's eyes pierce his son. "Seems the magician has vanished into thin air."

chapter nineteen

The birds sing happy morning songs as I get my tired body out of the Bug and join Luke and Ruthie in the school courtyard.

I take a sip from my McDonald's mocha. "Let's see the map."

Ruthie looks at Luke. "Turn around please." She twirls her finger in a circle.

Obviously used to her oddness, he complies without question.

Ruthie sticks her hand way down her shirt, her face scrunched in concentration. "I wanted to keep it protected, so I didn't shower last night. I even slept with my bra on, keeping the map safe. And cushioned."

"Noble of you," Luke says.

She rustles around a bit more before drawing out the paper and holding it up like the Holy Grail. "Perfectly safe . . . if not a little toasty."

I take the map and spread it out on the nearest picnic table. "There's the water tower. The school." I slide my finger across the drawn path. "But . . . where's the end?"

Ruthie straightens her blouse. "Every good treasure map has an X that marks the spot. What kind of loser map is this?"

Luke leans close and peers over my shoulder. "It's not complete. It can't be."

A breeze floats by, carrying his cologne with it. I struggle to focus on anything else but that familiar scent. "So when Red and Stewart were digging all over the place, they were just guessing."

"Then where's the other half?" Ruthie asks. "And who has it?"

When Wednesday night arrives, I am in serious need of some church. Our building isn't finished yet, so we meet at Truman High. Like I'm not there enough.

The worship pastor is doing an acoustical jam tonight, and it's just the calm my heart needs. Though I'm sitting next to Lindy and Matt, I focus only on the music, as if I'm the only one in the room. As the pastor sings a spiffed up version of an old hymn, I close my eyes and let the words wash over me, imagining that I'm singing just for Jesus.

When I moved into Jake's house, I would climb out my bedroom window and sit on the roof and just think. And pray. And read my Bible. But I haven't done that in such a long time. God may have blessed me with the gift of crime fighting, but I seemed to have let it take over my life. *Lord, help me to just slow down and find some peace again. I can't solve any mystery or help anyone with all this clutter in my head. Oh, and protect me from crazy carnival people who might've committed a murder or two.*

I watch Dolly sneak into a seat in the back. Cherry sits beside her. I glance across the cafeteria and see Mickey Patrick has noticed her as well. His smile is slow and contented.

After the service we file out into the parking lot. There, sitting on my mom's Tahoe, is Jake, holding a bouquet of flowers. Budge and I lag behind, but Mom and Robbie run right into his outstretched arms. Jake swoops them both up like they weigh no more than a feather each. He swings them around, peppering them with big smacking kisses.

"Let's go eat pizza," Jake says when Budge and I make it to the SUV. "I hopped an earlier flight to get here, and I'm starved." Jake waves at Dolly and Mickey, calling out an invitation to them too.

"Come with us," I say to Matt and Lindy, as they hover nearby. "The three of us haven't hung out in a while."

"That would be fun." Matt twists his class ring. "Lindy?"

"Sure. Like old times."

Thirty minutes later I'm thanking God that the only heavy thinking I have to do tonight is decide between pepperoni or sausage.

"So how were your matches this week, Dad?" Robbie sits on Jake's lap.

"Mostly I trained." Jake takes a giant bite, the cheese stretching from plate to mouth. "But a commentator got sick last night, and I got to sub at the last minute." He turns his megawatt smile on my mom. "It was awesome, Jillian. Most of it's on the teleprompter, but I got to wing it too, you know? They said it went so well, they want me to do some more events."

Mom picks at a breadstick. "So you'll be gone even more?"

The light in Jake's eyes dims. "No, I don't think that's what they mean."

"But you don't know?"

I turn away from the conversation, my own stomach in a knot messier than the emptied appetizer dish in front of me. And that's when I spot Luke sitting in a corner booth with Ashley—her brother nowhere in sight. Like a bad movie close-up, my eyes zoom in on the two. I shove my plate away, having suddenly lost my appetite. I know I broke up with him, so of course he's going to date other girls. But why not a nice girl from Tulsa? Or somewhere farther . . . like Poland?

She laughs over something he says. And my heart breaks. Just a little. He said to trust him—but this does nothing to convince me. What if their kiss at the carnival *did* mean something? I don't want to be someone who gets cheated on—like my mom was before Jake.

God, I have to move on and give up the bitterness. I'm just not going to look over at that table. "So how's the dog?" I ask Cherry, who sits between Dolly and Mickey.

"Peg's going to be okay. Once we got a good look at her, we could see she was in bad shape. She was starving . . . dirty. Who knows where she'd been or how she'd been surviving."

"It's really important you keep her a secret from Red and Stewart," I remind her.

"I know. But they're too wrapped up in the fact that Alfredo is on the loose to even care. Everyone at the carnival is a little jumpy right now."

"Are they afraid he's going to come after them? Maybe kill someone else?" I have to admit I didn't sleep that great last night myself. Kind of spooky having an accused killer out there—whether he did it or not.

"I think everyone's just on edge. But we did finally get a replacement for Alfredo today. The new magician starts tomorrow."

Mickey asks Cherry a question, and my eyes drift back to Luke and Ashley. His back is to me, but she looks like she's having a grand old time. He's probably telling her about his chess club or the vocab flashcards he keeps in his glove compartment. Surely she won't be attracted to that . . . like I was.

My heart seems to beat a little slower tonight. Everyone around me is wrapped up in someone else. Even Matt and Lindy have been talking nonstop.

"I can't believe your time on that half mile at last week's track meet." Matt takes a big drink of Coke. "How does it feel to break the school record by two seconds?"

Lindy laughs. "It was amazing. I wish you had been there."

His mouth curls around his straw. "Me too, Lind."

My phone rings in my purse, and I reach for it. "Hey, Hunter. What have you got for me?" The laughter and conversation at the table are so loud, I can't even hear him. "Hang on. Let me find a quiet spot."

I walk out the front door, the bell jingling as I exit.

"I don't have a lot to tell you."

"Um, not what I wanted to hear." The door behind me opens again, and Luke and Ashley file out. Great. If he kisses her in front of me, it will definitely suck up what little remains of my peaceful, easy feeling from church.

"Yesterday I caught her leaving the hotel. I got a grainy shot of her with my phone. I sent it to your e-mail just now. I couldn't follow her, though, so no idea where she went. But tonight? Bella, I've been standing in this hall for like two hours. Room service came once, but other than that, I haven't seen or heard anything. Well, I thought I spotted that hot chick from *Gossip Girls*, but I'm not sure. This is pointless."

"You can't just give it two hours and call it quits." Luke walks Ashley to her car, and though they stand close, he doesn't touch her. "Have you seen Christina there?"

"I've seen no one."

"What about getting the room next to hers and putting a glass to the door?"

"Does that really work?"

"You should try it and see."

Luke waves as Ashley drives away in a lipstick-red Mustang. No kissing. No hugging. Which means for me—no puking.

"Hunter, please don't give up on this. I know that woman in the hotel room is significant. I can feel it in my gut."

"Maybe you have Irritable Bowel Syndrome like me."

Luke sticks his hands into the pockets of his slouched jeans and walks my way.

"Go home, Hunter. You've done all you can tonight. But promise me you won't give up."

"You know, you're lucky I messed up so big. Otherwise—"

With one finger, I end the call and flip the phone from palm to palm.

"Hello, there." With his azure-blue eyes, Luke looks down where I sit on the sidewalk.

"On a date tonight?" I hope that didn't sound jealous. 'Cause I'm so not jealous. Not at all.

He sits beside me, his shoulder brushing mine. "So what are you doing out here?" he asks.

Okay, avoiding my question. I can take it. "I have Hunter spying on a hotel room in New York. Just getting an update." I glance at my watch. "In fact, I really need to get home to catch his e-mail." I could pull up the picture on my phone, but I want to see it full size. It might be a good lead.

Luke nudges my knee with his. "You seemed down today at school. And tonight you're sitting outside while the rest of your party is in there having fun. And you barely touched your food— that's not like you at all."

"How do you know? You didn't even know I was in there until you got up to leave."

He holds me with his gaze. "I knew the second you walked in the door."

My heart flips like Cherry on the trapeze. "Oh, reporter's instincts and all that?"

"Something like that." Luke's eyes dip to my lips before he regards me once again with concern. "Are you going to tell me what's wrong or not?"

"I don't know," I sigh. "Same stuff. I guess I feel like everything is out of order. Like spinning debris in a tornado—just pieces of stuff floating all around me."

"What kind of tornado trash are we talking here?"

I give a small laugh. "My dad's getting married soon, and so far I'm powerless to stop it. I'm no closer to solving the murder of Betty and—"

"*We're* no closer to solving the murder. You don't think Alfredo escaping is pretty telling—that he did it?"

"No. Maybe he did kill Betty, but Red and Stewart are involved. We both know that."

"What else you got going on in that head?"

I glance back to the restaurant door. "Mom and Jake are . . . in a weird place." *And you've moved on. Instead of pining for me forever like you were supposed to.*

He wraps an arm around me and pulls me to him. "I'm sorry, Bel. I'll pray for you."

I close my eyes and lean into him, pretending for just a second that he's mine and Ashley Timmons doesn't even exist.

"You really want to go home and check your e-mail, don't you?" he asks.

"Yeah."

He stands up and pulls me with him. "Go tell your family. I'll drive you."

In ten seconds I'm buckled into his 4Runner, filling him in on Christina and the Manhattan mystery woman.

"You know, maybe it's nothing. You tend to assume everyone is shady and look for the worst in people."

"That's not true. I just have this intuition." Or an unlucky habit of stumbling onto things I'm not supposed to. Like psychos and dead people.

"Face it, Bella. You don't trust anyone. Like right now, you're probably thinking Jake is going to end up screwing up and sacrificing your family."

It has crossed my mind. "But you have to admit I've been right. A lot."

"Maybe you should let this thing with your dad and Christina go. If he's happy, what's the problem?"

I twist in my seat toward Luke, tucking one leg beneath me. "Haven't you ever just had this *feeling* about someone?"

"Yes." He stops the vehicle in my drive and angles his head my way. "As a matter of fact, I have."

A strange tension hangs in the air as Luke's eyes stay locked with mine. My pulse skitters and begins to race like I ran Lindy's half mile.

"Bella, I—"

"Luke—" Our words overlap. I fumble with the edge of my shirt. "Do you have one of those strong feelings for Ashley?"

"Does it matter?"

A sassy barb immediately comes to mind, but I push the words away and opt for raw honesty instead. "Yes."

"Why?"

I contemplate the beaded necklace hanging down the middle of my shirt.

With a light touch of his fingers, Luke tilts my chin up. "Why does it matter, Bella?"

Why can't I just tell him I like him? That when I'm not thinking about a dead bearded lady, clown wigs, and a wacko fiancée, I'm consumed with thoughts of him?

He lets his hand fall only to lay it over one of mine. "Until you can explain that, there's never going to be an us. I have no reason to think it's anything more than jealousy."

I can't seem to find my tongue. I know I need to defend myself here—defend us. How can he just give up on pursuing me? The rules are changing right in this car.

He sighs and brushes his thumb over my palm. "You're a competitive girl. Is this just a game to you?"

I inhale all the air I can. "I don't know why being with you scares me, but it does."

Luke presses his head to the seat. "I scare *you?*" More chuckling. "That's a good one."

I laugh at his tortured tone. "I'm serious."

"I don't know why I'm explaining this, but Kyle left just before you got there."

"Of course he did." How convenient for Ashley that her brother had to go.

He removes his hand and rests it on the steering wheel. "Until you can trust me and just believe in us, then that's that. Kyle Timmons is a good friend and, frankly, so is Ashley."

"Can't we just—"

"No." In the dark vehicle I see the hard set of his jaw. "When you're ready, we'll talk. But as long as you're afraid of me, I'm not the right person for you."

Those words stab my chest. Who else could be more right for me than this yummy, infuriating boy? Why am I so messed up in the head?

"Are you going to continue seeing Ashley?"

He turns the key, and the 4Runner roars to life. "Good night, Bella."

"If I gave you a reason not to, would you?"

"You and I both know you're not going to do that," Luke says as I open the door. "I've proven I didn't cheat on you."

"Are you kidding? Hanging out with her seems to suggest the opposite."

"You know the truth." He pauses. "You know me."

"I don't know what to believe right now."

"Bella, you chose to let our relationship go, and I respected that. I still do. I'm not going to push anything."

"So I have to be the pusher?"

He nods.

"But if you go dating every cute, blonde reporter, it might be too late."

"Definitely a risk." He puts the SUV in drive. "Now you have to figure out if it's worth it."

chapter twenty

"Chocolate-chunk cappuccino ice cream." I pass my money through the window at the Dairy Barn drive-thru and try not to think about my dismal life. My e-mail from Hunter showed a picture of the back of someone's head. Like that did any good. And don't even get me started on Luke. "Better make the ice cream a double, please."* The man slides the glass closed with a nod.

"Did that guy look familiar to you?" Ruthie asks from the passenger side of my Bug.

"Didn't notice him."

"You didn't *notice* him? He was at least seven feet tall." Ruthie flicks off the radio. "What's wrong with you? You've been in a mood all day."

"Nothing. I'm fine." Or will be as soon as I have chocolate.

"You got a double scoop *and* you didn't even notice that man used to work at the carnival."

"Oh." I try to see into the window. "Did he?"

When the giant appears again with my ice cream, Ruthie leans until she's nearly in my lap.

"Lars, what are you doing working here? You're the tall man. Not the ice cream man."

He sticks his order pencil behind his huge ear. "I'm telling you, I've had it with carnival life. I want to be known for more than just being a giant."

I lick the top scoop. "I personally think serving ice cream is an admirable trade."

"You can't quit!" Ruthie yells. "We're your family, and family sticks together."

"Kid, you ain't carny folk. I've only known you for a month."

"But I had just written you into the encore performance for next week."

"Really?" His demeanor softens. "That's so sweet. Nobody's ever included me in a unicycle ballet before." Lars shakes his head, sending his long blond ponytail swishing. "No, you won't tempt me back. There are weird things going on there. Spooky things."

"Like what?" I ask.

He shrugs a shoulder the size of a small country. "I'm just saying things haven't been the same since Betty died and Alfredo went to the big house. Something ain't right on those carnival grounds. And when those trailers pack up and leave, I won't be going with them. I'm staying right here in Truman where there are so many opportunities."

"Like what?" I ask.

"The manager's already told me she'd teach me how to work the deep fryer."

"You gonna make chicken fried steak and onion rings the rest of your life?" Ruthie yells so close to me her blue spike jabs me in the neck. "You have a gift."

Lars sniffs, his blue eyes downcast. "What gift?"

"To entertain the children of the world with your outrageously weird tallness."

"I'm not going back. Fran quit too."

I try to bring this woman to mind. "The lady with the talking pig?"

"Yeah, he also oinks a few Elvis tunes, so it's a pretty big loss."

My ice cream drips onto my hand as the May sun seeps into

my car. "We'll see you later, Lars." In fact, I'll probably be by after tonight's show.

I roll up my window and aim my Bug toward the carnival grounds.

"You had an ice-cream sandwich for lunch," Ruthie says, staring out at a green field.

"So? Maybe I'm calcium deficient."

"Bella, just spill it. You've eaten enough ice cream to make Ben and Jerry name a flavor in your honor. What's wrong?"

I take a large bite and let the light coffee flavor settle into my taste buds. "Luke and I had this weird talk last night. And he basically said if we're ever going to get back together, I will have to do the pursuing." How boringly respectful. I mean, where's his sense of chivalry? His manly leadership?

Ruthie snorts. "Good for him."

"What? Whose side are you on?"

She flips down the visor and glides neon pink lipstick over her lips. "I'm on the side of love, Bella. Love. I just want you guys to be as happy as Budge and I. Every day I say, 'Thank you, Lord, for my Budgey Wudgey.'"

"If you make me yak up my cappuccino chunk, I'm going to stuff your leather riding jacket down your throat."

She applies a top coat of gloss and smacks her lips. "You speak of violent things, but I know it's coming from a place of hurt, so I won't take it personally. You should just go for it with Luke. He's a nice guy."

"He's also demanding, bossy, domineering, and intelligent to the point of being obnoxious."

"You know Luke didn't cheat on you."

"He's still hanging out with Ashley."

"He told you it was nothing more than a friendship."

"It doesn't look like just friendship."

"Lindy dove into the love pool. And look how happy she is."

"Happy? Every time I see her, she looks like her dog just got run over." Except for last night when she was hanging out with Matt again. She laughed and smiled the entire time.

"You got it bad for Luke Sullivan. The sooner you accept that and deal with it, the better. He won't be available forever."

"He was out with Ashley Timmons last night."

Ruthie cracks her knuckles and smiles. "She can be taken care of."

Moments later the sound of yelling greets us as Ruthie and I walk into the big top at the carnival.

"Cherry, you're so stupid! Don't let go of my hand!"

I flinch and look up. "Stewart's such a slimeball."

Ruthie nods. "I got a pair of nunchucks I'd like to introduce him to."

"Focus!" Red yells from the ground. "Cherry, take this seriously."

"I am!" She brushes sweat from her brow. "We've been practicing for three hours. I need a break."

"You've got about two weeks before I expect to see the Praying Mantis." Red glares at his niece. "I won't let you mess this up for my circus."

Even from where I stand below, I can see the hurt flash across Cherry's pale face. What a life she leads. Makes me grateful for my family—crazy though they are.

Red claps his chubby hands. "Back to the beginning. Try it again!"

"No." Cherry climbs onto the ladder and begins to shimmy down. "I'm taking a break."

"Cherry, you hop right back up there this instant! I'm warning you!"

"Or what?" She continues her journey until she reaches the dirt. "You're going to ground me—from work? That's all I do!" She stomps toward her uncle. "Maybe I want what other girls have. Like the chance to have lots of friends, go to dances, and take driver's ed! To sleep in a bed that you don't pull down the highway in a caravan."

"I told you her living with Dolly O'Malley was a mistake," Stewart says as he joins them. "Now little cousin thinks she's better than the rest of us."

"I do not."

Stewart's face pulls into a sneer. "You always have. You think you're privileged or something because of who your parents were."

Ruthie nudges me with an elbow. "This is better than those Latin soap operas I watch. And no subtitles."

"You want to know who my parents were, Stewart?" Cherry's voice packs a punch I've never heard before. "They weren't famous to me. They were kind and loving. And they cared about me. They didn't make me work all day long. And when I did work, it was because I wanted to and because it made them happy. I wasn't just some show dog."

"That's it!" Red pokes his finger in Cherry's face. "When Dolly comes tonight, we are having ourselves a little talk. And you can bet you'll be moving back here—where you belong. I don't know what crazy things that woman has filled your head with, but I will not have you disrespecting me. I took you in when you were an orphan with nowhere to go. Your parents left you nothing because all they cared about was this carnival. But you have a place to stay and food to eat because of me. If it weren't for me you'd be on the streets."

Tears gather like thunderclouds in Cherry's eyes. "My parents loved me!" With a choking sob, she runs away—right past the gathering crowd and out of the big top.

"We better check on her."

Ruthie follows me outside. "Just say the word and I'll get those nunchucks."

I catch sight of Cherry running to the back corner of the carnival grounds. She stops at the Ferris wheel and speaks to the guy cleaning it. He nods and walks to the control box.

"Oh no." I can see where this is headed.

"Want me to talk to Cherry?" Ruthie asks. "I'll jump on with her and you can just, um . . . text some encouraging words from below."

I lift my head toward the heavens and beyond until I find the top cart on the Ferris wheel. Gulp. "No. We'll go together." How is it I can ride a plane once a month with no problems yet can't get on a simple carnival ride without breaking out in hives?

Cherry walks onto the ramp and pulls the front latch of a cart.

"Wait!" I call. "We'll go with you."

The worker frowns and steps in front of us. "Miss, I don't think she wants to be bothered."

"We're her friends," Ruthie says loud enough for Cherry to hear. "And we want to ride too."

We walk to the cart, and I get in, scooting beside Cherry. Ruthie climbs in next, pulling the door closed and squeezing us in like toes in a stiletto.

"What are you doing? Go away." Cherry swipes at the tears spilling down her cheeks. "I want to be alone."

"Too bad." Ruthie gives the man a thumbs-up as he double-checks our door.

My heart squeezes as I look at the pain in Cherry's eyes. "Normally you'd be talking to Betty right now, wouldn't you?"

She sniffs and nods. "Whenever I had a problem, my mom would bring me out to the Ferris wheel, and we'd take a spin. Just the two of us. My grandpa bought this machine for my dad as a wedding present. Every cart is painted in a fairy tale theme. My mom loved it. This Sleeping Beauty one was her favorite." Cherry rubs a finger where elaborate paint swirls rise and fall. "After my parents died, Betty would ride with me in this cart when she knew I wanted to talk. She would have torn into Red today. She wouldn't have let him talk to me like that." Her voice catches. "And now there's no one to take up for me."

I pull her into my arms as best I can, given I'm plastered between the two girls sardine-style.

The Ferris wheel groans, and with a lurch, we're off.

"I'm so sick of being alone," Cherry whispers.

Ruthie leans on me and moves in for a three-way hug. "You're not alone. You've got us."

Cherry's laugh is small. "It's not the same, though. You have no idea what it's like to not have parents. To be an unwanted guest. I'm just a burden to my uncle."

You have no idea what it's like to feel this cart swing and imagine yourself plunging to the ground.

"You've got God too." The words tumble out of my mouth in a rush. "I know it's hard to see that he has a plan in all of this, but he does." Why are my cheeks burning? Why is it so hard to talk about God to people?

"I've gone to church with Dolly. We've prayed." The wind lifts Cherry's hair as we rise. "But how could I buy into that? Where's God in all this? Why was I left by myself? If there is a God, how could he just take my parents?"

I sneak a quick glance at Ruthie. I am so not prepared for this conversation. Why couldn't Cherry ask these questions to someone who knows her Bible a bit better? Or someone who's had lots of practice witnessing. I've had lots of practice shopping. But unless she asks me whether I prefer Gucci or Prada, that is pretty much not going to be worth diddly-squat.

"Um . . . you have to believe that there is a God, and he loves you." Ruthie could pick up the conversation at any moment. She *is* a pastor's daughter. I'm a plastic surgeon's daughter! Ask me about butt implants! But Ruthie's just sitting there leaning on the edge like she can't wait to hear what I have to say next. "Bad things happen. But I know that when we hurt, God hurts. He's not just some big, bad guy up there. He wants us to think of him as a father."

I release Cherry from the hug, and she rests her head back on the seat, staring at the clouds. My stomach rolls as the ride slowly revolves.

"What father would leave his kid stuck with Uncle Red and Stewart? What father would take away both my parents *and* Betty?"

"Cherry, believing in God isn't going to magically fix anything." Don't I wish it would. "And it's hard to trust in something you can't even see, but every day . . . God waits for you to try."

She closes her eyes and rubs her hands over her face. "I just want a life. Is that too much to hope for?"

"No," I say, trying not to glance down as we make another swoop. "And I'm going to pray that you'll have a family and love." I still feel like I'm just spewing words.

"Whatever. Unless you're ordering me up a total life transplant, don't waste your breath." Cherry signals to the carnival worker below, and he throws the lever. When the Ferris wheel stops, Cherry jumps out *over* the cart. No door, no waiting for Ruthie and me to get off. Just shimmies from the seat, leaps off the front, and hits the ground running.

Ruthie reaches into the pocket of her leather pants and gets out her Tic Tacs. "That went really well."

"Are you kidding me?" I set my teeth and count backward from five. "You could have helped me. Instead of letting me just flail in the water."

"I helped." She pops a mint into her mouth.

"Oh really? Tell me one thing of any significance you did."

"Prayed." Ruthie locks her eyes with mine. "I prayed the entire time you were talking." She reaches over and unhooks the door.

"You're quite the doubter, Bella Kirkwood. Anybody ever tell you that?" She hops out, leaving me sitting there.

"Miss, you want another ride?"

I glance at the worker standing by the control box. "No. Thank you."

"You sure?"

"Sir, I think that's about the only thing I am sure of."

chapter twenty-one

Today the weatherman predicted a nice breezy eighty-three degrees with zero chance of precip. As I watch Luke Sullivan walking my way, I think that guy clearly miscalled it. Because I see 100 percent chance of storm.

"What is this?" He slams down a piece of paper next to my mouse.

"Is that my exposé on nerd editors?" *And good morning to you too.* "I should have known it would hurt your feelings." He and I haven't really talked since we, you know, *talked.* I've kind of been avoiding him. It's all so awkward.

"Meet me in Mr. Holman's office. Now."

I definitely should've started this day with coffee. I look back to my computer and type a few more sentences. He can wait. Bossing me around like that. Who does he think he is?

"I would not push me this morning, if I were you," Luke calls out in front of the entire class. Every head in the room pivots from Luke . . . to me. Even our advisor, Mr. Holman, raises a bushy brow as he helps Ashley.

I stand up, smoothing out my funky Betsey Johnson skirt, and with a smile perfectly balanced on my face, I join Luke in the office.

He shuts the door behind us and motions me to a seat.

"I'll just stand, thanks."

"Sit."

Employing Haughty Look Number Four, I lower myself onto the edge of a chair.

He sits in the other one and pulls out the same piece of paper. "Back to our original question, what is this?"

I read the first line and sigh. "It's my column for next week."

"It's about birthday cakes, measles shots, and used books that smell."

"I write from the heart."

He takes off his tortoiseshell glasses and hangs them in the V of his shirt. I'm forced to look directly into his ocean blue eyes.

"This is rambling, lacks voice, and is full of grammatical errors."

"Maybe Ashley can fix it." Omigosh. Did I really just say that? "Or someone else on staff—if you think there's a problem or two."

But it's too late. I see the storm clouds roll out and that familiar arrogance take its place. "You know what I think?"

"You hope sweater vests come back in style?"

Luke wheels his chair closer to mine. "I think your mind's on overload. Between your schedule at the carnival, your family problems, and confusion about us, you can't even concentrate enough to write three cohesive paragraphs."

If I had gotten that morning coffee, I would've just spewed it. "Are you delusional? First of all, I don't work any more than you do." Though I do have the extra burden of clown feet and hair the color of Kool-Aid. "And I hate to burst your gargantuan ego, but I don't sit around all day thinking about you." Well, maybe just a few hours here and there.

"Your column's been weak the last three issues. As of right now, you're taking a break." He places a book in my hands.

"*Reviving the Passion of Nonfiction?*" Sounds thrilling. "Wow, I hate to borrow this from you. I know how you like to read it aloud to all of your dates." I better not have just seen his mouth quirk.

"Take the next week to read and review some work from published pros." His voice softens. "Relax your mind."

The book feels heavy in my hand, and I have to blink to block out the fantasy of braining him with it. "You can't just stop my column. Mr. Holman will never go for that."

Luke stands up, rubbing the back of his neck above his Abercrombie collar. "He will if I'm subbing a new column in its place."

My stomach plummets like the Zipper at the carnival. "Who?"

"Ashley."

Now I'm standing. "I cannot believe you. Let me guess, if I'd go out with you, you'd reconsider? Is this punishment until I come around?"

His look could freeze the Pacific Ocean. "If you think that then you don't know me at all."

"Oh, I know you all right. You're a control freak, and this is just more proof of it. I'm probably the first girl who's ever rejected you."

"The paper is too important. Your column runs on the front page, and lately it's not even worthy to be in it. I expect more from you, and until I see that progress, you're done."

"And you just *randomly* picked her?" I jerk my finger toward the classroom in Ashley's direction.

Luke takes a deep breath, doing that thing he does when he's considering his words and trying to be all uppity editorlike. "Everyone else is already writing all they can and worked to the maximum. But Ashley has yet to completely be integrated into the paper. Not that I have to explain myself to you, but she came to me with a great idea for a feature, and now would be the perfect time to use it, since there will be a big gaping hole where *your* work should go."

I chuckle once and shake my head. "You are so full of it, you know that, Luke Sullivan?"

He leans on the door, his arms crossed. "I'm sorry, Bella. I didn't handle this well. I lost my temper, and I apologize for my tone. But I'm being sincerely honest when I tell you that removing you from the paper for a week or so isn't personal. If anything, it's for your own good. I did it for Trinity Dermott out there last year, and now I'm benching you."

"Was Trinity also an ex-girlfriend?"

His tanned hand clutches the doorknob, yanking it with a twist. "You have your new assignment. Get to it."

"I think—"

"Leave, Bella." He holds the door wide open. "Before you say something else we're both going to regret."

By lunchtime I've printed out all of this month's articles with my name on them, read them a hundred times each, and worked up a seriously hideous headache. Luke is right. My writing has stunk lately. But still . . . to put Ashley Timmons in my place? He had to know that was a low blow. Even if her article last week on test prep anxiety was kind of clever. And funny. And well written. Still!

"Kirkwood, you gonna eat those fries? Can you believe when I got to the front of the line they were all out of meat loaf?" Ruthie steals a handful from my plate. "So I think my unicycle ballet needs a few more figure eights. A little more ribbon waving. Tonight I'm going to get crazy and do purple ribbon instead of pink. It will match my hair."

I stop picking the label off my water bottle long enough to notice Ruthie has once again colored her hair. It looks like Barney held her at gunpoint and took her hair as a hostage. "Very nice."

"Dang right it is." Budge pats Ruthie's teased-out ponytail. "My lady is hot stuff."

"So then he caught the pass and ran right into the goalpost. Knocked him out for five minutes."

Across from me, Lindy laughs at Matt's football practice story. "When is Corey Davis going to suck it up and get his eyes checked?"

"Last week he showed up in his golf shoes. Seriously, the boy needs contacts before Coach sidelines him forever." Matt takes a drink of Gatorade. "Hey, I was going to go sign up to help with the athletic banquet. Want to go talk to Coach and see what they still need?"

"Sure." Lindy stands up and grabs her food tray.

"There you are!" Bo Blades jogs toward her and wraps an arm around her shoulders. "I have a surprise for you in my car. Come on." He takes the tray from Lindy's hands and passes it to Matt. "Take care of this, will you?" Bo pulls Lindy out the cafeteria door, holding her hand like it's a state championship medal.

"Matt?" I watch him just stand there. Motionless. "You okay?"

He sets the tray down on the table. Takes a seat. "Have you ever wanted something, but didn't know for sure you wanted this something . . . until it was too late?"

"I assume you're not talking about the meat loaf."

He props his chin on his hand. "She was my best friend. I didn't want to mess that up. I was afraid if we didn't work out then I would have lost a girlfriend *and* a friend. But now I wonder . . . in playing it safe did I just blow it anyway? I mean, I could've had my chance."

"So you knew she liked you?"

He nods his freckled face. "Yeah. I knew."

"Wow. She did everything to get your attention this year."

"I know. Lindy was the brave one. What's wrong with me that I can't take risks? I can on the field and on the court, but in my personal life—I always play it safe." He glances toward the door. "And look where it's gotten me."

Ruthie steals another fry off my untouched plate. "You could tell her how you feel. I'm a firm believer in honesty."

Budge does a double take. "You told me you had a rare mouth disease for the first two weeks we dated so I wouldn't kiss you."

"I wasn't exactly lying. I was adding to my mystique."

"I had to call my doctor to make sure all my shots were updated."

"Awww..." Ruthie throws her arms around Budge. "That's the sweetest thing anyone's ever done for me."

"Matt, maybe you should just tell her how you feel."

He grabs a napkin and folds it over and over. "It's not that easy. I like Lindy a lot—but I don't know. It's kind of scary to think about committing to her in that way." He tosses the napkin down on the table. "Never mind. You wouldn't understand. All that stuff just comes easy to you."

My eyes slide across the room to where Luke sits with his soccer buddies. And Ashley Timmons. "Right. I'm just a natural."

~~~~~~

I park by Ruthie's motorcycle on the carnival grounds. I do an automatic scan of the lot just to make sure no escaped killer is skulking about. They seriously need to find Alfredo because I'm sick of having a twenty-four-hour-a-day case of the creeps.

"Hey."

"Oh!" I jump and spin around. "You—you scared me."

The new magician stares at me like he's memorizing my face. "Sorry. I guess you didn't see me behind you."

I look over the parking lot again. Just a second ago there was no one around. Where did he come from?

I nervously lick my lips. "I'm Bella." *And I'd give you my last name, but you look like the type who would Google me, find my house, and come over to show me your knife collection.*

"I'm, uh, Jensen. Artie Jensen." He angles his close-cropped head to the ground and speed walks right past me. "Have a good night."

"You too." Weirdo.

A few hours later I look out from the back curtain. The crowds are getting smaller and smaller every night. Soon the Fritz Family Carnival will be leaving, and if I don't break this case, I'll have nothing to show for it but a deep, abiding hate for honking clown noses and polka-dotted jumpsuits.

The performers meet in the center of the ring and take their final bows. The audience stands up and applauds as Red wishes them a happy evening and safe travel.

As I take off my wig and hang it on the hook, Luke steps into the changing area. "Bella, we need to talk."

I glare him down in the mirror. "I think we've said enough."

Ruthie sits down to pull off her giant clown shoes, not even hiding the fact that she's listening to every word.

"You know we need to discuss this."

"What are we discussing?" Ruthie asks. "I like discussions."

"Go away, Luke." I pull off my bow tie and place it in a plastic crate. "There's nothing more to say. You said my writing sucks, and you put Ashley in my place."

"Oh no, you didn't!" Ruthie slaps her thigh and laughs. "That is some serious drama, boy."

Luke shoots her a silencing glare. "I don't want to fight with you, Bella."

I pick up my purse and sling it over my shoulder. "Then I guess one of us should leave." I sail past him and head out into the arena. *God, why are boys so difficult? One minute I want to kiss him and tell him exactly how I feel, and the next I want to shove my rainbow wig up his nose and pull it out his ear.*

I walk by Cherry, who stands below the trapeze, gazing upward. "Hey, Bella."

"You did great tonight. You're just amazing up there . . . and the crowd loves you."

Her eyes dim. "My family doesn't."

"Well ..." I don't know what to say. "Dolly's crazy about you. You know she loves you."

The smile returns. "And Mickey."

"Is he spending a lot of time out at the house?"

Cherry unwraps her ponytail and shakes out her glossy hair. "He's there for dinner every night now. They're still a little nervous around each other, but it's kind of fun to watch."

Lord, I do not want to be in my fifties and still not have this love business figured out.

"Still keeping the dog under wraps?"

She nods. "It's our secret."

"Cherry, um . . ." I check over my shoulder for anyone nearby. "Stewart and Red have been going out late after almost every show and digging." I check for any signs of recognition. All I see staring back at me is cluelessness.

"Digging for what?"

"I was hoping you'd know the answer to that."

"No idea."

"Did Betty ever mention them having to find anything? Maybe they buried something the last time they were here?"

She scans her memory bank. "No. But how do you know they've been searching for something?"

"We've been following them." I catch sight of Luke across the way, sitting in the bleachers as if he's waiting for me. I struggle to rein my thoughts back to this conversation. "And this week I found the map they've been using to search."

Cherry drops her ponytail holder. "How? You didn't break into their trailer again, did you?"

"I might've wandered in there ... accidentally."

Her fragile hand flutters to her chest. "Bella, Red's never laid a hand on me, but I've seen it in his eyes. And I've seen him be less considerate to others—even his own son. You do not want to mess with him."

A chill flitters up my spine. "We have to figure out what they want."

"I thought you were solving Betty's murder."

"I think it's connected."

"Look out!" I hear Luke's roar before he shoves Cherry out of the way, taking me with her. As we hit the ground, a row of lights crashes around us. Glass sprays everywhere as Luke plasters his body over mine.

"Cherry!" Through the fog in my head, I hear Dolly's voice, distant and loud. "Cherry!"

The volume level rises as workers begin to follow the noise and congregate.

"Bella?" Luke lifts his head from my neck. "Bella, are you okay?"

I shove at his chest to push him off, but find there are two chests. Two Lukes. Two of everything. I lay my head back down. "I can't even handle one of you."

He rolls away and kneels beside me. "Can you hear me?"

"Of course I can." I look up into his eyes so full of concern. "You're always saving me." I roll my eyes and feel pain spike my temple. "It drives me totally nuts."

Luke's laugh is brief. "Obviously you're all right." He holds out a hand, and I take it. He slowly pulls me to a seated position, and my vision aligns into focus.

"What in the heck happened here?" Red stabs an angry finger toward the dirt where a small row of lights rests in pieces. "You've been working on lights, boy. You want to explain this?"

Luke gives my hand a squeeze and stands up. "I don't do rigging. Wouldn't even know how."

"It's Betty's ghost," says Ziggy, one of the clown midgets. "We're cursed."

"We ain't cursed!" Red shouts, throwing his hat to the ground. "It was an accident is all. Accidents happen, for crying out loud!"

"The girls could've been killed." Dolly wraps her arms around Cherry and aims her mama bear stare on Red. "I'm taking Cherry home."

Red's eyes glaze with anger. "I told you last night to bring her stuff back. She's staying here."

"No." Dolly whispers something to Cherry, and with a nod, the girl walks away. "This is no place for her to live right now, and you know it. As long as you're in Truman, she stays with me. And Red, if you want to fight me on this, you bring all you've got. If I got an attorney today, I know the first thing he'd tell the judge is how your niece almost got taken out by your equipment."

Red's eyes flutter and blink. "Now just a minute—she is my flesh and blood. You're just a distant cousin."

"Good night, Red." Dolly turns to me on her way out. "You okay, Bella?"

"Yeah." I feel my body tremble like I'm standing in the Denver snow. "Just another day on the job as a circus clown." I can't even work up a smile for my own lame joke.

Dolly shares a look with Luke. "Are you going to take her home?"

He nods once. "I'll take care of her."

Satisfied, Dolly heads toward the same exit Cherry used to make her escape.

"This ain't over, Dolly!" Red calls. His head rotates as he catches all the onlookers. "What are you people staring at? Get a broom! Get a bucket! Get this mess out of here!"

"Come on." With a hand under my arm, Luke guides me to my feet. "I'll take you home."

"I can drive."

He breathes out a small laugh. "Your stepdad's going to be proud of my body slam."

I cough as my lungs expand back to their normal capacity. "He'll have you fitted in a spandex onesie in no time."

As Luke wraps his arm around me and pulls me close, I snuggle into the safety of his side and try not to think about the fact that I could've been a splatter on the ground. But he saved me. *Thank you, Jesus. Omigosh, thank you, Jesus.*

The night air hits my face, and I suck it through my nose like I'm trying to breathe away the last few minutes.

Luke stops three steps outside the big top, and before I know what he's about, I'm flattened to his chest. "That scared the crap out of me." He presses me to him, lowering his head on top of mine.

I pull my arms around him and rest my cheek to his pounding heart. "But I'm here. Because of you. Thank you."

"Bella, we have to figure this out. I can't take much more of this." His hands caress my back, and I feel some of the trauma ease away.

"I know," I sigh into his shirt. "And I'm glad to know you're still interested in me."

His hands still. He pulls away. "I was talking about Betty's murder. And the map."

"Oh." *Why don't you just slam me on the ground again? It would be easier than this humiliation.* "Totally. Me too."

Luke quirks a brow and pulls my hair away from my twirling finger. "We should probably get your head checked. You took quite a hit."

"I'm fine." It's my achy heart that needs the assistance.

He wraps an arm around me loosely like a brother. Any sizzle that had been there is gone. All the heat blown out like a cheap firecracker.

"Y'all have a good evening."

Luke and I both turn as Artie Jensen throws a cigarette to the ground. He squashes it with his shoe.

"Good night." Luke draws me a little closer and steers me toward the parking lot.

"Be careful out there," Artie calls. "You might not get lucky a second time."

chapter twenty-two

"*A*nd that's how a bill becomes a law. Isn't that fascinating?" Robbie stares in eagerness at the faces around him. "Any questions?"

"Yeah." I smoosh the chili around on my hotdog. "Will someone pass the relish?"

It's an early dinner on this Saturday night before I go to work at the carnival. Since we're celebrating another rare evening of Captain Iron Jack being home, Mom wanted to dine as a family. Robbie picked Weiner Palace.

"Here's another round of root beers for everyone." Budge bends over to fill our mugs, and a plume from his turban sticks into my dog.

"Budge—please." I gesture to my plate. "You just got chili on your feathers."

He shrugs it off. "That's nothing. Yesterday I dropped it in the toilet."

Okay. I'll just skip the main course and move on to dessert. "Hey, is that Lars back there in the kitchen?" I catch sight of the giant man struggling with a bag of fries.

"Yeah, he started today. I guess the Dairy Barn caught him giving people double dips for the price of a single."

"What a brave, brave man." I don't know if I've ever had this much respect for a person in all my life. "You know, people think it's just ice cream, but to many of us, what he was doing was a ministry."

Robbie takes a bite of hotdog and comes away with most of it on his mouth. "But Bella, that's dishonest."

"That's what addictions do to a person, Robbie." Budge flips me with a hand towel and swishes away in his genie pants.

Mom cuts into her hotdog with a knife like it's prime rib. "I made an A on my philosophy quiz this week."

"Honey, that's great." Jake gives her a loud smooch on the cheek. "What classes are you taking for the summer term?"

She presses a napkin to her lips. "I told you I'm sitting out for a while."

"But we talked about this, Jillian. I want you to keep going. You can't stop now."

"You're right, we *did* talk about this. And the final word was that there was no way I could be a single parent three hundred days a year and go to school." Mom's voice lightens as she forces a smile for Robbie's watchful eyes. "It will be fine. Plenty of time to hit the books."

The tension is thicker than the Weiner Palace chili.

Mom turns her blue eyes to me and changes the subject. "Oh, Bella, I talked to your father. He said for you to be prepared for your bridesmaid dress fitting next weekend. Something about you and little Marisol having matching gowns."

"Can't wait. So Jake, how is wrestling going?" I never get to talk to the guy.

"It's been a challenge, but I like it. Training *and* performing doesn't leave a lot of time."

"And providing commentary," Mom adds.

"It's crazy." Jake's eyes light up. "I never was that good at public speaking, but this commentary stuff is almost more fun than wrestling. Hey, I hear you guys are going to have a watch party for tomorrow night's *Sunday Night Smackdown.*"

"Yeah, I guess Dolly's having a big dinner at her house after the evening service at church. Mom's the event planner and Dolly's catering." I put my drink down as Lars walks to our table. He lifts up a hand that could shield an entire town from rain and reads from a page he's holding. "Would you like anything . . . ? Shoot. I can't make out that last word. It got smudged with hotdog grease." He scratches his head. "Now I don't know what I'm supposed to ask you."

I take sympathy on the man who was like the patron saint of ice cream. "I think you wanted to know if we wanted anything else."

He drops his hand and considers this. "Okay. Sounds good. Well, do you?"

"We're good here, thanks," Jake says and returns to his discussion with Mom. Robbie just stares, his head cranked all the way back to take in the man who could've walked out of Jack and the Beanstalk.

"So, Lars, are you missing the carnival?" I ask.

He laughs, a deep belly chortle that nearly shakes the table. "Are you kidding? When I could have all this?" He gestures wide to the restaurant, and it pulls his already-short pouffy sleeves to his elbows.

"I was wondering . . . could you tell me about the night Cherry's parents died?"

Lars winces. "That was a horrible night. Things have never been the same for the carnival." He pulls up a chair and eases into it, the wood creaking in complaint. "It was a stormy night, so we had a smaller crowd. We were in Baton Rouge, stationed in a vacant Wal-Mart parking lot.* Red had only been with us a few years, and I remember he took to the center of the ring and announced Junior and Shelly Fritz. They were going to debut their new routine, the Praying Mantis. It was very risky, but those two"—he whistles and smiles—"they were good. Red had convinced them that this new trapeze act would put Fritz Family Carnival on the map. He said once word got out, people would be coming from miles around to see Mr. and Mrs. Fritz."

"What happened that night?"

"The performance started out so flawless. People were on their feet to get a better look—that's how good they were. Then—" He pauses.

"Yes?"

Lars closes his eyes as if he's stepped back in time. "Just as they were about to do the big finale, lightning blew out the generator. The electricity went out. Junior and Shelly both fell to their deaths. No net."

I replay the facts in my head. "Why wouldn't they use a net? All trapeze artists do."

He shrugs a round shoulder, sending the plumes on his hat to wiggling. "Our fiercest competition has always been an outfit called the Hickman Brothers Circus. They were doing a gig without a net—had some mighty fine aerialists—and were taking our customers. They were always a few steps ahead of us on the tour. So Red convinced Junior that going without a net was the only choice."

"But they were professionals. Experts. Was there any sort of investigation?"

"What are you saying?"

"I don't know." I'm no closer to piecing this all together than I was the day I first stuck on a clown nose. "I'm just trying to get to the truth."

"You think they were murdered? Like maybe the mafia? Some gangs? I saw this show about gangs on HBO once, so I know all about them."

"No, I don't think it's organized crime." But perhaps something just as sinister.

Lars hinges at the waist and leans over. "What about aliens?"

I look into his hazel eyes and can almost see the wide-open space behind them. "I'll let you know."

It's five o'clock when I walk into the big top. I head straight to the back of the tent where all the props are stored and where my small changing area is. I set my purse down on the ground, then reach for the box that contains my clown garb.

And there sits my long-lost flashlight.

I'm paralyzed to the spot as chills explode over my skin.

A hand clamps down on my shoulder, and I turn and scream.

"Shhh!" Luke covers my mouth, his eyes wide. "What are you doing?" he hisses.

I just stare at him, my eyes unseeing, my brain moving at a speed that could cause permanent damage.

"Bella?" His voice is a scratchy whisper. Then his eyes drop to the box. "Oh."

I swallow. "You didn't put it there, did you?"

He shakes his head. "I never found it. I even managed to sneak in Alfredo's trailer one more time." Luke leans down and picks it up, the pink metal gleaming under the dim lights. "It's definitely yours. And I think someone probably wants to send you a message."

I take my flashlight, my fingers sliding across Luke's palm. "They know I was snooping."

"And more than likely are smart enough to know you still are." His forehead wrinkles in a frown. "You okay?"

I inhale deeper, willing my breath to slow down. "Yeah. Just kind of caught me off guard." I quickly fill him in on my conversation with Lars.

Luke's voice is barely audible. "You think Red killed Cherry's parents?"

"Maybe he wanted them out of the way so he'd inherit the carnival."

"But Cherry—?"

"What if she's in danger?"

Luke's eyes widen briefly. "I was so focused on what could've happened to you when the lights fell last night . . ."

My heart does a small cartwheel.

"But what if you were just an innocent bystander, and the lights had been rigged to hit Cherry?" He rubs a hand over his face. "Or someone wants you out of the way because you're getting too close to her . . . and the truth."

"This case creeps me out more than the others have."

"That's why we need to work together." Luke watches me. "Got it?"

"Uh-huh."

His breath comes out in a huff. "Can you at least *try* to sound like you mean it? I'm serious here. No going into trailers by your-self—not even with Ruthie. No being alone with Red or Stewart or anyone from the carnival. We don't know what we're dealing with here, but it's big. And somebody could be out for blood. Not to men-tion Alfredo is still unaccounted for."

"You're kinda freaking me out."

"I *want* you scared." His hand latches onto my shoulder. "Do you get that? I want you scared enough that you're watching your back and never alone." Luke's hands slide down my arms. "Frightened enough that you'll be safe. Bella, I can't protect you every moment, and it's driving me crazy."

"Nobody asked you to protect me." But strangely enough, for once it sounds kind of nice.

"I think we should talk to Officer Mark. Update him."

"I agree."

Luke's eyes drop back to the flashlight in my hand. "Act like nothing's wrong tonight, okay? Can you do that?"

"Of course." It's becoming my specialty. "I need to go ask for next weekend off. No time like the present to show Red and Stewart that I'm not bothered at all."

"Let's go."

I hesitate for a millisecond before common sense takes over. That and the voice of my mother harping in my head. I follow Luke to the back of the carnival to the trailer area. We get to the edge of Red's just as the door flings open. Luke pulls me around the side, and we flatten to the wall.

"Well, William, this is the finest carnival of its size," comes Red's voice. "We have a long history of entertaining families *and* turning a profit. After we come out of our training season, we're gonna be better than ever."

I peek around the corner and see a short, white-haired man standing on the bottom step of Red's trailer.

"I certainly liked what I saw last night. I believe I'll stick around for this evening's show as well," the stranger says, adjusting his white cowboy hat.

"You do that. My son, Stewart, will make sure you have the best seats in the house. And if you feel so inclined, you can come back to the trailer after the performance and we'll discuss the contract."

The old man laughs. "It's always about money with you, isn't it, Red? Always was."

Cherry's uncle throws his head back and laughs. "William, you know I'd consider selling my soul for a good profit. So you *know* I won't hesitate to sell you the carnival."

Luke and I exchange a shocked stare, and I can't resist looking around the corner again.

"Your price is too rich for me, Red. I don't think I'm ready to sign over that check just yet."

I see Red slap the man on the back. "You just take your time thinking about it. In the end—Red Fritz always gets his way." A leering grin splits his face. "Always."

chapter twenty-three

People may think New York City is weird, but that town's got nothing on Dolly's house when it's packed with wrestlers.

"These little shrimp puffs are divine. Can you taste that tarragon?" Breath of Death pops one in his mouth and closes his eyes as if placing heaven on his tongue. "Dolly is amazing, Mickey. You should never let her go."

Mickey's gaze drifts over the crowd until he finds his ex-wife. "How right you are."

While Mickey still manages Jake's booming career, he's also been bombarded with requests from amateur wrestlers to train them, mostly former opponents of Jake's on the local circuit. I think Breath of Death is going to be his next breakout star—even though outside the ring, he's girlier than I am. Seriously, ten minutes ago he was quizzing me on my Zac Posen sundress.

I weave my way through the mass of people in Dolly's living room and head for her gourmet kitchen, where the food is spread out on two tables. Tonight's theme, courtesy of my mother's handiwork, is the fifties. The tables are draped in material that looks like pink poodle skirts. Vinyl records rest between the plates of food, and a rented jukebox plays "You Ain't Nothing But a Hound Dog." I expect Elvis to pop out any moment.

"Great party." Officer Mark grabs a cucumber and pops it in his mouth. "Wouldn't expect anything less, though. I always love a good Dolly-Jillian throwdown."

"They do work well together." I pour the punch into glasses that look like they're straight from an old time soda fountain. "I hear a lot of this stuff came from Sugar's Diner. Guess there's a ton of junk in storage from all their years."

He winces. "Sugar's is so old there could be dead bodies in storage for all we know."

"Speaking of dead bodies—"

"Bella"—Mark holds up hands of surrender—"don't start. I'm not here as a cop tonight. Just one of Mickey's boys having a nice evening out with the other manly men."

Breath of Death sticks his head between us. "Girl, I just caught a whiff of your perfume, and I *love* it!" He flutters his hand toward his nose. "Burberry, right?" The lummox of a wrestler laughs as he floats away, off to interrupt someone else's conversation.

I pick up my glass, covering my mouth. "You were saying?"

Officer Mark sighs and spoons out some spicy chicken dip. "It's weird that someone that in touch with his feminine side can crush a man's neck with his knees."

"So, Luke and I have been working at the carnival," I begin. "And there's a lot of weird stuff going on."

"Weird?" Mark frowns. "After Alfredo literally threw off his handcuffs and walked away, nothing would surprise me."

"Any leads on him yet?"

"No. Have you heard anything?"

I shake my head. "But there have been some strange occurrences at the carnival grounds." I fill him in, including my encounter with the crashing lights. "Luke and I don't know if it was meant for me or Cherry—or both."

"What makes you think it wasn't just an accident? Circuses

get thrown up really quickly, so quality and safety isn't always a top concern."

"I just know."

"Bella, if you're holding out information from the police, you have to let us know what you've seen and heard."

"But couldn't we share information—you and I? We're good friends—that's what friends do. Share stuff."

"Uh-huh," he smirks. "I'll remember that next time I want to borrow your flatiron and hairspray."

I reach toward a piece of hair sticking up. "Actually you could use a little—"

He slaps my hand away. "But it doesn't work the other way. *You* give us information. The end."

"You've helped me out before."

"*Before* didn't involve a murder."

"Well, actually it did. Both times." Psychotic killers seem to gravitate toward me.

"You know this is different." He adds more to his plate. "So tell me what else you've discovered—not that I approve of your snooping around."

"Last night I overheard Red talking to a potential buyer about the carnival. He's wanting to sell it."

Mark's hand stills on a serving spoon. "I guess the man's entitled to sell his own business. Does anyone else know?"

"I don't think so."

He shrugs and moves down the table. "Still, that's not really anything suspicious."

"I talked to a former employee yesterday who told me about Cherry's parents' death." I fill him in on every detail from Lars.

Mark puts his plate down and gives me his full attention. "Bella"—he chews on his bottom lip as if weighing a decision— "I already know a lot of this. The sale of the carnival is new information, but the rest, I knew." His eyes lock with mine. "Please believe me when I tell you that we have it under control. And also believe it when I say you need to stay out of the way. No more following people and hunting up clues."

"You know Red and Stewart are connected. Why can't you just call them in for questioning and confront them with some of this?"

"This is a delicate situation. And it's being handled as we see fit." Again with the intense eyes. "Can you trust me on this?"

My nosy-meter is off the charts. "What are you not telling me?"

Mark's cell phone vibrates on his hip. After a quick check, he hands me his plate. "Gotta run. But I'm serious about the warning. We know we can't stop you from working at the carnival, but just do your job and go home. Don't socialize with anyone there, don't go into any trailers, nothing." He pats me on the shoulder and gives me his I-know-best look. "You don't want to be responsible for ruining a very delicate investigation, do you?" He turns on his heel and disappears into the crowd, leaving me with a feeling as unsettling as brown guacamole.

I'm on the inside. Doesn't Mark get that? I'm close to Cherry. If I bat my eyes enough, I could probably get anything out of Stewart, and I'm there at the carnival almost every day. I'm the inside girl! What's wrong with *helping* the police?

A half hour later I'm sitting by Cherry and Dolly on one of the couches. Peg the dog rests in Cherry's lap, content to be petted during commercial breaks. Mom watches the *Sunday Night Smackdown* with fluctuating expressions of pride, excitement, and sadness as the camera pans to Jake, who gives a play-by-play of the action.

"He's really good," Dolly says. "Just a natural."

"My dad's the coolest." This from Robbie, who sits on Budge's lap in a leather chaise.

Mickey beams. "That's my Jake."

Actually it's my mom's Jake. But he seems to belong to everyone but her and this family lately.

When my phone sings, I get up and answer it in the dining room. "Hello?"

"Bella, it's me." Luke. The boy with the voice that could melt a Popsicle. "Can you meet me at the school parking lot?"

"Gee, Luke. It's a little late for a make-out session. But I guess I could brush my teeth and be there in ten."

"I'm serious, Bella . . . Actually I'm *dead* serious."

With hasty explanations to the party crowd, I walk out the door and into the steamy evening to my Bug. With my radio cranked up, I'm at the school four songs later.

I step into the passenger seat of Luke's 4Runner and inhale leather, faded cologne, and something else that is solely Luke Sullivan. "What's going on?"

He looks at me for a moment, taking in my spring sundress, then turns the key. "We're going to take a little drive."

"Is this about us?"

He pulls the SUV out and onto the road. "You know my conditions, so this couldn't be about us."

Because I have to be the one to initiate a relationship. Or even the next conversation about it. "Where are we going?"

"The Patton family cemetery."

"Why? Is Ashley going to be waiting there for me with a big ax?" Though it's balmy outside, I suddenly feel like turning the heat on. I'm cold all the way down to my Kate Spade flats. "I've never heard of this place."

"It's a small family-owned graveyard. The family's pretty much died out, so they use it to bury people in town who can't afford plots in the town cemetery." He turns onto Main Street. "I was doing a little surveillance tonight and stumbled upon something. I think

you're going to be very interested. Not that you're dressed for it."
His eyes slide my way again. "You look nice, by the way."

Heart flip-flops. "Thanks. If you had given me some notice, I
could've at least put on some black face paint."

A few minutes later Luke turns off on a dirt road.

"This isn't a cemetery." Creepiness radiating in full force now.

He shuts off the vehicle, reaches in the backseat, and grabs a
flashlight. "Ready?"

"Wait." I rest my hand on his to stop him. "What's going on?"

He hands me a dark running jacket. "We're going to walk down
the road a bit. About a fourth of a mile down is the back side of the
cemetery. We'll camp out in some trees. I brought that jacket for you
just in case you were decked out in sparkles and neon."

"Thanks." I slip my arms into the sleeves and imagine him playing soccer with it on. "Gonna tell me what's going on?"

"Betty the Bearded Lady is buried out here."

"Suddenly I don't really feel like paying my final respects."

"Apparently Red and Stewart do." He opens his door and steps
out. "They started digging her up about an hour ago."

chapter twenty-four

O we're going to see Red and Stewart breaking into Betty's coffin?" Well, here's the one time I wish he would've called Ashley Timmons instead. "And what—we're going to see if they'd like some refreshments?"

Luke locks his vehicle as I hop down. "No, we're going to see what they're looking for." He walks to my side and waits. "Can you handle this?"

"Uh, yeah." I snort. "Totally."

He slings an arm around me as we hit the dirt road. "Then why are you shaking?"

"Fever." I swallow hard and try not to think of Betty's dead corpse. "Probably the flu—just another reason I won't be making out with you tonight."

"Very thoughtful of you." He drops his arm and reaches for my hand instead. "Stick close to me. I know where I'm going."

This moment reminds me of last fall when he and I followed a bloodthirsty group of football boys into the woods at the lake. When they chased us out, we jumped in his 4Runner.

"Bella, I'm going to need you to trust me to get us out of this. Can you do that?"

I could hear the guys gaining on us. I remember yelling, *"Do something! What's your plan?"*

"*This.*" And he leaned in and kissed the life out of me. Fireworks zinged and popped in my head, and I just dove in and went along with it. For survival's sake, of course.

I wonder if he's thinking of that now. Or if he ever does.

"Bella . . . Bella?"

Luke tugs on my hand, and I realize he's been talking. "Um, yes. I agree."

I hear his small laugh. "You're not paying attention. I just asked you if you wanted to go home and snort wet spaghetti noodles up your nose."

I tug his hand right back. "Testing me?"

"Yeah, and you failed." He keeps walking and pulling me along. "I need you to be on your A game tonight. Just in case we have to make an emergency dash back to the car."

And in the dark I see Luke turn his head and look at me. Really look at me. And I know he remembers that night. My cheeks warm, and I smile at him.

"You ready?" he whispers.

For you? For this? To tell you I don't believe you were a willing participant in Ashley's kiss? "I think I might be."

Luke watches me for a suspended moment. For a slip of a second, I think he's going to kiss me. He reaches out a hand . . .

. . . and points beyond me. "Right this way." His attention refocused, he guides me off the road and through some trees. "Watch your step." He shines his flashlight on the ground as we traipse over grass that rises to my bare calves.

A few minutes later he's turned the light off, and I know we're almost there.

"Shhh." He pulls me around a tall pine and points to the left.

I peek around, and there, illuminated in their own spotlight, are Red and Stewart. Both stand with shovels in hand, knee-deep in the wet grass, sending the dirt flying into the air. They really are digging into that grave. If I were Catholic, I'd totally be crossing myself here. This is unholy! It's sacrilegious! It's . . . making me glad I slipped my camera into my pocket.

I watch in stunned silence for a few moments as the two plunge their shovels into the earth over and over. If I had any doubts they were capable of anything as vile as murder before, I don't doubt it now.

"Can't you dig any faster?" Red yells, his head barely visible over the ground.

"I'm going as fast as I can. I've been digging thirty minutes longer than you."

My left leg is tingling and numb by the time I hear a shovel hit metal.

"Got it!" Stewart yells. "Not much longer now."

Good. Because I seriously have to pee.

Time creeps in slow motion, and finally the digging stops.

"You do it."

"No. You're older. You knew her better."

Silence. Red mumbles something insulting to his son, then I hear the chill-inducing creak of the lid.

Stewart yelps like a girl.

"Would you shut up?" his dad bellows. "All we need is the cops out here."

"S-S-She looks—"

"Dead?"

Come on. One of you admit you killed her. Say something.

"Check out her neck," Red barks. "Hurry up."

Luke and I glance at one another as whining noises come from Stewart. Oh, to be able to see in that hole. Well, not see Betty. But to spy on those two buffoons—that would be priceless.

"I don't see anything."

"You know you're going to have to check in her blouse."

"It's not here, Dad."

"Check again!"

"Fine . . . oh, sick." Stewart's dry heaving noises have me turning my face into Luke's shoulder. He rests a hand on my head.

"Step back. Can't you do anything? Let me see her." More rustling around and grunting. "Nothing."

"I told you," comes Stewart's wounded voice.

"I don't understand. The map said it was around her heart."

I lift my head from Luke's shoulder, and we share a look. *Around her heart?* What does that mean? And what part of the map are they talking about? That's not on the version we have.

"You're sure that's what it said?" Red asks.

"I saw it, Dad. I saw it with my own eyes before that dog took off with it. But that's all I remember."

That's why they wanted the dog. Because Peg somehow had the other half of the map. But wait . . . if Stewart saw it before the dog ran off . . . I gasp as the thought hits, and Luke plants his hand over my mouth.

Ten minutes later we're shut safely in the SUV, and I give voice to one of the racing thoughts in my head. "Stewart either killed Betty or was in her trailer soon after."

Luke starts the engine. "Did you come up with that before or after you bit my hand?"

"I couldn't breathe."

"Likely story." He backs out of the field and steers us onto the dirt road. "If I have rabies, I'm giving Ashley all your assignments."

At ten o'clock, I'm in my car driving back out to Dolly's. When I wheel into the drive, most of the cars are gone. Budge's hearse is absent. No doubt he took Robbie home to be put to bed. But Mom's Tahoe is still here.

"Did you come back for more cake?" Dolly asks as I enter the living room.

"Um . . . came by to see if you needed any help cleaning up."

A brow lifts toward her teased bangs. "You came all this way to sweep and scrub down some tables?"

"Okay, I really just wanted to talk to Cherry about a few things."

Dolly jerks her head toward the back door. "She's outside feeding the dog. I swear, lately she gives her enough food to feed an entire kennel of Labradors."

I find Cherry by the pool, swishing her legs in the water as Peg rests nearby.

She looks up and smiles. "You're back?"

I ease down beside her on legs stiff from standing up so long. I weigh the contents of my brain, trying to gauge how much to tell her. How do you break it to someone that their parent-figure's grave was broken into?

"Cherry . . . Luke and I saw something pretty disturbing tonight."

"Oh. I didn't know you were still here when Breath of Death sang Clay Aiken during karaoke."

I blink twice. "Okay, though it seems impossible, I witnessed something even more frightening than that." I explain the scene Luke brought me to. I give Cherry a moment to absorb it.

"Why would Stewart and Red do such a horrible thing?" Her face is pale in the dim pool lights.

"They're looking for something. Whatever they've been digging for all over town, they were convinced it was actually *on* Betty." But if one of them killed her, wouldn't he have noticed?

"What do you think they're looking for?"

"I don't know. They said it was 'around her heart.'"

Cherry's feet still. "Look through town. Tear it apart. But the answer you seek. Is circled 'round my heart."

The air in my lungs stops. "What did you say?"

Cherry turns sad eyes to me. "It's the other half of the map."

"H-how could you know that?"

"The dog." She trails her hand down Peg's furry head. "She was gone for an entire day last week. I was crazy with worry, and it's not like I could ask anyone if they had seen her. But she came back to me." She pats Peg's neck, and her ID charm chimes in the breeze. "She's so smart like that."

"And ... ?"

"And she brought back the other half of the map." Cherry digs into the pocket of her shorts and pulls out a gnarled piece of paper. "It's the rest of it."

I unfold it and read the handwritten script.

Look through town. Tear it apart. But the answer you seek. Is circled 'round my heart.

"It's in Betty's handwriting."

"They didn't find anything tonight."

Cherry nods. "I'm scared, Bella."

"Maybe they'll find this hidden treasure or whatever, and then it will be over."

She lifts her eyes to mine. "That's not when it ends, and you know it."

I take a deep breath. "Then when do you think it's over?"

She stares into the darkness of the pool. "When I'm dead."

chapter twenty-five

$\mathcal{J}$ don't work at the carnival again until Tuesday. And by the time the three o'clock bell rings at school, my nerves are as fried as a funnel cake.

So many questions. Who put my flashlight on my clown uniform? Red? Stewart? Both? And if they do know I'm onto them, then why not just come out and say it? Why keep me around?

And as possessive of the carnival as Red is, why would he want to sell it now? Maybe he wants to get an eight-to-five gig in an office and provide a stable home for Cherry. Yeah, right. And I like K-Mart.

And this map? Where's this riddle going to lead us? Ever since Sunday night, that little rhyme of Betty's has been bouncing around in my brain. Circled 'round her heart? Why couldn't she have just said, "Hey, go to the water tower and take five steps. There it is." I mean, seriously, who hides clues in tacky poetry?

I drive straight home to check in with my mom and make myself a PB&J sandwich for work. The first week on the job, I ate dinner every night at the carnival. But a girl can't live on Sprite and hamburgers alone. Though I wouldn't mind trying.

I park the Bug in the back next to Budge's hearse and watch Robbie hop off the porch and do a double roll into the grass.

"Hey, Robbie!" I call. "Are you off to save the world?"

He squats low, his hands in karate chop position. "Yeah. I got secret intel that my cow needs me."

Every kid needs a pet. I have my cat. Lindy has a Lab. Ruthie has a lizard. But Robbie? His is of the bovine variety.

My stepbrother's red cape flutters in the warm breeze. "I have to be on my guard in case there's kryptonite on my path."

"Is that what you're calling cow poop these days?"

With arms outstretched, he flies away to save those in need, those in trouble, those who eat from troughs.

I open the screen door and step into the kitchen. Mom sits at the table, a pencil poised over her notebook. "Studying?"

She looks up and smiles. "Hey, sweetie. Yeah, I have my final Thursday." She pats the seat beside her. "How was your day? You look tired."

Can't imagine why. "Mom, what's going on with you and Jake?"

The pencil *thunks* as she sets it down. "Nothing for you to be worried about. We're just adjusting to his new career."

"You mean *he's* adjusting. We're just . . . here."

Mom's forehead wrinkles, and I wonder if she ever misses her quarterly Botox gifts from Dad. "Bella, basically overnight he went from working in a factory to being a national star. Do you realize by next Christmas they'll have a Captain Iron Jack action figure?"

"Good. If we get one, then he'll always be with us." I wince at the vinegar on my tongue. *Lord, why are nosiness and sass my spiritual gifts? Aren't I supposed to have something like peace, goodness, patience, and all that other sweet stuff?*

Mom shuts her textbook and puts her hand on mine. "I know I brought you to Truman on what seemed like a whim. But I knew marrying Jake was the right thing to do. I still believe that. And even though we didn't sign up for the way things are now, we have to have faith that it's all going to work out."

"I just don't see the end of it, though, Mom. Jake's just getting started. Let's say they retire him in ten years. Can you live like this that long?"

She nibbles on her bottom lip, her eyes on the table. "You and I aren't the only ones who didn't get what we bargained for. Jake spends every night on a bus. He wakes up each day and doesn't remember what town he's in. He misses his family."

"Then why doesn't he quit? Doesn't he feel guilty that you're the one taking care of his sons?" A year ago my mom and I couldn't have had a conversation like this. We barely knew each other. But now . . . we're friends. It's strange. But I like it.

"We're praying about it."

"For how long? When is enough *enough*?"

Mom leans over and curls her arm around me. I smile at the smell of her perfume, a fragrance she's worn all my life. It's just about the only trace of Manhattan left of her.

"Isabella, this is in God's hands. He told Jake and me both to pursue this. He didn't say go for this marriage and this wrestling career—then quit." Her fingernails trail meandering patterns on my back. "I'm going to be honest with you—things couldn't be more wrong. But it's brought me closer to God. Closer to you and the boys. And I know change is coming." She shrugs. "Could be tomorrow, could be next year. But the Lord didn't lead us through all we've been through just to desert us now."

"Mom?"

"Hmm?"

"When that change does come . . . can I have my own credit card again?"

"Bella?"

"Yes?"

"God says no."

Thirty minutes later I'm standing in the big top watching the progress of Stewart and Cherry's new routine. One swing suspends from the center of the trapeze area, and Cherry hangs from the bottom of it as Stewart is braced upside down above her. This new performance has more of a Cirque du Soleil feel to it, and I know it has to be challenging every muscle in her body. I can't imagine having to hold up your own body weight just by clinging to two ropes. And they've added a new element where Stewart will eventually unfurl her from a gigantic sash. It's pretty cool to watch, but I wouldn't want to try it.

"Amazing, aren't they?"

I turn my head as Luke approaches. He looks like he just walked off a Gap commercial, his hair curling at the ends, barely resting on the collar of his gray henley. He stands by my side, and my heart flutters like butterfly wings. I rein it back in and focus above me. "I think the new performance is too much for Cherry. Look at her arms shaking."

"She's determined to pull it off, though. She told me she wants to do this for her parents."

"You know Red wants them to nail this to impress the potential buyer."

Luke nods. "Let's hope that's all he wants out of the act."

"What do you mean?"

Luke's volume drops a notch. "This routine killed Cherry's parents. But you and I know that it might not have been an accident. So what if this is Red's psychotic way of repeating history?"

Chills flare on my skin that have nothing to do with Luke's preppy hotness. "That had crossed my mind. I just wasn't ready to put it out there and say it." It just sounds so evil. "But Stewart would have to be in on it. It's not like Red would kill his own son to get rid of Cherry."

"The question is when."

"And why. Why would he want his niece out of the way so badly?"

Luke watches the two flip until they've changed places on the swing. "Maybe he's jealous of her biceps."

"I know I am."

After the show, I pull off my sweaty clown jumpsuit and place it in the box. My neck is already hurting from looking over my shoulder every five seconds. Stewart and Red both treated me normally tonight. They pretty much ignored me—except for the occasional pervy stare from the younger Fritz. I would love to tell Stewart I would kiss Robbie's cow before I would even *consider* a date with him.

Ruthie, Luke, and I walk outside together, laughing over her unicycle ballet.

"It's not funny," Ruthie huffs. "Whoever had the bright idea to play Snoop Dogg instead of my usual *Phantom of the Opera* needs to be punished." She cracks her knuckles. "And I'm going to have some serious prayer time tonight until the Lord tells me how to go about my pain-inducing revenge."

"I had nothing to do with it. I just run the lights." Luke bites back a smile.

"So are we doing any surveillance?" Ruthie yawns. "These late nights are brutal on my beauty rest. Last night I fell asleep while Budge was telling me about this new game he created. I faded out somewhere between vector sequence and modchips."

I laugh. "I don't think it was your lack of sleep that knocked you out." More like Budge's computer lingo put her in a techie coma.

"We better back off for a while," Luke says, stopping at his 4Runner. "After what Bella and I saw Sunday evening, I don't think there's really any need to follow them. They don't know what they're doing."

Ruthie throws a leather-clad leg over her motorcycle. "I can't believe you guys left me out of that. Breaking into a dead lady's casket? I can't imagine anything cooler."

I can't imagine anything grosser. "We'll call next time."

"See that you do. You shouldn't keep something like that all to yourselves. It just isn't right." She throws up a gloved hand in a wave and zooms away. I stand there and watch her go, aware that she has a cool factor I couldn't achieve even if I had access to every one of my dad's credit cards.

Luke and I stand between our cars. Awkward. Silent.

"So, um . . . I read your latest article." He lifts his eyes from the blur that is Ruthie. "It's better."

I stiffen. "But not good enough?"

"You're distracted is all."

I listen for a hint of power-tripping arrogance, but don't hear it. "It was a perfectly fine piece, Luke."

He leans on his SUV, crossing his arms on his chest. "Nothing perfect about it. And as for fine, you're a better writer than that. I should be reading your work and thinking 'amazing' and 'creatively brilliant.'"

"Maybe you're confusing me with your new girlfriend."

With fire in his eyes, Luke pushes off the vehicle and takes the three steps that separate us. He stares down until I look up. "You have something to say, Kirkwood?"

"No." I don't know why that came out of my mouth. Like Ruthie, I'm just tired.

"I didn't think so." He shakes his head. "Because you're scared."

I draw up my spine. "I don't think *scared* girls watch men dig up graves." I give him the attitude-head-bob. "But maybe I'm wrong."

His smile could charm a snake. "You're scared of what's going on in here." He taps his own heart. "And honesty gives you that little nervous tick. *Real* scares you—admit it."

"I'm getting *real* mad. That doesn't frighten me at all."

Luke's face looms mere inches above mine. "You're jealous of Ashley."

"I am not—"

"You're so crazy about me, you can't think straight."

"Oh my gosh." I force a laugh. "Somebody needs to save you from yourself." Where're Ruthie and her nunchucks when I need them?

"And you're so prideful, you can't even see that your writing still needs work. Lots of work." Luke's voice dips low. "So quit taking it as a personal attack from your ex-boyfriend and consider it from the guy who runs the newspaper and knows what he's talking about."

Our eyes lock and hold. A clash of wills. Of friends. Of old flames.

"You really gotta do something about your split personalities," I breathe.

Luke pulls me to him and crushes his mouth to mine.

"I said I wasn't going to do this," he whispers on a kiss.

"S'okay." I pull him closer, my hands snaking up his back. "Don't mind."

His hands move up to cup my face, to tilt my head, to move his lips over mine again. "Bella?"

"Hmmm?"

I stifle a groan as Luke pulls away.

Still holding my face in one hand, he runs his finger down my nose. Over my cheek. I lean into his palm and just try to breathe. "What?"

"Do you know what this was?" he asks, his mouth near my ear.

"The warm-up?"

"A test."

My cozy smile drops. I step away.

"You're lying to yourself if you think you don't want to be with me."

"I—I"—am so mad—"it was the moonlight. It was the popcorn at nine o'clock."

Luke reaches out and brushes a piece of hair behind my ear.

"Face it—you're totally into your editor." He sighs dramatically. "I hope whatever is keeping us apart is worth it."

I stand there motionless, my tongue glued to the roof of my mouth as Luke climbs into his 4Runner. I should say something. I should yell—or maybe throw a shoe? What would Ruthie do? No. I can't moon him.

In my head fury wars with the theme song from *Pride and Prejudice* as the kiss replays in my head. Again. And again. When I glance back at Luke, I startle to realize he's waiting for me to get in my car and leave.

I give him a small wave. Yep. Going to my car. Unaffected. Absolutely unaffected. I kiss boys every day.

Starting the car.

I was born kissing boys. Boys better than you, Luke Sullivan.

Turning the key.

And that may have been a test for you. But that was just an act for me. Call me Reese Witherspoon because I have Oscar-worthy skills.

I put the car in drive and pull out of the parking lot, my brain on autopilot. His headlights shine behind me as we drive into town. At the four-way stop, I go right. He goes left.

I wheel the car into the school parking lot, put her in park, and indulge in a moment of banging my head against the steering wheel before I go on home.

"Stupid! Stupid! Stupid!" I'm *so* dumb. Why did I let him get the upper hand? Again. I like being in control. Me! This was my game. He can't just flip the rules on me.

Slowly raising my head, I take a few cleansing breaths.

I check myself out in the rearview mirror.

And see a cold-blooded killer in my backseat.

chapter twenty-six

$\mathcal{Y}$our brain does crazy things when there's a pistol aimed at your face.

Mine zooms on overload as I consider my options. There's jump out of the car. There's pray for the Rapture. And there's hope for aliens to beam down and suck Alfredo into the mother ship.

"Don't move," Alfredo says, the gun shaking slightly.

"If you shoot me, my mom will rip you in half with her bare hands." How in the world did he get in here? My car was locked—just like his handcuffs when he escaped. Dang, this guy is good. It's like you never see it coming. *Lord, I'd love to get through this alive—without peeing my pants.*

"Put your hands where I can see them. Rest them on the console."

I do as the man says, trying not to gag at the overripe smell coming from the backseat. "You seriously need a shower."

He rolls his eyes. "That's the least of my problems."

"And killing me is going to solve them?"

"I'm not killing you. I just want your attention."

I glance at the cold metal weapon. "You've got it."

"I didn't kill Betty."

"Uh-huh." I had begun to believe that myself, but now?

Alfredo rubs a hand over his bearded face. "I was set up. You have to believe me."

"Are you going to shoot me if I don't?"

He lowers the gun and sighs. "Look, people talk. I know you're like some supersleuth or something. That's why you're working at the carnival, isn't it?"

"How did you get out?"

"Dislocated bones help." The magician looks over his shoulder like a nervous cat. "I can get out of anything. It wasn't as easy as my own trick handcuffs—just two twists and a tug—but it wasn't impossible either."

"Two twists and a tug?"

"Yeah. The carnival cuffs. They're fakes, and if you move your hands right, they pop open."

"Alfredo, I don't know much about the law, but I don't think breaking out of jail is going to do much for your case. Your attorney probably isn't too happy with you right now."

Leaning forward, Alfredo wraps his arm around my passenger seat. The gun dangles loosely in his grimy hand. "I have to prove I'm innocent. Red and Stewart—those guys set me up." His eyes dart outside again. "Hey, could we, like, drive somewhere else? Someone's bound to see me here."

"Look, I've seen enough Oprah. You never agree to drive a guy with a gun somewhere. The second location is always where they find your dead, bloated corpse."

"I'm not a killer!" he shouts.

"If you want to talk, then talk." My voice tremors. This guy is seriously freaking me out. "But I'm not driving us anywhere, so say what you need to say . . . or kill me. Those are your choices." That sounded so much braver than I feel.

Alfredo closes his eyes and rests his head on the seat. "How did this all get so screwed up?" A few moments pass, and I begin to formulate a few escape plans.

"I loved Betty," he says finally. "You have to believe that."

"It doesn't matter what I believe. I hate to break it to you, but it's the judge you'll want to persuade." Seriously, does this guy know nothing about due process?

"You're the only one who can help me, though. My own lawyer thinks I'm guilty."

"Then who killed her?"

His mouth opens and closes on a hesitation. "Red and Stewart."

"What could they possibly hope to gain?" Again, the awkward pause. "I may have a small gift in crime solving, but I'm not a mind reader. Spill it."

"I don't know much. But I do know Betty was afraid of Red. She was anxious to get back to Truman. Said she had stuff to do. Something she had to get."

"Is that what Red and Stewart have been looking for?"

He nods. "Yeah. She had grown to trust me . . . but not that much. So I don't know what she left. Could've been money, incriminating photos, something for Cherry. I just don't know. But she would only tell me that she was the only one who knew about it, and she needed it to save Cherry."

"What does that mean?"

"I said I don't know!" His volume escalates with each word.

"Is this seriously all you have to bring me? I'm supposed to clear your name when you give me nothing more than your statement of innocence? And put that gun on the floorboard, will you? I can't concentrate with you waving that thing around."

"I heard you were bossy." He plops it on the floor without complaint.

"Alfredo, you have to really think about this. Scan your brain for anything weird Red or Stewart have said in the last year or so." An idea flicks to life in my own head. "I saw Red's payroll book. About the time you and Betty started dating, he gave you a raise. What's that about?"

"I loved Betty. I know we were an unlikely couple. Nobody bought it at first, but I loved her with all my heart. We were going to get married and take care of Cherry together."

"And then your sword found its way into Betty's chest."

Alfredo blinks hard, as if trying to push back the pain. "I want justice. Whoever killed my Betty, my fuzzy sweetheart—they must pay."

Ew. "You didn't answer my question. Why the sudden bump in salary?"

His eyes drop to the tan floor mat at his feet. "Times are really bad for the carnival. People started leaving before we even got to Truman, and they were not replaced. So I told Red I would work the job of two men, putting in almost eighty hours a week, and I would only ask for half an additional salary."

I study this man's outline in the glow of the streetlights. "Does Red know what he's looking for?"

"I think so."

"But he doesn't know where—even with the map."

"Map? You have Betty's map?" Alfredo straightens.

"So you know about it?"

"Of its existence, yes. That much Betty told me. You have to let me see it."

I lean back into the door and feel the handle press into my back. "I don't have to do anything." Crazy loon.

"If you let me look at it, it might make sense to me in a way that wouldn't to anyone who wasn't familiar with Betty like I was." His voice drops to a pleading whisper. "Whatever this is, it was important to Betty. And I think it has to do with protecting Cherry. I have to continue Betty's work and see this through. Then . . . I can let her go."

"Cherry thinks her life is in jeopardy."

"Then you must share the map with me. It's the only way. I won't let someone else die—not when I can prevent it."

"Where are you staying? How will I get ahold of you?"

"I can't tell you that." He settles back into the seat, slouching low. "But when you're ready to talk, put one of the carnival posters on your dash. I'll find you and leave meeting instructions."

"You've been hanging around the carnival, haven't you? Are you the one who let the horses out and all those other weird things that have everyone so spooked?" He says nothing. "This is illegal. I can't withhold information about a fugitive from the police."

He picks up the gun and moves it from one hand to the other. "Then tell them your life is at stake."

"Is that more blustery bravado?"

"Yes." He nods. "How'd I do?"

"Kinda scary."

"I learned a lot while I was locked up." Alfredo reaches for the handle and pulls. "It really is critical you not tell anyone you saw me. Cherry's life depends on it. I know you wouldn't want her death on your conscience for the rest of your life."

He slips out the door and disappears into the tree-covered lot beside the road. I watch him walk away until he blends into the night.

I have to call the police. Luke. Someone.

I flip on the overhead light and reach for my phone.

But it's gone.

Foiled by the magician.

He breaks out of handcuffs. He busts out of jail. And he steals phones.

Couldn't he just stick with pulling bunnies out of a hat?

chapter twenty-seven

By Friday morning I'm stressed to the point of snapping. I've been on edge ever since I found Alfredo in my rearview mirror. When I got out of school the following day, there, in my locked car, was my cell phone. Just waiting for me, as if it had been there all along. That Alfredo—it's like he can morph or something. He's an X-Man.

The rest of the week proved to be uneventful. No more bodies dug up. No more lights crashing at the carnival. And no posters in my car as a signal to Alfredo. I have yet to tell Cherry about my encounter. I've never withheld information from the police *or* my mom before, and I don't want to bring Cherry in on it. At least not yet. It's bad enough Luke knows. No need to upset anyone else.

"Bella, I still think we should talk to Officer Mark." Luke's voice is barely audible over the crowd at LaGuardia Airport. I press the phone closer to my ear.

"We've discussed this a million times."

"No, we've argued a million times. But I don't know that we've had a calm discussion yet." His voice drips with editor arrogance. "That's what I'm trying to attempt now, but so far it's a one-man job."

"Hey, I'm sorry, you're breaking up. Lousy reception in this airport." I hold the phone toward Ruthie, and she makes crackly noises. "Gotta go."

"Wait, Bella—"

"Yes?"

Silence on the other end. "I'm praying you have a good visit with your dad. I hope you find out what you need to know."

Wow. Hard to be snooty to a guy when he talks like that. "Thanks."

"And when you get back, we're telling Cherry everything. And maybe the police."

"Bye." I end the call and throw the phone in my purse.

Ruthie sips her Starbucks. "What did your boyfriend want?"

Why did I bring her with me to New York again? "He's not my boyfriend. And we were just having a small disagreement."

"You two wouldn't have anything to say to one another if you weren't arguing."

"I guess that would leave more time for making out." I smile as Ruthie spews her mocha. "I'm kidding." Mostly.

My purse vibrates with a text. Dad is here. Finally.

"Let's go get our bags and head to the *casa de crazy*." The teachers had a bunch of meetings today, so school was out and Ruthie and I were able to get an early flight. This gives me more time to get to the bottom of whatever Christina's hiding.

Ruthie walks along beside me, her blue and pink hair catching the stares of the occasional security guard. "So you're going to snoop a little this weekend, and I'm to provide the distractions. Just how is it I'm going to accomplish that?"

"Just be yourself."

In the taxi ride home, Dad updates me on his new highlights, his latest celebrity client, and his TV show developments. He asks few questions about me. It's a conversational rhythm I'm used to.

When we get home, I head straight for the kitchen, hug Luisa, then promptly ask her for any dirt.

"I know nothing. I see nothing. I hear nothing."

I stare my old nanny down. "In other words, you're afraid for your job."

She glances over her shoulder. "You would be to, if you were working for *Señorita* Beelzebub." Luisa makes horns over her head. "And little Marisol is her spitting image. *Querida*, I owe Maria Delgado two hundred big ones from a bad weekend of Texas Hold 'Em, so I must work. I can't give Christina any reason to replace me, you understand?"

"Do you find anything weird about her?"

Luisa hands a cookie to me and Ruthie. "This evening is bingo night at the church, and Father Joseph is the caller. It would take me all day to list what's strange about her, and I'm feeling lucky tonight. So maybe tomorrow we can talk."

She pats me on the behind and waddles away.

"What were you guys gossiping about?" Marisol peeps her head in the door. "Secret stuff?"

Ruthie looks at me and rolls her eyes. "I got three just like her at home. I can take her."

Ruthie and her sisters are the most violent preacher's kids I've ever seen. They could overpower Jake and his wrestling buddies any day. Not a dainty lady among them. It's like they were raised by a pastor *and* a pack of wolves.

"Why don't you show Marisol where the cookies are while I go talk to my dad." I give Ruthie a hard look. *Do not hurt this kid.* Any bloodshed would have a negative effect on the likelihood of my getting Dad's credit cards.

I hear Christina on the phone in the dining room and cruise past her down the hall to Dad's study. Knocking on the mahogany door, I step inside. "Hey, Dad."

He glances up from a phone call and waves me in. "Yeah, I'm really excited too. I know the show will be great. So I've got that list of ideas, and I'll just fax them to you, okay? See you at the wedding. *Até logo.*" Dad hangs up and smiles. "How's my girl?"

"Wow, were you just speaking Portuguese?"

He clasps his hands behind his head and leans back in his desk chair. "I've been seeing a language tutor. When we go to Brazil, I want to be able to communicate with the filming crew."

I settle into a leather wingback chair. "Dad, um, I wanted to talk to you about something."

He wags a finger at me. "You know you can't have that boob job until graduation."

Am I the only girl on the planet whose dad discusses these things like it's as mundane as getting a new sweater at Abercrombie? "No, I don't want to talk about that." Nor do I want anyone taking a knife to the girls, thank you very much. "I know it's none of my business, but I just wanted to talk to you about this prenup you've got with Christina."

His eyes narrow. "How do you know there's a prenup?"

"Marisol. She said you guys met with your attorney."

"Christina's attorney, yes." There's an edge to his voice, but I trod on.

"You didn't each have your own?"

"You know money's tight around here. I'm trying to rebuild my investments and prepare for the move. So we thought we'd save and just have one lawyer draw up the contract. Christina's was cheaper. I really don't see how this is your concern."

My expression is as innocent as a baby's. "Because I love you, and I worry about you. I know money's an issue, and I don't want to see you hurt." *And when you date losers, my inner radar goes off like a microwave timer.*

Dad's mouth grows into a smile. "I understand the accountant situation bothered you, sweetheart. But this time it's under control. I adore Christina and trust her completely. We want the same things. Besides, she didn't exactly walk out ahead of the game in the prenup."

"What do you mean?"

He lowers his voice a notch. "Usually in these deals, you settle on a percentage of your assets. But all she asked for was five hundred grand. Just a flat amount in the event of our divorce." He leans across his desk. "Bella, when the money for this show contract comes in, I'm going to be worth a lot more than that. So don't worry about your old dad. I'm getting a wife I love, and on the off chance it doesn't work out, I have a new career direction *and* my money."

"Uh-huh." Why doesn't this make me feel better? You have to be suspicious of the things that sound too good to be true. "So is there anything in the contract that would make the agreement void? I mean, what if she's cheating on you?"

"Like that's going to happen." He winks. "She's crazy about me. But our attorney advised me to just keep it simple. So no matter the reasons for a split, she gets the money. And I keep everything else. But listen, while I appreciate your concern, nothing is going to go wrong. Christina and I plan on having a long future together."

That's what Mom thought once upon a time too. "Okay." I walk to his side and kiss his stubbly cheek. "I worry about you sometimes. I love you, you know?"

He takes my hand and clasps it in both of his. "I love you too, my Isabella. And when you see me on that TV show, you're going to be so proud of your old dad."

"I am proud of you."

"But this will be even better." He gives my fingers a squeeze. "You'll see. It's going to be amazing."

"Can't things be amazing right here—in Manhattan?" Is it so wrong to want my dad close and not half a world away? Sometimes at night, I picture this fantasy where my dad starts to board the plane to Brazil, then turns around and runs back. He swings me around in his arms and says, "I couldn't leave you. Do you really think I could move so far away and leave my girl behind? You mean more to me than any job offer." And then we hug and laugh. And go shopping.

A shrieking Marisol explodes into the office and pops my fantasy bubble.

"What's wrong?" Dad opens his arms, and the little girl sails right into them as if she was custom made for that place.

"She—she scared me."

Ruthie peeks in her multicolored head. "I have no idea why she's so upset." She walks to my side. "One minute we were talking, and the next she went to freaky town."

"She hasn't spent much time with her big sister lately and is feeling a little down." Dad rubs Marisol's head as she glares at me and Ruthie like a pit bull about to strike. "Come on, let's go find Christina and raid the fridge for some ice cream."

"Okay," she sniffs.

My dad's hand curls around her small one, and I feel something grip in me as well. Right in the heart region. *God, am I ever going to get over this jealousy? It's not just that I'm envious—I'm hurt. Why can't he treat me with half as much care as he shows Marisol?*

The two slide out of the room, and I blink as Marisol sticks out her tongue just before she disappears.

Ruthie clenches her fists. "That little—"

I hold out my arm and block her charge. "Sit down. It's not worth it." I pick up my dad's discarded cell phone and quickly copy down the last number. I might need to call his contact at this Brazilian reality show and ask a few questions. For journalistic purposes, of course.

"Do you know what that little rat said to me in the kitchen?" Ruthie asks.

"She liked your hair?"

"It is looking good today, isn't it?" Ruthie gives it a pat. "No, that little skunk told me that if I didn't give her twenty bucks, she was going to tell your dad that I kicked her in the shins."

"She didn't mention any violence to Dad, so how'd you show her who was boss?"

"I might've accidentally let her see my slingshot." Ruthie shrugs casually. "Sometimes it just slips out of my pocket, you know?"

Later that afternoon I stand in the dressing room of Enrique's House of Design.

"You are lucky I let you back in my shop. You realize that, don't you?" Enrique flips his scarf over his shoulder and grabs his latte from a burger-deprived assistant. "I rescheduled the First Lady just to fit you and your"—Enrique sneers—"stepdaughter in."

Ruthie sits on the edge of her chair. "The first lady? Like Madonna—the first lady of pop? Or Paris Hilton, the first lady of spray tan? Or maybe Dolly Parton, the first lady of cleavage?"

"Silence!" Enrique shoves the latte away and rubs his temples. "Your talking is upsetting the creative vibes in this studio. I meant the President's wife."

"Somebody is snippy," Ruthie whispers toward me, loud enough for all to hear. "Do you think I should offer him some of my Midol?"

"I'll just try on that dress now!" I step in front of the designer with my most angelic smile. "Can't wait to see it . . . again."

"You scoffed at its beauty last time."

"I was young and foolish then."

He nods once. "Very well." He claps his hands, and the skinny assistant reappears. "Get me the Christina De Luna bridesmaid dress."

Ten minutes later I'm sneezing my head off and trying to secure the feather boa straps. "*Achoo!*"

"Come out so Enrique can fit it," Christina calls.

I waddle out in the tight confection. It's literally a pink trash bag with feathers hot-glued everywhere.

"Oh!" My future stepmother gasps when I step outside the

dressing room. "It's heaven, Enrique. I just lose my mind every time I see it."

Ruthie tilts her head to one side, then the other. "I can see why."

"Spin for Enrique," the man says. You have to wonder about people who refer to themselves in third person.

I turn in a half circle, and he grabs the extra material at my waist. "Ow!" I frown at the pins in his fingers. "You stuck me."

"Fashion is pain, darling."

I send a pleading look to Christina, but her eyes go wide in warning.

By the time Enrique finishes, the dress is too tight, I can't move, and I look like a reject from a cross-dresser's garage sale. "It's very tight. Having trouble breathing."

"You are a little blue," Ruthie says. "But it's a nice color for you. Complements your plumage."

"It's perfect as it is." Enrique spins on his heel and faces Christina. "You like?"

She clasps her hands over her heart. "It's a dream. And yes, it's just the right fit."

"Yeah, if your goal is to suffocate me." Which I don't doubt. "But if you expect me to walk in this, it needs to be let out some." Plus, I like my wedding cake. Gotta have room in the dress for that.

"If Enrique says it's fine, then it is." Christina laughs and tosses her black hair. "We would be foolish to argue with a genius, right?"

He chuckles as well, a high-pitched sound that would make a chicken give up her feathers.

"Achoo!" Ruthie's sneeze echoes off the walls. "Ah-ah-ah-choo!"

"It's her allergies," Christina says, helping Ruthie to her feet. "Nothing more."

"No." My friend points to my dress. "Actually, I think it's that frock of a—"

"We'll just step outside." Christina pushes Ruthie toward the door. "We'll be down at the corner drugstore getting her some decongestant."

"*Achoo!*"

The designer's eyes narrow as they exit.

"I'll change now." I shuffle back to the dressing room, my feet moving inches at a time.

"Do not disturb my pins."

"Wouldn't dream of it."

It takes me fifteen minutes to get the tube of fluff off my body. And I only stick myself six times—if you just count the ones that drew blood.

I sigh with appreciation as I slip into my Rock & Republic jeans and T-shirt. "Here you go." I pass the dress off to the assistant, who takes it with a look of fear. "Don't worry. I'm pretty sure it's dead."

Enrique meets me at the entrance. "Tell Christina the dress will be ready next Wednesday."

"Okay."

"And I will need to know who will be picking this one up. Her or her sister." He clucks his tongue. "When the flower girl's dress was picked up, there was a small security issue. I don't hand my art over to just anyone. How was I to know that woman was family?"

"What do you mean her sister? Marisol is only eight."

He fingers the ends of his scarf. "No. Last week I met the other one."

My brain shudders as if ice water just fell over my head. "What do you mean *the other one*?"

"The tall blonde." Enrique covers his mouth to whisper. "Though it's so obvious she's as real a blonde as Beyoncé. I don't know why she's not in the wedding, but I don't ask. I tell myself, Enrique, you must not butt into your client's business. Did I butt into Brad and Angelina's? No. I am a professional. But sometimes I do have a little talk with Katie Holmes. Not that she listens."

"Oh. Uh-huh. The blonde sister." Thinking . . . thinking . . . "I, um, come to Manhattan so infrequently I don't get to see her and Christina much. Plus, I like to devote most of my time to Marisol." *Dear God, please wait 'til later to strike me down for lying.* "You know, maybe you can help me. I was going to get Christina and her sisters a little wedding present to celebrate the fun day." I rest my hand on his arm like we're old friends. "I bought the most divine jewelry boxes from Tiffany's and want to have them engraved. Do you know how you spell her sister's name?"

"The little one?"

"No. The other one."

"I don't know." He shrugs off my hand. "I was not born to spell. I was born to design. I suppose it is like the car."

"What do you mean?"

Enrique stares at me as if I have cotton candy for brains. "A Mercedes. I would imagine it's spelled the same."

"Mercedes?" That's her sister's name? "Of course. How silly of me." I push open the door and gaze toward the street. "Thank you, Enrique. I have truly been enlightened today."

And now to find out who this Mercedes is.

And arrange a family reunion.

chapter twenty-eight

*Y*ou invited *who* over for dinner?"

"I've said it twice already, Bella. Mr. and Mrs. Penbrook and their son, Hunter, are coming over for dinner." Dad unknots his tie and leaves it dangling around his neck. "We've had this Friday night event planned for some time. I couldn't get out of it just because my daughter once dated their son. Jeff and I are still really good friends."

"Great. Just great." I stomp out of the living room and up to my bedroom. I need to find something to wear. What kind of outfit is appropriate for facing your ex after he cheated on you, then duped you on national television? "Hey, Ruthie, do you mind if I accessorize with your brass knuckles tonight?"

I flop next to her on the bed where she watches *Wheel of Fortune*. "That Vanna has such a cake job." She turns up the volume as a contestant buys a vowel. "That's what I want to be when I grow up. Well, either that or a brain surgeon."

"I didn't get a chance to talk to Dad about Christina. She walked in from work just as I was about to broach the subject."

"Bummer. Have you tried texting him?"

I think about this. "You want me to text my father that his fiancée is a lying schemer conducting shady dealings?"

Ruthie rolls her eyes. "Get with the times."

An hour later my old flame, Hunter Penbrook, asks me to pass the peas. I pick up the bowl, only briefly imagining dumping them over his head.

His smile is devilishly cute. "If you drop those in my lap, I will be forced to cause a scene." His hand brushes mine as he takes the bowl, and I realize I don't feel a thing. Nary a flutter nor a tingle. Why is it when Luke touches me, I instantly quiver like Jell-O?

Ruthie holds the dinner crowd's attention with her reenactment of her unicycle routine using salad tongs, the pepper grinder, and two stuffed mushrooms. My dad and Hunter's parents stare in amazement, while Christina studies her nails and Marisol stabs holes in her baked potato.

I take this opportunity to speak to Hunter. "You haven't called in a while. Are you still keeping tabs on that hotel room?"

"As much as I can. I told you I would let you know if I had anything to report."

"I like updates, Hunter. Updates."

"I do not miss your nagging."

I smile into my napkin and wipe my mouth. "I know. I'm too much girl for you. It's no wonder we didn't work."

"I've put in a lot of stalking time for you, so I wouldn't push it."

We share a laugh, and I realize once again, I have forgiven him. When Jesus said to forgive people to infinity, I assumed my ex-boyfriend was the exception. But it's kind of freeing not to be mad or holding a grudge. Besides, I need his cheating eyes on door number 857.

"You're a wily guy. Can't you draw her out of her room?" In a tiny whisper I fill him in on the new Christina development.

"Mercedes?" He chews this over. "I need a last name to get you any information."

"Christina's is De Luna. Try that."

"The woman is a hermit. If she leaves at all, it's while I'm at school."

I slice into my steak. "Maybe you could set up a hidden camera."

"And maybe I could go to jail."

"You'd do that for me?" I set down my utensils. "I'm touched."

"Bella, just give it up."

"How can I?"

"The wedding is June fifteenth. I think your best bet is to simply talk to your dad."

I nearly choke on my bite. "That's funny, I thought you had met the guy." I point toward the end of the table. "Dark-haired fellow. Works 24-7 and forgets I'm alive. He's the chap sitting across from your father."

Hunter glances that way just as the two men share a laugh. "It's good to see my dad happy. I haven't seen that in a long time."

"I'm sorry." I watch Mr. Penbrook high-five my dad as they share a joke. "I know he hasn't ever recovered from the accountant fiasco." My dad and Mr. Penbrook had the same bogus financial guru. Dad has slowly bounced back, since he lost cash and not his practice. But Hunter's father wasn't so lucky. He wasn't in the business of nose jobs and inflatable boobs, and ended up losing almost everything.

"It's okay. Things are turning around. He and my mom actually went on a date together last weekend. For a while I didn't think they were going to make it."

I know how that feels. "I'll bet you being out of the house and spying on that hotel room gives your parents even more alone time."

Hunter laughs. "You're about as smooth as a rattlesnake. But I'll get back to my Peeping Tom duties this week."

"Not just anyone would stalk a lady for me, Hunter." I pat his arm. "And I appreciate it. You're a good guy."

His eyes grow serious. "Really?"

"Yeah. And to thank you, I'm going to set you up with this girl I know named Ashley Timmons..."

On Saturday, Ruthie and I wake up late to find muffins on the kitchen counter with a note from Dad. The house is empty.

I pour myself a glass of juice. "Dad had to go in to work for a bit, and Christina took Marisol to dance lessons."

"'That kid neeths politeness wessons," Ruthie says around a full mouth of muffin. "She has no mannerth."

Says the girl who just spit out two blueberries. "I think we should get ready and pay my dad a visit. We have business to do."

"Whoa." Ruthie swallows her giant bite. "I don't have any business with a plastic surgeon. I don't want anything plucked, sucked, or tucked."

"We're just going to talk. I didn't get a chance to speak to him last night about that designer saying Christina had a sister."

"Maybe her sister's a member of a terrorist network, and Christina's only trying to protect your family. Or maybe her sister is a communist, and she and Christina have a plan for world domination . . . one plastic surgeon at a time."

I roll my eyes and take another swig of juice. "And this is why I'm the crime solver and you're the sidekick."

After a twenty-minute taxi ride, Ruthie and I climb out of the cab and take the elevator to my dad's clinic.

Walking into the lobby, I greet the twin receptionists. "Hi, Kim. Hi, Leslie." I have never been able to tell them apart, but Dad swears he can. He also swears they speak English, but I think their sole qualification is hotness.

"You go see your dad?" one asks.

The other shakes her bleach blonde head. "He very busy. Important client."

I smile at the two standing in front of a water fountain backdrop. "Good thing I'm his daughter and he *always* has time for me." I grab

Ruthie by the hand and lead her down the hall. "Walk quickly. Dad said they both have their black belts, so I don't want to push my luck."

Ruthie snorts. "Like I'm afraid of a black belt. Dude, I got street cred."

"Yeah, Main Street in Truman. I'm sure they're shaking in their push-up bras."

I zip us around a corner and power walk down the next hall. At the last door on the right, I rap my hand in a hearty knock. "It's me, Dad."

"Bella?" I hear him inside, getting up from his desk. The door opens a crack. "This better be an emergency. I'm with a client."

"Oh, it's a crisis all right."

His frown is not encouraging. "Like the crisis last year when you needed me to choose which shoes I thought looked the best with your skirt?"

"You should be glad I value your opinion." I try to peek in to see if his client is famous, but he stands in my way.

"Go to the nearest waiting room and hang out there. I'll get you when I'm through with my patient."

"Is it anyone I know?" I whisper.

He leans close. "Yes."

"Gonna tell me who it is?"

"Not on your life." Dad smiles and pats me on the shoulder. "But she was nominated for an Oscar last year."

Half an hour later Ruthie and I are back in his office, the surgery-requiring actress long gone. Dad is really crafty at protecting his clients' identity. I can't say it's a quality I respect about him.

"So tell me what brought you all the way to my office." Dad sits behind his desk and steeples his fingers. "I know it has to be something important or you'd be shopping right now."

"A girl can only shop so much," Ruthie says, eyeing the objects on his desk.

"Yes, I know." Dad grins at my friend. "And my daughter can shop *so much*, I sometimes think I need a second job."

Ruthie lifts a big rubber squishy ball. "What do you call this? A weight?"

I share a smile with my dad. "I call it a D cup."

"Ew." Ruthie drops it back to its resting place.

"State your business, Bella. I don't like to work late on Saturdays."

Oh, how to proceed? How do you tell your dad that his future wife is up to something? That you don't think he truly knows the real Christina? "Um . . . well . . . I have been having some weird moments with Christina the last few times I've been here."

Dad's leather chair squeaks as he lounges back. "Honey, you know she's been stressed with the wedding plans, her job, not to mention retooling my career with this TV show. The Brazil deal is a risk, and we're both staying pretty keyed up."

"A few weeks ago we were trying on dresses. And she told me she was going to call some clients and sent me to get a coffee. I came back early and saw her not on the phone. But talking to . . . some woman."

Dad's face is as bland as oatmeal. "Are you kidding me with this?"

"They were arguing. The woman had obviously come to meet her and talk. And Christina kept telling her that she wouldn't back out, that she would go through with their plan. Dad, I know it sounds crazy, but I just have this feeling."

"You're a teenager. It's called hormones."

"You got that right." Ruthie harrumphs. "Last week they took over my face in a zit attack."

"Okay, so yesterday I'm back at the same dress shop." Where I was again violated by chicken feathers and Enrique's assault on fashion. "And the designer asked me about Christina's sister. And he didn't mean Marisol. He said her blonde sister Mercedes had picked up a dress."

Dad leans an elbow on the shiny black desk and rubs the bridge of his nose. "You're giving me a stress headache. And stress headaches lead to crow's feet."

Oh, quit being such a girl! "Would you please listen to me?"

His hand drops with a slap to the desk. "I am. And I don't like what I'm hearing."

"Then can you explain any of this?"

"Bella, what is there to explain? I have no idea what you're talking about, but I'm sure it's all a big misunderstanding. We all know about that overactive, suspicious imagination of yours."

Beside me Ruthie bites her lip to cover a smile. That traitor.

"How do you explain her sister?"

"I'm sure Enrique was mistaken." Impatience flows with Dad's every word. "Marisol is her only sister, her only family. When Marisol was only a baby, Christina—"

"Yes, brought her from Brazil all by herself." On the back of a donkey. Or swimming the ocean with only a piece of driftwood. Or holding on to the wings of a swarm of migrating butterflies. "And do you really think it's in your best interest that your own attorney wasn't involved in your prenup?"

"That's none of your business." Dad stands up. "Actually none of this is. I believe you need to get back home. Now."

I jump to my feet and step toward the desk. "Dad, I know something's wrong here, and you're too blinded by Latin love to see it."

"Do you need me to call you a cab?"

A clock ticks on his desk as we fall into silence. Staring each other down like two enemies about to draw pistols. Instead of a father. And his daughter.

"I know this adjustment has been hard on you." The angles of Dad's face soften. "But you need to accept it once and for all that your mother is married and has moved on. And I'm going to be married. Your mom and I will never be together."

"Is that what you think this is about? Some juvenile wish for my parents to be together? I love my life in Truman." My words are pointed arrows, and I let them fire. "I can't imagine going back to how things were. I have two parents there who love me and are involved in my life."

"That's enough, Bella."

"Jake calls me from the road. Just to talk to me. My *stepdad* calls me more than my own father. And Mom makes me breakfast and goes to my school events. We have family game night and go to church together. And you think I want what we used to have?" I shake my head as a tear drips to my cheek. "I could never settle for second-rate parenting again. I have a real family now, and I deserve that. I deserve people who love me on a full-time basis."

He swallows and blinks. "You know I love you."

"On your terms." Now my nose is dripping. I'm totally snot-crying. "And you know what, Dad? It's not good enough anymore. I've been trying to get your attention for years. And I'm sick of it. I happen to be a great daughter. And I've changed this year, and you haven't even noticed. You know why? Because you never even knew me in the first place." I sniff and pick up my purse. "Let's go, Ruthie."

"Isabella, you stop right there."

But I keep walking. I'm done with this conversation. And done with trying to win my father's love.

chapter twenty-nine

Some people have their prayer closets. I have my prayer Volkswagen.*

I sit in my Bug Monday after school, my head on the steering wheel, and just spill my heart out to God.

Lord, my life pretty much stinks. Like week-old beans. Like Budge's shoes. Like the cafeteria on sauerkraut day. I left my dad's with nothing resolved. I don't know anything more about Christina and her mystery sister. I thought Marisol would cough up the details, but she played ignorant when I quizzed her two days ago. And Dad and I aren't even speaking. I just knew he would tell me how sorry he was. Nope. Nor did he act like he even cared a bit about all the info I dug up on his fiancée. He trusts her more than me, and she's totally shady! I need help, God. I need strength and wisdom and ice cream and sprinkles—

Tap! Tap!

I jump at the rapping on my passenger window.

Luke frowns down at me from the other side of the car. "Open up."

"Go away."

"You've been a hag all day."

"Take your sweet talk somewhere else." My cheeks burn with the embarrassment of just being caught whining to Jesus about my life. Most girls could've at least made it out of the school parking lot.

Luke leans his arms on the car and presses his forehead to the window. The breeze plays with his dark hair. "Talk to me, Bella."

I start the car. "Gotta go."

"Open this door or you'll be driving through Truman with a new hood ornament."

This image brings a small smile to my face.

"You have five seconds to unlock this door, or else I call your mother and tell her about your current pursuit of a murderer."

Click!

"Much better," Luke says as he slides in.

The car instantly smells like him, which only serves to muddle my head even more. "I don't have time for boys," I mumble.

"Bella, I've been thinking."

"You want to put me back on my weekly feature for the newspaper?"

"Not yet." He picks up a CD resting between us. "Been listening to some John Mayer?"

Luke and I have little in common. But one thing we do share is our closet love of all things Mayer. Seriously, I hear that piano and husky voice, and I melt on contact. Luke said it didn't have *quite* the same effect on him.

I snatch the CD back. "I have things to do, so I'll see you at the carnival."

He twists in the seat until his back is pressed to the door. "I want to know what's going on with you. You had at least three good opportunities to snip back at Ashley today in journalism, and you didn't take a single one."

I run my finger over the bumps and plains of the steering wheel. "Bad weekend with my dad." I tell him about Mercedes. "And when I confronted my dad with all this fishy stuff about his fiancée, he just blew me off. He is such a jerk."

"Jerk's a bad word? And here all this time I thought it was just your endearment for me."

"Do you know what I'd do if I were still living in Manhattan?"

His voice is as low as Mayer's. "Tell me."

"I'd go to a spa and just spend the whole day getting pampered and forget about all my troubles."

"I'll never understand the appeal of mud baths."

"I want my dad to pick me, you know? Just once I want to be his priority. I want to be able to look back on our relationship and know that I was well and truly loved."

"I like you."

I roll my eyes. "You don't count."

"You've made that abundantly clear."

"I mean nobody can replace my dad. Not even Jake."

"What about God?"

"He tends to forget to send me birthday cards," I quip. "It's just not the same. Yeah, I get he's the father of all fathers. But I want Kevin Kirkwood to man up and treat me right. I want to be . . . enough."

Luke pulls my hand until I'm leaning on him. "You are enough." He kisses the top of my head and wraps an arm around me. "Your dad has to be a selfish moron to not want to spend time with you."

"And to not listen to my voice of reason."

Luke's chest rumbles in a laugh. "That too. Maybe you could try talking to him again. Don't overload him with all your Christina stuff. Just tell him how you feel about the two of you."

"Honesty is so hard. Why can't people just say what they want?"

"I ask myself that question all the time."

I raise my head. Luke's fingers filter through the hair at my temple.

His eyes drop to my lips. "I'm not going to kiss you again, so don't even look at me like that."

"But you want to."

"But I'm not."

I lean in a centimeter.

"Move back, or you'll be the first girl I've ever elbowed in the ribs."

"Why?"

"Because I don't believe in hitting girls."

I smile. "No, why won't you kiss me?"

He removes his arm. "Because you're worked up about your dad. You're hurt and confused. If you kissed me, it wouldn't be about you and me. It would be about me being . . . an ice cream substitute."

"The honor couldn't get much higher."

He pats my knee like he's my grandpa. "Want to pray?"

"I'd rather make out."

Luke reaches for my hand again and none-too-gently tilts my head 'til it's bowed. "God, I pray for healing for Bella and for her relationship with her dad. I pray she would see that no matter what happens in her family, you truly are all the father she needs. Give her the strength and the courage to give all her pain to you. Help her see that not all guys are going to hurt her or leave her. Help her to trust the men you have put in her life. God, I pray that—"

"Lord, I ask that Luke realize I am a fabulous writer and let me have my column back. If this is dating retaliation, help him to get over it. I know the pain of not being able to have me right now is like a dagger to his black heart. And I—" Luke squeezes my hand 'til I shut up.

"Jesus, give Bella and me the wisdom to figure out our . . . friendship."

"And—" I get the hand squeeze again, so I let him continue.

"Give us the wisdom to deal with the carnival issue the best way. Help us to act with integrity and do what's right. And protect us."

Okay, let's wrap it up. "In Jesus' name, amen."

His thumb strokes across my hand. "Amen."

"I've been thinking about something." I watch my hand in

his and wonder if he knows he's still holding on. "This integrity business..."

"Yeah?"

"You want me to go to the police about Alfredo, don't you?" I ask.

"I'd sleep a lot better knowing we weren't doing anything illegal. Not to mention the thought of a guy charged with murder showing up in your car doesn't exactly give me nice, peaceful dreams."

Like a good facial, it finally sinks in. Luke cares about me. He genuinely cares about me. Not because my dad goes to parties with Hollywood elite. Not because my mom ruled Manhattan society. And not because I have a closet full of Prada, Gucci, and Zac Posen. He's been telling me this all along, and I just couldn't hear it. But my heart is still such a work in progress. I've come miles since moving to Truman, and I don't mean the frequent flyer kind. But it's still so scary. To be with someone and just be yourself. It's like going to Wal-Mart without makeup. Do I dare?

"Bella?"

"Mmmm?"

"Let's go talk to the police."

Way to rain on my warm, giddy moment. Men. They're so un-romantic. "Fine. But Luke?"

"Yeah?"

"You're a cute boy ... but you're no Rocky Road."

chapter thirty

*Y*ou did *what?*"

"Shhh!" I hold a shaking finger to my lips. "Keep it down, would you, Cherry?"

"But why would you tell the police about Alfredo?"

I want to say, "Sister, do you even *know* how hard that was?" Officer Mark was furious I had waited so long. Actually, furious doesn't quite touch it. I thought he was going to go all *Terminator* at the Truman PD.

"Withholding that information is a crime," Luke says. "And the police need all the help they can get to solve this case."

"But they think they already have their man—Alfredo." Cherry paces three steps in the big top, then returns. "And what's the harm that he's out? He didn't hurt you. And he didn't kill Betty. Alfredo says Red and Stewart did."

Luke crosses his arms. "What do you mean 'he says'?"

Cherry hesitates. "When I got to visit him in jail a few weeks ago. He told me everything he knew. And he said Red and Stewart had set him up."

"Has Alfredo approached you?" Why the sudden change in Alfredo's defense? This girl is not on the up-and-up. "Have you seen him since he escaped?"

"No!" Her eyes dart all around, then she lowers her tone. "I just know in my heart he's innocent. You weren't there. For the last six months Betty raised me. And I saw her fall in love with Alfredo. And he loved her. I've realized he couldn't fake that."

"Actually, he could."

"Bella," Luke warns.

Well, he could. Guys are like master fronters. "Cherry, when Alfredo and I had our little *meeting*, he seemed very interested in the map."

"Of course he would be. Betty told him it existed. Just not where it was."

"Are you sure you don't know where the map leads?" Luke asks.

"No. If I did, I'd be searching myself. Did Alfredo tell you why he wants to see it?"

Luke looks at me and nods.

"Yes." How to soften this? "He, um, said that you were in danger. That Betty was protecting you from something, and the map was somehow the answer to making sure you were safe."

Cherry's mascara-coated eyes widen. "You've known this for almost a week, and you didn't tell me?"

"I wouldn't feel left out," Luke mutters.

"Okay, so I'm not good at sharing information. I'm a bit of an evidence hog. And, Luke, if you don't quit rolling your eyes . . ." I focus my attention back on Cherry. "I don't think Alfredo is telling us everything he knows. I'm . . . I'm turning him over to the police tonight."

"Why?" Her voice is childlike. Desperate. "How?"

"Alfredo told me when I was ready to discuss the map, I needed to leave a carnival poster on my dash, and he'd contact me with directions to meet. So I'm going to put a flyer in my car tonight and wait for him to find me."

"I hate that part."

I turn on Luke. "Officer Mark said it was the only way."

"You know the drill." Intense eyes stare at me from behind his glasses. "Don't go anywhere alone, let me know where you are at all times, don't—"

"Luke, you drive me nuts."

He lifts a brow. "I think I proved that in the car when we almost—"

"Okay!" I cut him off. "Anyway, I'm not asking your permission, Cherry. I'm just updating you. This is your life we're talking about here, and I thought you should know. You need to be on guard too. If you see *any* sign of Alfredo or anything suspicious, you have to tell us. Or the police. Officer Mark is going to have a uniformed cop here every night and day."

Cherry bites her lip and looks in the distance at the carnival crew getting ready for the big show. "I was wrong to believe the police report and think Alfredo killed Betty. I don't care if his prints were the only ones on that sword, you're about to put an innocent man back in prison when he clearly escaped to solve Betty's murder . . . and keep me alive." She walks away on her muscular aerialist's legs.

"That went well." What have I done? Did I make the wrong decision? "Why is she suddenly so sure Alfredo didn't do it? What's changed?"

"You know you had to talk to the police," Luke says. "Let God handle the rest."

One hour and two snow cones later, I stand in the back and watch a white-gloved Ruthie juggle softballs as she turns circles on her unicycle. The crowd claps to the beat of Michael Jackson's "Bad." Only Ruthie.

I'm pulled away from the sight as Frank, the horse trainer, approaches. "You're Bella, right?"

"Yes."

"Note for you."

I open the folded notebook paper and scan the message. Ice explodes in my veins.

I know who you are. And I know what you're doing here.
Mind your own business, and I might let you live.
In the meantime . . .
I'll be sharpening my blade.

"Wait!" I run after Frank. "Who gave this to you?"

He shrugs nonchalantly. "I don't know. Some townie kid."

"What does that mean?"

"A customer. Some kid. Said a guy handed it to him and paid him with a buck."

"What did the guy look like? Was he skinny? Tall? Did he look like Alfredo? Maybe like Red?"

"I don't know! Who cares?"

"Can you find the kid again?"

"I'm up in five minutes. And I couldn't care less who sent you the love note."

"This is not a love note. It's—" A threat on my life. Visions of Betty race through my head. "Please. It's important."

"I wasn't even paying attention. I was messing with one of the horses out back. Couldn't pick the kid out of a two-man lineup."

I watch Frank disappear as my pulse escalates beneath clammy skin.

"Everything okay here?"

With a yelp I do a one-eighty and find the new magician standing right behind me. "Hey—" What's his name? "Um, Artie."

"Relax. It's just me." His face is void of all emotion, just like his monotone voice. "Everything okay here?"

"Did you send me a note?" What if it's him? I've had a weird feeling about this man from the get-go.

"Note?"

Does this guy ever speak in sentences consisting of more than three words? "Yes, a note. Did you send a note by way of a kid?"

"Get a scary message?"

"How did you know it was scary?"

Artie's eyes meander to the paper in my hand. "All your screamin' has me thinkin' in that direction." He spits on the ground. "Could be wrong. Can I look at it?"

With lightning speed, I throw my hand behind my back. "Nothing to see. Don't—don't worry about it." *I'll do enough for both of us.*

"Somebody threaten you?" he drawls. "I could help."

Oh, I'll just bet you could.

"Artie!" Red breaks through the curtain, his face as bright as his name. "You're up in thirty seconds. Get out there, you lazy mutt!"

"Yessir." Alfredo's replacement strolls toward Red, but before he disappears into the big top crowd, he turns around, his eyes as hard as bullets. "You be careful and watch your back. Anything could happen here."

My body convulses in a shiver, and I fight back the urge to ralph all over my clown shoes. Big inhale . . . big exhale . . . big inhale . . .

Officer Mark told me I had to tell my mom if anything else happened. But I can't. If someone's targeting me, then I'm close to the truth. And the sooner this is over, the sooner Cherry will be safe. And the right killer, whether it's Alfredo or a Fritz, will be behind bars.

I have to find Frank again. He could tell me who was around him with the horses. And perhaps *that* person could identify the kid who brought the note. The note that spells out my scary, sharpy, pokey death.

Ruthie steps behind the curtain, clutching a handful of roses. "How was I? I felt a little off tonight, like my emotional intensity wasn't quite there. But look at all this." She jerks her chin toward her multicolored bouquet. "My people love me."

"Great. Yeah." Wonderful. Cherry and I could both be dead soon. "Maybe you could throw your pretty flowers on my cold casket."

"Jealous much?" Ruthie snaps a bud from its stem and tucks it above her ear. "I mean, I knew you were envious of my mad figure-eight skills, but I didn't know it ran *this* deep."

I shove the threatening note in her face. "Read it."

"'I know who you are. And I know what—'"

"Silently."

Her lips move as her eyes scan over every word. "This is not good. In fact, I'd say it pretty much stinks."

"I need to talk to Frank, the guy who does the horse tricks. I'll be back."

"No way you're going alone. I don't want Luke mad at me." She grabs a water bottle and follows me through the back exit.

The generators hum and sputter as we make our way through the menagerie of people, trailers, and animals. I head toward the horse area.

I spot Frank's wife, Serena, brushing a horse the color of a cloud. "Have you seen your husband?"

Her head shoots up with a frown. "Why do you want to know?"

Ruthie steps forward. "He was asking me about unicycling."

"Oh really?"

"Yeah. I get a lot of requests for tips and instructional tutoring. I'm sure you know how that goes."

Serena sniffs and ignores us.

"Frank said he wants me to create a routine for you—a special love song."

Her grooming stills. "He said that?"

Ruthie nods. "He told me nothing could express his deep, burning love like a unicycle ballet."

She runs her hand down the horse's flank, then continues her brushstrokes. "It's his break, so I'd check the Ferris wheel. He's probably smoking with Kent, the guy who runs the machine."

"Thanks," Ruthie says and drags me by the hand. "Snap out of it. You're weirding me out." As we walk, she reaches into her deep clown pocket and pulls out her phone.

"Now is not the time to text a love note to Budge!" We hang a left at the carousel.

"I'm not," she barks. "I only do that on the minutes that end in an eight. And right now"—she consults her leather-strapped watch—"it's only nine twenty-two. So let's hurry this up. I thought of a new poem for my Budgy-wudgy-poo."

My urge to barf just returned.

"If you must know, I'm texting Luke."

I stop midstride. "He has you watching me, doesn't he?"

Ruthie finishes her message and drops her phone back in her suit. "Luke means business about keeping you safe." She does hubba-hubba eyebrows. "And about you in general. Come on."

I focus on the Ferris wheel and watch it come closer, spinning happy people in perfectly timed revolutions. They sit up there and watch the world, completely unaware that death could be lurking beneath them.

"Let's take the back way." Ruthie snakes behind the trailers and game booths, giving us a view that's like turning over a piece of embroidery, revealing the knots and guts of the carnival.

"Kent, I don't care how cute the ladies are!"

Ruthie and I stop at Red's bellow.

"I want you to take a ticket from each and every person. There are no free rides here! If I get one more report of this, you can find yourself a new job." From fifteen feet away, I watch Red point his stubby finger in the carny's face as Stewart stands by him and smirks. "Am I perfectly clear?"

"Yes, Mr. Fritz. No more free rides, I promise."

"I'll be watching you," Stewart says. Could this note be from Stewart? Is he watching me too?

"Is there a problem, gentlemen?"

"William!" Red's chameleon face changes to a look of pleasure as he sees his potential buyer. "I'd heard you were going to stop in tonight." The ringleader laughs. "Did you come by just to bring me a nice, big check?"

The man adjusts his cowboy hat. "I'm still weighing my options, Red."

"Well, you said you'd have an answer by tomorrow afternoon. So let's talk about those options, shall we?"

Red motions toward the trailer near us.

My heart lurches, and I hunt for a place to get out of sight. But not too far out of hearing distance. "Ruthie, over here."

We scutter behind the duck hunt game, resting against the cool metal of the building.

"Jonas, why don't you take your break now," Red suggests a little too nicely.

"But, Mr. Fritz, I just took one."

"Take it again."

I peek around and see the game attendant slip out of his box and walk away.

"Have a seat, William." Red gestures to one of the three wooden stools in front of the gun stations. "Now, what are you thinking, friend? Are you ready for all this to be yours?"

The old man takes off his beige hat and rests it on the low counter. "She is a beautiful operation. Seeing it in action sure helps. Some problems, but nothing a little TLC couldn't fix, I suppose."

Red twirls the end of a mustache curl. "A little TLC . . . and maybe five thousand dollars knocked off my asking price?"

"Oooh-wee!" William slaps his knee. "You sure do know how to make it hard to resist. But I still need some more time. It's between this carnival and the Mulligan family circus in Pittsburg. They have a heck of a trapeze show. It's like a Vegas act." The man looks meaningfully at Red. "Drawing a mighty big crowd, I hear."

Stewart speaks up. "So are we." He glances at his dad. "Me and my cousin Cherry have been packing them in since we amped up our own performance. And if you come back next Monday, you'll see what we've been working on all month for our big finale—before we start the tour in Kansas."

"Yes, William," Red says. "It's an aerial routine that you've never seen the likes of. Challenging. In fact, the level of difficulty is so great, it killed the former owners." Red lowers his head. "My own brother and sister-in-law, God rest their souls. But we're reviving it, and we will pull it off."

"I don't know." William returns his hat to his round head. "Next Monday, you say?"

"We're running two shows that night to celebrate our fiftieth anniversary and last night in Truman. First one runs at six. You won't want to miss it." Red digs into his pocket and pulls out two tickets. "I got some reserved seats just for you."

The man takes the tickets and smiles. "I guess I'll see you next Monday night then."

Red slaps him on the back. "And bring that checkbook."

The guys share a few more laughs, then Williams takes his leave. Ruthie and I exchange a look, and I shrug. I don't know what's going on. But it's weird.

I peek my head out again, only to jump back. Red and Stewart are still there, with Stewart facing my way.

"You gonna be ready for next Monday, son?"

"I told you I was."

"This is more than a performance. Got a lot on the line here."

"I said I was ready. I won't mess this up."

"You only got one shot," Red says.

One shot at the aerial routine? One shot at what?

"We go through with the plan just like we talked about. No backing out and no mistakes." Red's tone makes goose bumps sprout on my arms.

"You told William last week I was part of the package."

"I told him you were a powerful part of the Fritz empire. Let him think what he wants. We'll be long gone with a few million in our pockets by the time he realizes you're not in the deal. Can you handle two performances Monday night?"

"I'll be ready."

"I have big plans for the second one."

Ruthie and I stare at one another in a frozen tableau. *What does that mean?*

"It still bugs me that we didn't find Betty's hiding spot. That map doesn't lead anywhere—like a decoy. It's the riddle that holds the key."

Red laughs. "We got a buyer, Stewart. We don't need it! When you're driving your new sports car, I promise you, it won't bother you nearly as much." His cackling grows louder.

"I guess."

"Well, I know. I can already smell freedom, and it's worth every price."

Stools shuffle, and I hold my breath as I hear the sounds of Red and Stewart leaving. *Don't walk around this way.*

Seconds stretch.

Then only the noises of the carnival.

"They're gone," Ruthie whispers.

"Let's get out of here. I need to talk to Officer Mark."

"And plant that carnival poster in your car."

On quivering legs, I walk beside Ruthie around the game booth to the front side.

"Whew." Ruthie sucks in the night air. "That was pretty close. I was so scared Red and Stewart were going to cut through the back way to the big top and see us."

"Yeah, me—"

Something catches my eye, and I do a double take at the food booth in front of us.

Artie Jensen.

He stands across the way, holding a Snickers. And staring. His magician's eyes float down the grassy aisle to Stewart and Red in the distance. Then meander back to us.

He knows we were eavesdropping.

"Ladies." He holds up his candy bar in a salute. "Nice night for a walk, isn't it?" He pierces me with his deep brown eyes, and I swallow back fear. "You never know what you might stumble upon."

chapter thirty-one

You're moving up the wedding? You cannot be serious, Dad."

"Bella, I didn't call you to get more attitude. I called so you would have time to adjust to the idea and get your travel plans in order."

I slip into some red flats for Wednesday night church. "Don't you see what's going on here?" It sure isn't an apology. When I saw his number on my phone, I just knew he had called to tell me how sorry he was. "Christina knows I'm onto her. She knows the truth is getting ready to unwind right in front of her eyes like a big tangled ball of yarn." Okay, bad metaphor, but I'm exhausted. I haven't exactly been sleeping much these days. "Did you confront her?"

His sigh is impatient, as if he's barely tolerating me. "I asked her about her sister, yes."

"And what did she say?"

"That Enrique was mistaken. Mercedes is just her close friend, but in order to get the designer to let her pick it up, she had to tell him Mercedes is her sister."

"And you *fell* for that?" I'm so sure! "And what about the mystery woman who's staying in that hotel?"

"Also Mercedes. Look, Bella, this friend of hers has fallen on some really hard times, and Christina's paying her to run errands and do odd jobs."

"How convenient."

"Listen, young lady, you may not like Christina, but you will respect her. She's going to be my wife this Saturday—and your stepmother."

Gag. "Did you tell her about the conversation I overheard? What's this plan she has to stick with?"

"Again, she's helping Mercedes out. Not that I need to explain any of this to you."

"Yeah, I guess my own father isn't my business."

"That's not fair, and you know—"

"I'll see you this Friday. And I'm bringing a friend."

"Fine. And Bella?"

I plop down on my bed and drag Moxie into my lap. Her gentle purr does nothing to calm me. "What?"

"If you have any plans of ruining this wedding, you should just stay home."

"Is that what you want me to do—not even come?"

"Of course not." I hear Dad inhale and let out a ragged breath. "Whether you believe it or not, I love you. You're my daughter, and I want you there with me. I want to see you in all your feathery glory next to Christina and Marisol."

Mom yells from downstairs.

"I have to go. I have church."

"See you Friday?"

I run my finger over Moxie's jingley collar. "I'll be there."

"And no funny business?"

"No." My heart wilts in my chest. "I think you've got that covered all by yourself."

~~~~~~~~~

On the way to church, I ride in Budge's Death-Mobile. His hearse follows Mom, Robbie, and a newly returned Jake in their Tahoe.

"When did Dad roll in?" Budge yells over his screamo music.

"About thirty minutes before you got in from work."

He turns down the volume, apparently not finding the song "Road Kill Pizza with a Side of Cattle Prods" conducive to conversation. "Did you hear them fighting?"

"Yeah." How could I *not* hear it? "I somehow found my ear pressed against their bedroom door."

Budge sends me a sideways glance. "That happens. Kind of like I happened to find myself in front of the vent in the laundry room."

"The one that's connected to their room. Nice." I nod in appreciation. "Did Robbie notice?" It kills me to think of that little guy watching his new family falling apart before his eyes.

"No, I made him go feed his cow."

"What are we going to do?"

Budge swerves on the dirt road, barely missing one of Mr. Patton's ducks. "I've, uh . . . I've been praying about it."

I shake my head to try and dislodge the ear clog. "That's funny. I thought you just said—"

"I prayed about it, okay?"

"It's okay to admit that." I smile at his defensive tone. "You've really come a long way since you started dating Ruthie."

"She's all right." A grin spreads across his ruddy face. "A little psycho, but I dig her."

He does more than dig her, and we both know it. "I'm really worried about Mom and Jake. It's not working, Budge. Mom's mad all the time. Jake's never home. And the more successful he gets, the worse it will be."

"So you like it here in Truman?"

I pull my eyes from the road and face my stepbrother. "I'm about to weird you out, so brace yourself."

"Nuh-uh. Don't do it. Do *not* say—"

"I love you."

"Oh, man! Dude."

I start to giggle. "I love you and Robbie. And his stupid cow. And our rundown farm house. And your dad."

"I'm gonna have to pull off the side of the road and hurl."

"And I love our family dinners. I miss those, you know?"

"*What* have I done to deserve this moment?"

I plod on, talking right over his protests. "I'd even miss fighting over the bathroom. And this nasty hearse that at one time I was too good to even look at."

Budge laughs at the memory. "You were so stuck-up."

"And you were such a tool."

Silence hangs in the car as we stare at the back of our parents' Tahoe.

"I don't want to lose our family either," Budge says. "Robbie needs all of us. Together."

"Right. For Robbie's sake." We all need our family. "So what are we going to do about it?"

"That is so you, Evil Stepsister-O-Mine." Budge shakes a finger in my face. "You try to fix everything. But we're not going to do a thing."

"We have to. We can't just sit back and watch our family crumble in the name of spandex and body slams."

"Sitting back is exactly what we're going to do." He pauses, his mouth seeming to try to push out a difficult thought. "I, um . . . I know it's going to work out."

"What is this, Budge the Disney version?"

"No. I mean . . . I don't know, Bella." He shoves a chubby hand through his oversized 'fro. "I've just really been talking to God about this, and . . . I have a peace about it. Don't ask me how, but I know this is going to be okay."

"Have you been snorting mustard at the Weiner Palace again?"

Budge rolls down his window and lets the spring breeze inside.

"Yeah, it's nuts. I mean, what do I know? Up until recently I've been the church dropout. But I cannot shake this feeling."

I study his serious face. *God, it's like this trust issue keeps jumping up like a carp and slapping me in the face. Even Budge seems to be getting it. Why can't I?*

"Forget it." Budge jerks a hard left with the wheel. "It was stupid."

I let his words hang there for a moment before answering. "No. It's not." I take a cleansing breath and pray for a boost of faith. A Red Bull of belief. "If you say you have a peace about it, then that's that. God has obviously spoken to you." Why can't the Big Guy say these things to me? "Thanks for telling me." A trust lesson from Budge Afro Finley. What is the world coming to?

He cranks up the radio, and we sing—or yell—the rest of the way to church.

I push open the heavy door of the car and set my foot onto the parking lot. "Oh, and Budge?"

"Yeah?" He grabs his Bible from the back.

"You know you'd, like, donate a kidney if I needed one."

"You're right. I would."

I smile in triumph. The dude loves me.

"But only if I got a big, fat check."

Wanting a little distance from the frosty exhaust between Mom and Jake, I find Lindy and Matt and sit beside them. Matt's in the middle of a story that has my friend howling with laughter. They don't even stop to say hi to me. Just keep on talking. Keep on laughing.

"This seat taken?"

I look up to find Luke. He obviously got his hair cut after school, as it doesn't curl around his neck, but stands up in a deceptively messy pattern. Nothing accidentally messy about this boy.

"What are you doing here?"

He settles in beside me, his arm sliding against mine on the seat rest. "I didn't feel like driving all the way out to my church tonight. With all that's been going on, I'm kind of tired."

I narrow my eyes and scrutinize every twitch of his face. "You're checking up on me, aren't you?" Luke's church isn't *that* far out of town.

"Can a guy not visit a church without there being an ulterior motive?"

I point right at his button-down oxford. "Not you." But being next to him does give me some comfort. Even though I put the carnival poster on my dash Monday night, Alfredo hasn't contacted me yet. I'm still waiting. And stressing.

He settles his Bible in his lap and focuses toward the front. "Matt and Lindy seem to be getting along well."

"Don't change the subject." But I glance to my left. "Yeah, they are. I'm glad they didn't let their friendship get too off track." I turn back. "Romance can do that."

His eyes sear into mine. "Right. Good thing they played it safe and didn't end up dating." He looks over my head. "Clearly they got just what they wanted."

Bo Blades walks in and goes immediately to Lindy. Matt closes his mouth on the rest of his story as Bo hugs his girlfriend.

"Would you mind scooting down a seat?" Bo asks a blank-faced Matt.

"Here." I jump up. "We will." I give Lindy an encouraging grin. "No problem." But her happy face has disappeared. In its place is a sham of a smile that barely lifts her lips.

"I wanted to surprise you." Bo leans down and kisses Lindy's cheek. "I thought we could hang out after church."

"Yeah. That'd be great."

"There's a picnic packed for us in my truck. I brought all your favorite food—even homemade chocolate chip cookies."

She lets him take her hand. "Those are my favorites. You're so thoughtful to do that."

"I guess Matt never had a chance," Luke whispers. "Bo seems to be everything Lindy wants."

I shoot him a look that could melt ice cream. "You have something to say?"

"Just seems that the only one happy over there by you is Bo."

I refuse to humor him by looking at Matt and Lindy. But honestly, I don't need to. I know the gloom I'm going to find. Isn't there anyone I know who's content these days?

Luke yawns beside me. "I've always found playing it safe to be such a bore."

"Welcome!" the pastor says, taking the mic. "Tonight I want to talk about Noah and the ark. Ask yourself this: would you have had the faith to get on that boat? Or would you have gone down the drain like everyone else?"

Oh, come on. Could we not have a more comfortable topic? Like tithing? . . . Or adultery?

After church, the family gathers together at the Dairy Barn. I skip dinner and go straight for a double fudge sundae.

"Watched you on TV last Sunday night, Jake." I spear a banana and swirl it in some chocolate. "I like the new jazzed-up pirate costume."

"Thanks." Jake rests his arm around my mom's chair. "It's a little hard to wrestle with the eye patch, but it's specially created so I can actually see out of it."

"Hey, there's Officer Mark!" Robbie waves toward the door, a french fry dangling out his mouth. "Over here!"

Oh poop. I slink down in my seat and keep my eyes locked on my dessert.

"Jake, good to see you." The blue of Mark's uniform matches the navy of the dated restaurant curtains. "Jillian, I miss talking to you over coffee at Sugar's. It's just not the same without you and Dolly."

"I'm really busy with the kids." Mom's smile is as fake as the blonde streaks in her hair. "But I get lonesome for the diner crowd sometimes."

Probably gets more lonesome for her husband. And someone to talk to who's old enough to vote.

"Dolly seems to really be taking to that Fritz girl. I see them in town all the time." Mark steals a fry from Robbie's plate, sending my stepbrother into giggles.

"Mickey too," Jake says. "Any time I talk to him, that dominates the conversation. He loves that girl."

"It's a blessing Cherry came along." Mom hands Robbie an ignored chicken nugget from his plate. "It's drawn Mickey and Dolly together like nothing else could have. They go to church together, they eat dinner together, they go to the park. They've become a very tight family." I hear the teaspoon of jealousy mixed in her voice.

"Is that Bella over there?"

I don't miss Mark's sarcastic tone, so I also don't bother to look up.

"Bella, why are you hiding behind a menu?" Mom asks.

"Um . . ." Slowly I lower it. "I don't think this sundae is going to be nearly enough. Just checking out the milk shake options."

Mark ambles toward my seat. "Has Bella told you about the latest happenings at the carnival?" A table of blank faces stare back at the officer. "That's funny. I asked her to make sure you guys were in the loop since some *dangerous* incidents have transpired."

Mom blanches. "Dangerous? What are you talking about?"

"It's nothing." Mark's hand rests near my dish, and I give it a light jab with my fork. "Truly nothing."

"Dolly might've mentioned some weird stuff going on," Mother says. "But I didn't think it involved you."

"Oh, it always involves Bella Kirkwood." Mark smiles down at me. "Am I right?"

All I want is some peace and privacy to meddle into other people's business.

"Why don't you fill us in?" Jake levels me with a stare used to take down giants. "I seem to have missed something while I've been gone." He glances at Mom. "Maybe too much."

"Our little private eye here has been investigating a murder at the Fritz carnival."

My mom gasps. "I thought that magician did it."

"I don't think he did." I catch myself. "But I'm not investigating it really. I'm just, you know, hanging out and absorbing the atmosphere of the place. I might've *accidentally* run into a few suspicious facts."

"She also might've run into a set of lights that fell from the sky."

"Do you mind?" I hiss at Officer Mark.

"You said that was an accident. So this is why you insisted on working there." Mom shakes her head, and I can almost see the steam coming out her ears. "What else?"

"Um, I think Mark has to go now. Yep, Lars is yelling at you from the counter. Your order's—"

"Your daughter went to her car last week and found Alfredo, the accused murderer, in her backseat."

"Good heavens." Mom shoves her plate away. "I think I'm going to be ill. *How* could you not tell us?"

Jake stares down his friend. "Why didn't you tell me?"

"Bella assured me she would be speaking with you about it." He grins down at me. "I should've known. Nancy Drew here kind of likes to work solo."

Mark gives my parents the unabridged version of a story I'd title "Reasons Bella Kirkwood Will Be Grounded 'Til She's Fifty."

"That's it." Mom slams her napkin down on the table. "I've been so busy with everything that I haven't kept a good eye on you kids. Is there anything *else* I need to know?" Her eyes linger on Budge and Robbie.

Robbie bows his head. "I ate some glue last week. And when the teacher sent a note home ... I ate that too."

Budge's cheeks dimple in a grin. "Guess that makes me the angel of the family."

"You are not returning to work there, Bella," Jake says.

Mom swoops her head toward her husband. "Don't tell her what to do. You've been a parent for five minutes this month. *I'll* tell her how it's gonna be." Mom clears her throat and straightens her posture. "Bella ... you will not be returning to work there."

"What? I have to! You don't understand."

"I know all I need to know," Mom says. "And my decision is final."

"When will she ever learn?" Budge clucks his tongue. "Maybe you should send her to military school."

And maybe I should shove this banana up your nose. "Cherry's life could be in danger. And I am the perfect person to have on the inside."

"Apparently your life is in danger. And I will not even debate this with you." Mom shoves another nugget toward Robbie's hand. "We'll discuss it at home."

"Y'all have a lovely evening." Officer Mark has the audacity to wink at me as he walks away.

Mom steeples her fingers and leans on her hands. "Anything else I need to hear, Bella?"

I think about the threatening letter Frank brought me. "Uh ..."

"Spill it," she barks.

"I guess it's time you finally knew ..." I suck in a breath and just let the truth pour out. "Budge watches Hannah Montana."

chapter thirty-two

"*I*'ve sat behind that potted tree for weeks, Bella. I'm done. I'm through."

I stir the whipped cream in my mocha and look across the table at Hunter on the day before my father's wedding. The hustle and bustle of Manhattan carries on outside the Starbucks window as parts of my life grind to a shattering halt.

"The wedding is tomorrow afternoon. Just accept it and let it go. This fixation isn't good for you."

Beside me Ruthie blows bubbles with her straw. "You can't second-guess her hunches. They're always right." She nods at me with confidence. "The sidekick guidebook says I'm to defend you in the face of doubters."

"Thanks." I guess. "Hunter . . . okay, fine. It's over. You're right, I need to move past this and accept the fact that my dad is marrying someone else, and I'm sure there's a perfectly good explanation for all the weird stuff I've witnessed."

Hunter shakes his head, his expression grim. "That was too easy. You're up to something, aren't you?"

"Are you kidding me? I'm already grounded for eternity in one time zone." I brush my finger over a wrinkle on the napkin. "I can be mature about this."

Hunter snorts. "Oh, this is gonna be bad."

On Saturday morning I awaken with morning breath, a hankering for Luisa's waffles, and a renewed determination to nuke this wedding.

"Now don't forget." My dad takes a snicker-doodle out of the cookie jar. "I need you dressed and at the church by noon." He picks his TAG Heuer watch off the kitchen counter. "You slept late enough."

"I wanted to be refreshed for your big day." I bat my eyes and draw my big fluffy robe tighter. "Didn't want to have bags for the pictures, you know."

"You missed the bridesmaids' breakfast for Christina."

"I couldn't leave Ruthie. She'd feel left out." I elbow my friend.

"Yeah," she sputters into her chocolate milk. "I'm allergic to, um, quiche. I break out in a rash. Makes my butt itch."

Dad looks to me, but I only shrug. "Bella, don't let me down, okay?" After a pause, he walks to me, bends down, and presses a kiss to my cheek. "I do love you. You know that, right?"

I stare into eyes just like mine. "I'm working on it."

He acts as if he's going to say more, but straightens instead. "I have to go. I have some last-minute details to take care of, then I'm getting dressed at the church. Oh, and you and Ruthie will ride home with your grandparents. They'll stay here with you and Marisol tonight."

"Luisa will be enough of a chaperone for us." Seriously, on top of everything else, I cannot take twenty-four hours with my grandmother. She makes pit bulls look like lapdogs.

"No deal. Luisa's leaving after the ceremony to go on a church retreat."

"Where to?"

He slings his tux bag over his shoulder. "Caesars Palace. Vegas."

I watch him walk out of the kitchen and listen for the click of the front door. "Let's go."

Ruthie and I slide out of our robes, revealing our clothes for the wedding. I glance at my friend's skintight leather pants.

"What? I wanted to match your dress."

"Can you even breathe in those things?"

Ruthie frowns at her pants. "I guess it's a good thing I left the matching bedazzled bustier at home."

I grab my purse from its hiding place in the cabinet. Locating my phone, I call a cab. "Let's go wait on the front steps."

We get to the foyer, my hand on the door, when Luisa stops me. "Wait a minute."

I pivot and plaster innocence all over my face. "Yes?"

"The wedding isn't for another hour and a half. Where are you going?"

"We're off to save the world," Ruthie says.

Luisa looks to me for confirmation. I finally nod.

"Okay, then." She rolls her dark eyes at my dress. "But don't wrinkle that thing. I do windows, but I do *not* do feathers." She waddles away, muttering under her breath in Spanish.

When the yellow cab pulls up to the sidewalk, we rush inside. "Broadway Heights hotel. And there's a twenty-dollar tip in it if you can get us there in twenty minutes."

I was handing over a crisp Andrew Jackson in fifteen.

"So what's the plan?" Ruthie asks as we step inside the lobby of the hotel.

I stand in the middle of the vast space and just look around. I have no idea what I'm doing. Reaching into my purse, I feel around until my fingers touch my camera, my mace, and my Orbitz gum. All potential tools for detonating a wedding.

Ruthie taps her spiky boot. "You do have a plan, don't you?"

I consider this. "Yes."

"Oh, man. You don't." She covers her eyes with her hand. "The book warned me of times like these. When all your superpowers would go to your head."

I make a mental note to introduce this book to a blowtorch. "We'll figure it out when we get up to Mercedes' room. I just need to get in there so I can talk to her."

"And what are you going to say?"

"Would you quit asking these questions?" These questions that make . . . sense!

We ride the elevator to the eighth floor in silence. I chew on a glossy nail.

"You're kinda molting." Ruthie points toward some stray feathers on the floor.

"I don't have time to worry about this dress right now." I tug on a plumey strap and try to hold it in place. "We need to get in, force the truth out of her, and get out in time to stop the biggest disaster of my dad's life." Otherwise it will be the biggest disaster of mine.

"I still think we could've gone with my idea to hang Marisol up by her toes until she hurled up the truth."

I did give that one some serious consideration. But so far my questioning of that kid has gotten me nowhere. She's a locked box.

The elevator dings and comes to a whooshing stop. My breakfast jumps on my stomach like a trampoline.

"We could pull the fire alarm." Ruthie steps out and scans the walls of the hallway. "Pull it, and she'll come running. You can tackle her and—"

"Get arrested?" I guess that would give me a great excuse for missing the wedding. "I can't think." I'm so stressed! *God, I know I've got some dubious behavior going on here, but I checked my Bible last night. And there's nothing in there about causing a big stir to drive out a mysterious lady in hopes of stopping your father's nuptials. For a* second I thought I had found something in that chapter on animal sacrifices ... but no.

"I'll be back." Ruthie turns back toward the glass elevator.

"Wait!" I lower my voice. "Where are you going?"

"Just hang on to your feathers. I'll be right back."

This could be bad. Very bad. "Nothing illegal. And keep your clothes on!" I don't know why I needed to add that. But this is Ruthie. Anything is possible.

As she disappears behind the gold double doors, I walk down the hall and find the potted tree Hunter must've spent a good deal of time with. Easing down in the tight dress, I park it on the floor. And wait. And wait.

This must've been what Hunter felt like. No wonder he was so whiny. Ten minutes and my butt's already numb.

In the distance I hear the elevator ting again. "Bella?" comes a stage whisper. "Bella!"

I jump up, rub my tush, and peek my head around the corner of the hall. Sighing with relief, I see Ruthie. And then I see the cart. "What in the world are you doing?"

She is wearing a white smock, a billowy chef's hat, and is pushing a metal food cart. "Getting you into that room."

"How did you get that stuff?"

She moves her head in a jerky shake. "Don't ask. Just climb on."

I glance at the covered serving dishes on top. "Maybe we should pull the fire alarm."

Ruthie lifts the white cloth draped over the cart. "Get under here. Sit on the bottom, and I'll cover you up. When I push you inside the room, you can jump out and talk to her."

I guess it doesn't matter if we pull the fire alarm or not. Either way, I will not survive this day without being hauled away in cuffs. But desperate times call for ... mug shots.

"Okay. Let's do this." I slip under the tablecloth and with a few tries, finally get situated good enough to be covered up. "Oh my gosh. I'm like a pretzel in here." I'm so going to need a massage after this. And a really strong latte.

"My name is going to be Mavis," Ruthie says above me. "Mavis Durbinkle, the food service girl."

"Whatever gets you by."

"Mavis has had such a hard life. She needs this job."

I pull up a foot by its pink heel. "Write your autobiography later, Mavis. I have a wedding to stop."

My world goes black as Ruthie flops the white material over me and the cart. I hear her inhale big . . . then she puts us into motion. Oh shoot. Oh shoot. Oh shoot. Moment number 1,981,642 my mom would not be proud of.

My butt bounces with every rotation of the wheel, and the dishes clank a clumsy tune above my head.

Knock! Knock! "Room service," Ruthie drawls.

"Nice country accent," I whisper.

"Thank yew, sugah."

The door opens, and a loud *thunk* tells me it caught on the safety latch.

"Yes?"

I swallow hard and pray none of my feathers are showing.

"Room service, ma'am. Just fer yew."

"I did not order room service."

"It was sent up. Compliments of someone who said you'd need a little pick-me-up right about now."

Nice job, Ms. Durbinkle.

"I—I don't know. Who sent this?"

"The woman just said you'd know, and that she would talk to yew later. She popped her sweet li'l head in this mornin' and gave us the order. Dark-headed lady. Real nice." Ruthie stretches the syllables out like Laffy Taffy. "I think we have some chocolate goodies in here." My friend taps a serving dish, and I can feel it vibrate all the way to my Jimmy Choos.

"Okay . . . I guess come on in."

Ruthie pushes the cart, and it bounces over the carpet. "Oh, I see yer packin' up here. Are you leavin' us?"

"Yes."

"I hope it's nothin' we did wrong. We here at the . . . um, the . . ."

The Broadway Heights! It's the Broadway Heights!

"The *hotel* wants to make sure all our customers are happy as a pig in the mud. At least that's what my ex-boyfriend would say." A beat of silence. "Before he left me for another girl. But she was a hunter and a fisher like him. And Ezekial never could get past the fact that I couldn't skin my own possums."

Shoot me now.

Achoo! Ah-ah-choo!

Oh no. Mercedes sneezes three more times. It's my feathers!

"That's strange. *Achoo!* I had the hotel take away all the down pillows, but—*achoo!*—I seem to be—*achoo!*"

"Um, here we go. Here's some—oops! That's pea soup. That ain't right. I specifically asked for chocolate cheesecake."

"I'm afraid you're going to have to leave." Mercedes makes a whirling noise in her throat. "I seem to be allergic to you."

"No!" Ruthie cries. "It's not me. But I gotta serve yew some dessert now. Let's just uncover this other dish right here." Ruthie sticks her foot under the cloth and shakes it. It makes contact with my knee.

"Ow!" I slap a hand over my mouth. I have to move. I have to bail out of here and confront this Mercedes woman.

"I must insist you leave. I'm to catch a plane in a few—*achoo!*—hours to leave the country."

"Oh, I've always wanted to travel." More kicks beneath the cart. "Where are yew goin'?"

"None of your business."

"I've never been there."

"Please take the cart and leave at once!" The woman sneezes again. And again. "I'm calling management if you don't walk out of here right now."

"Yeah? Well, not before you see this!"

Light explodes in my eyes as Ruthie flings the cloth away. The tall woman's eyes go wide. She mutters a curse and reaches for the bedside phone.

"Stop!" I yell. "Stop. I won't hurt you." I move closer.

She doubles over and launches into a sneezing fit. "Get. Out."

"I know who you are."

"I don't care!" Her face is turning purple.

This isn't going well. I probably should've thought this out more. I figured she'd see me, see the dress, and know I was part of the wedding party, then fall at my feet, confessing the truth.

Ruthie lunges for the phone, but the woman knocks her hand aside. "Get away!" she screams.

"Mercedes, I just want to talk to you." I spy three framed photos across the room. The one in the middle is of her, Christina, and a younger Marisol. Surrounded by pictures of others I'm assuming are family.

"I don't know who you mean." Her left eye is swelling shut. It's not pretty. "But you have broken into my room, and I am calling the police."

Ruthie makes another try for the phone, but the woman throws herself on Ruthie and digs in her long nails.

"Ow!" My friend howls in pain. "I *knew* I should've brought my brass knuckles!"

I jump into the fray, only to trip over the train of my dress. Stupid feathers!

In a move worthy of any professional wrestler, Mercedes

clotheslines me with an arm, and down I go. She grabs the phone receiver and punches a button. "I need security. Room 857. Now."

From my position on the floor, I see her other eye taking on a gargoyle quality as well. Praying she can't see me, I race back to the cart, dig into my purse for the camera, and snap off some shots. But who would ever recognize this swollen creature?

"Come on!" Ruthie yanks hard on my arm and drags me toward the door. "Sprint like an Olympian!"

We run like mad to the stairwell. My heels dig into the carpet, and my feet cry out for mercy. *Please don't let us get caught! Please don't let us get caught!*

I lose a shoe at the fifth floor. "We need to separate!" I yell, kicking off the other heel. "They're going to be looking for two girls together. I'm going to get off at the fourth floor and ride the elevator. You go to the bottom floor and go through the kitchen. I'll meet you at the coffee shop half a block down. I won't leave until you show up." I wheeze out more instructions.

"Bella?" Ruthie calls as I pull open the fourth-story door.

My chest heaves. "Yeah?"

"I will never forget this."

"I know. I'm sorry, Ruthie."

Her face splits into a grin. "Are you kidding me? This is the best graduation present ever!"

"Remind me of that when we're wearing stripes." I shoot through the door and run down a series of halls until I reach an elevator.

It's all I can do not to shout a hallelujah when the elevator pings open and I step inside with a group of Asian tourists. When we hit the lobby, I shuffle close to them, completely invading their personal space until I'm emptied onto the street.

Freedom! Yes!

My dress straps long gone, I hold up the bodice with one hand

SO Over MY Head

and use the other to propel me down the street. At the sight of Manhattan Mocha, I slow down and sag against the building.

Thirty-one minutes later I sit at a bistro table inside and drum my fingers on a cup. Where is Ruthie? What if she got caught? What if the police have her? What kind of friend am I that I even dragged her into this twisted mess?

I lower my head to the table and bang it twice. "I'm the worst friend ever. I'm the worst—"

"If you get a bruise on your schnoz, that is *not* going to look good for the wedding pics."

I lift my head in a rush. "Ruthie!" Throwing my arms around my friend, I hug her close. "You made it! Thank God. You're the best sidekick ever!"

"Dude!" She goes limp in my arms. "Back off, okay? I don't even let Budge get *that* handsy."

"I'm so glad you made it. I was freaking out."

"When I went down to the kitchen, they wanted me to unload the dishwasher." She shrugs and straddles a seat. "I thought it was the least I could do."

I rest my head in my hands. "The wedding's in thirty minutes, and I've got nothing. I could try and show those pictures to my dad or people who know Christina, but who would even recognize that woman with her face all swollen?"

"Seriously. That chick looked like a bloated up shar-pei."

"It's over. I have to admit defeat and let the wedding go on. It was a half-baked plan anyway."

"The guide book said you'd have times of self-doubt." Ruthie reaches into her shirt and pulls out a frame. "Maybe you can show your dad this."

I snatch the picture and stare at Christina and her smiling family. "Aw, Ruthie. You're the best."

"Even without my slingshot."

Failure spirals in my gut. "But what does this really prove? Let's face it. I got nothing."

Ruthie takes the frame, unlatches the back, and hands me the photo. "Check it out."

I flip it over and read. *Marisol, Christina, and Sadie Vasquez.* "Omigosh." I dig through my handbag with frenzied hands until I find my phone. With trembling fingers, I pull up my ex-boyfriend's number. "Hunter?" I suck in a shaky breath. "I need you to meet me at my dad's wedding. Make sure your father is there . . . I think I just found their money-stealing accountant."

chapter thirty-three

adie Vasquez. Of course. It was staring me in the face the whole time.

"Can't you drive faster?" I yell to the cabbie.

"And roll up your window." Ruthie sputters and spits. "It's like a wind tunnel of feathers back here."

I press the phone more firmly to my ear. "Hunter, Christina De Luna is actually Christina Vasquez, sister of Mercedes."

"Sadie Vasquez." His words are as sharp as knife points. "The psycho who took my dad and yours for millions."

I grab Ruthie's wrist and check her giant alligator skin watch. "You have to stall the wedding. I'll never make it on time."

"What do you want *me* to do?"

"I don't know! But think of something." We come to a stop at yet another red light. Are there no green lights in this town? "I'm going to call my dad and tell him to wait, but I don't know if he's going to buy it. You find him and tell him you've talked to me, and I'm on my way."

"Got it. I'll wait for you inside the chapel."

The minutes tick by, and at one o'clock, when we're stopped yet again, I order the driver to pull over. "We're getting out here." I shove some cash in his hand. "Gonna have to run the rest of the way."

"Follow me!" I yell to Ruthie and take off down an alley on my bare feet. Three blocks later my phone rings again. "What?"

"Bella, it's no good," Hunter says. "Your dad won't even listen to me. He said he figured you wouldn't show up, and he wasn't going to wait. Something about Christina told him she knew you had made alternate plans for the day. I've been escorted out of the church."

"*Un*-believable!" Oh, my lungs are about to explode. And don't even get me started on my feet. "Go talk to him again. Tell him what I know. Tell him about Sadie."

"I tried. There's some big Brazilian goon guarding his door now. Says he's a friend of Christina's and the best man. He kicked me out and won't let me back into his changing room."

Without so much as a good-bye, I end the call and punch in my dad's number. Voice mail. I hit redial again and again. My own father won't take a call from me. How do you like that?

As I pound the dirt-encrusted pavement, I glance at Ruthie. She runs beside me like a track star. Even pace. Bouffant hair defying the laws of gravity and hair spray. Not so much as breaking a sweat.

"It's just around this corner." I think. Five blocks later I know I'm lost. *God, please help me. I need to get to my dad!*

I screech to a halt as a woman passes by, pushing a stroller of twins. "Hey!"

She casts a worried look and keeps going.

"Ma'am! Please stop, I need help."

She turns around. "Your dress is beyond help."

"I know that's right." Ruthie studies my torn frock, now minus the two bottom layers. I look like a flapper who got caught in a tornado of geese.

"Do you know where St. Augustine's Chapel is?"

The short brunette lifts a hand to block out the sun. "Yeah. It's two blocks north. Then turn and go four blocks east, and at the Y, head south."

North, east, south? Is she kidding me? "I need landmarks. Turn at the red bud tree by the fire station, hang a left at the playground. I do not speak this directional jibbity jab!"

Ruthie grabs me by the arm and offers the woman a sympathetic look. "Don't worry, ma'am. She just got cut from the Miss Manhattan Poultry model search, and she's feeling a little crazy. I plan on slapping her at the next street." My friend yanks me across the road and returns to running. "I can get us there."

"You don't know New York!" I scream over the passing cars.

She picks up the pace. "No, but I was a boy scout once, and I can tie a square knot, start a fire with gum wrappers, and know the difference between north and south."

I hold the pain at my side. "Um . . . a *boy* scout?"

"What they didn't know didn't hurt them."

So on faith and Ruthie's internal compass, I follow my friend through the streets of the city that never sleeps. And judging from the sludge on my feet, the city that needs to work on its sanitation.

"There it is!" Ruthie calls many moments later. "I see it!"

Relief duels with sadness. We're here . . . but it's twenty past one. The wedding was to be a short ceremony. And I'm sure with Christina tipped off now, the service was cut down even more.

Just as we approach the small yard in front of the church, I notice an olive-skinned man standing in front of the antique entry doors. He looks like a member of a Brazilian mafia.

"Ruthie . . . that guy's waiting for me. I know it. I'm going to need you to provide a distraction while I find another way in."

She gives him the once-over. "I can take him. I've watched a lot of wrestling lately."

Oh, Lord help us. "Just use your wits. Not your muscles. Or that slingshot tucked into the back of your pants."

"You can see it?"

"That and your panty line."

"That guy is kind of big." She swallows hard. "Isn't he?"

I pull her behind a nearby shrub. "Oh no." I shake my head. "No, you don't. You are not wimping out on me now. You, Ruthie McGee, are my sidekick. And I have never needed you more than I need you now. Do you understand me?"

She nods—slowly at first, then more certain. "I understand."

"You can do it. I believe in you."

"I sure wish I had that book."

"You don't need that stupid thing." I tap her temple. "Everything you need is right here. And in your heart. The truth is, you're all I've got here. But you know what?" I look into the heavily lined eyes of a girl who has become my closest friend. "I wouldn't trust this moment to anyone else. I'm glad you're here with me." I can't resist a slap to her butt. "Now go get 'em, partner."

She clutches her chest with a gasp. "Partner? Really?"

"Of course. Who wants to be a sidekick when you can be a dynamic duo?"

Ruthie lets out a happy sigh. "McGee and Kirkwood—mystery solvers."

Let's not go crazy. "Um, that's Kirkwood and McGee." I give her a playful shove and run toward the back of the chapel.

But not before I hear my partner in action.

"No way!" she squeals. "It's Brad Pitt! Oh my gawwwsh—I loved you in *Twilight*! Can I have your autograph?"

Limping like a peg-legged pirate, I jog around the brick building. Pink-dyed sweat trickles inside my strapless bra. I find a metal door and yank with all my might. Nothing. Locked.

At the back of the church, yet another door. Sealed tight as one of my dad's eyelifts. With clenched fists I beat the entrance, but no one answers.

"Are you kidding me?" I yell.

"You always were a drama queen."

I spin around, tripping on a remnant of the skirt. "Hunter! Why aren't you in there stopping this?" I'm too late!

"Because I knew you'd want the pleasure. Need a boost?" He points upward. Above us hangs a folded fire escape, leading to a window. "The bodyguard wouldn't let me near any of the other exits. He's sure not going to let you in." He squats low and holds out a hand. "May I?"

"I just want to tell you that I had a lot more dress on when I started."

My ex-boyfriend casts a doubtful look at my outfit. "I'm not judging."

I step onto his thigh and swing my other foot over his head until I'm sitting on his shoulders. With rubber knees I rise until I'm standing. "Don't even consider dropping me." He walks us beneath the window. "And don't even *think* about looking up what's left of my skirt."

"Wouldn't dare."

Hunter wraps his hands around my wobbly calves, and I reach my arms overhead. I feel the warm metal of the ladder and pull it down. "Look out below," I call as it grows toward the ground. I leave the safety of Hunter's perch and jump onto the rungs.

"Good luck," Hunter calls.

I shimmy up the rest of the way and push the partially opened window with dirt-streaked hands. Throwing a leg over, I crawl inside. Running out of the room, my feet slap all the way down a dim hallway as wedding music comes to a crescendo. The ceremony must be over. They're probably walking arm in arm down the aisle together as man and wife now.

"Dad!" I bellow. "Dad!" Must get to him.

I whisk down some steps, only tripping on one. "Dad! Wait!"

The stairs empty me into the small lobby. Smack into the burly man.

"Going somewhere?"

I look up at the beast. "You have to let me in there. That's my dad."

"I know all about you. Christina told me you'd try and stop the wedding." He shakes his bulldog head and smiles. A gold tooth winks back. "Not going to happen."

"Oh yeah?" Ruthie leaps out of nowhere, her slingshot poised. "Take this!" She fires away at the brute, pelting him with one rock after another. "Go, Bella! Go!"

I jump around the shrieking thug and yank open the sanctuary doors. "Noooo!"

Two hundred heads swivel my way. Whispers skitter across the aisles.

My dad stands at the end of the church, his hand over Christina's.

It isn't too late! They're not married yet! *Thank you, Jesus! I sooo owe you one! Or fifty. Okay, a million.* "You have to stop!" My voice echoes in the rafters as I speed toward my dad. "Christina isn't who you think she is."

"Get on with the ceremony," she hisses to the preacher. "I warned you his daughter might try and sabotage this."

I stop before them, and the balding minister nods my way. "It's true. She did."

"Bella, this is madness. I waited for you. You said you were coming, and I wanted to believe it." Dad takes in my disheveled state, his mouth tight in fury. "I held this ceremony off for twenty minutes hoping my only daughter would come through for me. And this— *this* is what I get?"

"You don't understand, I—"

"Christina was right. She said you'd try and ruin this day, and I didn't believe her."

"Of course she said that." I glare the woman down. "She's a liar!"

Gasps bounce all around the room.

"Bella, you need to leave." Dad lowers his voice. "Now."

"Listen to me. This woman"—I jerk my finger toward his waiting bride—"is the sister of Sadie Vasquez, your former accountant. Sadie, also known as Mercedes, is the woman who was staying at the hotel all this time. *She's* the woman I saw your fiancée plotting with. They're going to take your money—again."

Dad's brown eyes travel back and forth from me to Christina. "This can't be true."

"Believe it." I hold up my photo. "Check out this photo."

He squints and holds the phone close. "It looks like the face of a rhino."

"It's her sister!"

"Bella, I don't know, I—"

Ruthie takes that moment to charge through the doors. "Wait!" She plows right down the aisle. "I have proof!" She squeals to a stop, and with a heaving chest, pulls the framed photo out of her shirt.

"How does she do that?" Dad mutters.

I shake my head. "I don't know. It's like a Mary Poppins bag down there." I shove the picture into his hands. "Does this woman look familiar? It's Sadie. And you"—I growl at the woman who would've been my stepmother—"are her sister."

Marisol latches onto Christina's leg and begins to cry.

"I love you, Kevin," Christina says. "Please believe me. I love you."

I pull the picture from the black frame and show my father the names on the back. "She lied to you. This whole time, it was all a lie."

The evidence dangles in Dad's hand. "What about our future? What about the show in Brazil? Was that just a lie too, Christina?"

She shakes her head, her eyes brimming with tears. "Yes. At first. But I could've made it happen—somehow."

"But that wasn't the plan you and Mercedes had, was it?" I challenge as the pieces fall into place. "You had Dad sign that ridiculously generous prenup where you got a lump sum. An amount that would've been chump change to a guy who thought he had a multi-million dollar television deal."

Dad's eyes could freeze dragon fire. "You were going to leave me before the final round of contract negotiations were finalized, weren't you? Trump up some excuse for a quickie divorce?"

Christina throws herself on my father, her hands clutching his shoulders. "I didn't mean to fall in love with you." She rubs a manicured hand over her wet cheek. "You had that careless fling with my sister and just discarded her."

I glare at my dad. "You had an affair with your accountant?" No wonder she took all his money.

Christina continues. "Mercedes got away with your money, but it wasn't enough for her. She became obsessed. Desperate. Nothing I could say would reach her and her broken heart." She sniffs loudly. "I feared daily she would take her own life. One day . . . I promised her I would do whatever it took to avenge her honor."

What is this—honor-code according to *Sex and the City*?

"We formulated a plan. And I was to marry you, convince you there was a show."

"She knew where my weak spot was." Dad drops his head and pushes Christina's hands away. "Seduce my ego first, right?"

I glance back at the wedding crowd. They sit motionless on the edge of the pews, taking in every morsel of this living soap opera.

"I didn't plan on falling in love with you." Christina's voice is a weak whisper. "But I did. Do you have any idea how this has killed me?"

Ruthie cracks her knuckles. "Wanna brainstorm some ways we could make that happen?"

"You don't love my dad. Stealing his money isn't love."

Christina lifts pitiful eyes to my father. "I do care for you, Kevin. We could still work this out." Her voice lowers to a whisper. "Please don't send me to the police."

"You were actually going to go through with it." Dad glances down at a weeping Marisol. "Was it worth it? How could you do this to your little sister?"

"She's not her little sister."

Everyone pivots toward the doors. Mercedes Vasquez saunters down the narrow aisle. People rotate as she passes by, turning like dominos.

"You're supposed to be on a plane," Christina hisses.

"I couldn't leave without you." She ambles forward and joins our awkward grouping. Her wild eyes cut to me. "Nice dress, by the way."

"More of your sister's good taste." Even a crazy woman recognizes this frock is hideous.

Dad's laugh is ripe with disbelief. "What are you doing here, Sadie?"

"Mommy!" Marisol runs to Mercedes and clings to her pant leg.

"Mommy?" the church crowd echoes.

"That's right. This is my daughter—Christina's *niece*. If Marisol was Christina's sister, you wouldn't go looking for any long-lost relatives." She shakes her bleached-blonde head. "I knew this was over. First of all, I knew my sister couldn't pull it off." She stumbles to Dad and stabs him in the chest with a pointy nail. "And since your bratty kid here"—she tips her chin toward me—"messed everything up, I wanted to at least be here to see your face when you realized the woman you loved didn't love you."

"Don't say anything more, Mercedes," Christina pleads with her watery eyes. "It's time to go."

"I called the police fifteen minutes ago," Ruthie says. "I don't think you can get too far."

Dad runs a hand over his mouth like he's trying to wipe away a sour taste. "My own daughter tried to tell me. And I wouldn't listen to her." He looks at me with an unspoken apology. "What an idiot I've been."

Can't argue with you there, Pops.

Dad reaches out and brushes his fingers through Marisol's hair. "So you wanted revenge—fine. But how could you do something so heinous to this little girl? Who's going to take care of her when her mother and aunt are behind bars?"

Marisol turns her face to her mom's waist and lets out a wail that pierces my heart. Even brats don't deserve this.

Mercedes laughs as police sirens call in the distance. "I'll get off. We both will. It's a crime of passion. Who would ever lock me away after the horrible way you treated me, Kevin?" She pats her daughter awkwardly on the back. "And besides—her father can take care of her."

"Shut up, Mercedes," Christina warns. "Don't say another word until we talk to lawyers."

Dad's eyes widen as his tanned face turns the color of the white church walls. "No. I don't believe it."

Craziness shines in Mercedes' dark eyes. "Oh, did I forget to tell you?"

My father shakes his head. "That's not even possible."

The skin at the back of my sweaty neck tingles. "What? Dad, what's she talking about?" I don't feel so good.

Dad's tortured eyes flit from me to Marisol.

"That's right, Kevin." Mercedes cackles and pushes her daughter forward. "Marisol, dear . . . say hello to your father."

chapter thirty-four

$\mathcal{A}$t two a.m. I tiptoe downstairs, dragging my hand down the banister with each slow step. I'm sure there are conversations that every parent must have with his child that he dreads. The period talk. The alcohol lesson. The sex lecture. But they have to be nothing compared to the "Why Did You Have a Fling with Your Accountant and Have a Love Child" talk I must give now. Parents have no idea the burden of being a kid.

I check the living room for my dad, but find nobody but my grandfather snoring on the couch. An infomercial blasts from the TV, and noticing my grandfather's credit card in his hand, I hope he didn't just order the Sand Away Hair Remover.

Detouring through the kitchen, the floor is cold on my bare feet. I stick my hand into the cookie jar and extract two snicker-doodles. This chat requires reinforcement. Snagging a Sprite from the fridge, I plod on to the office. Still no dad. Between talks with his attorneys and the police, I haven't seen him since I left the church.

After completely searching the house, I ease the back door open, and that's where I find my father. Sitting in a metal chair on his tiny inch of grass, staring at the dark sky.

Slumped down in the seat, elbows on the armrests, he reclines back, still garbed in his crisp tuxedo shirt with the sleeves rolled to his forearms. Reminds me of the way Luke wears his button-downs.

But that's pretty much where the similarities end. This flawed man before me is hurting . . . damaged . . . and in need of an instructional manual more than Ruthie could ever be.

"Hey." My voice sounds harsh in the quiet evening air. "We missed you at dinner." I hand him a cookie.

Dad lifts his head. "You mean your grandmother drove you nuts, and you wish I had been there to intercede."

"Something like that." The woman lectured me on the improper etiquette of busting up a wedding. For two hours.

I sit down on the grass and contemplate the polka dots on my pajama pants.

"Ruthie asleep?" Dad asks.

"Yeah, she went a few rounds with Grandfather on Rock Band, and it totally wore her out."

"Your grandpa can't remember anything beyond 1966. How could he play that?"

"He has a surprisingly good grasp of everything Metallica ever did."

Minutes trickle by as I pick at some grass and try to think of something to say. Do I go with the blunt truth and say, "Hey, you royally jacked up. Again." Or maybe something deep and inspirational like, "The Bible says you can be lifted up on eagles' wings. Yeah, Dad, even you."

I inhale and decide to give it a go. "I—"

"Isabella—"

Our voices trip over each other, and my dad holds up a hand. "Me first." He pulls himself up in the chair and leans forward, resting his hands on his knees. "Bel, I messed up. I don't even know where to begin."

"You could try the beginning."

He nods. "Sadie—or I should say Mercedes—had been my accountant for years. She came highly recommended about nine years ago. We instantly clicked, and eventually one thing led to another."

"Like Marisol." Mercedes was in jail tonight, but Christina, who had confessed to being a small part of the embezzling crime, was out on bail and in a nearby hotel with Marisol. It still weirds me out to think I could have a half-sister. Does this mean I have to take her bra shopping when she's twelve? She'll probably strangle me with it.

"Marisol cannot be mine."

"But you've known her long enough."

"Not in that way. We began seeing each other about three years ago. You've got to believe me." He pushes his fingers through his hair. "Things got really awkward with Mercedes, and I ended it. It didn't go well. She went a little nuts."

"Well, obviously she matured. Because now she's full-on psycho," I say. "Did Mom ever know about Mercedes?"

"She suspected. But she was suspicious of every woman I met."

"Can't imagine why."

Instead of calling me on my disrespect, Dad nods. "And look where it got me. I've really done it this time."

"But why would Marisol stay with Christina?"

"I think that was Christina's choice. Probably knew Marisol wasn't safe with Sadie. I mean, did you see the woman?"

I take a bite of snicker-doodle. "She looked like Lord Voldemort's sister."

"As the police were cuffing the ladies, Christina told me Sadie has been getting steadily more unbalanced. She begged me to protect Marisol. Aside from the man I thought was my best man and television producer, Marisol has no family in America." He sends me a wary look. "I'm going to keep her."

"Marisol's not a puppy."

"No, but she's going to need a home. At least until Christina gets her stuff straightened out. I don't think she'll do much time. But Sadie—who knows."

I can't help the anger that spurts to life. "Do you seriously think you can take care of a kid? By yourself?"

"I've got Luisa."

The old bitterness bubbles up and threatens to spill over like a volcano. "So you're just going to let the nanny raise her. Like you and Mom did with me."

Dad straightens his spine. "I know I've messed up with you. Obviously your mom has made changes in the right direction. I can tell you two are closer." He sighs and looks at the ground. "But I'm still this huge failure to you. Right?"

This is probably the part where I rush to him, throw my arms around his neck, and say, "Gosh, Daddy, no! Don't say that about yourself."

"You're the best plastic surgeon on the planet." I twirl my finger around a dandelion and smile wistfully. "I remember sometimes I used to come visit at the office, and watching those famous people stroll in and out would be like stepping into a fairy tale. And they were all there to see my dad."

"But?"

"But then you never came home. You lived at that office. And when you were home, you just avoided me. And I thought when I moved to Oklahoma things would change. I thought *you* would change. How could you stand to let me go, Dad?" My throat thickens.

"I had to, Isabella." Dad slips out of his chair and sits on his knees in front of me, the tails of his shirt dragging the ground. "Your mother needed you, and you had this whole life waiting for you."

My bangs fall into my eyes, and I push them back. "And then I thought when I would come for my monthly visit to Manhattan that you would drop everything to spend time with me. I mean, to see your daughter forty-eight hours a month, who wouldn't make the most of it?"

"But not me," he says heavily. "I was too busy working."

I lift my head and look my dad directly in the eye. "You don't know what to do with me, do you? When I'm here—you don't know how to just be my dad."

"I guess you're right." His laugh is wrapped in bitterness. "Frankly, Bella, you scare me. I looked up one day and you were this young woman—a young lady I didn't even recognize."

"Because you didn't bother to get to know me. And now you're going to take on Marisol like you get to start over or something. You've got a daughter—me."

He rests his surgeon's hands on my leg. "I know my slate is far from clean with you. And you may not believe me, but I want to work on that. I don't think Marisol is my chance for a redo." Dad grimaces. "If you think I'm scared of you, you have no idea what I feel for that little tyrant."

"And now she's going to be your tyrant?"

"Maybe." He pats my knee. "But so are you. And I want to change, Bella. I do. For us. I want to be a better man. Maybe that's why I feel so strongly about taking care of Marisol. I know I have to change—for your sake. And mine. I've missed out on so much."

"Yes." Flashes of my life spin through my mind. Ballet recitals, first dance, skinned knees, my first short story Luisa hung on the refrigerator. "You have missed out on a lot. And that makes me sad. And mad."

"I don't want to be left out of one more thing. I don't want this rift between us to be how it is forever, you know?" Dad reaches out his ringless hand and closes it over mine. "Tell me what to do, and I'll do it. Because, baby, I have no idea."

A tear falls from my eye, and I brush it away with my knuckle. "I'm the kid, Dad. It's time you figured out how this parenting stuff works. Because I sure don't know."

He gives a weak smile. "You're right a lot, you know?"

"Maybe you could tell Mom that."

Dad pulls me to him and envelopes me in his strong arms. "I want my daughter." He smoothes my hair and presses a kiss to my temple. "I know I want my daughter."

More stupid tears fall and dampen my face. Must've been that Hallmark commercial I saw earlier. Because I am *so* not a crier. "Love is a risk, isn't it, Dad?" I think of all the breakups in my life, my family. And I think of Luke.

"It's worth it, though. You're worth it. I love you, Isabella Kirkwood."

Nose drips. "Right back at you."

"I'm going to figure this dad stuff out. I promise."

"Hey, Dad?"

"Yeah?"

"I hear credit cards are a great way to show affection."

~~~~~~~~~~

Later, as I push open my bedroom door, I'm greeted by the buzz-saw noises coming from Ruthie's open mouth. The stress of the day caught up with my crime-busting partner.

Or those pants finally cut off her circulation and she simply passed out.

I plop on the bed and stare at the ceiling, where the evil cherubs stand poised in their painted glory, ready to swoop down and attack. I feel so worn down. So drained. *God, everything is changing. Again. I'm not sure I'm ready for all this. A new dad. Maybe a new sister. I seriously need some Ben and Jerry's.*

I reach across the bed and grab my phone from the nightstand. It's ridiculously late, but I punch in the number anyway. Some moments just call for a comforting voice.

"Only a total idiot would call me at this hour."

I laugh at Luke's tired greeting. "Sorry to wake you."

"It's after two in the morning."

Luke sighs on the other end, and I hear the rustle of covers. "How did the wedding go? I texted you a few times, but you didn't respond. I took that as a sign you were being physically restrained somewhere in a padded cell."

I laugh again. "You make me smile, Luke Sullivan."

Three seconds of silence pass. "What's wrong, Bella?"

"I can't call and just be nice to you?"

"I'm sorry about the wedding. Did they leave on their honeymoon?"

I fluff a pillow under my head and let the sham cool my cheek. "One of these days you're going to learn not to doubt me."

"You stopped the wedding?"

"Yeah, you should've been there. It was a masterpiece of epically horrible proportions." I spend the next fifteen minutes filling him in on my day, not sparing any wacko detail.

"I can't believe it."

I grin into the phone. "Maybe you should put a little more trust in me."

"I don't think my trust in you has ever really been our problem."

I flush at his serious tone. "You have to admit I have good instincts."

"Except at relationships," he says. "And then . . . they suck."

The air hangs suspended in my chest. "I . . . I—"

"I'm through waiting, Bella. When you get back Sunday, I'm coming to your house. And you and I are going to have a big long talk. And I'm not leaving until you tell me exactly what you want."

"Okay." Sure. Yeah, I can do that. The thought of it gives me a strange barfy feeling, but surely that will pass. With ice cream.

"I didn't kiss Ashley Timmons. And you know that."

I let this go.

"Bella?"

"Hmm?"

"I'm glad I'm the one you called."

My heavy eyelids begin to flutter to my cheeks. "Actually, I went through the whole list of boys from the junior class. You were just the first one to pick up."

"Go to sleep." I can hear the smile in his voice. "You're beat."

I yawn. "Luke?"

"Hmm?"

"Thanks. I can always count on you."

"Never forget it."

chapter thirty-five

$\mathcal{W}$hat happened to coming home early Sunday?" Luke slides into the vacant seat beside mine in journalism on Monday. "Remember the talk we were going to have?"

I save my document and give him my attention. "The conversation you demanded?"

He doesn't budge. "That would be the one."

"Want to talk about it now?"

"Of course not. This is hardly the time or place."

But I saw that hesitation.

I let my brow rise just to the point of being flirty. "Afraid Ashley Timmons will get mad?"

Luke opens his mouth to speak, then glances across the room at his star reporter and occasional friendly companion who's not even bothering to hide the fact that she's eavesdropping. "I'll call you after the carnival performance tonight."

"Oh, I'll be there."

He slants his arrogant head. "Your mother forbade you to go."

I hold up a newly manicured finger. "She barred me from *working* at the carnival."

"And then she grounded you. You can't just slip out."

"It's a special night for Cherry. I'll talk Mom into it. The whole family's going." Well, minus Jake. He's taping a performance for

World Wrestling Television in Oklahoma City. He's apparently going head-to-head with some guy called Chainsaw. My stepdad said it's a promotion, so I guess the scarier the names, the higher up you are. When he's in a match with someone named Throat Slasher, I'll know he's really arrived.

"I don't think you should be at the carnival," Luke says. "It's not safe. Alfredo is still out there somewhere, and who knows what Red and Stewart have in mind for you."

"And it's safe for you?"

"Don't start that sexist routine with me."

"Um, I'm pretty sure *you* started it. You don't think you're in danger? They know we're friends and probably conspirators."

Attitude flashes in his eyes. "Nobody's flung stage lights on me yet."

I lean forward and drop my voice. "That could've been just for Cherry—if it was even intentional."

"We both know it was intentional. And I'm asking you not to go tonight."

"And I'm telling you no."

We stare each other down until my eyes burn from lack of blinking.

"Fine," he says finally. "Do what you want. I know you're going to anyway." He tosses a piece of paper on my desk. "Have a new article ready for your column next week."

"I'm back on?"

"Yes."

I stand up and clap my hands together. "Thank you, Luke. You won't regret this!"

"Don't even think of hugging me right now."

I step back. "Wouldn't dream of being so unprofessional, Chief." I wink and lean toward his ear. "I'll save that for later."

Plopping back down at my work station, I begin brainstorming ideas for my next column. Maybe I'll focus on seniors and the different graduation festivities. Or maybe I'll write about summer vacation plans.

I stop my mental list as a shadow looms over me. I see her reflection in my monitor and don't bother looking up. "Did you need something, Ashley?"

"Yeah, I, uh, just wanted to say Luke made me read some of the archived papers. And . . . you're a good writer."

Now this jerks my head upright. Ashley studies a spot on her shoe, and I notice her cheeks are tinged a nice, telling pink.

"Wow. Thanks."

"Didn't see that coming, did you?" She flips her long, blonde hair.

"No." I give her the closest thing to a real smile I can muster. "But thank you."

"I read all those articles on mysteries you've solved—the football boys' fraternity and the prom fiasco."* Ashley pulls her eyes from the ground and stares me in the face. "It was solid writing, Bella. And it was also good teamwork between you and Luke."

This thought brings a genuine grin to my face. "Yes, it was. We work well together." When we're not fighting.

"I picked up some writing pointers from your work." Her mouth hardens. "So now that I've got that nicety out of the way, I want to tell you that I'm going to give one hundred percent to pursuing your front page space *and* your ex-boyfriend."

I bring myself to my full height on my Stuart Weitzman heels. "Maybe you should go back and reread those pieces of mine. Because while you may have taken some notes on the mechanics, you obviously missed some common themes." I tick them off on my fingers. "One, I don't ever give up. So I may have been off my game for a few weeks, but I'm back now with all sorts of ideas—ideas that don't include you keeping my space as a regular feature columnist. And two, I don't believe in letting opportunities get away. So I'll be the one getting back with my ex. Not you. I'll be taking care of the final details this evening." I give her a condescending pout. "But I don't mind the competition, really. Keeps me on my toes. And reminds Luke that everything he wants is right here."

Ashley shakes her head slowly. "That's not what he said last night on the phone."

I narrow my eyes, and she catches my flicker of doubt.

"He said he's tired of your little games, Bella. So just prepare yourself. Your boyfriend's moved on. I wouldn't even waste your time talking to him tonight." Her voice drops to a whisper. "I'd hate to see a strong girl like you embarrass herself and beg." She pats me on the shoulder and walks on. "Just looking out for a fellow reporter."

Ruthie slides her cafeteria tray beside mine. "I feel so wrung out today."

Lindy bites down on a fry and sighs. "Me too."

And me three. Life is stressful. What would make me feel better is solving this mystery. And some new shoes.

"It's like I pour everything I am, my heart and my soul, into my unicycle ballet. And then there's not much left of me. The carnival is a soul sucker." She shoves her food away. "You know something is wrong when you can't even enjoy some high-quality meatloaf."

Matt lifts his head from his AP History homework. "You got Female Athlete of the Year at last week's athletic banquet, Lindy. I thought you'd be on top of the world."

She shrugs. "Yeah. I am." She says this with as much conviction as one would say *I love being grounded.*

"We haven't gotten pizza and gone to the park in a while. How about hanging out after school?" Matt asks. "You know, like the old days."

"That would be fun. I . . . um, just have to check my plans."

"With Bo." Matt rolls his eyes. "Didn't know he was in charge of your life and had to approve your schedule."

"I have a boyfriend now and things have changed."

Matt blinks away hurt, letting anger take over. "Fine. Whatever."

Speaking of the Track Star Romeo, Bo Blades walks to our table, his new Nike Airs a perfect match to his running pants. "Hey, Lindy." He squeezes her shoulder and sits down. "The Tulsa Oilers are doing a special benefit game this Friday." Bo holds up two tickets. "I thought you might want to go."

Lindy's smile wobbles. "I do love hockey."

"I know. I remembered you said that once. So when I heard it announced on the radio, I thought of you."

"You're always thinking of me. It's the perfect date."

"So I'll pick you up at five?" Bo laughs. "Well, maybe I better come by earlier. Last weekend your dad and I talked so long, we almost missed our movie. Dude, your dad is so awesome."

"Yeah." Lindy stares at her lap. "He thinks you're the best."

Bo squeezes her hand and stands. "I'll see you later. I promised a friend I'd pray with him before his sixth-hour test. I'll call you tonight. But not until after your *SportsCenter*, right?" He hums as he leaves.

"Bo, I can't!" Lindy jumps to her feet.

We all drop our plastic utensils.

He turns back to our table, still smiling. "What's wrong? You can't go to the hockey game?" He shrugs. "That's okay, Lindy. Maybe your dad and a friend can take our tickets. We can do whatever you want Friday night."

"I know." She bites her lip and steps forward.

Matt, Ruthie, and I lean closer.

"I . . . er . . ." Lindy wrings her hands, then lets the words just spew. "Bo, you're too perfect!"

He blinks twice. "Excuse me?"

Yeah, *huh?*

"You know all my favorite songs, my father adores you, you're the best Christian guy ever, you hold my doors open, and you know my every interest and dislike—sometimes even before I do."

"And that's a problem? Tell me what to do, and I'll fix it."

"That's just it. I know you would." Lindy folds and unfolds the hem of her T-shirt. "You're so perfect that I feel like *I* have to be perfect. And I'm not. I can't be myself around you."

Bo frowns. "I don't know what you mean."

"Did you know I always spill food on my shirts? Always. But when I'm with you, I feel like I have to watch my every bite. And I usually just stop eating after a few minutes because I'm so nervous."

"I didn't—"

"And you're so good to everyone, it makes me feel like I have to be on my best behavior all the time. But you know what? I get in bad moods sometimes."

"I'm sure everyone does."

"Not you, Bo. You're always happy. And it makes me uncomfortable. And you know what else? Your clothes are never wrinkled. Do you iron everything you wear? Even your T-shirts?"

"I guess I think it's important to look nice at all times."

"And you've never made me watch a stupid shoot-'em-up movie."

"I don't understand. I know you don't like that kind of stuff, so of course I would never do that."

Lindy's smile grows. "You're an amazing guy. But you're not *my* amazing guy. I can't be myself around you. I need someone as flawed as I am. Someone who also gets pizza on his shirts and occasionally makes me watch a stupid action flick because that's what *he* likes."

Bo rests his hand on Lindy's shoulder. "What are you saying here?"

"That you're pretty close to perfect. But that makes you perfectly wrong for me. I think you're an awesome guy. I do. But I've kind of lost myself in all of this. And it's time to get back to being me."

He casts a self-conscious glance at our table. We don't even pretend to look elsewhere. "Are you sure about this?" he whispers.

Lindy nods and pats his hand. "Go find your dream girl, Bo."

"Still friends?"

She laughs. "I knew you'd say that."

He drops his grip. "Let me guess, because I always say the right thing?"

"Because you're you."

"Um . . . do you think your dad would want to go with me to the game?"

"Definitely. I may have broken up with you—but he hasn't."

Bo gives Lindy his best reassuring grin, then walks away. Out of her life.

Lindy sits back down, and her sigh of relief could blow the ketchup off Ruthie's meatloaf.

"That was some good lunchtime entertainment," Ruthie says. "I give it four stars out of five. There wasn't any blood, or else I'd totally bump up the score."

I shoot Lindy a curious look. "I didn't see that coming."

She picks up her water and takes a drink. "I didn't either. But dang if that didn't feel good. Oh, and Matt, my schedule seems to be clear today for an after-school date at the park."

Matt's eyes go wide. "Date?"

"Yes. I'm asking you out."

My head jerks in a double take. "Who are you and what have you done with my friend Lindy?"

She only has eyes for Matt. "I am never more myself than when I'm hanging out with you, and I've missed you lately. I've missed us. And I realize you've never felt anything but friendship for me, but you need to know that I'm sick of pretending to be someone I'm not. And who I am"—Lindy straightens her back, squares her shoulders—"is a girl finally telling you how I feel."

"I—I, um…" Matt's face is as red as cherry Kool-Aid. "I . . . don't know what to say."

"Oh." Lindy's face falls. "Okay, yeah, sure." She picks up her tray. "I gotta go." With the speed that's earned her many a track medal, she leaves the table and heads toward the exit doors.

"You're just a chicken." Ruthie cracks her knuckles. "And if you don't go get her right now, I'm gonna tuck your head so far up your—"

"Wait!" Matt jumps up. "Lindy, wait!"

Ruthie and I follow him, as he runs to catch up with our friend in the hall.

"Lindy!"

She stops and slowly spins around. "What?"

Matt's lips struggle to form the words. "Um…" He stares at the white ceiling tiles over her head. "Would . . . would you like to go to the park today? On, um, a date?"

Lindy studies his face for a moment before she breaks into a wide grin. "Okay."

His head bobs once. "Then okay. I will, uh, see you there after, um, school."

"Don't forget the pizza."

His smile grows steadier. "No, I won't forget." He watches her walk away. "Oh, and Lindy?"

She turns.

"You have burrito on your shirt."

chapter thirty-six

"No, Bella. Absolutely not."

"But, Mom!" I pace the kitchen, torn between wanting to yell or stuff my face with Oreos. "I have to see Cherry's last performance."

My mother crosses her arms and gives me the stern look she's been cultivating for almost a year. "You should've thought of that before you left me out of so many details in your life."

"Those were trifling details though. I thought they would just bore you."

"Then I'm glad we've got this cleared up. So *next* time an accused murderer breaks into your car or someone tries to kill you with carnival equipment, you will know to clue me in."

"Right." I nod once. "I'll definitely do that. Let me just get my purse, and I'll go with you to the carnival."

Mom wags a finger. "Nuh-uh. You can stay home and clean the house."

Sometimes I really miss my old tuned-out Mom who I had wrapped around my finger. Those stupid parenting books. I think the first order of business in cleaning will be flushing those things down the toilet.

Mom snaps her fingers. "Oh, I almost forgot. Dolly and Mickey have been at the carnival grounds all afternoon keeping an eye on Cherry. I need you to go over to Dolly's and let Cherry's dog out."

"I can go all the way out there, but I can't go down the road to the carnival?"

"I've already checked in your car—there's no one hiding out. You go straight to Dolly's and right back." My mother plants a kiss on my cheek. "I mean it, Bel. If I see you at tonight's show, I will ground you for life. You'll be fifty and still won't be allowed to date."

"But—"

"No buts. Dolly is taking her new video camera, so she'll get it all."

"Are we ready to go?" Robbie does two swoops around the kitchen, his red Superman cape flapping behind him. "I didn't get my name on the board all week, so I get a funnel cake. And the rides close extra early tonight, so we have to hurry."

"Get in the Tahoe, Robbie. Budge will meet us there." Mom picks up her keys and gives me a final warning stare. "I'm serious. If you disobey me on this, there will be heavy consequences unlike any you've ever seen—including a long summer at your dad's."

"Ugh. Say no more. Like I want to be there right now." Just because Dad and I are on the mend doesn't mean that I want to spend too much time in Manhattan right now. Dad called this morning, and Marisol's already moved back in with him—indefinitely. Talk about a recipe for a nightmare.

Barely resisting the urge to throw myself on the floor and scream *No fair!* I watch Mom and Robbie pull out of the shrub-lined driveway and turn onto the dirt road.

Might as well get the dog task over with. Grabbing my own car keys—plus three more cookies—I slip out the back door and into my Bug.

My phone beeps, and I check the text. It's from Luke.

You + Me = Later.

I'm ready for our big talk. I think. And though I didn't get to speak with him the rest of the day, I'm pretty sure Ashley Timmons was just blowing smoke. Some girls and their insecurities. I mean, she's so full of it. Right?

As I buckle my seat belt and do my fifth check in the backseat for any unwanted passengers, I feel another wave of anger over how tonight has turned out. I can't believe everyone in town will be at the carnival, and I won't. After all those long hours in clown shoes and honky noses! And for what? To get grounded and locked away while the rest of the world is watching Cherry and Stewart. And probably while Luke is solving the mystery. By himself. Without me . . . and hopefully without a certain blonde reporter.

Ten minutes later I stop the Bug in Dolly's driveway. Using Mom's key, I unlock Dolly's massive front door and slip inside. The setting sun bounces off the large windows in the living room, making me want to flick on the TV and curl up on the overstuffed couch. I bypass the warm, inviting space and call for the dog.

"Peg! Here, Peg!"

Thuds resound overhead as the dog scrambles through the rooms above, then down the stairs.

"Hey, girl." I stand at the end of the long staircase. Peg lands next to me with a leap and instantly goes to sniffing. "Um, kind of intrusive there. Watch the nose. Watch the nose!" I would never sniff her butt. She could at least return the courtesy.

I reach down and run my hand over her furry head. "You ready to go out? Come on."

Peg's ears perk at that command, and her feet *clickity-clack* on the hardwood floor as I open the back door. "Okay, girl. Do your thing, and make it snappy."

Ten minutes later the dog has not returned, so I step outside. "Peg!"

I walk the grounds of Dolly's massive yard, calling Peg's name and searching high and low. Nothing. I even look over the side of the pool to make sure she's not floating face down, doing the eternal doggy paddle. But aside from some stray leaves, the pool is empty.

Where is that dog? This animal is all that Cherry has left of Betty the Bearded Lady. If I've misplaced Betty's only child, I will never get ungrounded.

And that's when it hits me.

Look through town. Tear it apart. But the answer you seek. Is circled 'round my heart.

That's it.

I know the answer to the riddle.

chapter thirty-seven

Peg! The answer has to be with that dog! Aside from Cherry, there was nothing more important to Betty.

Reaching into my pocket, I pull out my phone and call Ruthie. She answers on the third ring.

"This better be important. We're about to start, and I haven't done my pre-unicycle deep-breathing exercises yet."

"Ruthie, I need to talk to Cherry. Now."

"Fine. I'll get her. But some people need to recognize there's more than one star to this show . . ."

I continue yelling for the dog, but there's no sign of the furry beast.

Finally I hear Cherry's voice. "Yes?"

"This is urgent. I think I know the answer to the riddle, but I need to find Peg. I'm over here at Dolly's, and I let her outside. But that was almost fifteen minutes ago. Where would she be?"

The background noise of the carnival almost overpowers her voice. "I don't know. Probably out at the barn. She loves the horses."

"The barn's like a few miles away!" I'm not in the mood for a long walk.

"Yeah, you'll have to drive out there. She won't come back on her own, though. That's why you use the leash by the door."

"Oh. Right." Well, excuse me. Any dog that is intelligent

enough to work for a circus ought to be able to figure out how to pee and return home by herself. "I'll go out to the horse stables then. Thanks."

"Wait—Bella. You said you have the answer?"

"I think the answer is around Peg's neck. She's the missing piece in all of this. I'm going to check out her collar."

"Let me know what you find . . . and be careful out there."

Hopping back into the Bug, I beat it down the dirt road and turn into the field that leads to the horse stables.

The foreman drives my way in his beat-up Ford, and I roll down my window. "Have you seen Peg—the dog?"

He leans out his truck and spits on the green grass below. "Yup. Seen her around here nosing 'round my horses. Get her on back home, would ya? And close the gate when you leave the property. We're all checking out for the night. Going to the big top to see Cherry."

Who isn't? Oh . . . me.

I search in every building until my feet ache. My patent-leather flats are not dog-hunting shoes. Sticking my head in the last stall, I grin with relief. "Peg!" The dog runs from the side of a chestnut mare and sniffs my hand. A smart girl probably would've brought treats. Now how am I going to coax her into my car?

"Hey, Peg. It's time to go back home now, okay? You've had your big walk." And hopefully a big tinkle. "Let me see this collar here." I go to my knees in front of the dog. She sticks her nose in my hand as I try to wrangle with her tags. "What does this say here?"

"Thanks for the tip."

My head shoots up, and I'm on my feet. "Alfredo." I eye the magician with cold dread. "Wh-what are you doing here?" My hand slips into my pocket.

"Don't even think about going for the phone. In fact"—his arm shoots out and grabs my hand—"these ought to keep you from doing anything stupid." Alfredo wrenches my arms behind my back and slaps handcuffs on my wrists.

"What are you doing? Are you nuts?" My pulse escalates until it pounds in my ears. "Let me go."

"I don't think so." Leaning down, he coos to the dog. "What do we have here? So the answer's on the dog's collar. My Betty—she had a heart of gold, but she wasn't the smartest rabbit in the hat." His beady eyes narrow as he flips over the dog's name tag. "Nothing here! Just the dog's stupid name." He looks up at me with wild eyes. "It's a name tag. Cherry said you knew the answer was on the dog's collar."

"She called you after I talked to her, didn't she?" How does a runaway convict have a cell phone?

"Cherry knows I only want what's best for her. She trusts me— whether she should or not. She told me you were gonna turn me in."

"So that's why you haven't contacted me."

"This could've played out much differently."

"Have you been staying out here?" I remember Dolly saying Cherry had been feeding the dog—a lot. "Cherry's been bringing you food, hasn't she? She's known you were here the whole time. You've forced her to break the law."

"Shut up!" Alfredo blasts. "I only want what's best for her and—"

He freezes like a statue as a truck rumbles outside. I take advantage of the moment and scream like I'm on fire. "Help! I'm in here, I—*oomph*!" My words are lost as Alfredo plasters his hand to my mouth.

"Be quiet. This doesn't have to be like this, so cooperate, would you?"

I torque my head and glare. Like I'm going to let him just do—I shudder—*whatever* to me without a fight.

"Alfredo?" A familiar voice calls. "Alfredo?"

"In here!" my captor yells, causing the horse beside us to stir. "I got company."

Red Fritz steps into the dimming light of the stable. "You." His voice is as menacing as one of the villains on Robbie's cartoons. "This kid's been a problem from the moment Stewart hired her." He steps closer to me and runs a gloved finger down my cheek. "And then when I put him in charge of getting rid of you, he couldn't do that right either. You got her locked up good?"

I thrash against Alfredo, but he only drags me closer to him, ignoring the kick of my legs. "She's not going anywhere." He turns to me and drops his hand. "If you know anything about this dog's collar, you better tell me now."

"It's just a name. I thought there would be a map there on the back or something." I shrug with as much casualness as I can fake. "Guess I was wrong. But you do know the police are up-to-date on all of this, right?" I watch Red's eyes widen. "They know I was in contact with Alfredo, that my life was threatened, and that Cherry's in danger."

Red stoops down and grabs the dog's collar. "This is what I was called out here for? I got a fill-in covering the last half of the first show, and you drag me out here to read Betty's mutt's tags?" He peers closer. "Who would call an animal Peg Aurora Smith anyway? What's wrong with names like Spot or Fido?" He shoves the dog aside. "Waste of time."

"What do we do now?" Alfredo asks.

Red spears me with his beady eyes. "You know what to do. The girl goes with us. I got business to take care of during the second act." He smiles and pats his pocket. "I just sold the carnival two hours ago. So now I have a show to wrap up, a niece to kill off, and my own little disappearing act to complete."

Fear roars through my head like a New York subway. "What are you going to do to Cherry?"

"Wouldn't you like to know, you nosy little brat! You've been in my way ever since you went digging through Alfredo's trailer. Yeah, I'm the one who so kindly returned your flashlight. But you still didn't take the hint to butt out." Red blows cigar smoke in my face, and I blink against the burn. "Let's just say there will be a tragic accident during Cherry's second performance." He *tsks* his tongue. "And she will finally get that family she's been dreaming of—when she's reunited with her parents in heaven." Red holds his large stomach and laughs.

"Cherry's parents didn't die in an accident, did they?" As if I have to ask.

"It's taken awhile, but I've finally gotten what should've been mine all along." Red jabs his pudgy thumb in his chest. "I was the oldest. *I* should've been the one to inherit the carnival—not my brother."

I send a look of desperation to Alfredo. "Are you seriously going to stand by and let this happen?"

"Red's cutting me in on the deal." A wicked glint lights Alfredo's eye. "It's been me and him the whole time. He paid me to get Betty off his back."

"By killing her?" I charge.

"By dating her."

"Speaking of good shows!" Red claps Alfredo on the back. "Now that was an Oscar-worthy performance. Imagine—that woman ever thinking a man would be interested in her." His face sobers. "Take care of the kid and be in my trailer fifteen minutes before the final show is over."

Fear slides across my skin. "If you're going to kill me, you might as well tell me what you've been looking for."

Red laughs. "Doesn't matter now. I got the carnival sold, the check in my pocket, and soon I'll be a grieving uncle. Everything else can just stay buried." He waves a white hand over my head. "On second thought, bring the girl with us. We don't have the time or the resources to deal with her here." He moves his leering grin close to my face. "Don't worry. It will be painless—mostly. Just like Betty, I've found if I want someone killed well, I have to do it myself."

My brain shudders. That slimy, creepy, curly-mustached freak. *God, please help me. I'm too young and fashionable to die!*

Alfredo tightens his hold on my arms as Red motions him on. "Let's go."

"Peg Aurora Smith. Stupid name for a stupid dog." Red hops into his truck.

"Anything you want to tell me?" Alfredo stares at me with focused intensity.

"Nope."

"I had a feeling you wouldn't make this easy." His frown is sharp. "It'll only hurt for a bit."

I thrash against him as he pulls out a taser. "No!"

Violent heat pours through my body as I scream and drop to the ground.

The electricity stops and I grasp for breath.

"Now you got anything to say?"

I close my eyes and turn my head in answer.

Red's face splits into a smile as he hands the magician a roll of silver duct tape. "You two meet me in the truck."

My leg connects with Alfredo's knee but he holds up the taser. "You don't want to do that." He picks me up like a sack of feed and hoists me over his shoulder.

My mind races with options for escape.

And I think of the dog.

Because she's been the answer all along.

chapter thirty-eight

I stare at the floorboard of Red's truck and pray like my life depends on it. 'Cause, um, I'm pretty sure it does.

I have to get out of here! If only I could reach my phone. My body jerks as I force myself to breathe through my nose, slow and deep. *Don't panic. Do not panic, Bella.*

The vehicle comes to a rough stop, and the engine shudders into silence. "Get her out and bring her to the haunted house," Red says. "I've already missed more of the show than I meant to. Let's make this quick, because I sure can't miss my niece's Praying Mantis."

The door swings open and Alfred's hands pull me by my arms. "Nice ride, princess?" He heaves my body into his arms and over his shoulder, pinning my legs down with his iron grip, my bound ankles making my attempts at kicking pitiful and pointless.

The dark of the night covers us as the two men walk toward the haunted house. The eerie quiet of the closed rides does nothing to comfort me. *God, please rescue me. Save me from a really painful death. I have a cat to raise!*

I'm jostled onto Alfredo's bony shoulder as he climbs the steps into the dim spook house. My eyes search all around for anyone to help me. I scream behind my tape, but it goes nowhere.

"Throw her inside. Shackle her to that rail."

Alfredo does as Red commands. He drops me on the floor, and pain rockets through my body. He jerks my hands overhead and in two swift motions locks my cuffs to a rail. I donkey kick him with my duct taped legs, but he barely stumbles.

"Is she secure?"

Alfredo's nod is grave. "Don't you think this is clumsy—leaving her to die like this? You know they'll see the cuffs first thing."

"Who cares?" Red glances out the door. "We'll be long gone with a big check to share. If anyone knows how to stay out of sight, it's you." He throws down his cigar. "Are you sure she's secure?"

Alfredo's eyes laser into mine. "Two twists and a tug couldn't even get her out of these babies."

Tears flow unchecked down my face. No, I'm not a crier, but if there ever was a reason for it, surely this is it. And to die here of all places. Home of the worst job I've ever had. Well, aside from Pancho's Mexican Villa. And scooping poop at Dolly's. And getting attacked by the maxi-pad machine at the Summer Fresh factory. But, no, this *has* to be the worst. Because none of those other jobs resulted in my death.

"Light her up." Red runs his fingers down the curve of his mustache. "Don't worry, girl. Once the smoke gets to going good, it'll knock you out. You won't feel a thing."

I flop like a fish, yanking on the cuffs, screaming behind my gag. *Help me! Someone help me!* Panic fills my chest as I struggle to breathe.

"There's enough plywood on this thing to make one heck of a bonfire." Red checks his watch. "Ten minutes until Cherry's routine. Get to it."

Alfredo's wide eyes bore into mine again. Like he's trying to send me some sort of message, but I don't know what. Forgive him? Yeah, right. I'll consider that when my body is melting like a s'more.

The magician slams the door, and I'm thrown into darkness.

Seconds later, I hear something slide through the handle. I'm toast. Literally. *God, please.*

With ears attuned to every sound, I listen as the men work outside, my body jerking with every noise. Finally . . . silence.

Silence is not good. Silence means the fire has started. And I'm minutes away from the end. Why didn't I tell Luke how I felt about him? Why didn't I tell my mom I loved her today? Or call my dad. Or punch Budge in the arm. And Robbie—I'll miss that little guy and all his superhero fantasies.

Tears continue to drop on my cheeks, and I wonder if I could cry enough to douse out some flames.

I scream behind the tape as smoke filters its way into the trailer. *Please, someone see the smoke and call for help. It's my only hope.*

Smoke billows through the cracks of the haunted house, and a full minute passes until I see a flame lick the wall. I pull on the cuffs with all I've got.

Right this moment Cherry is getting ready to fall to her death. And there's nothing I can do to stop it.

And I'm about to burn up in a carnival attraction dedicated to horror. The irony does not escape me.

God, just let it be quick. I want to pass out from smoke inhalation just like Red said. That is possible, right? He wasn't just lying? Because I don't know if I can believe a word out of his fat, lying mouth.

I close my eyes against the smoke and hang my head. So many things I wanted to do still. Tell Jake he needs to fight for my mom. Let Luke know I'm over the moon for him, that I don't want to go another day without being the girlfriend of the bossiest, most arrogant boy on campus. I wanted to go to college and write for a university newspaper. Get married. Meet Prince Harry. Maybe marry Prince Harry and redecorate Buckingham Palace.*

The smoke. It's getting to me. I have to think. There has to be a way out of here. Now can't be my time. Not like this. *Lord, what do you want me to do?*

Why was Alfredo staring at me so hard? What was he trying to tell me? Think! I cough into my shoulder and recall every word that came out of that dirty crook's mouth.

Two twists and a tug couldn't even get her out of these babies.

Of course! The handcuffs. He was letting me know the cuffs are his magician's props.

I get to my knees and turn my head against the flow of the smoke. Flames eat at the wall and climb higher. Closer.

I twist the cuffs once. Twice.

And pull.

My hands snap loose of the restraints, and I nearly collapse on the floor. *Thank you, God!* Quickly, I rip off the tape from my mouth. My heart pounding, I feel for the seam at my ankles, as one anxious second passes into another. "Yes!" Finally, my fingernail snags the end of the tape, and I give it a pull, unwrapping my legs. "Help! Help me! I'm trapped!" Covering my mouth with my T-shirt, I pound on the wall in front of me.

I quickly look to the entrance, but the door is fully engulfed. No time to lose. Must get out.

Reaching into my back pocket, I rip out my phone. I punch in Luke's number. No answer.

"Luke, I'm trapped in the haunted house! Please come get me. Cherry's in trouble. Do not let her take the trapeze." *And get me! Find me! Rescue me.*

Now to call 9-1-1. A board pops overhead, and with a shout, I jump out of the way.

And drop my phone.

The roof is going to cave. I can't stop to find the phone. I just have to get out.

Using my hands, I fumble along the walls and try to locate a door. I know there's at least one more. People go into the haunted house, so they have to come out. I hope.

Splinters tear into my fingers as I grope along the rough wooden surface, moving along fast enough to stay ahead of the flames. But I know it could go at any time.

"Help me! Someone!" I scream some more then cover my mouth. The smoke—it's too much. Recalling Mrs. Bryant's ninth-grade health class, I stoop as low as I can to the ground, still searching for a door. I push past the light-headedness and keep moving.

"Bella?"

I freeze. Did I just hear my name? *Please, God!*

"Here I am!" I wheeze and cough. "In here!"

"Bella!"

Just gonna sit down for a second and close my eyes. So sleepy. Feeling oozy. Head spinning. Eyes sting. Throat raw.

Air flows over me, and I hear my name again. "Bella! Can you hear me?"

Then arms lift me up and cradle me close. Is this what dying feels like?

"Bella, hang on."

I nearly choke on the fresh air as it hits my lungs. I'm gently rested on the ground, and suddenly Luke's face looms near and aims close. Mouth open.

"Wait!" My lungs spasm as I wheeze. I push his face away and just move the breath in and out. I'm alive!

Luke sighs big and drops his head to mine. "You're okay. Thank God you're okay." He says this over and over.

"Luke?"

He doesn't move. "Yes?"

"Get off."

He lifts me to him and pulls close. "Some girls will do anything to avoid mouth-to-mouth."

I wrap my arms around him and just hold tight, letting the night air cleanse my mind and lungs. "Omigosh!" I shove him away and ease into a sitting position. "We have to save Cherry! Did you tell them not to let her go on?"

He frowns. "No, I heard the first part of your message and just ran out."

"We have to go." I stumble to my feet, and he helps me to stand. "Stewart's going to drop Cherry tonight. Red wants her dead. I heard the whole thing."

He looks back to the fully engulfed trailer. "I could kill someone myself right now."

"Save it for later. We have to go."

I take a step and pitch toward the ground. Luke pulls me up and plasters me to his side. "Are you sure you can make it?"

I just nod and keep up the desperate pace.

"What if we're too late?" My voice shakes.

"Cherry and Stewart were just going up when I left."

God, please let us get there in time.

I could cry with relief when I see the big top come into view. I keep praying as we draw closer and burst inside.

The fuzziness gone from my brain, I stare toward the center ring. "*Noooo!*" I grab Luke's hand, and we run toward the middle. Our voices drown in the sea of cheers from the crowd.

Cherry and Stewart suspend from an oversized swing from the ceiling. He hangs upside down by his feet and lowers Cherry by a giant red sash.

She glides down.

Down.

Down. It's too fast!

"Stop!" I yell, and it's as if time stands still. Can't get there fast enough. In the corner of my eye, I see a blur as Luke races ahead of me, arms extended.

Must get to Cherry.

Her body unrolls from the sash.

And empties toward the floor.

"Noooo!" The scream rips from my throat as I watch my friend pitch toward the ground headfirst.

Too late. Can't get there in time. Luke will never make it.

The entire room gasps, the crowd coming to its feet. Not part of the show.

Cherry's shriek pierces my ears, and I stare in sick horror as death waits to swoop in and capture this innocent girl.

Two uniformed cops fly ahead of Luke, arms outstretched.

The audience gasps again, and I have to shake my head to clear my vision. Is that . . . Artie Jensen with them?

Cherry torpedoes right into one of the officers, and the two slam to the ground, the red sash billowing over them like crepe paper.

I kick it into gear and race toward them. "Cherry!" She lies motionless on the man, her eyes glazed slits.

"Don't touch her!" Artie holds out a hand, then bends down to Cherry. "Can you hear me? Cherry, are you okay?"

She nods vacantly. "I don't know. My arm—it hurts."

The crowd of carnies pushes in, desperate to get closer. The audience stands in a hushed tableau.

"Back off!" Artie yells. "Get back now." He aims his head straight to the swing. "And, Stewart Fritz, I need you to know you're under arrest."

I blink at the man who fifteen minutes earlier would've been pulling bunnies out of a hat. "What?"

Artie Jensen holds up a badge. "I'm Detective Denny Whillock, Payne County PD. You have the right to remain silent."

The man finishes reading a hanging Stewart his rights, then gets to business running his hands over the unconscious officer, checking his pulse, behind his eyelids. Gone is the creepy magician. In his place stands a loud, brash cop. Unreal. He was in on it the whole time. I was working with the fuzz and didn't even know it! Awesome.

"Cherry, are you okay?" I drop down to the ground next to her. "Just stay right here." I spy Dolly and Mickey running across the arena. "Help's coming. Don't move."

Dolly and Mickey surround Cherry. "An ambulance is on the way," Mickey says, gingerly touching Cherry's limbs for broken bones. "Stay put."

Luke stands beside me and places his hand on my back. "They can check you out too."

"I'm fine." I smile up at him. "I think my hero got to me just in time. Want to go with me to make my statement?"

He laughs and clasps my hand in his. "Don't I always?"

I flash him my first smile all night. "It's like our standing date. You, me, and the Truman PD."

The detective formerly known as Artie Johnson fires off instructions into his phone as he sits with the downed officer. "I think he'll be fine. Took a pretty good hit. Probably got some broken ribs."

"That scared me to death." Mickey squats next to Dolly and Cherry. He wraps his arms around his ex-wife. "I thought I was going to die when I realized I couldn't get to you in time, Cherry."

Her smile is small. "It's okay. Everything's fine."

"No, it's not. And it hasn't been for some time." His scowl is fierce as his eyes sweep Dolly and Cherry. "Let's change that."

Dolly caresses Cherry's hand. "What are you talking about, Mickey?"

"I mean tonight—when Cherry was falling." He swallows hard. "For a second I thought I had lost it all again." He blinks back moisture in his eyes. "But I didn't. And I'm not going to let my family go again." He pulls Dolly closer to him. "You two are my family. We were meant to be together and nothing can stop that. I love you guys so much."

Dolly's voice is tear-clogged. "I love you too."

"I mean it, Dolly. This is it. The three of us—forever."

Dolly grins down at Cherry. "Can you handle that?"

Cherry nods and gives a weak smile. "I could probably handle it better with some Tylenol."

The paramedics surge through the growing crowd and place a stretcher next to Cherry and her hero.

Luke signals to one of the EMTs as he holds me close. "Don't look now, but here comes your mom." His hand rubs my shoulders. "She looks a little stressed."

I turn my head into his shoulder and smile. "I think I just got grounded—again."

chapter thirty-nine

I sit on the back of the ambulance getting the "Bella Special." This checkup routine is nothing new. Is my head cracked? How many fingers do I see? Does anything need stitches?

When Officer Mark passes by with Alfredo in cuffs, I push the EMT out of the way and jump down. "Wait!" Ruthie follows close behind.

Mark stops. "You did it again." His smile is reluctant. "I'm impressed, as usual, but mad that it had to go this far. You never stop, do you, Bella?"

I glance at Alfredo. "I didn't really solve anything this time. Just got in the right people's way, I guess."

"I would have come back for you," Alfredo says. "I would. But I had to save Cherry."

"You were never worthy to watch my unicycle ballet," Ruthie growls. "I should've shown you all the cool tricks *I* know with my switchblade collection."

"I couldn't figure you out." I step closer to Alfredo. "One minute you were harmless and the next, I was being shackled in a burning trailer."

"It all just went wrong. I didn't mean for you to get hurt."

"You were in cahoots with the man who killed your fiancée."

Alfredo shakes his dark head. "I loved her. Sure, I was paid to date her at first—and keep her out of Red's way. But I fell for Betty. And I did this all for her. She wanted Cherry protected at all costs, and I promised her I'd take care of that. I—I just didn't know how. I thought if I made Red believe we were working together, I could get close enough to get Cherry out of there. Take care of her."

"Your parenting skills leave something to be desired," Mark says.

"And then Red set you up for murder." The weird, jagged pieces of the puzzle begin to ease into place.

"Took me awhile to catch on to that," Alfredo says. "Red was telling me he had it under control and wouldn't let me hang. When I figured he was double-crossing me, I came up with the escape plan and decided to pull one over him—and get Cherry." Alfredo gives me that focused stare again. "You know how the dog's connected, don't you?"

I nod slowly. "Yes. I do."

"Take care of Cherry for me."

I glance to where she lies on a stretcher, surrounded by her new family and a detective. "She'll be well taken care of. You can cross that off your worry list—and focus on surviving prison."

Officer Mark laughs. "A guy who can do magic tricks? Oh, I have a feeling Alfredo here will be *very* popular with the fellas." He pushes Alfredo forward, and the two walk toward a flashing car.

Luke returns to my side. "Are you ready to put some closure on this?"

"Am I ever."

———

Hours later I stand next to the Ferris wheel with a small crowd of my family and friends, including Cherry, who insisted on being present, even with her broken arm and black eye.

"That's the seat." I point up to the third cart. A carnival worker pulls the lever, letting the wheel turn until the cart comes near.

"How did you know?" Cherry asks, pulling the safety bar open and stepping up.

"Peg's tag. Her middle name is Aurora."

"Who gives dogs middle names?" Ruthie asks.

"People who love their pets," I say. "Or people who want to leave a clue about where something's hidden. When I read the dog's tag, I remembered you saying the Sleeping Beauty seat was your mom's favorite on the ride."

"And Aurora was Sleeping Beauty's name in the story," Luke adds. "Pretty smart thinking."

I smile at his compliment. "Thanks."

"Allow me." Mickey steps in beside Cherry and tugs on the back of the seat until it gives. "Seems to be a panel here of some sort."

Ruthie fishes in her top. "Need this?" She pulls out a screwdriver.

"What? You'd be surprised how often that thing comes in handy."

Mickey shoves the screwdriver under the small panel and pops it off. "What do we have here?" He sticks his hand in the back of the seat then pulls it back out. "It's a key."

I read the tag. "Number 308." I look up at Mickey. "Lock box?"

"Only one way to find out."

I peek at my watch. "It's after ten."

Ruthie takes a pin out of her ratted hairdo. "Say the word, and I'll get us inside any bank in Truman." She holds up a hand. "Security systems are still a little dicey for me, but doors? No problem."

Mickey laughs and clasps the key tight. "I was thinking we'd just ask someone to let us in."

My friend snorts. "Amateur."

~~~~~~~~~~

After an unsuccessful trip to Missouri Savings and Loan, we caravan to the only other bank in town.

"Looks like one of our lock box keys all right." Joel Dean, the president of Truman National Bank, leads us into the vault. "This is a very unusual situation, and I'm not exactly following protocol here, but the records show Shelly and Junior Fritz do have a box paid through the rest of the year."

Cherry does a half circle in the stuffy room. "It could be a letter from my mom, something special of Betty's—anything."

Ruthie comes alongside Cherry. "I want you to know if it's money, I won't ask for a cut. Even though I am now officially Bella's partner, and since she solved this mystery, technically I did too."

"We'll both put our keys in the locks." Mr. Dean motions for Cherry to join him. "There we go. Just slip in your key."

I'm as nervous as a girl taking a pop quiz after a snow day. What could be in there that was worth killing for?

In the silent room, the click of the lock echoes off the walls. Mr. Dean slides out the metal box and places it on a nearby table. "Be my guest."

"Go ahead, sweetie," Mickey says, his arm around Dolly.

With a trembling hand, Cherry lifts the lid and peers inside. "It's an envelope."

Ruthie sighs. "Probably just a greeting card." She leans close and whispers in my ear. "I hope it's one of those singing ones. Those things are cool."

Cherry peels the envelope open and pulls out a piece of paper. Her eyes scan the document for what seems like an eternity. Finally, with wide eyes, she gasps and lets the paper fall to the ground.

Dolly swoops in to pick it up. "Well, if that don't beat all. It's a will. From Cherry's parents, naming her as beneficiary of their estate, which is the Fritz Family Carnival." She holds the paper to her chest. "You own the circus, Cherry."

"That's why Red wanted you gone," I say. "He wanted to sell it and keep the money himself."

"And make sure you weren't around to contest it," Luke adds.

"He thought he had the perfect plan. And Betty knew it was here. She must've created the map to throw him off the scent."

Ruthie shakes her head in misery. "I can't believe I donated my artistic talents to those slimebags."

Mickey grabs the will and reads it over. "So I guess the sale of the carnival is null and void now, since Red wasn't ever the rightful owner. Cherry, what do you want to do? It is your legacy."

Cherry pulls out a chair at the small table. "I want a family, not a full-time job. It was important to my parents, but that's when we were together. I just want to stay here with you and Dolly."

"And Peg," Ruthie pipes in. "Don't forget the dog."

"And to think." My brain swells with the possibilities. "If Peg hadn't have come back, we would never have known any of this."

"Betty had a heart of gold." Cherry smiles at the thought. "But she wasn't especially creative."

"I guess it worked out like God intended." Dolly goes to her young cousin and wraps her arms around her. "He was in this the whole time."

"Crazy as it sounds"—Cherry's eyes find mine—"I do believe you're right. Because suddenly everything that seemed so wrong . . . feels just right."

chapter forty

When girls are silent, everyone knows we're mad—or up to something. But when guys play the quiet game, it's just a big mystery. It could be anything from *I'm ticked* to *I need a cheeseburger.*

"You haven't said two words since we left the bank." I stare across the dark SUV at Luke, watching the way the city lights play on his skin.

He drives right by the carnival parking lot where my car waits, but he keeps going.

"Um . . . if you're planning on running away with me, I should warn you I have a psychotic friend with lethal talents."

Luke continues driving until he reaches the city park. Pulling into a spot, he kills the engine, walks around to my door, and holds it open. "Let's talk."

I step outside and notice he doesn't offer me his hand. "Okay." What does this mean? Was Ashley Timmons right? Did Luke reach his expiration point for how much of my waffling he could take? Can't a girl change her mind? Can't a girl play hard to get? It works in the movies!

Luke gestures to the swings. "Take a seat."

I lower myself into a seat that cups my butt in ways that remind me I'm no longer six. "Luke, I've been wanting to tell you that I—"

"Bella"—he paces the dirt mound in front of me—"I can't take this anymore. You obviously don't want a relationship from me, aside from friendship, and I've come to realize despite all your flirting, that's your final answer."

"But I've been flirting because I—"

"If you don't trust me by now, after all we've been through, then there's nothing I can say or do to help you or change your mind. You have to work this stuff out on your own. But I won't be waiting for you when you get it together." He drags his fingers through his hair and continues wearing a trail in the ground. "I realize you've seen a lot of crap and guys have let you down. But I've more than proven myself. I thought at some point you could just follow your heart and see what we had. But now I know you're just not ready. And I'm backing off, okay?" He stops abruptly and drags in a deep breath. "I don't know what I am to you . . . but it's not your boyfriend."

I watch a star fall in the sky beyond his shoulder. Leaning back, I push off with my feet and swinging once, I jump out right in front of Luke.

"You're always talking." I shove his shoulder. "Always telling me how it is. Well, do you want to know how *I* think it is?"

His Adam's apple bobs. "I don't think so."

"I think you're the most amazing guy ever." I watch him try to control his look of shock. "You're one of my best friends. You make me laugh, you're scary smart, and I always know you have my back. And Mr. Editor, more than anything, I want to be your girlfriend. And maybe I will be looking over my shoulder and waiting for something bad to happen between us, but that's just going to take some time." I step forward until we're nearly nose to nose, and I clasp his hands in mine. "I'm crazy about you, Luke Sullivan. Tell me you're still into me. Because if you've decided I'm too much trouble, I fully intend to sic Ruthie and her slingshot on you."

His lopsided grin has my heart tripping. "I'm still going to be bossy in journalism."

I roll my eyes. "Tell me something I don't know." Pivoting on my heel, I walk back to the swing and sit down.

Luke follows. He wraps his hand around the chains and bends down, his lips a breath away from mine. "I thought I had lost you tonight."

I search his face. "We've suffered through maniac football players and that tiny explosion at prom. What's a little smoke and flames?"

"Are you sure this isn't just hero's syndrome? I save you and you get all gushy?"

I can't help but laugh. "I never gush. But I also don't share. No more hanging out with just Ashley and her brother. It's not that I don't trust you. But that girl is on the prowl."

He nods. "Done. I'll only hang out with one Timmons—Kyle."

"Are you positive Ashley is out of the picture?"

"She was never even an option. I'm afraid you're it for me. It's kind of like a disease. I call it the plague of Bella."

"You say the most romantic things, Chief."

"I am a writer."

I cover one of his hands with mine. "You might break my heart."

"It's possible." With gentle fingers, Luke caresses my jaw. "But I'm sure gonna try not to."

Luke pulls on the swing until his lips are a feather-light brush against mine. I slip my arms around his neck and curl my fingers in his hair. With his careful touch, I block out thoughts of evil and death. Memories of the haunted house burn away like ashes as I stand up and crush my mouth to his.

He rains small kisses on the side of my lips, my forehead, and my cheek . . . then pulls my head to his chest and strokes my hair.

"Luke?"

"Hmmm?"

"How are we going to handle dating and the newspaper?"

He rubs the tension at the base of my neck. "I tell you what to do and you'll ignore me."

"So . . . like normal?"

"Yeah."

"Sounds good."

Nothing like an attempt on your life to extend your school-night curfew. When I walk into my living room, it's almost midnight. And the whole family is there.

Including Jake.

"Bella, good heavens." The big guy rushes to me and nearly chokes me in his hug. "I came as soon as I heard."

"Um, Jake?" I step away. "Why are you still in your pirate uniform?" I stare at his gold vest and black stretchy pants.

He shakes his head. "I was getting ready to go against Chainsaw when Mickey called. I rented a car and drove like a maniac. Are you okay?"

"I'm fine." I'm more than fine. I'm Luke Sullivan's girlfriend! And I'm happy. "You didn't need to drive all the way back just for me. We handled it."

"That's what I tried to tell him." Mom sits on the couch with her feet curled beneath her. Robbie lies in her lap, passed out and wrapped in his cape.

"Close one tonight, sis." Budge wiggles his bushy brows. "I almost got my bedroom back."

"You can bet your Wiener Palace flair I wouldn't give in that easy."

"I'm sorry." Jake clamps his arm around my shoulders. "I should've been here."

I lean into him. "Hey, relax. We understand."

Jake angles his head toward Mom. "No, there's no excuse, and I've worn out your patience in understanding . . . I quit tonight."

"What?" Mom lurches to her feet, accidentally dumping Robbie to the floor.

"Ow! Hey, what gives?" The little guy rubs his head.

"On the long ride back to Truman, I had a lot of time to think. And I'm sick of living without my family." Jake kisses me on the head. "I almost lost one of you tonight"—he frowns at me—"again."

I shrug. "Narrowly escaping death does seem to be one of my pastimes."

"Jake, you can't just quit the WWT." Mom moves beside us, and the wrinkle between her brows would have Dad breaking out the Botox. "This is your dream. You've worked too hard."

"For what?" Jake throws up his hands. "To leave you alone to raise our family? I need to be here—for you, for the boys, and for Bella."

Mom slants her eyes my way. "Keeping up with her does seem to be a full-time job."

"Jillian, I want my family back. This isn't a decision I've just made in the heat of the moment. I've been thinking about it for a while now, and I know this is the right thing to do."

I step aside as my mother curls her arm around her husband. "Are you sure? What will you do, Jake?"

Budge groans and flops onto the couch with his brother. "Dad, you can't go back to the pad factory."

"If that's what it takes. I'll do whatever I need to do to support this family and be at home with the ones I love."

"I think we should all join hands and sing a song now," Robbie says. "Maybe a nice inspirational Josh Groban number?"

"Dude, my gag reflexes are already being pushed to the limit." Budge reaches for his Coke on the coffee table.

"Are you sure about this?" Mom asks.

"Looking at all your faces, I've never been more certain of anything in my life."

"Aw." She gives Jake a quick kiss on the lips. "Group hug! Come on!"

Robbie, Budge, and I reluctantly make our way to our parents, piling arms and hands until we're one big wad of family.

"I love you, guys," Jake says.

"Love you!"

"Love you too!"

"Ditto."

We stay like that for a long while until my heart overflows, my arms ache, and ... my eyes burn.

"Budge ... did you fart?"

"Oops."

Ah, family.

They may be crazy, but I'll take them—the good, the bad ... and the stinky.

chapter forty-one

"Ruthie looks great in her graduation cap and gown," Luke says beside me, fanning the both of us with a program in the heat of the evening.

I watch my friend walk across the stage on the football field. The principal hands Ruthie her diploma, and she grins wide for the photographic moment. She shifts down the line to the superintendant, who frowns, then moves Ruthie's tassel to the other side.

"Her hat is pretty clever." Budge snaps a picture on my other side.

"And totally Ruthie." Only Ruthie McGee would forego the graduation beanie and wear her motorcycle helmet. "But I like how her hair is in school colors."

Luke intertwines my fingers with his and leans over to Budge. "Has she decided what she's going to do yet?"

"Yeah. She had lots of offers, but she took the full ride from Tulsa University."

I blink. "That's funny. I thought you just said—"

Budge grins. "I did. My Ruthie-poo is one humble genius. Turns out she pretty much set the curve on the ACT last year. And of course, every college wants her for her unicycling ballet skills."

"Of course." I laugh and clap for my friend as she leaves the stage.

"Did you see the paper today?" I ask Budge.

"Yeah, great article, you two. Pretty cool to get published on the front page of the *Tulsa World*. Wouldn't you know Stewart would end up singing like Justin Timberlake in tight undies? And to think, Cherry's parents had entrusted Betty with the key to the will. They all knew Red was bad news."

"And Alfredo," Luke adds. "I guess we'll never know if he really did fall in love with Betty."

"I think he did." Even though the jerk nearly killed me, I still believe there's a good heart in there somewhere. And love just found him unexpectedly.

It happens to the best of us.

I lean into Luke's side and stare at the clouds lazily rolling along overhead. Truman, Oklahoma—who would've thought this would be home sweet home? Jake will start his new job next week as a commentator for World Wrestling Television. The show was furious that he left, but when my story hit the press, and the world knew why Jake left his match that night, America fell in love with my wrestling stepdad. And soon WWT was calling and begging him to come back. And he did. On his terms.

Dolly proposed to Mickey last night at Sugar's diner over a piece of lemon chiffon pie. That's right—*Dolly* proposed. Mickey and Cherry said yes.

And then there's me.

I don't know what will happen with my dad. We're talking more now, but it's still awkward. Seventeen years is a long time to know someone—but not really know them. So we're working it out. And now that he's the temporary parent of an eight-year-old, he needs my support. Actually he needs the support of the entire National Guard, but so far they haven't returned his calls.

And I'm just taking it day by day—my relationship with Luke, my attempts to get a raise in my allowance for that new Chloe dress, and my new decision to keep my nose out of other people's business. It's just too risky! After all, God has given me a lot to live for.

The graduates toss their hats in the air, and my eyes nearly bug out of my head when I see Ruthie's helmet take out a science teacher on its descent.

I curl my arm around Luke's waist and walk toward the seniors to hug some friends.

"Excuse me."

I turn at the tap on my shoulder and smile. "Yes?"

A teenage girl steps close. "I've heard all about you, and I think I have your next job for you."

"Oh no." My laugh is a tinkling bell on the wind. "I'm out of the business."

The girl doesn't move. "I think my boyfriend is cheating on me, and I want you to investigate."

Luke's smile is slightly indulgent. "She's retired."

"Yeah, I can't help you." I'm walking the straight and narrow path.

"Oh." Her face falls. "That's too bad. My aunt is a buyer for Gucci, and I was going to pay you in purses."

I eye her shiny green bag with appreciation. "Well . . . we could at least talk about a down payment."

To some, God gives the gift of encouragement, of teaching, maybe of mercy. But to me? Nosiness.

And I've never been one to turn a gift away.

acknowledgments

$\mathcal{J}$f I had to write a book by myself, I'd still be scratching incoherent sentences in a one-subject notebook. It takes a lot of people to throw these things together, and I'm grateful for every soul who had a part.

It is with huge amounts of gratitude that I thank:

Natalie Hanemann, my fabulous editor at Thomas Nelson. Thank you so much for all you've taught me and for putting up with all my crazy e-mails and ramblings. And for understanding my pain and heartache over any video with Jillian Michaels' name on it. But we are gonna be so toned this time next year. (Okay, you will. I have too much of a dependent relationship with Ben and Jerry's. But I'll cheer you on from afar.)

Jamie Chavez, another amazing editor. I'm so lucky to work with this dynamic duo, and Jamie, I appreciate the friendship, the travel advice, and for pointing out all the dumb mistakes I make in every book. Like how there aren't three days in a weekend. But you have to admit—it's a nice idea.

My family. Things always get crazy during deadline crunch time, and I'm so glad you haven't locked all your doors and windows so I'd move on to another family. Thank you for embracing the inevitable fact that you are stuck with me. And that I require lots of chicken and steak dinners.

My friends. For still talking to me after I turn into Deadline Medusa. Y'all are the best. Thank you for the laughs, the movie nights, and all our traveling adventures. And for tolerating my airplane takeoff/landing freak outs. It's not that I'm scared. I'm just dramatically concerned.

Chip MacGregor, the best agent and Ameri-Scotsman on the planet. Your zippy one-liners make my day, and your career advice is top-notch. I can't imagine entrusting these big dreams to anyone else. Thanks for believing in me. (Hum Josh Groban as you read this paragraph for maximum effectiveness.)

Erin Valentine, once again you have been such a huge source of help and support. Thank you for prereading the sloppy drafts, even when they make no sense and require a PhD in crazy to even read through them. I couldn't do this without you.

The sales and fiction staff at Thomas Nelson. Thank you for everything you do, and for making the job of writing books so worthwhile. I love you guys!

My blog family at jennybjones.com. You guys are the most awesome Web family ever, and I love hanging out with you every week. You seriously brighten my days.

My readers, the most amazing people on the planet. A handful of years into this writing life, and I still cannot figure out why anyone would read my little stories. Voodoo? Trance? Brainwashing? I dunno, but please don't find the antidote. I'm grateful to every one of you and pray for you often. Thank you for being a part of the ministry of fiction. Pass it on.

Jeff Spivey, funeral director extraordinaire and former classmate. Thank you for answering my questions about burials without even blinking an eye. I don't know how I can repay you for the information on digging up bodies, but if you figure out its favor equivalent, give me a shout.

Tony Humphrey, a hero of a fireman and medic. I appreciate

the help with answering my questions. Thanks for lending me your expertise. And for not laughing at my crazy inquiries. Or turning me over to the police ...

Ken "Bubba" Whillock, of the Arkansas State Police, for all the procedure assistance. That taser info might come in especially handy. Thank you for keeping Arkansas and Bella Kirkwood safe.

Joel Dean, king of all things techie. I'm so thankful for your help through this series and for putting up with my dumb computer questions. I appreciate your time, patience, and for keeping your eye rolls to yourself.

Finally, a huge acknowledgment to God. Every book takes me on a spiritual theme. I intend it for the characters, but somehow I get pulled in along for the ride. I'm so grateful for all You're teaching me and the countless ways You're blessing me. God is good. All the time. (Pass that on too.)

all access with Jenny B. Jones

CHAPTER FOUR

1. Page 19: I actually have a mentally challenged cat. He is very pretty, but there's nothing between those fuzzy ears but vacuous space. But he means well. And that has to count for something. I got the cat at a donut shop. And that's not really relevant to anything, but I've always liked that detail about him. Especially since there's not much to say about the poor, simple soul.

2. Page 24: When I was in high school, I traveled with the track team and kept time just so I could hang out with my athletic friends. During one meet they needed some team points and talked me into doing a new event—speed walking. I agreed to do it. And I looked like a robotic chicken.

CHAPTER SIX

3. Page 39: I also don't eat small, green, squishy things. When I was a kid and my mom would make me eat peas, I would take them like pills and swallow them whole. They still make me gag.

CHAPTER FOURTEEN

4. Page 107: At this point in the book I became aware of how much

lighter than usual the spiritual theme is. But it's kind of intentional really. A Charmed Life series is not really about teaching major lessons, but more about seeing how a Christian girl does life. I know I don't get a big obvious word from God every single day. And my days and weeks are often not best summed up in themes. In *So Over My Head*, I wanted you to see a normal girl living her daily life as a follower of Christ. A totally normal girl. Who solves mysteries. And narrowly avoids murder. And finds herself in life-threatening situations on a regular basis. Totally norm!

CHAPTER TWENTY

5. Page 143: Ben and Jerry's is my favorite ice cream. My dream job is to be a taste tester for them. And even though I send them my application and resume every single month, they have yet to call me. I don't know why. I'm so qualified! In fact, given all the ice cream I eat, I might be a tad overqualified. But even if they never hire me, I'll continue doing my own taste tests for them. Pro bono. (But if they would like to reimburse me for all the Ben and Jerry plugs in my books, I don't take cash. Just some Chocolate Fudge Brownie. Oh, and maybe a little Strawberry Cheesecake.)

CHAPTER TWENTY-TWO

6. Page 166: A carnival that lasts for months might sound crazy to you, but where I live they set up and stay most of the summer—usually in abandoned parking lots. Usually with lots of reptiles on showcase. I seem to always forget to stop by . . .

When I was about ten, my grandfather took me to a circus that had come to town. It was my first one. It was also my last. I have always been more than a little sensitive when it comes to animals, and I couldn't stand seeing those poor animals there. That is why in this book it's strictly an equine show. Oh, and one collie.

Chapter Twenty-Nine

7. Page 214: I don't know if I should tell you this one. Nope—don't think I will.

    Okay, yes. I will. But don't judge...

    I don't have a prayer closet, but I do have a prayer bathroom. I am REALLY easily distracted, so when I need to buckle down and pray and haven't really been able to accomplish that, I'll go to a specific bathroom in my house and sit on the floor and pray. Why? Because it's so hygienic. Wait, no, that's not it. I guess because there are really no distractions. I don't take my phone. I can't see the TV. I can't see the refrigerator. And sitting on the cold floor is good motivation to stay focused and not linger in an ADD haze. During book deadline crunch time, I also will take my laptop in to the bathroom when I can't do anything but find excuses not to write. Now all that is a little bit crazy (and slightly gross), so I'm gonna have to ask you to keep that just between us. It will be our little secret.

Chapter Thirty-Five

8. Page 271: Like Bella, I was on my high school newspaper. We were not allowed to write anything that might ruffle even one feather, so I wrote fascinating pieces like, "English Teachers are So Nice" or "The Amazing World of Physical Science." Riveting stuff. Our advisor was affectionately known as Cosmo Bob, whether he knew that or not. That name was passed down from class to class for decades—because he was there forever. We also handled the yearbook, which was convenient because if you're on the yearbook staff you can make sure you and your friends are in there. A lot.

Chapter Thirty-Eight

9. Page 289: Buckingham Palace. I went there a few summers ago.

Well, I mean I went to London and visited the palace. As a tourist. Sadly, not as a guest. (But there's always next year . . .) You can see my pictures at jennybjones.com/2007/08/22/vacation-pics-london.

You cannot take any pictures inside the palace. Nor can you take any drinks or snacks, which is a total letdown. Though outside her majesty's palace, you can buy her own brand of ice cream. After I saw that Queen Elizabeth had her own ice cream, my respect for her totally shot up. This almost makes up for all those sensible shoes she wears. Almost . . .

reading group guide

1. What do you think the title means?
2. After Luke's ex-girlfriend returned to Truman High, Bella didn't handle it very well. What would you have done in her situation?
3. In a carnival or circus, things are often not what they seem. Where else was this true in the book?
4. What's some advice you'd give to a friend who's struggling with a parent's remarriage? What would God want her to know?
5. When Jake gets his dream job as a pro wrestler, things didn't quite turn out like he or the family thought. How so? Describe a time when getting what you wanted wasn't quite all you thought it would be.
6. Bella ultimately forgives Hunter, her cheating ex-boyfriend, and resumes a friendship with him. Was this the right thing to do or should she have stayed away from him?
7. Communicating in families is often hard. Why do you think Bella's dad wouldn't listen to her warnings about Christina? Why do parents sometimes not "hear" you?
8. If God sat down and had coffee with Bella, what would he tell her she needed to work on?
9. How has Bella and Budge's relationship grown?
10. What tips would you give Bella's dad for repairing his relationship with his daughter? Where would he even start?

11. 1 Corinthians 1:9 promises us that God is faithful. In what ways do you see this in the book? Where have you seen this in your own life?

author to author

$\mathcal{T}$he Thomas Nelson Fiction team recently invited our authors to interview any other Thomas Nelson Fiction author in an unplugged Q&A session. They could ask any questions about any topic they wanted to know more about. What we love most about these conversations is that they reveal just as much about the ones asking the questions as they do the authors who are responding. So sit back and enjoy the discussion. Maybe you'll even be intrigued enough to pick up one of Rachel's novels and discover a new favorite writer in the process.

JENNY B. JONES   RACHEL HAUCK

Jenny B. Jones: What is your favorite thing about writing for the lady folk?

Rachel Hauck: I love romance, encouraging women to achieve their dreams and destiny in God through stories. It's a great way to "see beyond" ourselves and what great possibilities life has to offer.

JBJ: You have a series you've co-written with recording artist Sara Evans. What was it like to work with her and meet her?

RH: Sara is great to work with. She's very fun and down to earth. Meeting her was very natural, like we were meant to do this project together. She felt a little like a sister.

JBJ: I think your books are great for teen girls as well. What are some of the themes you've dealt with lately in your books and how could a teen relate to that?

RH: Finding the right guy, making the hard decision to follow God no matter what your friends are doing. Knowing we are a called with a purpose. I've dealt with sexual pressures, parental relationships, teen pregnancy, and good old fashioned heartbreak.

JBJ: So, what inspired you to start writing?

RH: I always wanted to be a writer. I kept journals for seventeen years and the reflections of that desire are evident in my diaries. But I was a career girl in the corporate software world for many years, then about a year after I married my hubby, a story started forming in my head. Took forever to write, but that's how I got started.

JBJ: What advice would you have for teen girls who also have a huge, mongo dream?

RH: One of my favorite worship leaders, Kim Walker-Smith said it best. Pursue God above all else. He will lead you to your destiny. I know that's been my testimony. People ask me, "How'd you get published?" Or "How'd you hook up with Sara Evans?" My answer is always, "Surrendering my plans to God." See, He really does give us the desires of our hearts. Meaning, if we surrender to Him, ultimately what we desire, He gives to us. It's a surrender but "get back" sort of cycle. Your identity and worth is not in what you do, or your success or even failure in this life, it's who He says we are: Beloved.

JBJ: I love that. That's awesome—that His love is both enough and more than enough. Tell us, if you weren't a writer, what would you be?

RH: Lost. Ha! Seriously, I have no idea. A singer maybe?

JBJ: And just an FYI, Rachel is also a worship leader and has an amazing voice. But when not belting it out for God or your next career, what does fab-o author Rachel Hauck like to read in her spare time?

RH: I read Amazon. "Look Inside" was the best invention next to McDonalds. I also love romantic comedies.

JBJ: Me too! Whether it's YA or books for adults, it's my favorite genre. We'd love to know what is one techie convenience you could not give up?

RH: iPhone. I love my iPhone.

JBJ: I've heard of those. My phone wants to BE one of those. What's something you wish you could go back and tell the teen Rachel?

RH: "Oh, grow up." Since teen Rachel lives with me in the form of diaries and letters, I can get a glimpse of my thought processes. I was both foolish and wise. I'd tell teen Rachel to study harder. And that the guy you think is the greatest to ever look your way will pale in comparison if you wait for the one God has for you. And oh, save your money, girl! What were you thinking?

JBJ: Super advice. Girls, did you hear that? Okay, Rachel, you were just elected president. What's the first FUN law you would institute?

RH: Tax cuts.

JBJ: And there you have it, ladies, the wonderfully talented and inspiring Rachel Hauck. I love to read her books, and I know you will too.

To learn more about Rachel Hauck,
visit her website at RachelHauck.com

New York's social darling just woke up in a nightmare:

Oklahoma.

Problem is, it's right where God wants her.

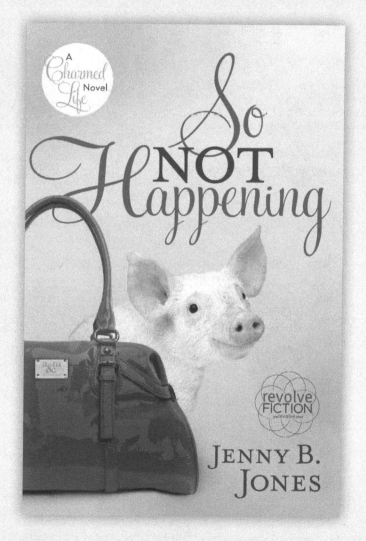

THOMAS NELSON
Since 1798

VISIT JENNYBJONES.COM

Bella is getting used to life on a farm, but will she survive starring on a wrestling reality TV show?

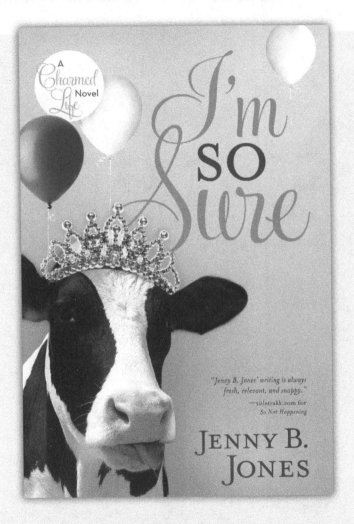

THOMAS NELSON
Since 1798